How to Be a Wallflower

Eloisa James

W F HOWES LTD

This large print edition published in 2023 by
W F Howes Ltd
Unit 5, St George's House, Rearsby Business Park,
Gaddesby Lane, Rearsby, Leicester LE7 4YH

1 3 5 7 9 10 8 6 4 2

First published in the United Kingdom in 2022
by Piatkus

A CIP catalogue record for this book is available
from the British Library

ISBN 978 1 00412 742 9

Typeset by Palimpsest Book Production Limited,
Falkirk, Stirlingshire

*This novel is dedicated to all the women
who dream of being wallflowers*

CHAPTER ONE

Germain's Hotel
Mayfair, London
March 15, 1815

Miss Cleopatra Lewis looked at her reflection with satisfaction. Her hair was pulled into a dowdy knot, and the jet beads encircling the high neck of her gown made her skin look sallow rather than interestingly pale.

On the other hand, the black fabric made her hair turn from auburn to fire red.

'I need a turban,' she told her dresser, who was scowling as if Cleo's appearance gave her indigestion.

'You must be jesting!' Gussie cried with all the horror of Lady Macbeth confronting her cowardly husband. 'You're trying to provoke me.'

Cleo allowed a chill to creep into her voice. Years of managing her own fortune – including Lewis Commodes, the wildly successful, if indelicate, business she had inherited from her father – meant that she had long practice in squashing rebellion. Though Gussie, who had dressed her mother

1

before her, had all the boldness of a member of the family.

'I am resolved, Gussie. A turban, if you please.'

'You'll look a proper quiz!' Gussie retorted. 'Not that you don't already, with that high neck.'

'That's the idea,' Cleo said, mustering patience. 'I plan to be a wallflower while living in London, and it's important to dress for the role.' She gave her maid an apologetic smile. 'My appearance won't reflect your abilities.'

'You look like a crow as got his head stuck into a red paint pot.'

'I am in mourning,' Cleo pointed out.

'Your mother – heaven rest her – has been gone almost these ten months, so half mourning at the most. Your mourning gowns were respectable but never frumpish.' Gussie sucked in a dramatic breath. 'It's more than I can bear.'

'You must bear it, just as I must bear the tiresome series of events that makes up the London Season,' Cleo said. 'I promised my mother I would debut. But that doesn't mean I have to collect a train of followers who will waste my time. The obvious solution is to become a wallflower.'

'Barbarous,' Gussie moaned. But she began poking through a trunk to the side of the dressing table. 'The only turban we have is a Mameluke cap, out of date these *three years*!'

'Think of it as a new role. I couldn't have a better maid, given your background in the theater,' Cleo said encouragingly.

'You as a wallflower is a casting choice that I would never make. You was never meant to be a wallflower.' Gussie straightened, holding a limp length of gray fabric. 'I didn't care for this cap even when your mother dressed it up with feathers.'

'Costumes make the role,' Cleo reminded her. 'Just think of how many plump Henry VIIIs turn out to be lean and hungry without their padding.'

'What of your grandfather?' Gussie demanded, shaking out the layers of gray muslin that made up the turban. 'The viscount will probably be mortified to find you looking like a quiz. You know how your mother regretted being estranged from him. Mrs Lewis would want you to make the old gentleman happy, especially since you still haven't managed to meet him.'

Gussie's right, her mother announced, deep in the recesses of Cleo's mind. Cleo had been somewhat dismayed to find that in the months after Julia's death, some errant part of her memory persistently offered up her mother's commentary.

It was because Cleo missed her so much, of course. Julia had dazzled: clever, witty, beautiful. Erratic, but always entertaining.

'I'll wear an ordinary gown to meet him tonight,' Cleo promised. 'He and I have exchanged several letters. I warned the viscount that I have no wish to marry, and that I plan to be a wallflower when I join him at society events. He indicated that he will happily sit with me at the side of the room.'

From what Cleo had gleaned through their correspondence, her grandfather, Viscount Falconer, was lonely and desperately sad about Julia's death. Unfortunately, his daughter hadn't bothered to stay in touch with her family after she married – and then it was suddenly too late. Julia had died without even knowing that her mother had passed away a few years ago.

One of Julia's last wishes had been that her parents would launch their granddaughter into society, a prospect that Cleo did not find exciting. She would prefer to spend her time expanding Lewis Commodes into one of the most powerful business concerns in Europe, as well as learning French, improving her vocabulary, and visiting Paris once Napoleon was evicted.

The prospect of joining the viscount for the Season didn't make her nervous. Julia might have been a free spirit, but she periodically recalled that she was the daughter of a viscount. Cleo had mastered ladylike comportment by the age of ten.

Yet even at that age, Cleo had preferred to shadow her father in his office rather than practice quadrilles with a dance master imported from London to Manchester at huge expense. A yawning feeling of boredom loomed at the very thought of accompanying her grandfather to one ball, let alone night after night of them.

Gussie was entertaining no such foibles. 'You can try to be a wallflower.' She started to fit the

4

cap over the hair coiled at Cleo's neck. 'It'll never work. It'll be like when I played the flower seller in *My Fairest Lady*! You'll walk into a ballroom. There across the room you'll see a tall man with piercing eyes—'

'I'll promptly look the other way,' Cleo interrupted. 'Don't forget that Reggie Bottleneck played the hero, Gussie, and he got two women with child, though the production only had a four-month run.'

Gussie grimaced. 'Not *his* piercing eyes. Better ones.'

'I know too much about men,' Cleo told her. 'I don't need one of them getting in my way, not to mention claiming my fortune. Just look at all the men who Mother . . . well, with whom she was acquainted.' Not to mention that rat she'd been betrothed to.

'May heaven rest her, your mother had a tender heart for a leading man. Drat it!' Gussie muttered as the turban dislodged a couple of hairpins and Cleo's curls sprang free.

A soft heart was a tactful description. Julia rarely met a handsome actor whom she didn't instantly adore – and invite to her bed, both during her marriage and after her husband's passing. Cleo had decided early in life that nurturing illusions about her mother would be disastrous.

Her levelheadedness was precisely why her father had left his fortune to his fourteen-year-old daughter, rather than to his wife. On occasion, Cleo had made use of it by paying off a particularly fervent lover who wouldn't accept that Julia had lost interest in him.

Cleo's opinion of the male sex had fallen lower and lower as actor after actor strode through her mother's bedchamber door.

'I'm not tenderhearted, like my mother,' she said flatly. 'I'm . . . I'm inimical to men.'

'Word of the day?' Gussie asked. 'I'm thinking "inimical" means you don't like men, which, begging my pardon, miss, we both know isn't true. You were betrothed to Foster Beacham only a year ago.'

'Briefly,' Cleo stated.

'You can't let one broken engagement sour you on the pack of them.'

'I shan't. I would simply prefer to cater to my own interests rather than someone else's. Still, Lord Falconer is my only relative, and I shall enjoy spending time with him. Which reminds me that I meant to send a note asking him to recommend a modiste. I need everything from gowns to parasols in – in wallflower mode, if you see what I mean.'

'Your mother hated drab clothing.' Gussie paused. 'Heaven rest her.'

'You needn't say that quite so often,' Cleo said.

'Mrs Lewis wasn't restful, was she? I hope that she's at peace now.'

'Mother's version of heaven likely includes a great many handsome actors, and as many romantic plays as anyone can watch.'

That's right, Julia murmured, with a naughty chuckle.

'Half mourning suits my mood,' Cleo said, prompted by her mother's commentary. 'I needn't want to wear black any longer, but I miss her.'

Gussie put her hand on Cleo's shoulder for a moment. 'The sadness will go away with time. You do realize that French modistes won't want to dress a wallflower?'

'They will create whatever garments I require,' Cleo stated, confident in the power of the almighty pound.

'We'd do better with a costumier. My dear friend Martha Quimby has her own emporium and outfits the best theater companies. It was her da's, but she renamed it after herself when he died. Drury Lane Theatre Company won't buy costumes from anyone else.'

'I don't want to stand out,' Cleo warned.

'That's not how it worked in *My Fairest Lady*, nor yet in that other play your mother loved so much, *So Dear to My Heart*. Remember *The Highland Rogue*? The heroine—'

'Exactly: those are *heroines*,' Cleo interrupted. 'Think of me as a bit player, Gussie. I need to be costumed accordingly.'

'A wallflower, I can't promise. You just don't fit the role, miss, if you don't mind my saying so, no matter what you're wearing. But Martha would do her best.'

Cleo glanced at herself in the mirror. Her reflection looked back at her: passable features, blazing red hair mostly caught up under the turban, a

7

pointed chin that she secretly disliked. In her opinion, what would make her a wallflower wasn't only her clothing; it was her expression. She was too old at twenty-two to bother with looking demure, let alone shy.

'Men from the gentry and nobility want ladylike wives,' she pointed out.

Gussie shook her head. 'You're being naïve. Trust me, you will be catnip to a tomcat.'

'Nonsense. Gentlemen fondly believe they're desirable. If you aren't interested, they scamper off to women who will flatter them.'

'Your mother – may heaven rest her – would chase after any fellow who caught her eye, but it didn't make them fall in love with her, did it? Most times she lost interest, but others dropped her and disappeared.'

'Men are easily distracted by the next pretty face they see,' Cleo said, not bothering to add that her mother had been the same.

Gussie chuckled. 'Not when they see something they *really* want.'

'Pooh,' Cleo replied. 'I don't care what men really want or don't want. I shall spend time with my grandfather as Mother wished. After I've learned French, I will travel to the Continent. Enough fussing with the turban, Gussie. I have to be back here by four in the afternoon to meet with the hotel manager as he's considering a renovation with our commodes.'

Gussie pulled the turban a bit lower on Cleo's ears.

'Didn't Mother pin an emerald brooch in front as well as the feathers?'

Gussie nodded, with the air of someone biting her tongue.

I hate to think of my lovely daughter in London – with curls that resemble a bushy hedge in autumn, Julia observed in the depths of Cleo's mind.

'Perhaps we can fit in a visit to a milliner,' Cleo said.

'Martha also makes headdresses,' Gussie said, eyeing her critically. 'You look more like an old maid than a wallflower. May I point out that one follows the other, like night and day?'

Cleo shrugged.

'Lip color?'

She shook her head.

'It's not natural,' Gussie said mournfully. 'What if we was to meet that piercing-eyed gentleman right here on a London street? What then?'

'He'll walk straight by me,' Cleo told her. And smiled.

Frightened off by that turban, her mother put in, having the last word, as usual.

CHAPTER TWO

An hour later, Cleo's carriage drew up before a large building with a striped awning. A sign hung from the second story: *Quimby's Emporium: Purveyors to Drury Lane Theatre & More.*

The carriage was toasty warm, but a fretful spring breeze tossed scraps of paper along the sidewalk.

'Your muff,' Gussie said briskly, handing over a velvet puff, trimmed with swansdown, in a somber dark blue that matched Cleo's pelisse.

Once on the sidewalk, Cleo saw that the store's bay windows held a dressmaking form clad in a gown sewn all over with golden spangles. Given its starched ruff, it might have been fashioned for a queen, albeit one on the stage, not in Westminster.

'Mother would have leapt at the chance to wear that gown,' she said, feeling a pang. Sometimes it seemed impossible that such a vivid, passionate person could simply disappear after a short illness.

'Quimby's costumes entire casts,' Gussie said, following Cleo's head groom, Chumley, up the short flight of steps to the front door. 'That

10

includes queens, maids, and old maids – excuse me – *wallflowers*.'

Chumley pushed open the door and waited until Cleo walked past him. The front door opened directly into a large chamber with two curtained enclosures to one side, and a gracious seating area encircling a low platform on the other.

'Martha is usually here to greet people,' Gussie said, taking off her pelisse and hanging it on a peg on the wall before she bustled over to help Cleo. 'Chumley, you guard the mistress's belongings. No saying who might walk in, and this muff came from Paris.'

Cleo smiled at the groom. The whole household was used to being bossed around by Gussie. 'Thank you, Chumley,' she said, handing over her gloves.

'Mind them gloves,' Gussie ordered. 'That swansdown trim is murder to clean. No getting that pelisse wrinkled either!'

'Yes, Miss Daffodil,' Chumley said obediently. He backed against the wall, holding the pelisse, muff, and gloves as if they were made of fine crystal.

'Martha will be upstairs,' Gussie said, 'though I'll have a word with her about leaving her establishment without a soul to guard the door.' She headed straight toward a broad flight of stairs in the rear of the chamber.

The stairs led to another large chamber, this one containing two clusters of women, many of whom appeared to be weeping. Cleo paused in the

11

entrance, but Gussie rushed forward, heading for a stout woman in the middle, presumably her friend Martha.

Cleo stayed where she was, looking around with curiosity. The ceiling was very high, and the walls were lined with shelves holding bolts and rolls of fabric. Lace and ribbons spilled from half-open drawers. One corner held a tall vase full of curling multicolored feathers, so long that they looked like exotic ferns.

Dress forms clad in half-constructed garments were scattered about. Unlike the dress forms she was used to, these had round, cotton-stuffed heads, presumably so an entire ensemble could be designed at once. A pope's miter, thick with jewels and golden embroidery, graced one head; the form was clad in a sweeping white silk gown draped with bands of gold embroidery.

Gussie was hugging her friend, so Cleo wandered over to another form, this one wearing a misty gray gown under an exquisite spencer, very severe and cut in sharply just below the bust. The gown could be worn in the morning, but adding the jacket transformed it into a walking dress. The wrists ended in corded rows forming Vs at the wrist.

Her mother had had a veritable lust for brightly colored clothing. Secretly, Cleo had sometimes thought Julia's garments were garish, if fashionable. To Cleo's mind, the design of a frock was irrelevant if it had been constructed from bright orange silk with an apricot overlay.

This gown had elegant lines, but it was reserved. Powerful. The woman who wore it informed the world that her lack of general's stripes was merely an accident of birth. The silk felt smooth and heavy. If a bonnet had one of those long lavender feathers . . . No, that would call too much attention to herself.

'He can't do that!' Gussie cried sharply, behind her. 'I'm sure it's illegal.'

Cleo turned. Her maid was still hugging Martha.

'How can he possibly move you wherever he wishes? It's impossible. There must be a law against it. You should write to the constable. The king! Write to His Majesty!'

'I won't, I just won't,' a young woman sobbed. She was drooping on the shoulder of an older seamstress, who was patting her and staring into space.

'We have arrived at an uncomfortable moment,' Cleo said, walking over to Gussie.

'Martha is being forced to move, Miss Lewis,' Gussie cried.

'You must be Mrs Quimby,' Cleo said. 'I'm so pleased to meet you. Gussie has told me of your emporium.'

Martha bobbed a curtsy. 'It's a pleasure to meet you, miss. I've just had some bad news, or I'd be more cheerful.'

'Have you lost your lease?' Cleo asked. Her father had left her a number of plumbing establishments, and although her man of business dealt with many of the day-to-day activities, she had necessarily learned a great deal about leases.

'I wish it was so simple,' Martha said, sighing. 'A few months ago, I decided to look for an investor, Miss Lewis. The theaters aren't steady with payments, you see. They open for a season, travel about the country or Europe. Then they come back and need a bishop and four gowns for the lead actress within a fortnight.' She waved her hand toward the dress forms.

'I can see that would pose a problem,' Cleo said sympathetically.

'Quimby's prides ourselves in making up a gown within a week. If an actress leaves a company, I'll have a new wardrobe made up for her understudy in no time. Sometimes my seamstresses just sit about, with nothing to do. But the lack of steady money tests the soul.'

'That does sound challenging.'

'My solicitor found us an investor to give us a fixed amount every other month. I was so happy.' She stopped and wiped her eyes.

'Does your investor wish you to leave the West End?'

'Not just the West End, nor yet London, but England itself,' Martha said, wringing her hands. 'He plans to move us, lock, stock, and barrel, to New York City. Which is in the Americas, you know, in the colonies.'

'Not colonies,' Cleo said absently. 'They won that war some twenty-five years ago.'

'I know, I know, I just forgot,' Martha said. 'Oh, do stop crying, Peg. If you don't want to come with us, you needn't.'

'Then what would I do?' the young girl cried, lifting her head from the older seamstress's shoulder. 'I've a son at home. And if I go over the sea, my babe will turn into an American, and my da will never speak to me again!' She threw her apron over her head and resumed sobbing loudly.

'Why on earth would your investor move you to New York?' Cleo asked.

'He's American,' Martha explained. 'He's buying up everything. He bought a bunch of them early Shakespeare books so he can put them on display. He's taking actors too. I heard that he's paid Reginald Bottleneck to go over there.'

'Good riddance to bad rubbish,' Gussie put in. 'That'll be a relief for the parish as has to support Reggie's ill-begotten babes.'

Condoms! Julia commented in Cleo's head. *I told that boy about French letters years ago and he never listened.*

'Bottleneck is the lead at the Drury Lane,' Martha said, shaking her head. 'What are they to do without him? He's been playing Robin Hood to full houses. What's more, half the cast of *The Honeymoon*, including the lead, Louisa Siddows, say they're going over there. That gray gown —' She pointed a trembling finger. 'That gown is for Louisa's next role! Now I'll be out the cost.'

'No, you won't,' Gussie said, patting her on the

15

back. 'If you're going to New York, and Louisa is going to New York, she can wear it there.'

'The Drury Lane commissioned it for a play they are putting on,' Martha pointed out. 'Who knows what role the American theater will put her in? She'll likely be in frills and ribbons, playing a girl of seventeen. That silk cost a fortune.'

'*I'll* pay for it,' Cleo intervened. 'If you can remake it to my measure, of course.'

Martha narrowed her eyes and looked Cleo up and down. 'I can do that.' Her eyes welled up. 'But I don't have time. I'll be in New – New York, and you'll be here! He wants to us to leave *immediately*!'

'Let's all sit down,' Cleo said, leading Martha over to a comfortable grouping of chairs by the window. Four women followed.

'My head seamstresses,' Martha said, blotting her eyes. 'Miss Lewis, these are Mrs Peebles, Mrs Andrewes, Mrs Rippon, and Miss Madeline Prewitt. Mrs Andrewes can sketch any gown after no more than a glance. Miss Prewitt paints the sketches, so the directors can set the scene in their head.'

'My pleasure,' Cleo said, nodding to each. 'I'm happy to introduce you to Miss Gussie Daffodil, my dresser.'

'Everyone should go back to work,' Martha said to her seamstresses. 'No matter what happens, I promised the bishop's costume by five o'clock tonight, and there's all the interior seams left to

16

do and one of the gold bands unfinished. With luck, we can have the bishop done by teatime.'

The seamstresses fanned back onto the floor, taking the clergyman's robes to pieces and separating into sewing circles before each of two large windows.

'So, the financier offered to back you,' Cleo said, turning to Martha and Gussie, 'without informing you that he intended to move your emporium to another country?'

Martha dabbed her eyes. 'The contract, the offer, was pages long, so I suppose the news might be hidden inside. We've been so busy with the opening of *A Midsummer Night's Dream* at the Covent Garden. All those fairies . . . Gossamer wings for four, and they kept ripping, so we'd have to start over.'

'You didn't closely read the contract,' Cleo said sympathetically.

'My solicitor, Mr Worting, didn't say a word about the Americas until this morning!' Martha cried.

'Deception like that should be illegal,' Gussie put in. 'Sue him, Martha! Put him in prison! Both of them!'

'If she already signed the contract, I'm afraid that a judge will insist that Martha does indeed have to move Quimby's to New York,' Cleo explained.

'Actually, I haven't signed,' Martha sighed. 'I only discovered it when Mr Worting brought me the papers to be signed this morning. I flatly

17

refused. But how can I not go forward with it? I already had debt, and when I thought I had an investor, I went ahead and bought some lovely French silks, that gray, for one. As well as gowns from the Duchess of Berrow. So now I owe even more.'

'You bought the gowns from an actual duchess?' Cleo asked with interest.

'Directly from the duke's man of business,' Martha explained. 'We buy gowns whenever ladies don't want them anymore, so we can remake them. I'm known for making an actress from the East End look like a duchess. Now I can't pay for the silk and gowns, and the rent, and salaries are due at the end of this week. I won't be able to pay them either.' She began wringing her hands again. 'Mr Worting says I don't have any choice. He said it's not his fault, and I should have read the contract.'

Cleo had a shrewd idea that Worting expected a healthy bonus from the American in thanks for delivering one of England's top costumiers. It was exceedingly rare to find a woman running her own business, and the solicitor might have taken advantage of Martha in any number of ways. Men were always trying to do it to Cleo, thinking she couldn't read a ledger.

'Mr Worting said I should expect the investor to come here, demanding I sign that contract,' Martha said, taking a ragged breath. 'How can I say no? I'll end up in the workhouse, and all my girls with me.' She glanced around the room, at the women bending over various parts of the bishop's costume. Her eyes filled with tears again. 'I've worked so hard to build the emporium. My granddad started it as a stall, years ago.'

Gussie leaned in and kissed her cheek. 'America isn't so terrible, Martha. I heard that the Spanish dug gold mines and then just left them be. You can pick up a chunk of gold right from the ground. You can get rich!'

'I don't want to be rich,' Martha said, hiccupping. 'I just want to keep Quimby's right here in London where we belong.'

'I'll be your investor, Mrs Quimby,' Cleo said, making up her mind. 'Quimby's is an *English* costumier, and ought to stay in our country. We can't let some American stroll into London and steal our heritage.'

Gussie clapped her hands together. 'Perfect!' she crowed. 'Miss Lewis can help you to no end.'

Martha's brows knitted together. 'Do you mean your father or man of business, Miss Lewis?'

'No, I mean myself,' Cleo responded, unsurprised by Martha's assumption. Though the seamstress was also a business owner, few women owned their own companies. 'How much did the American promise you as a monthly investment, and what were the arrangements for repayment?'

'Paying my current debts and three thousand pounds up front,' Martha said, 'with a thousand pounds every other month for two years, with the expectation that—'

Cleo raised her hand. From the floor below she heard a deep, rumbling voice and the sound of boots. Heavy boots. Not gentlemen's boots.

Martha's eyes rounded. 'It's him!' she gasped.

Chumley was directing the man up the back stairs.

'Mrs Quimby,' Cleo said, leaning forward with some urgency. 'Trust me.'

'You can!' Gussie squealed.

Martha nodded to Cleo.

'Please shake hands with me.' Cleo rose, holding out her hand, and Martha stood as well.

'You can call me Martha,' the lady said.

Cleo smiled at her and turned the seamstress's hand over. 'Sewing calluses?'

'Indeed,' Martha whispered. 'Oh, dear. Oh, dear.'

The boots were pounding their way up the stairs now. This was no gentleman mounting the steps; he walked with purpose, his heels sharply striking the wood.

Fortunately, Cleo was accustomed to the men who worked for Lewis Commodes. Moreover, her mother's penchant for leaving home and accompanying traveling theater companies around the country had necessitated that Cleo often found herself chatting to theater managers and, for that matter, solicitors when she had to pay off an unhappy lover – or his wife.

She linked her hands together and waited.

Gussie wound an arm around Martha's waist.

'Don't you worry, my dear. My mistress may look young but she's an old soul.'

Cleo had to smile at that. She felt old. Part of it was grief for her mother's death. But part was . . . exhaustion, perhaps. Or, equally likely, the result of her mother's predilection for racketing around the country in a theatrical wagon.

The American didn't just enter the chamber: he burst into it. It wasn't a matter of speed. He simply had the sort of character that dominated a room.

Partly because he was *big*. Big and rough. She'd never given America much thought, but she could imagine this man making his way through untamed forests in the snow.

Yet here he was in London, his dark hair looking as if it'd been in a high wind. It hardly needed to be said that his hair wasn't brushed forward in the currently fashionable style; unruly curls tumbled over his head like one of those Italian statues they had in the British Museum.

His features were harsh, his jaw remarkably strong, and his nose too. He certainly wasn't a gentleman, unless this was what all American gentlemen looked like. It was rather fascinating, like seeing a disheveled lion padding its way down Oxford Street.

And his chin –

She was staring at the fellow, which was fantastically rude and quite unlike her. 'Good afternoon,' Cleo said, walking toward him.

His gaze brushed over her and landed on Martha.

'Mrs Quimby,' he said, striding toward the costumier and ignoring Cleo entirely, 'I am told by your solicitor that you declined to sign the contract earlier this morning.'

Cleo blinked.

That didn't happen to her.

She wasn't vain, but she was a wealthy young woman whose mother had painstakingly taught her how to catch a man's attention. Julia, after all, had considered a day wasted in which she didn't attract male notice. Obviously, clothing *could* make a woman into a wallflower.

Or invisible, however you wanted to put it.

The puffy gray turban wasn't *that* unattractive.

Her mother begged to differ, but Cleo wasn't in the mood to entertain impertinent comments from deceased relatives.

Slowly she wheeled about to watch as the American started talking to Martha about his offer. A spark of amusement curled her lips. He thought she was not worth a greeting, did he? Yet given that handshake agreement with Martha, he stood in *her* emporium.

With that, her smile turned into a grin. Lately, life hadn't seemed very interesting. Life with her mother had been full of adventure, exhausting adventure.

But besting this man, with his lack of manners and dismissive behavior?

It would be a pure pleasure.

CHAPTER THREE

'**M**rs Quimby,' the American was saying, with a distinct note of impatience.

His voice had a roughness that caught Cleo's attention. She was used to accents that could be put on and off at will. Actors were chameleons. For example, Gussie, who harked from the East End, could speak in refined tones, thanks to her time on the stage. Her own mother, Julia, was raised in the heights of society, even though she had chosen to forsake it. Yet she often dropped her elegant accent in order to make an actor feel more comfortable. Or, in other words, seducible.

'Only yesterday your solicitor informed me that you had agreed to my offer,' the American continued.

Cleo thought about sitting down and watching the encounter like a scene in a play. But she might need to intervene at any moment. She stayed where she was, edging to the side so she could see the financier's face. His chin was absurdly strong, suggesting an obstinate temperament.

She loathed stubborn men: they were so often underqualified and overpresumptuous.

'I did agree,' Martha replied. 'Before I changed my mind.'

'She did!' Gussie confirmed.

'I broke off negotiations with Winch's Costume Emporium when I was told you had agreed to my offer,' he barked. 'You can't just change your mind. This is a matter of business, Mrs Quimby. We had an agreement.'

'No, we didn't,' Martha retorted, folding her hands at her waist. 'You may have had several conversations with my solicitor, but I signed no papers.'

'Martha didn't sign a paper,' Gussie cried. 'You can't carry out your Machiavellian machinations, you villainous scoundrel!'

Cleo found herself smiling again. Gussie's voice had abruptly taken on the intonation of a proper young lady because she was quoting from one of her favorite plays, *Love's Dominion*.

In contrast, the American's voice seemed intrinsically part of him. He would never change its intonation to play the part of a king or seduce someone of lower rank. It was all of a piece: the scruff on his chin, the broad shoulders, the gravelly voice, the . . . the rest of him.

'Why didn't you sign the contract?' he demanded. 'If you're angling for more money, I have to tell you that your current debts reduced the value of my offer considerably. I can assure you that once I expand this enterprise, you will become a very wealthy woman.'

24

'I don't want more money,' Martha said. 'I've made other plans. I found another investor.'

'No one will give you the support that I offered,' the American stated. 'Did you read the section where—'

'I didn't have time to read your offer,' Martha said, cutting him off.

His eyes went from frustrated to forbidding. 'Am I to understand that you refused my offer without even reading it? Am I to be given no chance to bid against whoever stepped in?'

'Yes, I did. I am,' Martha told the American, displaying a near manly gift for obstinacy.

Cleo didn't feel a bit of guilt at the idea of thwarting this brash man. The American rebellion had happened before she was born, but she knew the facts of it. They were a wild and undisciplined people who wouldn't agree to pay taxes, even for tea. They'd rather drink coffee, simply to avoid taxes.

Which said about everything that needed to be said, given that coffee was a vile drink that tasted like fusty beans.

No wonder the American had been tricked by a solicitor who hid information for personal gain. Trying to abscond with unsuspecting people and take them to New York City, wherever that was.

Geography was not Cleo's strong suit. Govern esses had periodically joined her parents' household, but they invariably left within the week, not caring for their mistress's fascination with the stage – particularly her extramarital relationships with handsome actors. Her kindly, retiring father had given his wife her freedom, and spent his time in his offices.

Not your business, darling, her mother observed.

Pushing away that unhelpful comment, Cleo waited to see what happened next between Martha and the American. It felt as if it had been months, perhaps a year, since something so interesting came her way. Lately, the world had been flat and gray, but now her blood was fizzing with something close to excitement.

'I am refusing your offer,' Martha said firmly.

'Why?'

'Because she had no idea that you intended to move her business interests to New York City,' Cleo put in, moving to stand next to Martha, across from Gussie.

He glanced at her, his brows drawing together. Anger was flickering in his eyes, but he seemed to have himself under control. Cleo's lips started to curl into a smile, but she stopped herself. No matter how enjoyable she found his offended look, it would only enrage him if she laughed.

In her experience, men were incapable of accepting that they might – sometimes – be a figure of fun.

'Are you Mrs Quimby's daughter?' he demanded.

'No.'

'Then what the devil have you to say about it?' His impatient gaze slid away, and he turned back to Martha.

'You concealed the truth about the move,' Cleo pointed out. 'Your preliminary offer was laughably insufficient, considering that you expect Mrs Quimby to leave her family and friends, not to mention eschewing the steady income resulting from her connections with the best theater companies in the kingdom.'

Cleo gave herself a silent huzzah for using 'eschew,' a word of the day from two weeks ago. Slowly but surely, she was enlarging her vocabulary.

He didn't just glance at her this time; he turned his entire body and looked her up and down. Cleo didn't like the glint in his eye, mostly because she couldn't interpret it. Men often responded to her with either a lascivious or a condescending attitude, but he didn't seem to display either.

He certainly wasn't admiring.

'Does England allow women to be solicitors now?' he demanded.

Cleo had been grief-stricken for nearly a year; irritation was a salutary change. 'They do not,' she told him. His eyes drilled into hers. It would be a misnomer to label that gaze condescending: appalled, perhaps.

Like many other men, he likely believed that women had no place outside the home.

Arranging her face into an innocent expression, as if she were merely answering a tourist's inquiry, she beamed at him. 'British women are not yet invited to attend university, nor the Inns of Court.'

Her smile had no effect.

'Then what in the bloody hell are you doing, butting in with your opinions of a matter that doesn't concern you?'

'Rude!' Gussie hissed.

Martha coughed. 'Sir—'

'It concerns me,' Cleo said, cutting her off, 'because you are standing in *my* establishment, Mr whatever-your-name-is from America. I own Quimby's. In England women *are* allowed to be investors, and I am one of them.'

'You've been doing a rotten job of caring for the emporium,' he retorted, giving each word a sharp edge. 'It was an act of pity on my part to offer four thousand pounds for an establishment deep in debt that seems to have kept only happenstance records and can't account for most of its inventory!'

'Yes, I can,' Martha interjected indignantly. 'I can lay my hands on every feather that enters this workroom. My girls are not thieves, if that's what you're implying!'

His jaw flexed. 'It is my understanding that a theater commissions a costume for a fixed amount, am I right?'

'Yes,' Martha replied hotly, folding her arms over her sturdy bosom.

'After which, you create the costume. According to your own records, you pay no attention to the profit you expect from each gown. From what I understand, you add feathers and silver embroidery with no consideration to whether an extra feather will take you from profit to loss.'

Martha's chest visibly swelled, and her cheeks turned red. 'You know nothing of the art of costuming, you . . . you Yankee!'

He gestured toward the sewing circles. To a woman, the seamstresses were gaping in their direction. 'Just how much will the costume they are working on have cost on completion, Mrs Quimby? Do you have any idea?'

Martha glared at him.

'Your opinion is irrelevant,' Cleo said, before Martha could launch into a speech that might reveal how hastily they had agreed to work together. 'I am Quimby's new investor. I offered Martha five thousand pounds immediately, with a thousand pounds a month for the next two years; we will share profits.'

His brows drew together. 'My plans for expansion of Quimby's will make it far more profitable than it can possibly become here in Britain, where theaters are limited to London. In America, theaters are popping up in every city. I own three in different localities, and I have plans to acquire more.'

'London is full of theaters,' Martha retorted.

'They are owned by different people. My theaters will put on the same play, at the same time, in different cities. All costume measurements will be created, Mrs Quimby, in New York City and sent out for alteration by local seamstresses. I'm sure

29

you agree that it is far more profitable to sew the same gown four times.'

'Far more boring,' Cleo said coolly. 'My plans for expansion do not involve repetitive work. Quimby's will soon be creating garments for gentlepersons as well as for theaters, and I fully expect my investment to double before the two years are finished.'

The American's eyes narrowed. 'French modistes dominate that market,' he told her, his tone just a hair from insolent. 'Your endeavor will fail.' He looked back at Martha. 'This woman will drive your emporium into the ground with her foolish ideas. Trust me, a duchess will never order her clothing from a costume store.'

'I don't see why not,' Martha protested. 'My clothes are as well made as any of them made by those supposed Frenchwomen. Most of them really are from the East End and putting on a fancy accent.'

'I grew up with Madame LaClou,' Gussie put in, 'back when she answered to Batilda Forks.'

'A duchess is already acting a role,' the American said, with the insufferable air of lecturing to students at a parish school. 'The last thing Her Grace wants is for the hoi polloi to recognize how very little separates nobility from commoners: a matter of silk, a feather or two, and supposed blue blood.' His curled lip showed that he was fully in agreement with his countrymen as regards the aristocracy's claim to being a ruling class.

Cleo was struck by the irrelevant thought that, accent or no, he would have made a remarkable stage actor. Thanks to her mother, she had met many leading men, and none of them could dominate a room the way he did now.

For that matter, he could be a nobleman, stalking the floor of the House of Lords.

The good news was that she wasn't her mother or a theatrical director, and didn't give a damn what this American devil thought of her.

Even better: she suddenly thought of an idea that might save Quimby's.

'Thank you for the counsel,' she said, ladling gratitude into her tone. 'So many men try to keep their crumbs of business advice from women, afraid that they will be outdone, I suppose. You don't understand me, however: I propose that Martha outfit young ladies and their mothers who are *attempting* to join the peerage. Those women who desperately need the appearance of ladies to match their ambitions.'

Martha didn't blink an eye at Cleo's announcement. 'There's no one better than me at taking a young woman from the country and outfitting her so that every man in the audience thinks she's a princess. What's more, I can do it in a week, and modistes require well over a month.'

The American scowled. 'Where's the profit? You are describing a quixotic, foolish act of charity. You will lose money on each gown, just as you will lose money on those bishop's robes.'

'The young ladies whom Quimby's will serve can afford *very* expensive garments,' Cleo told him, making her voice kindly, as befitted his ignorance. He was an American. What did he know of the English elite? 'London is full of industrialists like yourself, sir. Men whose fortune stems from business, rather than inheritance. Last year, the lord mayor's daughter married a viscount – and the lord mayor is a fishmonger. A very, very wealthy fishmonger.'

His eyes sharpened, and Cleo felt a pleasing jolt of energy. He grasped her proposal.

'As more and more successful entrepreneurs bring their daughters to the marriage mart known as the Season,' she elaborated, 'their family members will need to be outfitted, from head to toe. We will make their daughters look like ladies since they – perhaps foolishly – wish to marry gentlemen.'

One side of his mouth hitched up. 'That foolishness may be the first thing we agree upon.'

'Quimby's will give the ladies a fighting chance to achieve that dream,' Cleo said, throwing him a dark look. 'Their looks and dowry must do the rest.'

The American had a thoughtful expression as he registered the force of her argument. Which was very pleasing, since Cleo had only thought it up in the last five minutes, driven by the wish to best him.

'Martha made me look like a proper lady when I played the lead in *My Last Duchess*,' Gussie said.

'I was a fair treat.' She nodded at the American. 'You'd have to imagine me, just a slip of a girl from the East End, and Martha no more than one of her da's junior seamstresses. I was the talk of London. I could have married a duke, iffen I wished!'

Cleo didn't care if the American was affronted. He was just the sort of man whom she felt inimical to. To whom she felt inimical? She was never quite sure of her grammar.

Who she despised, in plainer English.

No, *whom* she despised.

A muscle pulsed in his jaw. 'A pipe dream,' he said, turning to Martha. 'You'll end up even more embroiled in debt, trying to outfit ladies as well as actors. You should come to America and do what you do so well, Mrs Quimby: make costumes for the very best theaters.'

A pleasant thought occurred to Cleo. She could make certain that her American agents never sold him any commodes. He would be very sorry for his rudeness when he was unable to befit his water closets with the newest piping.

In his theaters *or* his own house.

'What is your name?' she inquired.

The man gave her a searching look, his brow twitching when he reached her turban. 'My name is Jacob Astor Addison.'

'We have nothing more to discuss,' Martha said. 'Even if I hadn't agreed to new financing, you are not a man I care to do business with, given that you concealed your intention to move Quimby's to a foreign country – and offered me three thousand pounds that you're now claiming was four thousand.'

Mr Addison's brows drew together . . . *again*. At this rate he was going to have a crevice between his brows by the age of forty. 'Any chicanery belongs at the feet of your solicitor, Mrs Quimby. I was very clear about the move, and I offered four thousand pounds.'

'That's as may be,' Martha said tartly. 'Mr Worting is no longer my solicitor, just as *you* are not my investor.'

'In that case, would you be so kind as to formally introduce me to your new investor, Mrs Quimby? I'd like to make her acquaintance.'

His words were calm enough, but his eyes were dark and furious. Gussie might even label his gaze 'piercing,' but given Gussie's frown, her maid had suddenly realized that reality wasn't romantic.

Far from being a hero, this man was a growling despot, shocked to find that the world hadn't fallen into place at his feet.

'Unfortunately, life is full of disappointments,' Cleo told him. There was something – well, powerful – about him, for all his attire, and she almost dropped a curtsy but kept herself upright. 'My name is irrelevant as I have no intention of letting Quimby's out of my hands.'

'You bought this establishment in order to thwart me, didn't you?' he demanded.

Cleo laughed at that. 'Nonsense. I know nothing about you, Mr Addison. I've never heard of you, so I have no interest in thwarting you, though I am happy to support a fellow female business owner. To put it in terms that you will understand: I don't give a damn about you or your theaters.'

In the recesses of her mind, her mother frowned; Julia felt that ladies should behave in public, whereas Cleo held that ladies as portrayed on the stage – never cursing, for example – existed only in the male imagination.

'Then why would you—'

She cut him off again, because they'd heard enough from the American, with his piercing eyes and uncompromising mouth. 'My motives are purely financial, as were yours. Since you've offered me business advice, allow me to do you the same favor. It was remarkably careless of you to attempt to buy an establishment and move all the souls who work there across an ocean without ever entering the building or speaking to the owner yourself.'

If the temperature in the room had been cool, now it was rising sharply. Sadly, it seemed the American didn't care for financial counsel, no matter how kindly offered.

Cleo realized she hadn't felt so cheerful in recent memory. 'Quite likely you are often the victim of outright robbery,' she continued, ladling on the sympathy. 'You offered four thousand pounds for this establishment, but Mrs Quimby was offered only three. Mr Worting was stealing from the both of you, thanks to your cavalier behavior in not speaking personally to the owner of the establishment you hoped to buy.'

Anger faded from his eyes replaced, to her surprise, by wry amusement. 'You're right. I have a friend here, a duchess, who warned me that British women were not to be crossed.'

'How nice that you have friends,' Cleo said. She nodded toward the stairs. 'Mrs Quimby asked you to leave, Mr Addison.'

His anger hadn't moved Cleo, but the smile that turned up his lips now? She felt a crumb of discomfort. She *never* responded to male wiles. Growing up around her mother, it had begun as a defense and hardened into a character trait.

'I don't care to leave yet,' he stated, leaning against the wall and crossing his boots. They were sturdy and definitely not the footwear of a gentleman.

Cleo turned her back on him. 'Martha, shall I return tomorrow for a fitting of that gray gown?'

In truth she meant to bring a solicitor with her and draw up a simple contract that they both understood and agreed upon.

'No, no, Miss Lewis, I shall come to you,' Martha said, dropping a curtsy.

'Germain's Hotel,' Gussie said, giving her friend another hug.

Cleo walked toward the stairs at the back of the room, telling herself that she was imagining the feeling that Addison's eyes were on her. She was certain that he planned to offer Martha six thousand pounds the moment she left the shop.

She was equally certain that Martha would turn down even ten thousand pounds. Addison had no idea what it meant to move a British woman to the wilds of America, taking her away from the establishment that her grandfather had founded.

She occasionally came across businessmen like him, with few scruples and no capacity for regret. They had no real roots, and assumed that money could sway people to betray theirs.

Addison didn't even wait until she was out the door. Gussie was holding Cleo's pelisse when his voice echoed down the stairs.

'Quimby's will suffer, financed by a woman.' He didn't sound condescending, merely matter-of-fact. 'If you indeed plan to take up your investor's reckless plan, you'll need more than a monthly contribution. In order to keep your costs down, you must create direct relationships with silk manufacturers in Brussels and feather merchants in Antwerp. Men prefer to work with men.'

Cleo held up her hand. Gussie, eyes round, didn't make a sound. Her groom, his hand on the door latch, froze as well.

Above, Martha snorted. 'I'll hire someone with the needful body parts, Mr Addison. That's easily done.'

'Someone like Mr Worting? If you came to America with me, Mrs Quimby, you needn't worry about thieving employees. You could concentrate on being a costume designer, one who never worries about sordid details such as the price of satin.'

'I, a woman, built this costume shop into the best of its kind, Mr Addison,' Martha told him. 'Isn't my skill the reason you want to uproot my business and move me to New York? To this date no one has refused to sell me either silk or feathers.'

'Your company is on the verge of ruin, because you pay too much for those items. Worting shared your books, remember?'

'It won't be from now on,' Martha said with a confidence that made Cleo's lips curl into a smile. 'Me and Miss Lewis will turn Quimby's into one of the most powerful emporiums in London. I always knew that I could dress the gentry, because I do it on the stage, don't I? I take their old clothes, pull them apart, and make them better than they were in the first place.'

'Your skill is remarkable,' Addison said, his voice taking on a silky note. 'That is precisely why I wish for you, and only you, to build not just a single costume emporium, but a series of them in America. As I said, I own theaters in Boston, New York, and Philadelphia.'

'Since I don't know where those cities are, I don't care,' Martha told him. 'Now, if you don't mind, sir, I need to get back to the bishop's robes.'

'If I can't buy your business directly, I must warn you that I plan to acquire Quimby's from Miss Lewis,' Addison stated, surprising no one.

At that, Cleo laughed aloud, not caring if the sound floated up the stairs, and followed her groom out the door.

'Oh, he is a beast!' Gussie cried once they were safely in the carriage. 'A beast! I heard as if those Americans were a rough lot, wild as can be. Martha had a lucky escape, miss, a lucky escape.'

'I agree,' Cleo said, smiling. 'Gussie, will you please summon my solicitor this afternoon? I shall lay out initial terms, and tomorrow we'll meet with Martha to determine what will best serve her interests.'

'They don't even drink tea over in that country,' Gussie said, not listening. 'Beasts, not men, miss, and that's the truth of it! Uncivilized. You could just tell, couldn't you? Dressed like . . . like a carter, that's what he was. His neck cloth was that carelessly tied: I could see his neck! It's the lack of a civilizing brew, miss. The whole place is mad.'

'Once Napoleon is dealt with, I want to visit Paris. Perhaps after that we'll travel to America,' Cleo said. 'I should like to visit one of Mr Addison's theaters.'

'We'd have to bring our own tea,' Gussie pointed out. 'And you said after your mother died that you'd never darken the door of a theater again.'

'I could make an exception for one of Mr Addison's theaters,' Cleo said. It would give her a great deal of pleasure to witness one of the inevitable mishaps that mar a theatrical evening, from a lackluster lead actor to a convoluted, boring script.

Audiences were so prone to losing patience and letting fly with a volley of rotten vegetables. American audiences were likely even more unruly than the English.

She linked her hands and smiled out the window.

CHAPTER FOUR

7, Cavendish Square, London
Residence of the Duke of Trent
The same evening

'Bad day?' the Duchess of Trent asked, gesturing to her butler to hand a glass of canary wine to her houseguest, Jacob Astor Addison. He had the slightly wild-eyed look that her American friends sometimes got after a day wandering about London.

Merry loved her adopted country, but it had taken several years to adjust to the British knack for condescending while radiating self-righteousness.

'Yes,' Jake said. He took a healthy gulp and put down the glass. 'Extremely irritating. I met one of those eccentric English ladies you were telling me about at breakfast, the ones you suggested I marry.'

He shuddered. Luckily he had no need of Merry's assistance, since he had already chosen a charming and decidedly non-eccentric American lady. 'She was wrapped up in black from head to toe and fierce as a turkey cock. By the way, wasn't Trent supposed to return home today?'

41

'I want to hear everything about her!' Merry exclaimed. She wrinkled her nose. 'Unfortunately, Trent sent a letter saying that he will be delayed for weeks, perhaps another month. When we were first married, we were never apart. But these days I can't uproot the children, the tutors, and nannies, not to mention the dogs.'

'It's George, isn't it?' Jake said, showing how well he knew her.

It was true that she'd spent years moving the ducal establishment so that the family stayed together. But now . . .

Merry reached down and pulled one ear of her beloved bulldog, who lay at her feet, his head on her slipper. 'George is ten years old. I can't leave him, and he doesn't travel well.'

Jake leaned down and peered at her dog. 'He looks healthy, Merry. I'd give him another year. It's just as well for your reputation that I've decided to move. I can't stay here for a month in your husband's absence.'

'Move? Where?' Merry's eyes kindled. 'I'm happily married, and everyone knows it. No one would —' She caught herself.

Jake burst out laughing. 'No one would imagine you'd lower yourself to me, would they?'

Merry smiled at him over the rim of her glass. 'You're good-looking, in an American mold. But there's your clothing . . . More to the point, my husband *is* a duke, and English people cannot imagine anything more seductive than a title.'

'Poppycock. They would gossip, and you know it.'

'But I will be wretchedly lonely by myself. It's the Season, you know. I need you to escort me around.'

'No, you don't,' Jake said, not bothering to sound sympathetic.

One of the best things about Merry was that she was self-sufficient. 'Besides, I shall be at Germain's Hotel, near enough to play escort if you insist.'

'Germain's,' Merry said, knitting her brow. 'Why?'

'She's there.'

'The eccentric Englishwoman? Is she unwed? No, she can't be if she's staying at Germain's Hotel. Is she a widow? Jake, what are you up to?'

'I have no idea if she's married or not, and I don't care,' he replied, pushing away a suspicion that he was, in fact, slightly interested. But only because her husband would be a curiosity to any red-blooded male, since he –

No, she was *Miss* Lewis.

Relief unexpectedly shot through him.

'Unmarried, not a widow, and definitely staying at the hotel,' he said. 'I don't suppose you know a Miss Lewis?'

'I can't bring one to mind,' Merry said, frowning, 'and I've been making up an invitation list for a large ball we'll put on in May. Do you think she's a member of polite society?'

He hesitated. Miss Lewis had all the attributes

that he associated with a lady – but she cursed. Even Merry only said, 'Well, spit.'

It could be that Miss Lewis had ambitions to marry into English society, which would explain her plan for expanding Quimby's. It wasn't a bad idea. In fact, it might be brilliant.

Except that his plan to centralize costumes for a number of theaters was just as good and would require a smaller financial outlay.

'What did she look like?' Merry asked, tapping her bottom lip with a finger.

He shrugged. 'Hair tucked under one of those turbans. A pointed chin, a bit witchy. Sharp eyes. A bluestocking, I'd say, but primarily an investor.'

'Definitely not wellborn, then. Unmarried ladies are never allowed to dabble in financial affairs. Still, a great many women who aren't members of the *ton* attend larger events. I may have noticed her, even if we were never introduced.'

'Because their fathers are fishmongers and the like?'

'Exactly. Last year—'

While Merry told him all about the lord mayor's daughter who married a viscount – a story he already knew from Miss Lewis – Jake's mind wandered.

He wanted Quimby's.

Martha Quimby was a genius, one who could easily oversee costuming for multiple theaters.

It was his considered opinion that directors and even actors could only do so much to make a performance a success. The magic of the stage was bound to the visible. Audiences longed for the mirage: to see a princess, even if they knew perfectly well that the actress had been a scullery maid only a few months earlier.

For the last two weeks, he'd been attending the theater every night, suffering through plays, looking for the best actors – and costumes. Mrs Quimby had an uncanny ability to create stage magic.

The thought confirmed his gut reaction: no other such emporium would do. The only thing Martha Quimby lacked was hardheaded business sense, and he could supply that.

'That doesn't explain why you plan to move to Germain's,' Merry said, wrapping up her story.

'Miss Lewis bought Quimby's out from under me,' he said, his voice grating.

'Oh, she did, did she?' Merry laughed outright. 'Not used to competition? Welcome to Britain, Jake! We Americans love to think of ourselves as revolutionaries, but I assure you that English-women are a force of nature.'

'I'm moving to Germain's because I intend to acquire Quimby's Emporium from her, one way or another,' he said grimly. 'She ripped it away out of pure . . .' He didn't know how to explain it. Not spite, because she'd never met him before. 'She plans to expand the business, but I could swear that she made up the idea on the spot.'

'Will her idea work?' Merry asked.

'Possibly,' he said grudgingly.

45

'You're such a curmudgeon. It will be a brilliant success, won't it?'

'My proposal will be more profitable. I am moving to Germain's because I need to get Quimby's out of the hands of Miss Lewis. I already sent my valet over to take appropriate chambers.'

Merry bit her lip. 'You're not planning to *seduce* Miss Lewis, are you?'

His head jerked back. 'For God's sake, Merry! Have I ever given you the impression that I'd become so corrupt?'

'I'm sorry,' she said hastily. 'I just don't see how—'

'I shall speak to her. Convince her.'

'To give up Quimby's?'

'To give up her plan for the emporium. She has no idea how exhausting it will be to form relationships with silk manufacturers, feather merchants, even cotton mills. She doesn't understand the enormity of the endeavor.'

'So, you plan to *talk* her into giving you what you want?' Merry shook her head, eyes dancing with amusement. 'That will never work.'

'Yes, it will, if I have the chance.'

Merry broke out laughing. 'Promise me you'll come to dinner the night after you speak to her?'

'I live to entertain,' Jake said dryly.

'In return, I shall find out who your Miss Lewis is,' Merry said. 'I have friends who pride themselves on knowing everyone in London worth knowing, by which they mean everyone with money.'

46

'Invite her to dinner?'

George woke up and got to his feet, looking rather like a small barrel with legs. 'I shall,' Merry promised, standing up too. 'This elderly gentleman will be waiting for his bedtime snack and then we're both off to bed.'

Jake rose and bowed. 'Your Grace.'

'Ass.' She swatted him again before she left the room, followed by a footman bearing George on a velvet cushion like a royal diadem.

If said diadem snuffled and snorted.

CHAPTER FIVE

15, Charles Street, London
Viscount Falconer's townhouse
March 16, 1815

At the age of seventy-two, Martin Mountgarret-Lennox, Viscount Falconer, was no stranger to grief. His wife had died without knowing if their daughter Julia, who'd run away at the age of seventeen, still lived. And when Julia had died, ten months ago, he'd had no idea. The thought hurt, a physical pain in his chest.

When the library door opened forty minutes later, he hadn't moved.

'I'll find my way into the gloom by myself, Ponder,' a husky voice announced. 'Though a drink wouldn't go amiss; a touch of the Massougnes cognac, if you would.'

Elias Byng-Stafford, known to his friends as Byng, advanced into the library holding his lit cheroot over his head like the North Star. 'What in the bloody hell are you doing, sitting in the pitchy dark like a troll under a hill?'

He went straight to the mantelpiece and used

his cheroot to light both candelabras, revealing that he was clad in an emerald-green smoking jacket embroidered with peacock feathers. 'Aren't we expecting a visit from your granddaughter this evening?'

'Where did you get that absurd costume?' Falconer asked, not really caring.

'Burghart & Davidson,' Byng said, dropping into a chair. 'Up and coming, near Savile Row. You aren't going to adapt Brummell's gloomy aspect, are you? All that faith in black, as if sober dressing would lead to sober living. The man's trying to protect himself from shame with a starched neck cloth, and it ain't going to do it.'

Falconer didn't bother to answer. He didn't give a damn about clothing.

'The cloud of despair hanging around your shoulders suggests that you're thinking about your daughter,' Byng said, sucking his cheroot like a draughty chimney.

'Cleopatra, my granddaughter, wrote that she and Julia traveled to Stratford in a theatrical wagon. My wife would have been horrified,' Falconer said, his voice growling from his chest.

Byng raised an eyebrow. 'Julia did always dance to her own drummer. I liked her.'

Falconer's hand tightened into a fist again because he had loved his daughter dearly, and for twenty years he had never given up hope that she would return home. He'd paid a small fortune to Bow Street Runners over the last two decades, but

49

they hadn't found her . . . until a letter arrived from Miss Cleopatra Lewis, his granddaughter.

Her married name explained why the Runners never located Julia.

Who in the hell was Lewis?

He didn't like the name Lewis; it was commonplace. The truth was that Falconer had always thought that his daughter would come home to him one day.

But he'd been wrong. Shortsighted. A blind, affectionate fool, because it seemed his daughter never gave him a second thought, even when she was widowed, or her husband ran off, or whatever happened to him.

'They can't have lived year-round in a theatrical wagon,' Byng said. 'Where did Cleopatra grow up?'

'Manchester.'

'Manchester!' Byng said with undisguised revulsion. 'Undistinguished ambiance and a sad want of civility and culture.'

Falconer slammed his fist onto the arm of his chair. 'We raised Julia like any other young lady. What happened, Byng?' Agony rumbled through his voice, but Byng was his oldest friend, and they didn't keep secrets from each other. 'Why the hell would my daughter travel about in a shambles of a theatrical wagon rather than come home? We weren't monsters. We didn't beat or starve her.'

Byng nodded. 'She was a happy child. But she never fit into polite society, did she? She had too much ebullience, too much *joie de vivre*.'

50

The door opened, and Byng leapt to his feet. 'Ponder, thank God. You can leave the brandy—'

His voice broke off.

'Miss Cleopatra Lewis,' the butler announced, moving to the side.

A ravishing young woman walked through the door: blazing red hair knotted at her neck, porcelain skin marred only by a spray of freckles over her nose, the kind of curvaceous figure that made men instinctively check their pockets for a stray diamond ring.

Falconer froze. The only sound in the room was the click of the door closing behind the butler. His granddaughter had her grandmother's bluish-gray eyes, but the spark of mischief in them was pure Julia. His heart clenched again at the impossible thought that he would never again see his daughter.

'Cleopatra!' Byng exclaimed, moving forward.

Falconer's gouty foot was propped up on a stool, giving him an excuse to stay seated. He felt as if his heart was juddering like a carriage without springs.

'Good evening!' she said, strolling into the room. 'I certainly don't have to wonder who my grandfather is, do I?' She headed straight for Byng. 'Mother would have loved that peacock coat.' She brushed a kiss on his cheek, and said, 'Her last words were of you. She loved you very much and deeply regretted not having seen you in so long.'

Falconer was bracing himself to rise, but grief hit him so sharply that he sank back.

Byng opened his mouth, caught Falconer's eye, and stayed silent.

Cleopatra showed no signs of discomfort, nodding at Falconer in a friendly way before she turned back to Byng. 'I rarely indulge, but I think this is an occasion, don't you? May I have a cheroot as well, Grandfather?'

Without a word, Byng flicked open his enameled case. Cleopatra took one, walked over to the candelabra, and lit it.

'I hope that I didn't impose by calling you Grandfather, rather than Lord Falconer,' she said, turning around. 'Mother did train me in courtly manners.' She looked at Byng. 'Won't you introduce me to your friend?'

'Actually, *I* am your grandfather,' Falconer said, forcing the words from a chest grown too tight for breath.

'*What-ho!*' Cleopatra said, giving him a charming smile before she dropped a curtsy, albeit a lopsided one that kept her lit cheroot away from her skirts. 'It is a great pleasure to meet you.'

'Please forgive me for not rising.' He waved at his bandaged foot. 'Gout, I'm afraid.'

'I believe that is quite painful,' Cleopatra said, walking toward him. 'You have my sympathies . . . Grandfather? Or would you prefer Lord Falconer?'

'Grandfather,' he said, the word resounding oddly in his ear.

'Now I think on it, Mother had your hair and your nose. A Roman nose, she always called it.'

52

For a second, Cleopatra's composure wavered, and Falconer saw raw grief in her eyes. It was reassuring, somehow. He wasn't the only person desperately sad because Julia was no longer in the world.

Cleopatra glanced over at Byng, who was staring at the two of them with fascination. 'You, sir, are so well-dressed that I thought surely my mother had inherited your sartorial flare.'

Falconer cleared his throat. 'May I introduce a dear family friend, Mr Byng-Stafford? He is staying with me for the Season.'

Byng stepped forward and bowed.

'Miss Cleopatra Lewis,' she said, curtsying again. 'Though I'd prefer that you and my grandfather address me as Cleo. I try to avoid ill-deserved comparisons with the Queen of Egypt.'

'Please be seated,' Falconer said, gesturing toward the chair opposite him.

'Did you have a pleasant journey?' Byng inquired. 'I'll shout for the butler, as he unaccountably forgot to offer you refreshment.' He got up to do so.

'Did you travel here with the theater company?' Falconer asked.

'No, no, I mustn't have been clear in my letter. Mother and I didn't *join* the company,' Cleo said, waving a hand. 'Mother was what one might call a devoted admirer; five or six times we accompanied a troupe on tour for pleasure. Until we reached Stratford, which is where I've been for nearly a year.'

She gave Falconer a rueful smile. 'Mother was insistent that she be buried next to Shakespeare. You'd be shocked by how difficult it was to get her within shouting distance of the Bard. It's taken months of wheedling, and in the end, I had to promise to build a new steeple.'

'A new steeple,' Byng repeated, eyes round, seating himself again.

Cleo nodded. Getting to her feet, she moved toward the fireplace, and tossed the cheroot into the flames. 'I always forget that smoking is more pleasurable in imagination than reality.'

Then she walked back until she stood just before Falconer's stool. 'My mother lived in a state of excitement, leaping from one dramatic situation to another. Yet as I told Mr Byng-Stafford, she was terribly sad not to have seen you and my grandmother again. She asked me to come to you.'

He cleared his throat. 'I would have – I would have liked to attend her funeral.'

Her smile wavered again. 'She didn't wish you to know of her death until I had managed to bury her next to Shakespeare. She . . . she wanted you to be proud, I believe.' With a gentle sweep of her skirts, she sat down beside Falconer rather than across from him.

Ponder opened the library door. 'You rang?'

'The Massougnes,' Byng ordered. 'Three glasses, and on the double.'

'Make up a bedchamber for my granddaughter,'

Falconer added, giving Ponder a commanding stare.

Some butlers are thrilled to be butlering for the nobility and prance to do their master's bidding. Not Ponder. As a matter of principle, he disapproved of anything his supposed betters might request. He was rarely surprised, and frequently annoyed.

Yet even he felt moved to respond to this news, raising a hairy eyebrow. 'Your granddaughter, my lord?'

'Miss Lewis,' Falconer snapped, thinking that he ought to find a more biddable butler. Someone who wouldn't regularly imply that he was demented, which he was not.

Cleo intervened. 'As a matter of fact, Ponder, there's no need to prepare a chamber. I'm residing at Germain's Hotel, just around the corner.'

Ponder likely realized that his interests aligned with hers, since he promptly retreated, closing the door behind him.

'A young lady cannot stay in a hotel! It isn't safe nor proper,' Falconer protested.

'I don't travel alone, Grandfather,' Cleo said gently. 'It takes a great many people to keep me presentable and entertained. As for safety, I appoint a groom to the corridor outside my suite.'

'You really are Queen Cleopatra, aren't you?' Byng said with a crack of laughter.

'There's nothing particularly regal about taking a suite and housing my staff nearby,' Cleo said.

'You do plan to stay in London as we discussed in our letters?' Falconer asked, disliking the uncertain note in his own voice.

'Of course,' Cleo said, to his enormous relief.

'Join me for breakfast tomorrow?' he asked.

She shook her head, smiling. 'Tomorrow I must apply myself to gathering a proper wardrobe.' She twinkled at Byng. 'I don't know if my grandfather has warned you, sir, but I intend to debut as a wallflower, since I am uninterested in marriage. I shall need a complete wardrobe to fit the role: gowns, pelisses, oh, everything.'

'But surely, dinner tomorrow?' Falconer asked.

'Your grandfather has an appalling butler but an excellent cook,' Byng told Cleo.

'I would be most happy to join you,' Cleo said. 'Mother had a portrait done by Thomas Lawrence last year. She asked me to give it to you, Grandfather, so I shall bring it tomorrow.'

She gave Falconer a smile so sweet that his vision blurred. Julia had smiled at him like that when she was a young girl.

'Oh, dear,' Cleo said sympathetically. 'I do have my mother's smile, don't I?' She leaned forward and kissed his cheek. 'I will spend at least three months here, Grandfather. Well, not *here*, but in the hotel, as I am very comfortable at Germain's, and I fear that your butler and I would not be friends. Where is that cognac, one might ask?'

'He doesn't approve of my drinking,' Falconer said.

'How lucky that I am not living with you. Ponder would find himself and his luggage outside the door. I cannot bear people who express the opinion – in my case – that a young woman should neither drink nor smoke. I shall return to the hotel and have a brandy in his honor.'

'I am looking forward to introducing you to my friends,' Falconer said, making up his mind that he would introduce Cleo to every eligible man in polite society. His granddaughter was witty and beautiful; she would never be a wallflower, even in a potato sack.

'Unfortunately, the Duke of Trent is happily married,' Byng said. 'You would have dazzled him.'

'I don't wish for a duke or a lesser soul,' Cleo said. 'I'm quite ineligible for such an honor, and I meant it when I said I plan to be a wallflower. An unmarried one.'

Falconer winced. 'Are you illegitimate? That is . . . I . . . We didn't raise Julia to—'

'No, no,' Cleo said. 'I wasn't born until an acceptable fourteen months after my parents' elopement. But I have met any number of eligible men and they find me unsettling. Since I share their distaste, marital harmony is unlikely.'

'Gentlemen won't find you unsettling; they'll be on their knees before you,' Byng exclaimed, echoing Falconer's opinion.

'In my experience, men jump up from their knees to embrace me, mistakenly believing that unwelcome caresses will sway my refusal,' Cleo replied. 'I dislike being treated like a hothouse pineapple, which is another excellent reason to become a wallflower.'

'A pineapple?' Falconer asked.

'Sweet, expensive, and there for the taking,' Cleo explained.

'No woman in my family has ever allowed herself to be manhandled,' Falconer declared.

'Do you kick them?' Byng asked.

'I stab them with my umbrella,' Cleo replied cheerfully. 'Or my fan, depending on the environs. Most of my accessories are equipped with a pointed end guaranteed to fend off a man without killing him.'

'Excellent,' Byng said, nodding. 'I suppose one wouldn't wish to kill.'

'Not due to a kiss, no matter how unwelcome,' Cleo agreed.

'I don't care to have one of my relatives living in a hotel,' Falconer said. 'It doesn't look right.'

'Nothing about me is going to look right to polite society,' Cleo told him. 'I will not enumerate my deficiencies, but trust me, they exist.'

'You are a viscount's granddaughter, which is good enough for anyone!' Falconer exclaimed, reversing himself.

'You might as well accept that you'll be all the rage,' Byng put in.

'Nonsense. I'll be a wallflower. To be brutally frank, my inheritance stems from the sale of commodes.'

'Commodes, as in the new water closets, the ones that flush?' Byng inquired.

When Cleo nodded, Falconer thought she had a point about her ineligibility. 'My gouty foot keeps me from dancing, and I shall enjoy sitting with you.'

'Excellent,' Cleo said, smiling at him.

'I have a granddaughter,' Falconer said wonderingly, after the door closed behind her. 'Cleopatra.'

'Cleo,' Byng corrected him. He grinned. 'Lucky man.'

CHAPTER SIX

The next morning

Germain's Hotel occupied an entire block in the most expensive area of Mayfair. It was clad in buttery marble, like a courtly pretender to the House of Parliament. Every pillar had a ruffle, and the iron railings outside were torturously curled into fleurs-de-lis. No fewer than four men in impressive livery stood outside, springing to attention when Jake jumped down from his hackney.

The most imposing of them moved forward. Imposing, in this context, meant a cannonball of a belly and excessive braiding on each shoulder. He bowed.

'Mr Astor Addison, allow me to introduce myself. I am Farragut, your majordomo for the extent of your stay at Germain's.'

'How the devil did you guess who I am?' Jake asked.

'Germain's prides itself in knowing its guests,' Farragut replied.

Jake cocked an eyebrow. 'Even the American ones on their first visit to this country?'

'Grooms sent by Her Grace, the Duchess of Trent, delivered your luggage,' Farragut said stiffly. 'They were kind enough to describe you so that we could welcome you.' He glanced down at Jake's boots. 'They understated your informality.'

Jake threw Farragut a glance that made him start to blink rapidly. Then he headed past the man toward the shallow steps leading to the entrance.

'If there is anything I can do, Mr Astor Addison, to make your stay with us more comfortable,' Farragut said in a far more polite tone, trotting after him, 'you may ring for me day or night.'

'Just Addison will do.'

The majordomo led Jake straight through a large reception chamber, waving his hand in the direction of the dining room. 'Germain's dining room has a dress code; gentlemen must wear a coat and cravat.'

They climbed to the second floor, where Farragut pushed open a pair of double doors with a flourish. Jake walked in to find his valet, Moggly, vigorously polishing a brass candelabra.

Farragut's brow furrowed. 'You appear to be dusting, Mr Moggly. I can assure—'

Jake raised a hand. 'Save the conversation for when I'm not in the room.' He nodded toward the door, and Farragut withdrew, albeit with a distinctly indignant air.

61

'I have something to tell you that will make you happy, Moggly. I decided to stay in London for the time being, which means I'll have to order a new wardrobe.'

His valet put down the candelabra. 'Sir?'

'All of it, head to foot.' Jake paused. 'No, not foot. I can't give up these boots. The British find them so irritating. Everyone seems to stare at them. Even Merry told me to get rid of them, so I'll wear them when I visit her, of course.'

'Her Grace, the Duchess of Trent, asked me to inform you that you are bid to dinner tomorrow, and you'd "better show up or she'll skin your gizzard." That's a direct quote, sir. Prefaced by "Well, spit." Which I took to indicate disapprobation.'

'Merry as a duchess rather boggles the mind,' Jake said.

'May I ask why you require a new wardrobe, sir?' Moggly asked.

'I wish to blend into polite society. British society,' Jake said, somewhat untruthfully.

'I know how to disguise you as a gentleman,' Moggly said, with the tragic look of someone wounded to the bone. 'I've had plenty of practice.'

'English clothing will give me something extra, a touch of British elegance. I am interested in pursuing a business proposition with a lady staying here in the hotel. I have to look the part.'

The valet's nose went directly into the air. 'Ladies do not reside in hotels.'

'Her name is Miss Lewis. I assure you that she is in this hotel, as that is why we moved here.'

'Oh, *that* lady!' Moggly's eyes grew round as shillings. 'Miss Lewis has taken one of the two royal suites on the third floor. Her lady's maid calls herself a *dresser*, and she is attended by a flock of footmen, plus grooms to guard the corridor.'

'Excellent,' Jake said. 'So how will I encounter her?'

'You won't,' Moggly said. 'A private staircase leads to that floor.'

'What else did you learn about her?'

'She's the granddaughter of a viscount. Her suite has a private dining room and parlor.'

'No father in residence?' From what Merry had told him, the British guarded their daughters as if they were raw eggs, liable to crack and spoil.

Moggly shook his head. 'Miss Lewis is an heiress. She's dining with her grandfather, the viscount, tonight.'

Obviously, the hotel was rife with gossip. It was going to be challenging to reach the heiress.

He hadn't grown a fortune by the age of thirty by giving up at the first sign of an impediment.

He never gave up. Ever.

'Get me some livery,' he told Moggly. 'The hotel's, obviously, so I can get around her grooms.'

'You're going to court a lady while wearing the costume of a *servant*?' Moggly gaped like a dying codfish.

'I have no intentions of courting her,' Jake said, stripping off his shirt. 'A business proposition, remember? Ring for a hot bath, and then go downstairs and nick some livery, the coat at least. We'll wait for an evening when she isn't dining with her grandfather.'

'I shall *not* steal, even when commanded,' Moggly retorted. 'I suppose I can bribe one of the footmen.'

'Good idea,' Jake said. 'Cheaper than ordering a new wardrobe.'

Moggly shook his head. 'Your mother would be appalled, sir. Appalled.'

Jake tossed the shirt at his head.

CHAPTER SEVEN

Four days later

'*S*elon Monsieur Rousseau,' Cleo said to Monsieur Carnal, her French tutor, '*les animaux sauvages sont toutes bonnes.*'

The idea was nonsense, but she didn't know how to say so in French. Wild beasts weren't noble or good. Not that she'd ever met a bear or a lion, but she had the distinct feeling that Monsieur Rousseau hadn't either. Surely a lion would be pleased to gobble up a Frenchman for breakfast.

Her tutor had eyes that seemed too large for his egg-shaped head. Whenever she broached a sentence in his native language, horror made them appear to be on the verge of bursting out of his face. Cleo found it unnerving.

'*Tous bons, pas toutes bonnes,*' he snapped.

Cleo obediently repeated the sentence with the correct grammar.

Monsieur Carnal sighed and gave up. 'For tomorrow, please prepare a comparison of the brilliant essays of François-Marie Arouet, also known as Voltaire, to those of Rousseau, with

65

particular attention to this essay on the difference between man and beast.'

'I don't care for Rousseau,' Cleo observed.

'Only fools misjudge Rousseau,' Monsieur Carnal retorted. 'He is a superb observer of the human condition. I had hoped that you would be able to read Voltaire in the original by this time, but we must satisfy ourselves with a translation.'

He placed a small book on the table with a thump.

'Right,' Cleo said unenthusiastically. 'Thank you, Monsieur Carnal.'

Her tutor headed for the door without another word.

'Did that man just imply that you're a fool?' Gussie asked, getting up from the corner of the sitting room where she waited during Cleo's lessons.

'Yes,' Cleo said.

'He's the fool,' Gussie said. 'Considering that three months ago, you couldn't say a word, you're a miracle. Babies take years to learn to talk!'

'I loathe Rousseau. After reading his tedious essay, I was seized with a desire to walk on all fours just to prove the man wrong. *Marcher à quatre pattes*, to say it in French, because even though Monsieur Carnal thinks I'm hopeless, I *am* learning the language.'

Gussie frowned. 'There'll be no crawling for you, miss. You're too old for that.'

'Perhaps I'm too old to learn French.' Cleo

walked over and peered at herself in the glass over the mantelpiece. 'I might end up with a furrow in my brow from all this learning.' She kept thinking about the ferocity with which Mr Addison had responded to the news that he had lost Quimby's.

A pleasant feeling coursed through her body at the memory. It was satisfying to convince a plumber that a woman was capable of understanding the importance of a threaded pipe. But it was even more fun to steal an emporium from under a financier's nose.

'Why not take yourself into the dining room?' Gussie suggested. 'There's a nice warm fire burning; have a glass of sherry. You can clear your mind.' She handed over the scandal sheet she'd read during the French lesson. 'Much better than a nasty philosopher saying that men should crawl on all fours.'

'That's not precisely his point,' Cleo said.

'The gossip column is good,' Gussie said. 'It has a duke's love letters. Writing to his mistress, needless to say.'

'Hmm,' Cleo said, tucking the scandal sheet under her arm. 'That does sound interesting.'

'A body has to relax after all this learning. You're likely to burst your brain, miss. Burst it right open. Would you care to dress for dinner tonight?'

Cleo glanced down at her delightful gray walking costume, which Martha had delivered that very morning. 'I haven't many choices until we order more gowns from Quimby's. No, I shall stay as I am.'

'Take your fan and be sure not to injure your complexion by sitting too close to the fire,' Gussie ordered. 'I'll go downstairs, miss, so I can sponge and press a morning dress. I ordered pheasant, as they say the chef has a French way with the bird.'

The third floor of Germain's Hotel was divided between two large suites, with a common corridor in between. Cleo's chambers connected to each other in a line, so she entered the corridor only when she wished to leave the hotel. Her dining room was charming, decorated in robin's-egg blue with white accents. One end held a dining table, and the other a seating arrangement before a fireplace.

One of her footmen, Robbins, was sleepily leaning against the wall but he jerked upright.

'Look sharp,' Gussie told him. 'Miss Lewis would like a glass of sherry, the dry kind, mind you. Then go tell the kitchen that she'll have her evening meal now. You can pull up that small table before the fireplace, and be sure to stay outside the door in case she wants something.'

Cleo accepted a glass of sherry and sat down beside the fire. For a time, she occupied herself by reading a column boasting of 'salacious events,' which lived up to its promise. Apparently, a lady caught her lord entertaining his lover in the bedchamber, upon which she shot a pistol at the pair, luckily hitting the chandelier rather than the bed.

The accompanying illustration would have made her mother laugh; Julia had been – alas the target of many an angry wife.

No matron ever invaded my bedchamber, Julia informed her, which made Cleo realize that her mother's voice had been silent throughout the day.

The thought made her sad – but not tearful, which was progress. And she quite enjoyed her *pheasant à la braise* once it arrived, though she hadn't had much of an appetite in the last few months.

After the meal, Cleo began wrestling with French philosophers and their pointless wish to define the difference between men and beasts. She didn't look up when the door opened and Robbins announced, 'Household staff, miss,' before retreating to the corridor.

'I don't care for a sweet course,' she said, paying no attention to the footman – until he stopped directly before her.

Her brows drew together. She recognized those boots, although they appeared to have been polished since she first saw them in Quimby's.

She looked up, and sure enough, the American financier was looking down at her with a genial smile, as if he had every right to walk into her private dining room.

'What on earth are you doing here?' she asked, feeling curious rather than alarmed. Addison was large and imposing, but she was certain that he posed no threat. Besides, she could always jam the sharpened end of her fan into his ribs and call for Robbins.

Addison had stuffed himself into a suit of the hotel's crimson-striped livery, clearly designed for a man with a slimmer build.

'I've brought you a French brandy,' he said, nodding down at the silver tray he carried.

The livery was a terrible disguise. He still looked like a burly American financier. Not precisely a gentleman, but the kind of man who would never agree to work for anyone else. He was too broad-shouldered, too energetic, too commanding to be a servant.

Possibly even to be a gentleman.

Of course, American 'self-made' men were a different species.

Without waiting for a response, he set down the tray. Wheeling about, he plucked another goblet from the sideboard, returned, and dropped into the seat opposite her.

'Not only did I not invite you to my rooms, but I did not give you permission to join me,' Cleo said, allowing her voice to cool.

'In that case you wouldn't be able to enjoy this brandy,' he said, opening the decanter. 'I have it on the best evidence – gossip from the depths of this hotel – that you will appreciate what I am offering.'

He handed her a glass and took one for himself.

'So how was your day? Bought another company? I myself found some excellent scene painters, happy to move across the ocean.'

'Mr Addison!' Cleo said. 'You cannot simply barge into my private dining room.'

'I didn't "barge,"' he protested. 'I paved the way with French brandy. What's more, my valet paid a pound for this uncomfortable livery.'

'A waste of money,' she said, pushing away the book of French philosophy. Despite herself, she was prickling into an oddly awake state. Her mother's death had been so unexpected: one moment Julia was sweeping about, making eyes at the lead in *The Tempest*, and then she was gone.

Afterward, it was as if cotton wool descended into Cleo's brain, muffling the world around her.

But now . . .

'Every businessman knows that sometimes you must make an expenditure to ensure a later profit,' Addison said. 'My valet swears he has been camouflaging me as a gentleman for years, so he enjoyed the project of disguising me as one of the hotel staff.'

Cleo registered the crinkles at the edge of his eyes when Addison smiled and felt a qualm. She didn't care about men's expressions. She prided herself on being calm, whereas her mother relished feelings. Uncomfortable feelings.

She took a sip of amber-colored brandy, which slid through her veins, spicy and warm. 'What on earth is this?' she asked, despite herself. It was the brandy equivalent of her gray dress: demure, sober, and rich.

'Renault & Company Réserve, Champagne cognac, made for the Parisian restaurant La Tour d'Argent. I bought a case of it from a Frenchman the other day, intending to ship it all back home, but sharing a bottle with you was a more appealing prospect.'

She sat back and took a bigger sip. A true lady would likely be screaming for her footman, but Cleo's life had not infrequently presented her with odd circumstances.

'There's a hint of fruit,' she said, tasting it again.

He nodded. 'Cherry, or *cerise*, which makes it sweeter than many French brandies.'

'Showing off your knowledge of brandy or languages?' Cleo asked, raising an eyebrow.

'They say downstairs that you are learning the language from a prickly Frenchman,' he said, swirling his glass. 'You might as well analyze brandy the way the French do. Last time I was in Armagnac, they chattered endlessly about *cerise* and *figue*.'

'Figs?' Cleo asked. At his nod, 'What else do they say about me, downstairs? And how do you know?'

'I am in residence on the floor below you. My valet is an inveterate gossip, so he knows everything from your taste for brandy to the fact that you eat like a bird. Why is that, by the way? Your frame seems to be of an adequate size. You're not one of those frail women. Are you trying to trim your figure, as my mother terms it?'

He kept his eyes above her chin, but even so, Cleo leveled a frown in his direction. 'You've broken into my suite under false pretenses to offer commentary regarding my appearance?'

'You know damned well your figure is acceptable,' he said, eyes meeting hers over the rim of his glass.

Which made her feel a little disconcerted. Addison wasn't gazing at her with lustful or lascivious eyes. His gaze was direct and somehow even more disconcerting for it.

He apparently considered the subject of her figure closed with 'acceptable.' Along with 'adequate.'

'So why are you learning French?' he asked. 'Do you plan to sell commodes on the Continent?'

'My reasons for learning French are not so industrious,' Cleo said, pushing away her conviction that her figure was a good deal better than 'acceptable,' particularly when flattered by her darling new jacket. 'I've made up my mind to amend my deficiencies.'

His eyes flickered over her face, and he shook his head. 'I don't see any deficiencies. I do think you look better with hair. Without that bandage you had on your head.'

A chuckle escaped her. 'I gather you are not planning to flatter me into selling you Quimby's.'

He shrugged. 'Polite conversation is overreliant on fawning compliments. If you wish me to

73

elaborate on my opinion of you, I am willing to do so. Reluctantly. I'm not very good at it. My friend Merry regularly complains that I have no command of appropriate adjectives.'

'What would those be?'

'She was annoyed the other day when I neglected to say that she looked as youthful as the day she was born. Or some such.'

'Flattery would not make me more amenable to hearing your proposal to acquire Quimby's.'

'As I thought. So, why French?'

'I didn't have a governess as a girl and learned no languages. I plan to make an extended trip to Paris. Perhaps visit Cognac and Armagnac as well. I do love brandy, and their food is far better than that we cook in England.'

'"Better" is arguable. It's certainly fancier. The French never saw a liver that they didn't want to make into a rissole and plunk down in front of an unwary customer,' Addison said. 'In Paris I had a cock's comb served up to me. Laid across the plate like a scarlet feather.'

Cleo was taken aback, but he seemed serious. 'Was it good?' she asked cautiously.

'It did pass through my digestive system, if that's what you're asking.'

'I was not!' Cleo said tartly.

'In as many words you were.'

Cleo had to suppress a smile. Addison was reck-lessly ungentlemanlike. Her mother would have been horrified.

74

Not necessarily, her mother observed, in the depths of her mind.

'Since we're on the subject,' Addison continued, 'I can tell you that French drains are excellent, but their commodes are not, so they could use your intervention.'

'Stop smiling at me like that,' Cleo ordered. 'We are not friends.'

'What are we, then?'

'Not even acquaintances.'

'I beg to differ,' Addison said, his eyes glinting at her. 'I wish to be friends. Unless I am wrong, you've decided not only to deprive my theaters, but to destroy my future happiness altogether.'

'And how, pray tell, shall I do that?' Cleo inquired. The brandy was giving her an irresistible wish to giggle, and she *never* giggled.

'You plan to ban me from Lewis Commodes,' he said, a little smile playing around his mouth. 'My wife will loathe me for it, and then she'll leave me for a man whose house is fixed up with the best water closets.'

Cleo barely stopped herself from jerking back. 'You have a wife, Mr Addison?'

'Not yet. Though I plan to marry soon. Won't you call me Jake? All my friends do. Are you certain that you don't wish for a sweet course? This brandy would be complemented by an apple tart.'

'How do you think they'll respond, downstairs, when they discover a supposed hotel footman sitting at my side?' Cleo asked, shaking her head at him. 'There would be a frightful scandal. You aren't so keen to buy Quimby's that you think to compromise me into a forced marriage?'

'Absolutely not.'

She gave him a direct look. 'Just in case I furnished you with an idea, Mr Addison, you should know that such tactics will never work with me. I don't give a damn about my reputation. I've already weathered that particular storm.'

'You refuse to marry me?' he asked. His eyes were dancing over the rim of his glass. It was extraordinarily provoking.

'Yes, I do,' she said, keeping her voice even.

'If it gives you peace of mind, I'll point out that I haven't proposed to you, and I have no intention to do so. Under any circumstances, including scandal.' He laughed aloud. 'To be frank, only a madman would go to such an extreme measure merely to acquire a costumier, excellent though Martha Quimby may be. I am not mad.'

His eyes were disconcertingly honest. A flash of irritation zipped through her. Unmarried men did consider her attractive enough for marriage, especially with a fortune in the offing. She may have chosen to be a wallflower, but she certainly didn't have to be one.

Whereas Addison seemed to believe that neither a fortune nor Quimby's was enough to make up for her personal deficits.

Even *with* hair. Of course, hers was very red.

His brows drew together. 'Am I to understand that some rogue tried to compromise you?'

'Yes. Though he didn't put on livery to do so.' Cleo took another sip of brandy and let its comforting warmth slide down her throat. Addison's opinion of her was irrelevant. She didn't care what an American thought of her.

What *any* man thought of her.

'Appalling,' he said, looking as if he meant it. 'To reassure you, Miss Lewis, I have no plans to court you by fair means or foul, no matter how delectable the prospect of gaining Quimby's might be.'

'I am happy to hear it,' Cleo said. She was aware of a crawling sense of embarrassment, and her cheeks were turning pink. She had misinterpreted his laconic reference to her figure, thinking that he was attracted to her.

'Acceptable' didn't equate to 'marriageable.'

'When I marry, the lady in question will be serene and . . . domestic, for lack of a better word,' Addison put in obligingly. As if she cared. 'Unless I'm much mistaken, you are a woman who wakes up in the morning and then charges about, solving problems.'

'I do not charge about,' Cleo corrected him.

'No? You remind me of my mother.'

'Is that a compliment?' This was the oddest conversation Cleo had ever had. Somehow the American had managed to settle down opposite her as if they were old friends.

77

'I am quite fond of my mother.'

His eyes were an interesting color: indigo, she decided. 'To return to the subject, Mr Addison, why are you in my dining room? Did you think to bribe me with brandy?'

'No,' he responded. 'I know few people in London, and I thought that you and I might have much to talk about. After all, both of us tried to buy a costuming establishment. It's not as if we were in competition for a china teacup. Surely that unusual circumstance gives us grounds for any number of conversational topics, other than one's digestion, I mean?'

'Men and women do not generally discuss business,' Cleo observed.

'I am not very good at the trivial conversation. I enjoy talking about facts. Money. Contracts.'

Cleo took another sip of brandy. Addison wasn't attracted to her as a woman. Instead, he appeared interested in what she might say. She had to admit that it was a heady emotion, more appealing than flattery.

Even the certainty that his attention was a tool to convince her to give up Quimby's didn't extinguish the appeal.

'I'd like to know more about your business concerns,' he said. 'I gather Lewis Commodes are the best on the market.'

'They are. My father invented the sliding valve that is integral to our design,' she told him.

'What does that do?'

'It uses standing water to seal the bowl's outlet, which stops foul odors,' she explained. 'His first inventions were for vehicles. But my mother's complaints about water closets were so vigorous that he turned his mind to commodes.' She couldn't help smiling. 'He could solve any problem. For example, his iron-strapped pipes last far longer than wooden ones, which quickly rot.'

'I'm trying to visualize the arrangement,' Addison said, frowning.

'What about you, Mr Addison? What interested you in theaters?'

She felt as if they were playing a game, like two five-year-olds rolling a ball back and forth. Except that Addison was no child and certainly not gentlemanly. The breeches of his livery were as tight as his coat. His thighs were unattractively muscled.

She glanced away, because some primitive part of her relished the way those muscles flexed when he moved his leg.

'Like you, I inherited the business from my father.' He idly turned his glass, making sparks of firelight glint off the crystal. 'I find you far more interesting than I, Miss Lewis. I had imagined that your plan to expand Quimby's came from a personal impulse to join polite society. But they say downstairs that you are a viscount's granddaughter. Surely a blue-blooded member of the nobility would have had a governess to teach her French?'

He leaned back in his chair, eyeing her quizzically. The lion at rest, Cleo thought irrelevantly.

She shrugged. 'My claim to blue blood is diluted since my father was a blacksmith's son. My parents eloped, and I did not grow up in the viscount's household.'

'How long ago did you inherit?'

'Eight years ago, now, at age fourteen. I had a trustee until I was eighteen.'

'After which you grew the concern,' he guessed, one side of his mouth pulling up into a wry smile.

'Indeed, it has doubled in size in the last three years,' Cleo said, faintly surprised that she was sharing details. 'My father enjoyed inventions. He was not interested in the details of how one brings a product to market. I was, and am.' She drank off her brandy and put down the glass.

'My uncle, John Astor, credits his wife with the growth of his fortune,' Addison said.

Cleo nodded. 'The trade in fur? And more recently, the opium trade.'

Addison's eyebrow flew up. 'You are well informed.'

'You are not the only one with the ability to make inquiries. I will say that the report cost me considerably more than the pound you paid for that livery.'

He cleared his throat, looking at his glass rather than her. 'Why did you pay for an investigation?'

'You are not a man who is used to losing,' she said flatly. 'In the event that you declared war on my ownership of Quimby's, understanding of my rival would be a shield and weapon. I must say that I'm surprised to see you disguising yourself in livery, Mr Astor Addison, formerly Mr Astor. The report described you as straightforward.'

He winced. 'A glancing blow.'

Cleo found that her lips were curling into a cheerful smile. 'I hadn't suspected that you would come up with a nefarious plan to invade my chambers and talk me into changing my mind.'

His eyes darkened. 'I am not interested in compromising you, Miss Lewis. There's nothing nefarious about my visit.'

Somewhere deep inside, Cleo was still struggling with a feeling that he needn't be *quite* so dismissive; at the same time she was cheering her (obviously correct) use of 'nefarious.' 'I was referring to the bribe that surely you are about to offer me,' she replied, keeping her voice matter-of-fact.

'If it would work.'

'It would not. I have no need for money.' She said it gently because she was aware how much men disliked a refusal. 'Though that's not the point, is it? Many without need are driven by greed. I have sufficient funds. I shall grow Quimby's for pure pleasure, and because I'm interested in helping its proprietor, Martha Quimby.'

'I have no need for money either.' His eyes locked with hers. 'We are alike in that, Miss Lewis.'

'Would it head you off if I assured you that Martha – at least in my estimation – will not succumb to your lure?'

'Everyone has a price,' Mr Addison said. 'I will admit that Mrs Quimby's price to leave this

81

country would likely be exorbitant. I am not a man who likes to pay a dime more than what something is worth.'

Cleo summoned a charming smile and aimed it in his direction like a weapon. Showing that he wasn't an idiot, he flinched. 'I anticipate that you will come up with another plan to acquire the emporium, Mr Addison. But now it is time for you to leave. I must return to wrestling with French philosophers.'

'I do indeed have a plan,' he acknowledged. And then, 'I am fluent in French, if you would like assistance.'

'No, thank you. Good night.' She inclined her chin in farewell.

'My school days are far behind me, but I'm certain that French lessons will be improved by strong drink. I will leave you the brandy.' He rose. 'I look forward to seeing you again, Miss Lewis.'

She looked up at him. 'I appreciate your vigor in pursuing your goals, Mr Addison, but you will not be allowed into my chambers again. I may not be vulnerable to being compromised into marriage, but I value my privacy.'

He smiled at her. 'I believe we shall meet at Vauxhall Gardens in a few weeks, if not sooner.'

She frowned.

'With your grandfather, Viscount Falconer. It seems that he and one of my dearest friends, the Duchess of Trent, are well acquainted. Merry told me last night at dinner that he has accepted an invitation to join her party in your name as well.' He bowed, a brisk gesture from a man with no interest in social niceties. 'Miss Lewis.'

When the door closed behind him, Cleo leaned back in her chair. Addison was . . . He was troublesome.

It was merely because she'd never met a businessman like him, of course. As a sex, men tended to be condescending at first, and cowed thereafter. Condescending, given they thought a woman would blush at the mention of a privy. Cowed and resentful, after realizing she held the patents and thus all the power.

Mr Jacob Astor Addison was not cowed. A crumb of disquiet stirred in her stomach. How far would an American businessman go to get what he wanted?

The thought made her head ache, so she began pulling pins from her hair, her mind drifting from Addison to Foster Beacham, the man whom she had come close to marrying the previous year.

She had truly liked Foster. He was a member of the Drury Lane Theatre company, an actor who would surely be a lead in a year or so. He had blue eyes like Addison's, except the American's were dark blue, almost navy. Foster's eyes were sky blue and shone with admiration, desire, and supposed love. He had even taken to throwing her yearning glances from the stage.

Her mother chose that moment to pipe up after staying silent throughout the conversation with

Addison. *I told you that you should have tossed him back into the sea, darling. They get so pesky when they're besotted.*

Cleo hadn't minded the idea of a besotted husband until she discovered that Foster was holding secret conversations with one of her competitors in the plumbing business. He wasn't in love, but greedy, and their engagement was off, no matter how stridently her fiancé protested that he was merely trying to learn the trade.

Foster was neat and trim, a sleek, handsome man who knew his figure was one of his best assets. No man could pose more of a contrast to Addison, who acted as if his body didn't exist. His muscles just carried him through life, as opposed to being flexed for a lady's appreciation. Addison threw himself into the chair, whereas Foster invariably seated himself with a view to displaying his excellent posture.

What's more, Addison was *big*. The tight livery emphasized what she'd noticed on their first meeting. He was tall and broad.

Cleo couldn't help admitting to herself that his body . . . well.

A glance at him was potent, like the French brandy. Look at him too long, even under her lashes, and a suspicious warmth spread through her limbs like sticky honey. Embarrassing. *Absurd.*

She swallowed. She so prided herself on being contained that it was a shock to realize that part of her was like her mother, after all.

A member of the human race.

A person subject to lust.

My daughter, Julia supplied, but Cleo firmly banished the voice.

It had been comforting to hear her mother's commentary in her ear, but she needed to learn to live alone, without Julia, especially when it came to matters of desire.

The honest truth was that her mouth had gone dry when Mr Addison smiled at her. She'd had to keep her gaze away from his tight breeches. From the shape of his tool, tucked behind his placket, its thick length perfectly clear to the eye.

She pulled out the last pin, and her curls tumbled down past her shoulders. Shaking her head, she let her hair fly around her shoulders and then began plaiting back a few strands in the front to keep it out of her eyes. Fingers nimbly working, she forced herself to acknowledge another truth.

She, Cleopatra Lewis, felt lust, like every other human. No, like both animals and humans. There was nothing there that a French philosopher could use to distinguish humanity from beasts.

She had always told herself that she would never be enslaved by the feeling, the way her mother was.

She *wasn't* enslaved.

She could refuse the feeling, reject its effects, disguise it as disdain –

All of those were ladylike skills. In fact, ignoring

desire was proof positive that she was not her mother's daughter. She poured herself another slug of brandy.

These uncomfortable feelings would fade in no time.

CHAPTER EIGHT

7, Cavendish Square, London
Residence of the Duke of Trent
The back garden

After asking for Merry, Jake was ushered into the garden behind the ducal townhouse, which he hadn't seen before. It was palatially large, with the Thames lazily flowing at the bottom. Rather than being set out in neat quadrangles, like most gardens he knew, winding curves and clumps of flowers broke up the space.

He had a dim memory that Merry used to talk about designing gardens when she was a girl. If so, she'd created one to live in, with a permanent croquet installment at one side, a frivolous little gazebo by the river, and plenty of grass to run about on.

Just then the duchess herself jumped out from behind a stout oak tree, a wooden sword in her hand. At his shoulder, the butler sighed almost soundlessly, and said, 'Her Grace is currently occupied, Mr Addison, but I am certain she will greet you shortly.'

He retreated into the house. All three of Merry's children were chasing her across the lawn with high-pitched screams, waving their own swords. At first, he thought they were pirates, but realized they were all wearing white kitchen cloths tied over one shoulder, clearly improvised togas. So, ancient Rome.

Merry caught sight of Jake and waved. 'One minute,' she called, sounding a little winded. She pulled herself upright, thrust her sword into the air, and shouted, '*Non ducor, duco!*'

Jake's Latin was far behind him, but he agreed: a duchess leads, rather than being led. 'Definitely not pirates,' he murmured, strolling onto the battlefield.

Her eldest, Thomas, also known as Thomas Cedric John Allardyce, the future seventh Duke of Trent, howled 'Mama!'

'You're not supposed to take a stand yet,' the next eldest, Fanny, cried reproachfully, planting the tip of her sword in the grass. '*Gladiator in arena consilium capit.* The arena is over *there*, not here.' She pointed at the gazebo at the bottom of the garden.

'Yes, but darling, I'm longing for lemonade, and Mr Addison has come to visit,' Merry explained. Then she shouted again, '*Non ducor, duco!*'

Her youngest, Peter, didn't mind the script change. '*Sic semper tyrannnis!*' he retorted, trotting toward his mother, sword outstretched.

'Thus always to tyrants,' Jake translated,

impressed. The child couldn't be more than six, but he already knew how to threaten violence in a second language, always a useful skill.

'Darling, remember what I told you—' Merry called, but the sturdy little gladiator tripped over his own feet and slammed his forehead into his own weapon on the way down into the grass.

Merry knelt down to mop up tears with the hem of her gown, glanced at Jake, and pointed toward the gazebo, so he strolled off in that direction.

Thomas jumped in his way and dropped a credible bow. 'Good afternoon, Mr Addison. Do you know Latin?'

'*Oderint dum metuant*,' Jake stated.

'Let them . . .' He puzzled it out. '*Let them hate so long as they fear!* Excellent!' He ran away, presumably to share Caligula's wisdom with the family. Once under the shade of the gazebo, Jake dropped into a comfortable chair and waited for Merry.

It didn't smell of London behind the duke's townhouse, but of freshly mown meadow grass and river water. A few fat bees were lazily swirling over Merry's flower beds, and a willow tree trailed its branches into the water. The river turned yellow-green near the shore, so probably not too deep, though Merry had prudently erected a fence to keep her children on the shore.

'You were right,' Jake told Merry once she collapsed into a seat beside him and demanded to know all about Miss Lewis. 'A conversation was completely ineffective. She won't give up Quimby's.'

Merry was kind enough not to smirk. 'I told you she wouldn't. If she's anything like her grandfather, Viscount Falconer, you haven't a chance.'

'Who would have thought it?' he said with some disgust. 'You told me that a lady was never allowed to invest her own money.'

'Normally, they are not,' Merry said. 'Miss Lewis appears to be a true original. So, she wouldn't listen to you?'

'She listened,' he said. 'But she is damnably certain that her idea has equal merit to mine.'

Merry leaned forward and bellowed at her children, who were following a footman indoors. 'Don't forget George!'

Thomas veered under the shade of an oak tree and grabbed the handle of a red wagon.

'Riding in style, is he?' Jake asked. He could make out the plump shape of the elderly bulldog being pulled at top speed over the grass.

'The poor dear has something wrong with his hips. Otherwise, he'd still be dashing around the battlefield,' Merry confirmed. 'At any rate, you need to find another costumier.'

'I want Quimby's,' Jake said glumly, knowing he was going to have to settle for second-best. 'Martha Quimby could have easily become one of those faux French modistes, but my impression is that she likes the challenge of coming up with bishop's robes one day and fairy wings the next.'

Merry nodded, leaning back in her chair and wiggling her bare toes. Her eyes followed his to her feet, and she said, 'Don't you dare become prudish in your old age, Jake.'

'I'm not old,' he protested. 'I'm jealous.'

'Last year, Trent and I commissioned costumes from Quimby's for Lady Buckinghamshire's masquerade.' She turned to a tin bucket set in the shade, ladled lemonade into crystal wineglasses, and handed him one.

The drink smelled fragrantly like sunshine and the Italian countryside. 'How were you costumed?'

'We were the North and South Star. I had a gown of silver tissue, and Trent was in a waistcoat and breeches of the same fabric, with a blue silk mantle. Our capes were starred all over with plated silver stars, and we had wings too, gorgeous gauze ones. Trent refused to wear his wings, but I loved mine.'

'I'm astounded that you talked Trent into silver breeches.' Jake didn't know the duke terribly well, but he would have sworn the man didn't strut around like a peacocking fool. He wore respectable black and spent his time doing respectable things. Like overseeing steam engines being built in Wales, which was what he was doing now.

'Trent wanted us to dress as a monk and nun. It wasn't easy to persuade him,' Merry said, a naughty smile playing around her mouth.

Jake sighed. 'Since I cannot convince Miss Lewis to sell, I've been wondering if I could change Martha Quimby's mind. I'm not welcome at the emporium—'

He broke off.

He could think of one way by which he *would* be welcome at Quimby's.

Extremely welcome.

He narrowed his eyes. Merry had offered her husband something Trent couldn't refuse – and in exchange, the duke had donned silver breeches: *Trent*, who'd been clothed in respectable black whenever Jake met him.

Obviously, His Grace didn't give a damn about his dignity.

If a duke could wear silver breeches, so could he.

Jake had never lost a battle, and he didn't intend to now. If it took silver breeches to win a war, why then the war was easily won.

'What do you think of my clothing?' he asked.

'Anyone can tell that Weston didn't make your coat,' Merry said.

'I'm going to order a new wardrobe – from Martha Quimby. She can't afford to say no.'

Merry frowned at him. 'How will that convince Miss Lewis to allow you to buy Quimby's? If anything, you will confirm her ideas about tailoring.'

'Not if I commission *gaudy* clothing,' he said, a smile curling his lips. 'Not if my clothes are garish, and I tell everyone who made them. I'll escort you to events and boast about how Quimby's made me fashionable.'

After Jake's uncle, John Astor, married his aunt Sarah, they started selling fur, a smelly, dirty business. 'Until we could afford to move to

Broadway and Vesey, we lived with that smell,' his aunt had told him once. 'My sisters scoffed at me. Your grandmother refused to pay me a visit. But it was worth it, Jake.' They had built their first fortune out of the fur trade.

This was a parallel situation.

He would deliberately wear tasteless clothing and invite polite society to deride him, a task that – being not so polite – the Brits would relish.

'Brilliant,' Merry breathed. 'Though a bit mean-spirited.'

'The British invariably expect an American to be taken advantage of, so they'll believe it. Brits love to scoff behind a foreigner's back, Merry. You must have experienced it yourself.'

She rolled her eyes. 'Have I! You should have been here when the news leaked out that I was nursing my own children. You'd have thought I had sprouted horns.'

'If they ridicule me, no one will consider buying clothing from Quimby's. Especially those who are uneasy about their standing. Terrified of being thought gauche.'

'You're right,' Merry said reluctantly. 'But it's not kind. Poor Miss Lewis has an excellent idea, and you'll ruin it for her, not to mention damaging her investment.'

'I'll head off her plan before she loses any investment,' he corrected. 'Quimby's would presumably expand into the modiste business next Season. Instead, she'll sell me Quimby's after this Season.'

93

'Not at a discount,' Merry said sharply. 'If you're ruining her plan for expansion, Jake, then you must pay her an appropriate amount.'

Jake had already decided that on his own. 'I'll pay her over double what it's worth and give Mrs Quimby an extra two thousand pounds as well. You should have seen the gown in the window of her emporium. It glittered like a tin roof in the sun. I'm actually doing a favor for any fish-monger's daughter who would end up clad in spangles.'

'I don't feel good about it,' Merry said, frowning.

'All's fair in love and war,' he said. 'This is war. Do you feel it's unfair simply because Miss Lewis is a woman? If she were a man, would you feel the same?'

Merry grimaced. 'I see what you mean.'

'I respect Miss Lewis as an investor,' he said. 'But the ballroom is a long way from the stage. How could she know whether the garments created at Quimby's are fashionable or overly theatrical, garish, and tasteless? Her own clothing is prim.' He thought about the gown she'd worn the first time they met. 'Even puritanical.'

'Have you thought about the fact that you will have to wear those garish garments? *You* will be donning apricot-colored breeches, gloves with fringes, rosy cravats.' Merry clapped her hands, apparently dropping all her reluctance. 'Oh, Jake, I'd pay for your wardrobe myself, just for the pleasure of seeing you dressed like a peacock!'

'I'm going to do it,' he stated. 'I'll return to Quimby's next week.'

'Not until you warn Miss Lewis, Jake. It's only fair.'

'I suppose I could tell her that I intend to offer her a sum commensurate with her projections, even though the woman came up with the idea in order to spite me.'

Merry scowled at him. 'For goodness' sake, listen to yourself! You sound like a disgruntled schoolboy who can't bear to lose.'

Jake grinned at her. 'Every time I start thinking about how much I like you, I am jolted back into remembering how glad I am that we didn't marry.'

'That was never an option since you didn't ask. I've been married nearly a decade, Jake. A *decade*! I can scarcely believe it myself.'

Jake eyed her. His childhood friend had betrothed herself to a few rogues back home before she shook them off and decamped to London. She was a beautiful woman who had grown only more lovely for being cosseted by her duke. 'Stop fishing for a compliment; you look well enough.'

Merry pounced on that. 'You're supposed to tell me that I haven't aged! You always were a bit of a misanthrope, and you seem to have only grown worse in recent years.'

'I dislike exchanging trivialities,' Jake said, feeling a pang of pity for Merry's husband. She never overlooked deficits in a man's character, as any well-mannered lady would do. 'You know you're striking. Don't pretend you're miffed, because I know you're not.'

'You're frightfully arrogant,' Merry told him with the impunity of someone who'd known him since the age of ten. 'Acerbic wouldn't be going too far.'

'I'm not acerbic!'

'Acerbic when you're annoyed. Harsh when you're angry. Thank goodness we didn't marry. They would have heard us bellowing from Boston to New York, like stags clashing on a mountaintop.'

'Like Roman gladiators?' Jake asked, finishing his lemonade. 'Am I to believe that you don't argue with Trent?'

'Occasionally,' Merry said, a note of caution in her voice.

Jake reached over and poked her. 'Fibber.'

'We may disagree now and then,' Merry conceded. 'But do fess up, Jake. I had a letter today from my aunt saying that you had formed an understanding with a young lady, but she neglected to tell me who it was. You never mentioned anyone! Tell me about her.'

'Your aunt was referring to Miss Frederica Cabot.'

'My cousin Frederica? *That* Frederica?'

Merry's voice had risen to an ill-mannered squeak, though Jake decided not to mention it. 'The only Frederica I know.'

She cleared her throat. 'I find it hard to imagine the two of you together.'

'The lady is attractive, wellborn, and has a charming temperament. My mother likes her.'

'Yes, but she—' Merry stopped and bit her lip.

Jake gave her a look that indicated further commentary was unwelcome. Frederica was to be his wife, after all.

'Don't glare at me,' she said, obviously unmoved. 'Frederica certainly comes from a good family. But you wouldn't dream of calling her Freddie, would you?'

'I don't want to marry anyone named Freddie.'

Merry rolled her eyes. 'Have you imagined being married to Frederica, Jake, *really* thought about it?'

'Would I name the lady, had I not? I proceeded as with any merger, assessing the facts for and against. I will admit that my mother's approval swung the balance.'

'When it comes to choosing a spouse, someone who will be with you for the rest of your life . . .' She shook her head.

Jake reined in his irritation. Merry planned to share her opinion, whether he wanted it or not. 'Yes?'

'I've made only a few visits to Boston since I left a decade ago,' Merry said, tapping her mouth with a finger. 'Frederica must be eight years younger than I am, so I don't know her well.'

'Ten, actually. She's nineteen,' Jake said. 'Whereas you are near thirty—'

Merry gave a little shriek and swatted at him again.

'And I jumped over that landmark last summer,'

he continued. 'You are beautiful and beloved, Merry. Age shouldn't frighten you. Have some backbone.'

'There,' Merry exclaimed, 'that's *exactly* why you and I would have had a quarrelsome marriage. I couldn't stand it if my husband referenced my age so casually.'

'Frederica won't mind.'

Merry muttered something that sounded, confusingly, like 'Moo.'

Jake raised an eyebrow.

'More lemonade?' Merry asked brightly.

'You might as well tell me,' Jake said, accepting another ladleful.

Merry took on the grave air of someone revealing state secrets. 'Are you aware of Frederica's abiding interest in livestock? Last time I was home, she enthused throughout the meal about a stoneware pitcher featuring a heifer.'

'I have no interest in crockery; she can set the table as she wishes.'

'Do you recall the costume party for your eighteenth birthday? Frederica was there.'

'She was?'

'She came as a cow.'

'She would have been seven or eight years old! I'm sure she was adorable.'

'Her mooing was eloquent.'

'Frederica has interests other than livestock.' Though now Jake thought of it, their last conversation had been about cattle herding.

'Crewel embroidery,' Merry said, nodding. 'She

is working on a set of chair seats featuring short-horn cows. And how do I know? Because she told me at length!'

'My mother taught me that women's arts are to be taken seriously,' Jake said. 'You do remember that Mother opened a cooperative a few years ago in which women exhibit and sell their handmade goods, don't you?'

'Of course I know that! She and I have a lively correspondence. I enjoy hearing about her endeavors.'

'My mother is tiring to be around,' Jake said flatly. 'I decided long ago that the mother of my children would be a calm woman with no particular interests outside the home.'

Merry put down her glass with a click. 'You are an anachronism, Jake. I would wish better for you than a tepid marriage to a woman with a growing collection of china cattle.'

'I've never met a woman whom I liked as much as you, so perhaps my unmarried state is your fault,' Jake offered.

'You would never have wed me even if you had returned to Boston for my debut,' Merry told him, her eyes alight with laughter. 'I'm not peaceful, remember? Nor biddable, because that's what you really want. You want a wife who won't cross you, only praise you, and thinks you're the most wonderful person for miles around.'

'There's nothing wrong with that,' Jake said.

'Not if you feel the same about Frederica,' Merry

said, leaning in to kiss his cheek. 'But you don't, do you?'

'I shall feel that way when I come to know her better. She's young.'

'She will *always* be younger than you.' Merry looked at him guilelessly. 'When you are seventy, she'll be a sprightly sixty-year-old, sitting at your bedside, enthusing over a Hereford – her favorite breed, as I recall.'

'Damn it,' Jake said, shaking his head. 'No wonder you had to come to England to find a husband, Merry. When Frederica agrees to become my wife—'

'So, you haven't proposed?'

'I shall propose on my return from England. I bought a ring a few days ago.'

'Oh, lovely! Is that what was delivered from Rundell & Bridges this morning? May I see?'

Jake pulled the small box from his pocket and Merry flipped it open.

'It's exquisite,' she breathed. 'Why an opal? Is that Frederica's favorite stone?'

'I was buying a gift for my mother, and it caught my eye.'

'Do you even know what she fancies?' Merry asked. 'Here's a thought, Jake: What if a cattleman comes along and snatches her up while you're in Britain? Please notice that I didn't suggest he might *lasso* her.'

After which, she howled with laughter, having amused herself.

100

Jake didn't care to put the obvious into words. Given that Frederica – along with most of society on the far side of the Atlantic – was aware that he was contemplating a proposal, the lady would remain unmarried until he returned from England and fell on one knee. Though he would likely just hand over the ring and be done with it.

'Of course, your father was an Astor, and you made your own fortune, and you do have a nice nose,' Merry said, recovering. 'Do stop scowling at me, Jake. Obviously, ladies have given you too much attention. My husband says that before marrying me, ballrooms made him feel like the only red-blooded creature in a swamp full of horseflies.'

'Not a bad description,' Jake observed. 'Did you know that horseflies slice a hole in your skin and drink the pooled blood?'

Merry yelped. 'Enough! It's astonishing that Frederica will take you on in all your sharp-tongued glory. And your mother is happy with your choice?'

'Certainly. In the last year, my mother has paraded any number of quivering maidens before me, including Frederica.'

'Quivering?'

'Would you prefer radiant? Fair as angels? Eyes like dark blue pansies?'

Merry shook her head. 'You'll have to be less dismissive if you want a happy marriage, Jake.'

'My wife will take me as I am,' he stated.

101

She tapped her chin with one finger. 'Since you haven't yet proposed to Frederica, I'll introduce you to a young lady or two here. I still think you would be happiest with an original, a British lady who is unimpressed by your lineage and your fortune.'

'No, thank you.' He paused. 'Frederica's eyes are blue, Merry, and opals are her favorite stone.'

Merry leaned over and brushed a kiss on his cheek. 'Then I apologize for teasing you, old friend. If you don't mind my asking, what will Frederica think if she learns of your new wardrobe? Many of my friends carry on a vast correspondence with American friends and relatives. She's bound to find out.'

He shrugged. 'She's not the kind of person who bothers about such matters.'

'Perhaps you should write to her,' Merry suggested.

'We don't correspond,' Jake said. 'I don't even write to my mother.'

'*I* write to your mother!' Merry cried.

'What on earth for?'

'She's one of my favorite people. Yours too, for all you pretend to find her annoying.'

'Write to my mother about my new wardrobe if you wish. I expect she'll find my plan to win Quimby's amusing.'

'May I mention the opal ring?'

'Certainly,' Jake said indifferently.

He couldn't help wondering what it would have been like to wed a woman like Merry.

102

Frederica would never play gladiator in bare feet and a faded dishcloth. She was charming and placid. He rather liked her affection for cows.

No, he was right.

Miss Frederica Cabot would make an excellent wife and mother. She enjoyed embroidery and painting landscapes, quite good ones. Trees, hills, and yes, cows, but who didn't like a nice cow on the wall?

At the end of a long day, he would walk into his house to find Frederica sitting in a pool of candlelight, working on her embroidery, a welcoming smile on her face.

Merry might be his oldest friend, but she didn't understand him.

The last – the very *last* – thing he wanted was an 'original,' whether English or American.

CHAPTER NINE

15, Charles Street
Mayfair, London
Viscount Falconer's townhouse

Viscount Falconer had spent the day more energetically than was his wont. He had made his butler's life a misery, demanding that the nursery be cleaned and aired, in case Cleo would like to see where her mother grew up.

Not that Julia ever spent much time in the townhouse nursery; his wife had been of the opinion that children should stay safely in the country, away from coal smoke. Having had years to regret his parenting choices, Falconer no longer agreed. If they had seen more of Julia as a child, would she – would she have been more attached to them, to be blunt?

It was a question with no answer, so he shook it off and returned to badgering his cook into creating delicious morsels that his granddaughter might enjoy.

When Cleo walked through the door, Falconer

had his stick at hand and clambered to his feet to greet her.

'Grandfather,' Cleo said, coming over and kissing his cheek. 'Do sit down; there is no need to stand on ceremony between us.'

Falconer rather gratefully sank back into his chair. 'Byng will join us soon, and I invited two guests, one of whom is a young lady, so you aren't surrounded by ancients as you have in your other visits.'

'I don't mind being in company with you and Byng in the least,' Cleo said, sounding sincere.

'I asked Ponder to put out sherry and ratafia, so that we can serve ourselves.' It was a tacit acknowledgment of the fact that the butler would probably wait to serve them until dinner was called, out of pure peevishness.

'Ratafia,' Cleo said, wrinkling her nose. 'Made for ladies with the assumption that they have a sweet tooth. May I pour you a glass of sherry, Grandfather?'

'Just a touch,' Falconer said. 'The doctor says that alcohol spurs on my gout. I had to give up caviar and foie gras.'

'Doctors should be taken in moderation,' Cleo said, smiling at him as she handed over a glass.

Falconer felt a hiccup in his chest again at that smile. She was so *like* Julia and yet so different. His daughter would never have worn that gown, for example. Or would she?

As a girl, his daughter had blithely insisted on

wearing breeches and riding astride in the country. Julia had battled her mother over her debut ball, demanding to wear scarlet and purple, although other young ladies would be in pastels. She had always wanted to sparkle and shine, to stand out from every other woman in a room.

Cleo, by contrast, wouldn't be out of place at any elegant gathering. Her gown was misty gray silk, clenched under the bosom the way women's dresses were these days. She wasn't in full mourning, but she wasn't sparkling either.

Yet the pearls on her necklace were nearly the size of quail eggs. He cleared his throat. 'I gather that your father, Mr Lewis, is no longer alive?'

'My father died several years ago,' Cleo said. 'His parents had passed away before him, and I never met them.'

'I had no idea where Julia was, or whether she was alive, until I read your first letter,' Falconer said, loathing the rasp in his voice. A man wasn't supposed to show weakness . . . but he felt weak.

His granddaughter was silent for a moment. 'Mother depicted her elopement as a great adventure. I am unsurprised to learn that she neglected to leave you and my grandmother a letter. She rarely imagined the distress her escapades caused to others.'

'Was Julia – was she happy?' Falconer asked, pushing the words into the air.

'For the most part,' Cleo said. 'Perhaps it is more accurate to say that she enjoyed sadness as much

106

as joy. Luckily, my father didn't pass away until I was of an age to take over as a steadying force in her life.'

'We would have accepted her marriage,' Falconer said. 'She—'

Byng joined them in a wave of chatter, settling only when he had a glass of sherry in hand.

'We are discussing Julia's husband,' Falconer told Byng. 'Was Mr Lewis an actor?'

'An inventor,' Cleo replied, and hesitated. 'The son of the blacksmith on your country estate.'

Falconer drew in a sharp breath. The entire county knew that their daughter had been abducted – or run away from home – but his blacksmith had never said a word. Not a word. No wonder he had up and left for Scotland the following year, without a by-your-leave.

'Mother adored the story of their elopement,' Cleo continued. 'Father rode up on a white horse to a ball at Windsor Castle, swept her onto the saddle, and they galloped into the night.'

'The ball was actually at this townhouse, and someone saw her willingly climbing into a hackney carriage,' Falconer said flatly. 'We were afraid she'd been kidnapped.'

Cleo winced. 'Mother's flair for storytelling did not include deference to the truth.'

'Nicely put,' Byng said, grinning. 'Unless Julia changed, she thought the truth should defer to her.'

'True,' Cleo admitted.

'Did you grow up in penurious circumstances?' Falconer asked, feeling sick to his stomach.

'Thankfully, no,' Cleo said. 'Father had already invented a practical and sought-after chain for use in the undercarriage of large vehicles when my parents married. When I was twelve, he invented something even more desirable: a sliding valve for use in commodes.'

'My goodness,' Byng exclaimed. 'I had sliding valves and S-traps put into every water closet only a year ago! Don't tell me that your father owned Lewis Commodes?'

Cleo smiled at him. 'I know commodes aren't a respectable way to earn money, but I am grateful to have inherited the concern. These days, Lewis Commodes are to be found in water closets from Eton College to the naval barracks.'

'A lady doesn't mention financial circumstances,' Falconer said, before he thought better of it.

'Luckily, I can choose the moments when I wish to appear as a lady,' his granddaughter replied, patently undisturbed by his reprimand.

An angry thumping sound in the distance suggested that a groom had lost patience waiting for the butler, Ponder, to answer the front door.

'That will be an old friend of mine, Madame Dubois, and her charge, Lady Yasmin, daughter of the Duc de Castiglione,' Falconer said. 'Lady Yasmin is the granddaughter of the Duke of Portbellow. She was raised in the French court – frankly, Castiglione is one of the nouveau titles created by Napoleon – and His Grace says that his granddaughter needs to be brought up to snuff.'

'If the lady was raised in Emperor Napoleon's court, she ought to be more than up to snuff,' Cleo pointed out.

'I have heard that Lady Yasmin enjoys brandy and bawdy jokes,' Byng said. He twinkled at Cleo. 'You'll be bosom friends.'

'To return to the question of financial circumstances, I am fortunate enough to be a lady in command of a more than respectable fortune,' Cleo said, clasping her warm hand around Falconer's gnarled one. 'Why on earth would I turn over my well-being and my estate to a man, whether titled or not?'

'You would never again have to travel the length of England in a theatrical wagon,' Falconer said, feeling slightly desperate.

'Our wagon was an elegant conveyance, designed by a French artist,' Cleo said. 'It cost as much as a small house. I have rented a mews to store it, as well as stable my horses. I would love to show it to you someday.'

'At your earliest invitation,' Byng exclaimed.

Out in the corridor, Ponder was relieving the ladies of their pelisses. There was one question Falconer hadn't let himself ask so far. He closed his eyes. 'What happened? How did Julia die?'

'Mother caught a chill,' Cleo said, her hand tightening on his. 'The company was performing

109

Shakespeare's *Tempest*, pouring buckets of water from the top of the theater to the stage to give the illusion that the ship was sinking. The whole front row got wet. She refused to leave, though the theater was draughty. She was fond of the actor acting Prospero and wanted to see him play the famous last scene, in which the magician drowns his books.'

Falconer drew a deep breath and opened his eyes.

'Mother didn't regret anything except not seeing you and her mother again. She loved her life.'

'Thank you, my dear,' Falconer said. 'It is helpful to know that.'

The drawing room door opened. 'Madame Dubois and Lady Yasmin Régnier,' Ponder said, looking at the ceiling with the air of Saint Sebastian watching a flight of arrows launched toward his chest.

Cleo gave her grandfather's hand another squeeze and then came to her feet, helping him to rise. Byng was already toddling toward the door.

The young lady who strolled past Ponder's shoulder was the most eye-catching woman Cleo had ever seen in her life, and that was after years of frequenting theaters.

Would have given me a run for my money, Julia commented, sounding amused.

Lady Yasmin had hair the color of old guineas, and eyes that even by candlelight appeared to be violet. Add a scarlet lip and a gown that barely skimmed her nipples, and she could have strolled onto any stage in a leading role.

Following her was an older woman with a strong nose, whose clothing veered between those of Queen Elizabeth and Queen Marie Antoinette. She wore three starched ruffs, one on top of the other, around her neck. But her gown kept to the correct narrow silhouette, albeit with the addition of an upside-down ruff at the hem.

'Madame Dubois, Lady Yasmin, you both look well,' Falconer said. 'May I introduce my grand-daughter, Miss Lewis?'

Cleo was rather proud of the way her grandfather pulled himself upright and bowed. No one would know he was in pain. She dropped into a deep curtsy. 'Good evening, Madame Dubois. Lady Yasmin. It is a pleasure.'

'Your gown is surely French,' Lady Yasmin observed, after they were all seated.

Cleo thought about answering in her language, but decided their acquaintance was too slight to embarrass herself. 'Indeed, it was created by a Parisian exile living in Manchester.'

'You must give me her name, if I remain in this country long enough to need new garments,' Yasmin said. They were seated beside each other on the settee while the others caught up on gossip.

'Do you plan to return to France?'

'Actually, I hope to stay here. But alas, my grand-father finds me quite unlikable.'

'Surely not!'

111

She laughed. 'Surely yes. Your grandfather seems to be a dear, but mine is oh so fierce. He was never inclined to care for me due to my mother's naughty behavior.'

Cleo let out a startled exclamation. 'My mother created a scandal as well!'

Yasmin raised an eyebrow. 'If you'll forgive me, you look the essence of a British gentlewoman.'

Just so might Queen Marie Antoinette have described the hoi polloi. Though Yasmin wasn't being insulting, merely curious.

'My mother fled this house to marry the blacksmith's son,' Cleo said. 'I am an heiress due to sales of commodes, which is even more scandalous, though my grandfather is nurturing fond hopes that I might still find a husband during the Season.'

'Commodes?' Yasmin asked, with a puzzled look.

'Water closets,' Cleo said cheerfully. 'Lord Falconer did just inform me that I oughtn't to speak of financial matters.'

'And my grandfather has given me a similar warning!' Yasmin said with a delighted smile. 'I too am an heiress. My disreputable dowry was bestowed upon me by my mother, who was one of Emperor Napoleon's mistresses during his marriage to poor Josephine. The emperor was very, very generous to her. My grandfather, the duke, is mortified, and has forbidden me to mention my misbegotten fortune.'

'Goodness.'

'He doesn't seem to understand that I needn't

obey him in any respect, which has confirmed his worst fears.' She added with a naughty twinkle, 'I am not unlike my mother.'

'Whereas I am my mother's opposite, which may explain my grandfather's current good cheer,' Cleo said.

'The duke suffered an attack of vapors upon seeing my gown this evening,' Yasmin confided. 'His dearest hope is that Madame Dubois will find me a stern husband who will lock me in a tower.' Lady Yasmin's disposition was clearly as dramatic as her appearance.

'That's not very kind. I'm sorry,' Cleo said.

Yasmin wrinkled her nose. 'It's no wonder that my mother fled. Does your grandfather also hope to marry you off?'

'I'm afraid so.'

'Bah! Being one who grew up in the court, you understand, I cannot pretend to excitement at the idea of an English husband. Or the English Season, for that matter.'

'My mother described the Season as a savage assault on one's senses,' Cleo said.

'More tedious than savage, so far,' Yasmin said. 'Young English ladies, coddled to a high shine like ponies off to auction, who curtsy if someone even squints at them. I feel as if I am bobbing up and down like a cork on the waters. They are poorly educated, what's more.'

'So am I,' Cleo admitted. 'I've hired tutors because I'm appallingly ignorant.'

Byng leaned over. 'There's nothing unladylike about ignorance.'

'Your mother loathed her governesses and spent most of her time escaping lessons,' Viscount Falconer added.

'She and I are – *were* – patently unalike,' Cleo said.

'How lucky you are in your granddaughter, Lord Falconer,' Yasmin said. 'My grandfather finds me a sad trial.'

'Don't reveal your faults with such relish, *ma poupée*,' Madame Dubois put in.

Cleo made a mental note to inquire about the meaning of that French phrase.

'What are you studying?' Falconer asked Cleo.

'French, philosophy, astronomy, music, literature – but not dramatic – and watercolors. I seem to have no painting or musical skills, but I persevere.'

'I can help with French,' Yasmin offered with a smile.

'That would be very kind of you,' Cleo said, smiling back.

'We ought to go in to dinner before Ponder decides the first course is wasted and throws it away,' Byng said.

With a timing that suggested he was hovering outside, ear to the door, Ponder opened the door. 'Dinner is served.'

Madame Dubois looked up. 'Nonsense. I have not finished my sherry.'

'The food will grow cold,' the butler opined.

'It is your responsibility to make sure that is not the case,' Madame ordered. 'You may leave us.'

Ponder left.

Yasmin leaned over and whispered in Cleo's ear, 'There are moments when I fear that Madame may marry me to someone before I realize what happened. She is *formidable*!'

No need to translate that word.

CHAPTER TEN

The following evening

Jake climbed the private staircase to the third floor clad in his uncomfortable livery again. After spending the day unable to get Miss Lewis out of his mind, he realized why.

It was his conscience.

He'd always had an overactive conscience, at least from his family's point of view, given that it led him to eschew his uncle's trade in opium.

John Jacob Astor, his uncle, saw the opium trade as just another business endeavor, but Jake didn't agree. The ensuing family battle had led to Jake changing his last name to Addison.

Jake had thought about writing Miss Lewis a letter informing her of his plans to order a garish wardrobe. But then Moggly informed him that Miss Lewis was eating dinner in her suite once again. It would be easier to tell her in person.

She was the most irritating woman he'd met in his life, from the top of her gleaming red curls to that porcelain complexion. Who would have thought she had hair that color?

116

Though it made sense.

Stubborn nose. Stubborn jaw. Stubborn mouth.

Her hair wasn't just red: it was *blazing* red. Even woven into a complicated knot, he could see that it was as unruly as she was.

Her curves would have made him feel weak at the knees back when he was a youngster. Luckily, at the age of thirty, he was far past such a response to a lady.

Still, when she had leveled blue-gray eyes at him and commanded him to leave her dining room, he discovered an ancient truth: one never knows oneself.

He *had* felt a trifle weak at the knees.

The only other woman he knew who was so independent was his own mother, who stemmed from a Boston family that claimed to have arrived in America on the *Mayflower*. Before his father died, the two of them had battled over everything from the merits of chicken to quail, Astors to Cabots, geraniums to roses.

Miss Lewis had a similar character, that of a woman who had never entirely given herself to a man and never would.

His fortune and his lineage – Astor was a name that excited women like a salt lick did deer – were enough to make him a target of every fortune-hunting mama in America. Even changing his name to Addison had had no effect. He was tired of the way women's smiling faces turned toward him the moment he entered a New York drawing room.

Not in England.

Merry had told him as much, and here was the proof. When Miss Lewis smiled, it was from the pure glee of thwarting him.

Of course, he wasn't really attracted to her.

Halfway up the stairs between her suite and his, he heard a sharp voice from behind him. 'You! You're not allowed on this staircase!'

Jake swung around.

A stout footman was scowling at him. 'You're new, aren't you? Only guests are allowed to use the private staircase.'

'Yet you are here,' Jake pointed out.

Red stained the man's cheeks. 'Take this and be grateful that I don't report you downstairs and have you turned off without a shilling.' He thrust a tray into Jake's hands and turned to go.

'Take it where?' Jake asked his back.

'Back to the kitchens, of course!' the man snapped. 'Suite 302 wanted apple tart but he's gone to bed instead, the old fool.' With that, he disappeared around the curve of the stairs.

Jake looked down at the silver tray in his hands.

A warm, fragrant piece of apple tart. Fate had taken a hand.

A young footman was sleeping against the wall outside Miss Lewis's dining room, suite 301, his mouth ajar. He didn't stir when Jake pushed open the door.

She had hitched her seat close to the fire tonight.

Her head was bent over a book, scowling at the page, her quill frozen in thought.

Something had changed.

He blinked before he realized: red hair spilled around her shoulders, falling onto the small table. Her ringlets caught the gleam of firelight and curled down her back, making her resemble a fairy-tale illustration of a delightful, endangered princess.

He glanced down at the silver tray he held.

Was it princesses who cast spells with apples? Or evil witches? He was bringing *her* the apple tart.

'Oh, for goodness' sake, it's you again,' she said, looking up, and frowning. 'I thought you were a footman, a real footman this time. I told you not to return.'

Yes, he intended to marry Frederica. But he was a man.

Miss Lewis was so beautiful, cheeks flushed by the warmth of the fire, that any man would picture what she might look like after being thoroughly loved.

The thought made his heart kick up a beat. Surprising, that. It seemed he didn't like thinking of other men ogling her, which made him a hypocrite. No more than he would wish for men to ogle Frederica, he told himself. No gentleman likes to think of a female acquaintance beset by leering eyes.

'I was handed an untouched plate of apple tart,'

he said. 'Given that I suggested a tart would complement the French brandy, it felt like an act of Providence. I should like to begin again.'

'What on earth do you mean?' An enchanting little pucker appeared between her brows. Red eyebrows. How had he not noticed that when they first met?

'We are natural friends, rather than enemies,' he said. 'As such, I plan to share with you the details of my plan to convince Martha Quimby that she would rather specialize in theatrical costumes than expand her business into society.'

'I see.' Her lower lip was caught in her teeth. 'That is unusual among businessmen, I must say. I am more accustomed to double-dealing.'

'I don't care for it,' he stated. 'It won't take long to explain my plan.'

'Very well.' She nodded toward the chair opposite, curiosity shining in her eyes.

Jake set down his plate. The tart glistened between them: apple slices peeking between a lattice of flaky crust. He picked up two goblets and the decanter from the sideboard and poured them both a drink before he seated himself.

He leaned forward and held out his hand. 'Miss Lewis, may I introduce myself? My name is Jacob Addison, and I would very much like to make your acquaintance. I am an American financier. I made my fortune in fur, but when my uncle turned to the opium trade, I broke away and began investing in theaters.'

Her eyes flew from the tart to his face. 'And costume emporiums?'

'As well as other entrepreneurial concerns. I pride myself on honesty, which means I truly did offer four thousand pounds for the emporium. I have a plan to change Mrs Quimby's mind that I want to share with you.' He hesitated. 'I would rather be friends than enemies.'

Amusement transformed her face. As he had told Merry, Miss Lewis's face in repose was a bit witchy, given her pointed chin and large eyes. But when she smiled?

That wide, beaming smile?

Damn.

He felt the shock of it down to his toes.

She took his hand and gave it a firm shake. 'How pleasant to meet you, Mr Addison. My name is Miss Cleopatra Lewis. My grandfather is a viscount, but I am more interested in plumbing and commodes than in polite society.' She glanced down at the tart and then up at him. 'Also, French brandy, apple tarts, and costume emporiums.'

The plate was accompanied by cutlery; she handed him a spoon. 'Won't you share this beautiful tart with me?'

Her smile went straight to his groin.

'I'd love a bite or two,' he said, surprised by the gruffness in his voice.

'If we are to be friends,' she said, 'I suppose you'd better call me Cleo, though not in public. I am serious about not being involved in a scandal, you know. I have no plans to marry, and certainly not—' She broke off.

He burst out laughing. 'Certainly not to me? Merry, the duchess whom you will meet at Vauxhall, informed me that even if I remained under her roof during her husband's prolonged absence, no one in polite society would gossip.'

Cleo raised an eyebrow. 'Why is that?'

He was disconcertingly aware of the arch of that eyebrow and the color of it: darker than her hair, but still distinctly red. A color that cast normal eyebrows in the shade.

'Apparently, I am well enough in an American kind of way,' he replied. 'But I gather that no one with my background or looks could offer competition to a duke, especially given my disreputable clothing and lack of a title.'

She was bent over the plate, cutting the tart in pieces, the way his nanny had when he was young. He couldn't see her eyes. 'I think your friend gives you too little credit, Mr Addison.'

'Jake,' he said. 'If I am to call you Cleo, then you must call me Jake. In public or private.'

'I don't think your clothing is precisely disreputable,' she observed, still not looking at him. 'Though my dresser, or lady's maid, was shocked by a glimpse of your neck. You might want to buy a wider neck cloth to wear during your stay in London. Do have some tart.'

He obediently spooned up a piece, trying to shape his expression into friendly lines as he chewed. As best he could. It wasn't a quality he worried about much in his daily life, but he knew perfectly well that if Cleo's face looked witchy in repose, his was worse. Forbidding and grim, or so he'd been told.

'Is there something wrong with exposing one's neck?' he asked, after swallowing.

'Gussie was an actress of some acclaim,' Cleo told him. 'She played a lady on the stage so often that she is far more ladylike than many in polite society, or so I tell her. As she ages, she is veering toward a duchess, as least as regards her sensibilities.'

Jake still wasn't sure why a duchess would be appalled by a man's neck – and he thought Merry hadn't even noticed – but he ate another bite of tart rather than inquire further. Chances were that most duchesses don't run around the back garden without stockings, so obviously the one duchess whom he knew wasn't a good model.

In fact, the whole concept of 'lady' was somewhat foreign to him; he'd spent too much time in Oregon Country working in the fur trade. Deep in the forest, a woolen scarf and a knife are the best accoutrements.

'Mmm,' Cleo said, savoring the tart. 'It's not just apple, is it? There's something else, elderberries, I think.'

Jake shifted in his seat. Her eyes had turned dreamy merely from one bite. He cleared his throat. '*Confiture*,' he replied, giving it the French name. 'The chef has added a little jam to the filling.'

She smiled again, and he discovered to his utter surprise that she had a dimple. A delightful dimple in her right cheek, and none in her left. Desire sliced through him like a knife, and his whole body tightened again.

'I've never met any man quite like you,' she observed. 'My father did not speak French, knew nothing of jam, and wouldn't have been interested in visiting Europe. He liked cold chicken, the English countryside, and beer.'

'So do I,' Jake said, pushing away the absurd thought he'd had about her dimple. Of course, he didn't want to – 'Also coffee and pickles.'

She wrinkled her nose. 'Coffee tastes like fusty old beans.'

'Good coffee does not,' he told her. 'I'll brew you some, one day. An excellent cup of coffee is something to be revered.'

'The way we British do tea? Here, have another bite.' She poked some tart over onto his side of the plate. 'I'm not trimming my figure, but I'm not terribly hungry.'

He instinctively glanced at her bosom before he hastily stuck the pastry in his mouth. The *confiture* married sweetness to tart apples, but he scarcely tasted it. He swallowed, and a sentence came out of his mouth, unbidden. 'You should not trim your figure, ever.'

Cleo blinked at him, clearly startled.

124

'I have not given up my plan to convince Martha Quimby that she would be happier making costumes than attiring members of polite society,' Jake announced, jumping into the awkward silence.

She raised one of those eyebrows again. 'How will you do that?'

'Tomorrow I shall order a complete wardrobe from Quimby's. The Duke of Trent is out of London, and I plan to escort his duchess to several society events, wearing Quimby's garments.'

She laughed. 'You believe that Martha will be put off by the idea of dressing an American?' Her eyes rested thoughtfully on his shoulders. 'She may well charge you by the ell for fabric. Is your plan to bankrupt the emporium due to your size?'

Jake scooped up another bite. 'You've hardly eaten anything, whereas I am outsized already.' He held it up to her lips. 'Have this.'

Her lashes swept up, and their eyes met. Dimly he registered that Cleopatra Lewis's gaze was not helpless or, for that matter, innocent. Her eyes were deep as the evening sky when it turns from blue to gray. They were knowing, older than she appeared, curious, amused . . .

Desirous.

It felt like the most triumphant moment of his life. He *knew* he caught a hint of desire, even though a moment later her eyes seemed to register nothing but polite inquiry.

He cleared his throat. 'Once I wear my new

garments to society events, Quimby's reputation for elegant attire will suffer. I'm American, remember? Untitled, no blue blood, too large, unattractive, and all the rest of it. Merry told me once that my jaw was hard as hammered iron, and she didn't mean it as a compliment.'

A burble of laughter came from Cleo's lips. 'You are depending on your unattractiveness to discourage people from ordering clothing from Quimby's?'

'The nature of the wardrobe I intend to acquire will inform insecure purchasers – such as those you intend to target – that the emporium is better suited to creating clowns out of Americans than clothing a future viscountess. I plan to branch out into color.'

At that, she burst into giggles.

'Flowered fabric,' he said, enjoying the sound of her laughter. The reserved air that hung about her had fallen away. 'Embroidery, pastel cravats, lacy cuffs. All manner of extravagance. Spangles and silver thread.'

'You're planning to make yourself look like a circus master and frighten off all the prospective buyers,' she said, still giggling.

He nodded. 'Precisely.'

'I don't know why I'm surprised. Look at you.' Cleo waved her fork.

Jake glanced down at the deucedly uncomfortable coat he was wearing.

'I can't think of an English gentleman who would

be caught in servants' clothing,' she told him. 'Not even literary ones. Romeo wouldn't have stolen into Juliet's household wearing livery. Gentlemen are too aware of their consequence.'

'I'm not a gentleman,' Jake stated. 'I'm an American.'

'So, you have no fear of garish clothing,' Cleo said, nodding to herself. 'That's clever . . . *very* clever.'

'Thank you.' He ate the last bite of apple tart.

'But it won't work,' she said with utter confidence.

He frowned. 'Why not?'

'Because I too am ordering a new wardrobe from Quimby's,' she said, giving him that dimpled smile again. 'Martha has already taken my measurements. New gowns, pelisses, and even headdresses. They will be exquisite. *And* my grandfather has managed to coerce me into accompanying him to any number of society events, so if you will be a walking advertisement for absurdity, I shall be the same for would-be viscountesses.'

Her lips were gleaming with French jam. Jake was struck by an impulse to lean forward and lick it off that was so strong he felt it to the depths of his . . .

Gut.

Not lower.

'Your attire will be balanced by my gowns,' Cleo added, pointing a fork at him in a markedly unladylike fashion.

'How will you know if your wardrobe is appropriate?' he demanded, the irritation he felt at his unruly and unwanted emotions leaking into his tone. 'After all, you haven't been presented to the queen. Perhaps your taste is garish.'

'It isn't,' she said serenely.

'You are rash to imagine that you will do Quimby's a service by wearing their garments,' he persisted. 'I actually think that you are playing into *my* scheme. What if your taste aligns with that of your father rather than your mother? In short, what if the clothing you order is fit for a plumber's wife, rather than a viscountess?'

She shook her head, eyes still amused. 'My mother was aware of her status and trained me as such. What's more, I spent several years following theater companies on tour. I know a great deal about fashionable clothing, because not only did I observe it on stage every night, but audiences are often more interesting than plays.'

Jake frowned. 'Following? What do you mean?'

'My mother and I accompanied Drury Lane's traveling company across England, albeit in our own wagon.' She leaned back and sipped her brandy. 'She wasn't loyal to one company; our first such excursion was with the Covent Garden company, which means that I can attest that the costumes Martha creates are far superior to those that appear on rival stages.'

Jake didn't know what to make of her story. His own theater companies hadn't yet formed traveling versions, though he had it in mind for future expansion. He'd never imagined that eager audience members would accompany a troupe. 'Are you a devotee of theater?'

'Oh, dear, no,' Cleo said. 'In fact, if I never enter another theater, I shall be perfectly happy.'

'Your mother, then?'

Her eyes were wry. 'Indeed. My father died when I was fourteen, and shortly afterwards my mother commissioned her own wagon and announced that we would accompany the Covent Garden troupe to Scotland.'

'That must have been a shock.'

'Yes, but I fell in love with the countryside. We didn't have to make good time, you see, so we rambled through side roads and stopped wherever we wished. I particularly adore brewing tea and drinking it out of doors.'

'I never travel anywhere without a destination in mind,' Jake admitted.

'Your visit to France?'

'I am planning a concern that will supply wine and spirits to restaurants and households in New York and Boston. Disrupted at the moment by the war, but I have every belief that the Seventh Coalition will banish Napoleon once again.'

'I wondered why you had been talking to cognac makers. Unlike you, I love to travel without a destination in mind. There's nothing more glorious than a village common after a rain when cobwebs are picked out with silver—' She broke off. 'I can be boring on the subject.'

'I am not bored,' Jake said.

Cleo wrinkled her nose. 'I used to irritate my poor mother to no end trying to get her to admire elderberries.'

'What do elderberries look like?' he asked.

'A gorgeous dark violet. I think they looked like sapphires, but my mother called them the devil's toenails.'

Jake's brain was fizzing with a foolish desire to pull her into his arms; instead, he broke into laughter. 'I can't say I ever thought about the devil's feet, let alone his toes.'

'Elderberries are dangerous unless cooked,' she explained. 'Thus they might send you right to hell, if you were heading in that direction. Have you traveled around America?'

'In the west, yes. I can't describe things as well as you, but once we were in a deep forest, full of snow, and a bright red cardinal swooped down through the branches.'

'I think snow is beautiful.'

His heart thumped at the way her face lit up. 'Tell me.'

'One of my favorite memories is a spring day when snow dusted the daffodils and celandines; it came down in puffy flakes that reminded me of cherry blossoms.' Cleo smiled. 'From heaven, not a tree. But equally important, if we hadn't been in a caravan, parked by the side of a meadow, I never would have seen it. City streets are the same everywhere.'

Jake reached out and pushed a ringlet behind her ear before he thought.

Her hand flew up to her head and her eyes filled with horror. 'I forgot that my hair is down.'

'There's a lot of it,' Jake said, wishing for the first time in his life that he had the gift of gab.

Composure fell over her like a veil. Cleo gave him a tight smile that signaled she was about to send him on his way.

He didn't want to leave. It was a gut-deep feeling, and as a rule, Jake followed his instincts. He wanted to stay here with a red-haired dimpled witch and . . . listen to her tell him about berries or trees or anything else she wanted.

Argue some more. He liked the way her eyes smoldered at him.

Likely a reaction to all those syrupy glances women usually threw him.

'Just look at the gown you're wearing now,' he said, distracting her before she could boot him out the door. 'No marriageable miss will order a gown from Quimby's after they see what you're wearing. You look as gloomy as a graveyard.'

It wasn't polite, but it was accurate. She was wrapped up like a storm cloud, in a severe jacket with a military air. Even if the fit showcased a figure that would bring a man to his knees.

Sure enough, Cleo's eyes sparked with irritation.

'I did warn you that Merry calls me acerbic and harsh by nature, didn't I?' he added.

'Is that an excuse?' He had the idea that her ears were going red, but it was hard to see because of all her hair.

He cocked his head. 'Do you want me to add that you're beautiful, etcetera? I can if you wish.' She looked so infuriated that he couldn't help grinning at her. 'I can play Romeo to your Juliet. I've seen the play more times than I could wish, since it's a staple in every repertory. "Two stars twinkle in your face."' He peered at her. 'Gray stars, I gather.'

'That's not one of Romeo's lines!'

'Blue stars?' he asked, leaning closer. She smelled flowery, but spicy too. Like the spicy burn of a good brandy. As compared to sweet, feminine ratafia.

Cleo was a general, a queen. Most women were – He broke off that thought.

'You'd think that a theater impresario would be more knowledgeable about Shakespeare,' she was saying. 'You've got Romeo's line entirely wrong. You are deliberately trying to provoke me.'

'What's an impresario?' he asked, ignoring her last comment.

'A theatrical organizer. From the Italian *impresa*. Like' – she gave him a wry smile – 'Regina Mingotti who managed her own opera company here in London.'

'I have nothing to do with productions,' Jake told her.

'I thought you adored the theater!'

'Far from it. I can't stand Shakespeare, as a matter of fact. Romeo burbles on forever, the way no dignified man would. Here, I remember a whole line: *The brightness of her cheek would shame those stars.* The stars being the ones in heaven, not the ones he just said were in Juliet's face. A repetitive and unclear reference.'

She gave a little choke of laughter at that, and Jake leaned back in his chair. 'So, you tell me, Miss Cleopatra Lewis, do you think Romeo would have been gassing on about stars and jewels if Juliet had walked into that ball wearing a gray dress that covered her up from the chin to the toes? In my opinion, he would have gone stargazing in some other woman's face.'

'You know nothing about fashion,' she told him, shaking her head. 'I adore this gown, and so would have Juliet. I've never seen anything like this jacket.'

'That's not a good sign,' he said helpfully. 'Given as you're a plumber's daughter.'

'You sound frightfully snobby. What sort of American are you?' she demanded, taking a deep breath.

Which did wonderful things for her bosom. Needling her was so enjoyable, especially when her cheeks flushed.

'The fur-trapping kind,' Jake said. 'We Americans consider a plumber far more useful than a viscount, to be honest.'

Laughter rose in his chest at the way she scowled

at him. 'Juliet was likely wearing a nightdress when she wandered out on the balcony,' he pointed out. 'Frankly, the gowns that ladies are wearing these days resemble nightdresses. You should—'

'Don't say another word!' Cleo ordered, holding up a hand. 'You are maddening me, quite deliberately.'

'That's true,' Jake admitted.

'Well, then, stop it!'

'Why? I'm enjoying it.' He leaned forward and gave her a wicked smile. 'And so are you.'

CHAPTER ELEVEN

Cleo was *not* enjoying it.

In fact, she hadn't been so irritated in months. Not since she discovered that her fiancé was sneaking around behind her back making plans to sell Lewis Commodes.

Jake Addison apparently thought her exquisite ensemble befitted a plumber's wife. What did he know? He was just an American. An unattractive one at that, as confirmed by a real duchess.

The fact that *she* seemed to find his jaw . . . his whole self . . . wildly attractive just confirmed how unladylike she was. Ladies certainly wouldn't appreciate his sculpted muscles. They definitely wouldn't feel something that she admitted was raw lust.

Lust, it seemed, was irrational, if powerful.

She pulled herself together and changed the subject. 'My mother would have enjoyed the gaudy clothes you intend to order,' she said, trying to make her tone informative and friendly. 'I can probably advise you on precisely how to make them as eye-catching as possible.'

Too late she remembered that any help she gave him would be a mistake. A business mistake.

Jake grinned at her. 'Not to belabor the point, but as I peacock around London in clothing that your mother might have appreciated, the mayor's daughters will be terrified. Moreover, as you stroll around London wrapped up in two-day pudding, anyone who wasn't terrified by me will be disheartened by you.'

A flash of anger went up Cleo's backbone. 'Two-day pudding? How dare you!'

'Pudding takes on a grayish tinge,' he pointed out.

'I am dressed in half mourning,' she told him icily. 'I am grieving for my mother.'

'I am sorry. When did she pass away?'

'Ten months ago.'

She couldn't fool herself that his eyes were brimming with sympathy, and indeed, he didn't bother to offer another platitude. 'I remember the feeling,' he said instead. 'My father died just over two years ago. My point is that between your drab clothing – no matter how relevant to your emotions – and my garish costumes, the *ton* will not flock to Quimby's.'

Cleo's jaw set. 'I plan to remain in half mourning for two more months in honor of my mother.'

'On the worthy side, it allows Martha Quimby to show range. Garish *and* gray.'

Despite her irritation, her lips quirked up. 'You're not helping your own cause. You should be secretly reveling in the fact that my clothing will frighten polite society instead of making such a point of it.'

'I'd rather win fair and square. That's how we do it in America. Anyway, my clothing will be frightening, yours merely dismaying.'

'The British are just as interested in fairness as Americans. I have never engaged in unscrupulous dealings of any kind.' She gave him a fierce stare. 'Ever!'

Did she have to put a hand over her bosom?

Naturally, Jake's eyes dropped to her breasts, which were handfuls. More than handfuls. Curved and heavy and . . . He couldn't think of any more appropriate words because his body surged with inarticulate passion.

Not that those words were appropriate. He could just imagine her response if he described her breasts as big handfuls.

He *wanted*. He wanted to take her in his lap and kiss her happy, and then trail a hand over her bosom and make her more than happy.

Jesus.

What was happening to him?

'Well,' he said briskly, 'you know all the details of my plan, and I needn't badger you any longer. Wouldn't be gentlemanly, would it?'

'As if you cared about being gentlemanly!'

'I don't when it comes to namby-pamby rules about boots and hats and the like. Wide cravats versus a glimpse of a man's neck. To me, the definition of gentleman is something different.'

She looked at him curiously.

'Honor is the most important aspect of a gentleman,' he found himself telling her, surprised. He never explained himself.

'Courtesy is crucial to the definition,' she noted.

'Not if courtesy results in failure to tell the truth.'

'I pride myself on controlling my temper, but you keep managing to – to—'

'Annoy you?' Jake said, grinning at her. 'Infuriate might be going too far.'

She raised a finger. 'One, you twice steal into my chamber under false pretenses. Two, you inform me that you have no wish to marry me. Three, you plan to undermine the excellent plan I've made to grow an emporium that I bought, fair and square!'

'My lack of a proposal is on the list?' Jake said.

She scowled. 'Due to rudeness and discourtesy – like your other ungentlemanly behavior.'

'Think of me as American,' he advised. 'That's what Merry does. And she insults me frequently.'

Cleo had the horrid feeling that he was enjoying himself. In fact, she couldn't persuade herself otherwise, given that his eyes were alight with laughter.

'Go,' she said, flapping her hands and getting to her feet. 'Go, before I lose my temper and throw the decanter at your head.'

'My mother once threw the family dog, Percy, at the butler,' he said, rising.

'She threw a *dog*?'

'Luckily, our butler was excellent at rounders, and Percy is small and plump.'

'I adore this gown,' she blurted out, before she could stop herself. 'The moment I saw it on the dress form at Quimby's, when you were there, I asked Martha to fit it for me.'

'I also saw it.' His eyes roved over her, from her collarbones to the tips of her toes. 'Tells the world that you're sad, which is the point, of course. It covers up every inch of your cleavage, which means that the next mayor's daughter is unlikely to find a spouse.'

'Men look past such shallow attractions when they seek a wife,' Cleo told him.

'How do you know?' He gave her a sardonic look. 'You are *Miss* Lewis, after all. Men don't care to marry nuns. I know, because believe it or not, New York and Boston have polite societies of their own and I rank at the very top of both.'

'How fortunate for you,' she said tartly. 'It's typical of a man to think that a woman who doesn't show rash enthusiasm for a husband must be ready to join a nunnery.'

He took a step closer, but she held her ground. 'Do you plan to order gray dresses due to your mother's death – or because you wish to warn off suitors?'

Cleo scowled at him. 'Grief is not to be questioned.'

His shrug was an easy movement, a shifting of those massive shoulders. 'Why not?'

'You – you *shrugged* at me.' She might not have had a governess's attention for long, but she understood the gesture was considered gauche.

'True.'

'You shrugged at the mention of my mother's death!'

'Cleo, I am not the sort of man who's good at smooth conversation.'

'Believe me, I noticed,' she said with feeling. 'In our first exchange, you shared details about your digestive processes.'

Jake knew perfectly well that he was making a mess of it, but damn it, he had an important point to make. 'Merry and I are close friends because she has never expected me to lie to her.'

'I pity her,' she said stonily. 'I gather you have a few more truths you'd like to share.'

'Your eyes were sad when you talked about your mother's love of theater. I am not saying that you didn't love her. But my father died not so long ago, remember? I know well that the first overwhelming grief fades away.'

'Mine hasn't faded away.'

'Your eyes were furious when you told me that you never planned to marry. And that you had weathered a man's attempt to compromise you. '

Cleo flinched, and Jake's heart skipped a beat.

He took another step toward her. 'I can understand why you wish to warn off suitors.' He took a last step so that he was standing directly before her and tipped up her chin. 'You need not wear

140

a gown that can double as a suit of armor. You can reject any proposal that comes your way and laugh in his face, if you wish.'

She lifted her eyes to his, her expression frosty. 'I need no reassurance from you, Mr Addison.'

'You are named after the Queen of the Nile. The name is enough.' He lightly touched a curl. 'Added to your hair. Your eyes. Your laugh.' The firelight behind her shoulder made her hair richer and darker, her skin flawless.

She didn't glow because of firelight, but because of her own spirit. Her intelligence and reckless courage and a passion for life that extended to admiring the beauty of poisonous berries.

He didn't know how to put any of that into words. 'Your lips,' he added.

She said nothing for a moment and then crooked her mouth into a joyless smile. 'An itemization delivered without adjectives, but delivered, nonetheless. Thank you.'

At that moment, he gave in.

Cleopatra Lewis had conquered him without a single come-hither smile.

In the back of his head, he reshuffled his life goals, and an impetuous, exasperating, utterly desirable British woman stepped to the fore.

Thinking faster than he had in his entire life, he said, 'You claim that the British are fair, and I claim the same for Americans. I have an idea. You will order *my* wardrobe from Quimby's, in bright colors. I will order *yours*, in half mourning.'

141

She shook her head. 'Why on earth would I allow you to order my clothing? Let alone do the same for you?'

'Because it would be fair, Cleo. We'll spar like the honorable people we are: I will try to win Quimby's for you, and you will try to win Quimby's for me.'

'That's utterly absurd! You seem to be over-looking the fact that I have already won the emporium.'

He had to admit that she had a point, but he was playing a double game: he no longer gave a damn about Quimby's. He needed a reason to see Cleo: a solid reason that would give him the time and space to win a woman who seemed damned near unwinnable – because she couldn't be courted by conventional means. At the moment, if he asked her to dance, she would conclude that he was trying to cozen her into giving up Quimby's.

'Martha deserves a chance to decide whether she prefers to use her imagination, clothing everything from fairies to monarchs,' he said. 'If your plan succeeds, she'll spend much of her time measuring tiresome young women whose ambitions don't match up to reality. How many viscounts are available to marry fishmongers' daughters?'

Her brows drew together.

'It would be equitable,' he added, keeping his gaze somber without a hint of desire. Though he felt it, all right. Carnal desire gripped his limbs, but he refused to reveal it. 'I will use fair means to convince Martha Quimby that clothing the gentry is tiresome. When ordering your clothing, I will give her the opportunity to create a wardrobe that befits a duchess.'

Cleo pressed her lips together. 'I want to be a wallflower, and I plan to order clothing that will match my ambition.'

Jake's mouth fell open. She pictured herself a wallflower? Not even layers of gray fabric could disguise her, any more than livery was disguising him. 'You can't ask Martha Quimby for a miracle!'

She gave him a perplexed look. 'There's nothing miraculous about it. I don't care to be the center of attention, that's all. Some women wear gowns that are translucent. My mother—' She broke off. 'I don't want to look naked, and I shall never dampen my petticoats.'

'I wouldn't order such a gown,' Jake promised, revolted by the idea of men leering at her legs.

Cleo raised both eyebrows this time. Damn it, who ever imagined that a woman's eyebrows were erotic? But hers were: winged, slender, derisive, thoughtful.

His control slipped another notch. He bent his head until his breath feathered over her lips. 'Cleo.'

She met his eyes, fearless, amused. *Desirous.*

'Have you ever been kissed by a servant, Queen Cleopatra?'

'Never.' She didn't move.

'Your mouth doesn't match your dress,' he whispered. 'Dress severe, lips plump and generous. Dress stern, mouth curving and delicious. Dress dismal, lips colorful, rosy.'

Her lips curled. 'You *do* know adjectives, it seems!'

'A few.' His lips touched hers. 'Irresistible.'

She drew in a breath, and he followed the air, his tongue sliding into her warm mouth. He let his hands settle on her narrow shoulders, not pulling her closer, just holding her, making her the still point in a spinning world.

Her tongue brushed his, and he felt it down his legs. She tasted fresh. Not sweet and docile: never that. Her tongue tangled with his, rather than retreating shyly.

Her arms ringed his neck, and his sigh of relief went from his lungs to hers.

Kissing Cleopatra Lewis took all his concentration. Their tongues slid by each other, every touch fueling desire, making lust spear down Jake's spine. When she drew away slightly, he nipped her lower lip.

Her eyes flew open.

A dimpled smile, not angry, not sad. Not – thank God – offended. But then she wouldn't be. It was as if they'd had a conversation without words, one in which he begged, and she consented. Or in which she demanded and he . . .

'Should I apologize?' Jake asked, his voice husky. He had never given Frederica even a gentle buss on the cheek, but he had the dim idea that a man should routinely apologize for kissing a lady. 'As a gentleman, I mean. Courtesy demands?'

'Only if the lady didn't enjoy the kiss,' Cleo informed him.

'I wouldn't presume to know your emotions.'

She snorted at that.

Snorted! No lady made such an inelegant sound, but Jake kept that observation to himself.

'Jake Addison, you've done nothing in the time we've known each other but inform me of my own emotions: sadness, anger, frustration.'

'Lust?' he suggested, realizing the moment the word left his lips that he should have offered a more poetic term.

Her eyes narrowed.

'Desire,' he amended quickly. 'Lust is something that only plagues men. Ladies long, and men lust.'

'Oh, there are women who experience lust,' she said, her voice wry.

Something in her eyes told him to change the subject. 'Perhaps lust for apple tart.' Then he kissed her again because, damn it, her lips were irresistible and she desired him, no matter how the emotion was labeled.

She tasted like Cleo and fiery brandy, making his body heavy and taut, blood pounding through his veins. She kissed him back, her mouth open, her tongue playing with his. Her hands slid to his shoulders and clung.

A woman he slept with once told him that his shoulders resembled those of an ox. He had the feeling that Cleo liked his strength, for all she'd made fun of the ells of fabric it would take to cover his body.

His hands shifted slightly until his thumbs could stroke her neck, a caress that meant her pulse thundered under his fingers. And her tongue followed his, back to his mouth.

He wasn't luring her.

She had captivated him, rather than the other way around. His mind blurred, rules he was taught at his nanny's knee evaporating as if they never existed. As if the world was encompassed by one man and one woman.

Cleo pulled back again. 'We have to stop.'

'Of course.' If her voice was husky, his had a rumble of desire that no one could mistake.

'It must be the plumber's daughter in me coming out.' Cleo's voice was careless, even sophisticated, but her cheeks burned with color. He let his hands fall from her neck. Deep in her eyes, he saw shock.

The same shock he was feeling.

'That kiss cannot happen again,' she told him, visibly reassembling her composure. 'I enjoyed it; I wouldn't wish you to think that I did not. But . . .' Her voice trailed off.

'You are not a woman who dallies with near strangers,' he supplied. Not that they were strangers now, and never would be again.

146

'Exactly.'

Her voice was firm, but he had the sudden idea that a flash of hurt had crossed her eyes. What had he said?

'I don't make a habit of kissing strange men, and I shall not begin with you.'

'Familiar men?'

She blinked.

'Do you make a habit of kissing familiar men?' He was fairly sure that his voice was even, and not a growling, jealous burr.

'I am a very quick hand with a sharpened umbrella. My umbrella isn't at hand. But we shan't do that again, Jacob Addison, no matter how friendly we become. This was a mistake.'

He nodded, though his entire body and soul disagreed with her. But Cleo was alarmed, every sinew of her body tensed and ready to retreat. Or go to battle.

'An indiscretion brought on by French brandy,' he said lightly. 'We'll think no more of it. Tomorrow, may I order you a wardrobe, Your Majesty of the Nile?'

It took a moment, but Cleo reassembled herself into a dignified woman, though her cheeks still burned rosy, and her lips were swollen by kisses.

'A wardrobe for a lady's London Season is frightfully expensive,' she told him. 'I shall pay for my own clothing.'

'Of course. Will you order a wardrobe for me?' He couldn't stop himself from reaching out and nudging a curtain of red curls behind her ear. 'Your hair . . .'

'I know,' she said. 'Red as fire, etcetera. Believe me, I've heard all the terms that could possibly be applied.'

He shook his head. 'I didn't mean that.' He could hardly tell her that her hair was the most erotic thing he'd seen in his life. That the mere sight of locks sliding over her chest had turned his cock to a steel bar threatening to break from his overly tight breeches.

Mischief sparked deep in her eyes. 'You'll allow me to order whatever garments I wish? Flowered and spangled and fringed?'

'As long as you give me the same latitude. I promise to remain within the bounds of half mourning. My mother wore lavender and violet for six months after putting away her blacks. White and cream with black trim.'

'You must remain within the boundaries of good taste,' she ordered. 'I'm serious about dampened petticoats, no matter how fashionable they are. I want to be a wallflower.'

'I understand.' The devil made him succumb to temptation. 'Do you wear a long corset? It makes a difference in the design of a gown, as I understand it.'

Cleo was no Puritan. Her chin rose and she met his eyes jauntily. 'Short. No whalebones necessary.'

Any man would have celebrated his control: he

148

didn't allow himself to glance below her neck. Now he knew that her breasts were not fenced in by the bones of a sea creature, merely lifted and supported –

No.

'What about drawers?' he heard himself say.

Her lips curved into an impish smile. 'My under-garments come from Paris, and I have no need of more.'

Game to the lady.

'You minx,' he whispered.

She looked back at him, fearless, laughing.

Words had left Jake's control, replaced by an image of Cleopatra Lewis wearing a silk shift with a wide neck, falling down one creamy shoulder, red hair scattered over the pillow. His body tight-ened even more, his mind jumping to a ready image of Cleo in the throes of abandoned pleasure, the queen lying under him, her eyes languid, cheeks, *breasts* –

He took a step back.

He wasn't a gentleman in the courteous, courtly mold, perhaps, but he was an American gentleman. Merry's question echoed in his mind. Of course, he wouldn't seduce Cleo, if she were seducible.

Honorable men do not seduce maidens after sneaking into their chambers under false pretexts, wearing servants' clothing.

He jerked his coat down so that it did a better job of covering his erection and took another step backward. 'I shall bid you good night.' He moved to pick up the silver platter, the empty plate, the brandy glasses. 'Tomorrow morning in Quimby's?'

'We should order our wardrobes separately, because otherwise they will not be a surprise.'

He never would have thought that the Miss Lewis he had first met was so – so naughty. Mischievous.

'I don't like surprises,' he said, honestly enough. 'You are surprise enough, Cleo. Besides, how will you choose my clothing if I'm not there to be measured? I cannot choose fabrics without holding them against your hair. I can't possibly describe its color to Mrs Quimby. You were wearing a dishcloth on your head, remember?'

That didn't come out properly. Merry would swat him.

Cleo bit her lip and glanced at him from under her lashes. 'A dishcloth?' Her voice wobbled. 'You really thought my turban was so unattractive? That I . . . was . . .'

His heart dropped. Apologizing had never been his forte, any more than flattery. 'I'm sorry.'

She snapped her chin up and burst into laughter. 'Ha! If we're to be friends you'll have to be more polite, Jake. I learned womanly wiles at my mother's knee.'

'You were mocking me?'

'Only a trifle. It's tempting when you come out

with oafish comments like that. For your information, I was wearing a fashionable turban that cost at least two guineas a few years ago.'

'Impossible!'

'You, sir, know nothing of fashion. My hair is easily described: fire, apples, etcetera.'

He shook his head. 'The only adjective that comes to my mind when I think of your hair is erotic.'

Satisfyingly, her mouth fell open, if only for a second. 'Well, now I *know* that you were kissing me in order to win Quimby's.'

'Now I know that *you* know nothing of men.' He pulled her into his arms and covered her lips with his, even though he had just promised himself that he would leave her chambers. Immediately.

The drive to kiss her smashed his resolution to be a gentleman. The ferocity of desire he felt was unlike anything he'd ever experienced. It was as if he had lived for this day, this woman, her lips, her mouth, her closed eyes, her sweetness.

Her. Cleo.

'Damn it all,' he whispered a moment later. 'You've undone me, Cleo.'

Her eyelashes opened slowly. 'Time for you to go, Mr Addison.' Were her eyes gray? At the moment they seemed blue as deep waters.

'Tomorrow morning for the fitting.'

'No more kissing, though.' She gave him a wry smile. 'I won't pretend that I'm not attracted to you, Jake. But I am a lady and not free to follow my inclinations in these matters.'

He took a breath, preparing to say things for which he had no words.

She cut him off. 'I'm fully aware that you have no interest in compromising me, and I assure you that I am unperturbed. A mere kiss is irrelevant, no matter how enjoyable.' With that, she gave him her dimpled smile, came up on her toes, and kissed his cheek.

'Tomorrow, Mr Addison.'

He managed to bow.

He was used to challenges.

His father had been enraged when he turned to the ungentlemanly fur trade. His uncle had been furious when he rejected the idea of the opium trade. His mother had been aghast when he changed his last name to Addison, considering it an insult to his deceased father.

All those battles faded into insignificance.

Winning Cleopatra?

She held all the cards. Their kisses took his breath and language, leaving him with an inarticulate wish to growl, pick her up, and find a bed.

Any bed.

She, on the other hand, was teasing and dismissive. Warning him, in so many words, not to try to seduce her out of Quimby's.

Clearly, she had no idea just how much their intimacy affected him. He felt desperate, unhinged by desire: she coolly made fun of him, pretending to flutter her eyelashes at him.

His jaw set. She was his, even though she had no idea of it. Even if he had to sell all his theaters in order to persuade her that he cared nothing for Quimby's.

Even if she didn't feel the same as he did.

Yet.

CHAPTER TWELVE

When Jake bowed, Cleo didn't even consider a curtsy. For one thing, he was dressed as a servant. For another . . .

She was lucky to be standing upright. Her limbs felt sleek and limber, as if they would curve easily around a man's hips, a thought that made warmth flare in her cheeks.

Jake had kissed *her*. As a person. As herself.

She had enjoyed kissing Foster, her erstwhile fiancé. His breath had been pleasant, and he didn't clasp her too tightly. Yet he never made her breath catch until she nearly found herself panting. His kisses never made her think of other lascivious pleasures, of *other* kisses one could share . . .

Never.

She knew all about lovemaking. Julia had been nothing if not descriptive in accounts of *affaires*. Cleo still remembered her mother holding forth over dinner about the importance of a woman's ability to satisfy a man with her mouth.

Her father had quietly left the room; fourteen-year-old Cleo remained behind, sitting silently, trying not to envision such a disgusting thing. Trying to pretend that her own mother wasn't describing such an indecent act. Avoiding the eyes of the footman waiting by the sideboard.

She'd actually forgotten about that dinner and the searing combination of humiliation and horror until now.

Until an American man murmured something while kissing her, his voice aching with desire, and the memory popped right back into her head.

Without disgust.

Jake hadn't pushed against her while they were kissing but there had been one moment when he shifted his weight, and his tool pressed against her thigh.

It made sense that he was large; it went with his overall size. She was no silly miss, for all she was a virgin. Her mother had nipped any such inclinations in the bud years ago, so Cleo had known instantly what throbbed against her. She had never given the question any thought, but now it occurred to her that such impressive masculinity might be desirable.

She watched silently as Jake opened the door to the corridor and left, tray in hand. After the door closed, there was a rumble of voices as he spoke to the footman outside. Cleo sank into her chair, knees wobbly, and pushed her French studies aside.

Julia's comment was succinct: *Huzzah!*

She should examine what just happened to her: a near stranger had kissed her and she had turned to flame. But she didn't want to think about it. Her mind shied away.

It wouldn't happen again. The kiss was engendered by brandy and proximity. No wonder social rules decreed that young men and women should never be alone.

They had slammed together like two bulls she once saw in a village fair. More gently, but with equal fervor.

She found herself staring at the fire, drumming her fingers on the chair and comparing their kisses to those she shared with Foster, who had responded to her refusal to marry him by trying to kiss her into compliance.

If Foster and she had kissed like that, would she have rejected him? She liked to think she would, that control of her business interests was more powerful than desire.

But she wasn't entirely sure. Addison – Jake – was dangerous. After living with her mother's tempestuous emotions, she had been certain that she would never feel anything like desire.

Possibly wasn't even capable of such feelings.

As Cleo had seen it, marrying Foster would have taken her away from a life she was tired of. He had promised to leave the stage, which meant no more endless performances, histrionic actors . . . her mother. Whom she loved fiercely but didn't want to live with.

It was all so complicated that she ended up staring at the dying fire for another hour.

Foster had been a companion. A friend, she had thought. A spouse who would be calm and – and honorable, except he wasn't. After she discovered the truth, she'd seen so clearly that she had allowed herself to be blinded by a fortune hunter with a trim figure and a ready smile.

The comparison to Jake Addison was jarring and unwelcome.

Foster had schemed behind her back to profit from her inheritance. Jake had returned to her room to confess the details of his plan to convince Martha to sell him Quimby's.

He had put all the power into her hands. He would wear whatever she ordered for him.

Gaudy, he said. Bright colors, even flowers. She knew little of men's clothing, but she thought there was a chance that embroidery would draw attention to his masculinity. While other men – Foster – would be diminished by wearing pink silk, Jake might only look more powerful.

If that happened . . . Well, every man in London would be knocking at Quimby's door, begging to be made into an American beast, albeit a beast in a flowered silk waistcoat.

She would be punctiliously fair and order exactly what he demanded, no matter the outcome. Byng suddenly leapt to mind: her grandfather's friend, swathed in his extravagant embroidered smoking jacket.

A smile curved her lips.

Byng would know exactly how to turn a man into a peacock.

CHAPTER THIRTEEN

Quimby's Emporium

Jake walked into Quimby's first thing in the morning.

'Mr Addison,' Martha said, looking dismayed.

He raised a hand. 'I'm not here to try to convince you to move to New York, Mrs Quimby. I wish to order a wardrobe. Head to toe. Parasols, boots, the whole of it.'

'Men don't carry parasols!' she gasped.

'Oh, really?' he asked. 'I had the idea that gentlemen in the United Kingdom were bent on protecting their skin. Whatever it is that men do carry over here, I'll need it. I'm going on the Season. That's the British term, isn't it?'

Her eyes couldn't get any rounder. 'Mr Addison, I don't think . . .'

'No need to think,' he pointed out. 'You can charge me whatever you like, to make up for the affront of nearly signing a contract to take you to America.'

'But you are returning to America,' she pointed out.

159

'Not any longer.'

'No?'

'No, I've decided to take a wife here, and she's someone you know well.'

'Not . . . not Miss Lewis!'

'Precisely.' He paused. 'It might be better if you didn't share that information, Mrs Quimby. I don't want to put her off.'

Her expression told him exactly what she thought of that.

'Already put off, you think?'

'Mr Addison,' Mrs Quimby said, clearly choosing her words with care. 'You don't . . . The other day, you stood there in the presence of the lady in such a coat as I would be ashamed to sew, with no hat and your hair mussed, and your boots . . .'

'I like these boots,' Jake said, glancing down at them.

'You can't wear them to society events,' Mrs Quimby said flatly. 'I have to be honest, though you do deserve the worst for trying to steal me away to America.'

'It was your solicitor, Worting, who kept the truth from you, not to mention the thousand pounds he planned to pocket.'

'He's a wart,' Mrs Quimby said, obviously disgusted. 'But the fact is that I can't help you, Mr Addison. It's nice that you're thinking of marriage, and I'm sure there's many a suitable lass in the Americas who would take you . . . as you are.'

Jake burst out laughing. 'If you won't help me,

Mrs Quimby, where do you advise that I go? Isn't there a street full of tailors somewhere in London? I recall my uncle telling me that he has all his coats made . . . Is there a fellow called Weston around?'

Mrs Quimby bridled. 'Highway robbery! The most expensive tailor in the city. You're not fit to be out on your own, Mr Addison. First you let Mr Worting take advantage, and now you're going to stroll into that den of thieves, as innocent as a newborn lamb!'

Jake tried hard to look innocent. 'You think Weston might raise his prices when he sees me coming?'

'That, or show you the door,' Mrs Quimby said. 'But no, because everyone knows as how there's an American over here buying up anything that catches his eye. He'll fleece you. Likely he *will* sell you a parasol and make a fool of you for carrying it, for a jest. A jest that will cost you a guinea or more!'

'I'll never find a bride under those circumstances,' Jake said gravely. 'I need your help, Mrs Quimby.'

'I expect that the thieves are on you as thick as gutter mud,' she said, sighing. 'Have you checked to make sure that those Shakespeare plays you bought aren't just tea-stained versions of a player's book?'

'I have,' Jake assured her. 'I'm very good at pricing what I buy. I know, for example, that

161

Quimby's is a far better costume maker than Winch's.'

'That is true,' Mrs Quimby said, giving him a genuine smile. 'They make nasty, cheap garments over there. What if the play outlasts its run? The theater must commission all new costumes. Mine will last a company a year or more!'

'Are you sure you won't consider coming to America?' Jake asked.

'Never!' She straightened up, her eyes glowing. 'An Englishwoman I am, and I'll die the same.'

'Then won't you help me?' Jake asked, ladling his voice with pathos. 'I do mean to coax Miss Lewis into marrying me. If you leave me in the hands of Weston, I'll be robbed blind. But you, Mrs Quimby, *you* would know how to outfit me.'

'It's true that I've taken many a rough actor and turned him into a gentleman,' Mrs Quimby said, squinting at his shoulders. 'You're not the right shape, I don't mind telling you. Too big around the chest. You'd have to do something about your face.'

'Not much I can do about my face.' Jake was thoroughly enjoying himself now. 'I was born with this jaw, more's the pity.'

'Milk baths,' Mrs Quimby muttered. 'You're not the right color for a gentleman.'

He raised an eyebrow.

'Gentlemen are pale, and you're brownish, as if you gallivant around in the sunshine.'

'That is exactly why I thought that Brits might have taken up parasols,' Jake pointed out.

162

'It wouldn't matter on the stage,' Martha told him. 'You'd have to put on a thick base coat of face paint. But it wouldn't do for you to be wearing paint to a ball.'

'I understand,' Jake said, keeping laughter out of his voice with some difficulty.

'Milk baths, cucumber on your eyes, perhaps a gentle bleach? A gentleman's gentleman would know what to do.'

'My American valet will do his best.'

'Once I list all the clothing that a man requires to look gentlemanly, you might change your mind. It's going to cost you a pretty penny. I fit a hero with two or three changes of costume at most, but you're going to need far more than that.'

Jake didn't have the heart to mention that he did own fancy clothing, made in Paris. But it was all left back in his two homes in New York and Boston – two cities with quite fine societies of their own. He'd been attending balls and the like since he was a stripling. Yet he had no evening clothing here, so Martha would have to outfit him from head to foot.

Martha shook her head. 'How are you to get invitations, Mr Addison? It's not like the theater, you know. You can't just pay to sit in the front row. Them balls, they don't let people stroll in off the streets, no matter how nicely dressed they are. If that was the case, Reggie Bottleneck would be married to a duchess's daughter right now.'

'I have a friend who's a duchess,' he assured her.

She frowned at him. 'I don't believe you, Mr Addison, and neither will anyone else. Just present yourself as a wealthy eccentric from America. Don't pretend to be anything more than you are!'

'I won't,' Jake said, smiling at her. 'That is excellent advice, Mrs Quimby, and I shall take it to heart. But I *am* very close friends with the Duchess of Trent.'

Mrs Quimby eyed him suspiciously. 'You are?'

'You clothed her as a North Star,' he reminded her.

'Course, now I do remember that she's an American. You're friends with a duchess,' Mrs Quimby said, obviously astounded. 'Here I am, worried that you won't get a single invitation. They do call her the *American* duchess.' She dropped into a seat. 'You truly will be going around polite society, won't you?'

He nodded.

'Bless my soul and whiskers,' she whispered. 'I've the Haymarket production coming up as well.'

'I need to be as elegant as Miss Lewis,' Jake said.

'Bless me,' Mrs Quimby said, fanning herself with a scrap of cloth that she had snatched up. She looked up, her eyes damp. 'I've gone from being terrified about moving to the colonies or being destitute, to dressing friends of nobility.'

'Life,' Jake said, nodding. 'One moment you're a free spirit and then next you're on the verge of marriage.'

Mrs Quimby took a deep breath. 'I'll have some sketches made up for you, sir.'

'There's a twist. I shall be ordering Miss Lewis's wardrobe, and she will order mine.'

Mrs Quimby's voice rose to a squeak. '*Miss Lewis will wear what you order?*'

'She will. I'll tell you now that I'm not ordering anything like that gray dress you put her in. Conversely, I will wear whatever she orders for me.'

'I thought it was an evil day when you caught sight of Quimby's,' Mrs Quimby said. 'I'm big enough to say as I was wrong.'

Jake grinned at her. 'That day, I walked in here furious with you, and here I am, not so long after, with . . . well, not with a bride, but at least with the hope of one. We're good luck for each other, Mrs Quimby.'

'Martha,' she said. 'You call me Martha.'

CHAPTER FOURTEEN

'Grandfather, you mustn't!' Cleo exclaimed, rushing forward to rescue the poor footman being poked in the back by the viscount's cane.

'They're liable to spill me onto these steps,' Viscount Falconer complained. 'Watch as you go, fellow!'

Her grandfather had adamantly refused to be left at home when Cleo arrived, requesting Byng's aid. Given that the viscount's gout was particularly painful in the morning hours, he was reclining on a litter carried by four hearty footmen rather than walking on his own from the carriage and up the steps to Quimby's Emporium.

They entered to find the bottom chamber of Quimby's thronged with people. Several of Martha's seamstresses were clustered around a low pedestal, two of them with sketching paper, others with measuring tape. A box of pins had scattered on the carpet.

In the middle of it all, standing with his back to them, was Jacob Astor Addison.

With a silent intake of breath, Cleo realized that

Jake wore only a pair of sleekly fitted breeches and – oddly – a length of shimmering violet silk over one shoulder that spilled off the pedestal.

Gussie instantly shrieked and clapped a hand over her eyes.

Cleo did not.

Such a ladylike response didn't even occur to her. Instead her eyes opened wider, and she caught every lineament, every muscle. Strong legs . . . burly, even. Thighs like the trunks of oak trees. A taut, muscled arse. His body narrowed above it and then flared out to shoulders that seemed constructed for manual labor.

One of his shoulders was slashed by an old scar. No, not one scar: three.

Three white streaks curved across his wide back and tucked into his waist. Her stomach clenched, following the realization that he might well have died from such a brutal wound. The scars were bleached and cruel against the golden hue of his skin.

Not gentlemen's skin.

He wheeled about.

Cleo instantly looked away.

Too late. The maleness of his chest was emblazoned on the inside of her eyelids and perhaps even in her bone marrow. His muscles were grooved across his stomach, as if made to guide a woman's touch below his waistband.

She wanted to trace them, to follow the line of his scars and know the story behind them.

That unwelcome emotion, desire, swelled up inside her again.

She was getting to recognize it, shameful though it was. Desire was a longing spark in her chest and a warm glow between her legs. It ran through her, deep as . . . as the ocean, she thought irrelevantly.

Due to her mother, obviously.

Inherited from Julia. Though, thankfully, Julia didn't offer any commentary.

Without planning to, Cleo found that she was smiling a welcome.

'Let me off this litter,' her grandfather barked. 'No, not like that, fool. Get me to my feet. Hand me my cane. You, whoever you are, cover yourself so that these womenfolk don't faint. We already have one invalid in the room.'

Up on the platform, Jake laughed and tossed the length of silk to a seamstress. Cleo's grandfather hobbled to a chair, and Cleo followed him, sitting down and taking his hand.

She and her grandfather had fallen into a happy friendship. She stopped by once a day, sometimes merely for tea, sometimes sharing a meal. His hand curled around hers, knobby from arthritis but still strong.

'Now,' the viscount said, slamming his stick against the floor, 'where's the owner of this establishment?'

Martha Quimby stepped forward, hands clasped before her. 'I am she, my lord. Mrs Quimby, the owner of the emporium.'

'I am Viscount Falconer,' he announced. 'Dismiss this naked fellow so that my granddaughter can order a monstrous amount of clothing. Men's clothing, because I damned well don't understand the world any longer, but that's what she wants to do.'

Cleo's hand tightened around his. 'Grandfather, the fellow is Mr Addison, and the clothes I order will be worn by him.'

Off to the side, Byng was caught in a paroxysm of silent laughter.

'We have measured the gentleman,' Martha said, nodding. 'My lead seamstress, Mrs Andrewes, has begun making sketches of clothing that will turn Mr Addison into the most elegant man in all London.'

'Impossible,' her grandfather said flatly. 'That fellow will never look refined. Not a monstrous body like that. Legs that could hold up an elephant.'

Jake had stepped off the platform and pulled a white shirt over his head. Peeking from under her lashes, Cleo watched as he stuffed the shirttail into his breeches.

He walked over and bowed before them. 'Miss Lewis, what a pleasure to meet you again.'

Cleo inclined her head. 'Mr Addison, good morning. Grandfather and Byng, may I present Mr Jacob Astor Addison? Mr Addison, these two gentlemen are my grandfather, Viscount Falconer, and a dear family friend, Mr Byng-Stafford.'

'Good morning, Lord Falconer. Mr Byng-Stafford,' Jake said, bowing again. His bow was respectful but abrupt, not part of a choreographed series of gestures intended to impress the onlookers with his grace.

Because he wasn't graceful, Cleo thought with amusement.

'I don't understand what my granddaughter has to do with you,' Falconer grumbled, examining him.

Jake's eyes were thoughtful, amused. Perhaps she could find fabric that precise shade of indigo blue.

'My lord, Miss Lewis and I are friends,' he said, bowing again, 'as well as business rivals. Your granddaughter outbid me for this very establishment.'

'Good Lord, your voice is a piece with the rest of you,' Falconer remarked. 'Thundering and twanging at the same time. I can never understand Americans.'

Cleo gave him a narrow-eyed look.

The viscount sighed. 'Mr Addison, how pleasant to meet you.' He held out his hand. 'Forgive me if I don't rise.'

Perhaps her grandfather expected that Jake would bow over his hand? He shook it.

'Any relation to John Astor?' Byng asked, coming forward.

'My paternal uncle,' Jake said, shaking hands with Byng as well. 'I'm named after him, as a matter of fact. He is John Jacob Astor.'

'Then why are you called Addison?' the viscount demanded.

'I changed my name.'

'You *what?*'

'I chose to become an Addison,' Jake clarified.

'But you are an Astor,' Byng said.

'I do not hide my relationship to my family, but I decided to change my name.'

Cleo gave her grandfather's hand a squeeze. 'Mrs Quimby has sketches to show us.'

'In England, we value our relatives,' her grandfather announced. 'How'd you get that monstrous scar?'

'A gift from a bear,' Jake said, with a wry smile. 'I spent a few years in the wilder regions of America, working on fur contracts with my uncle.'

'Looks like the bear almost got its revenge,' the viscount remarked.

'Mrs Quimby, may I look at some of your sketches?' Cleo asked, feeling a tinge of desperation. Her grandfather was a force of nature, and so was Jake. She had a slight fear that they might start shouting at each other.

'My understanding is that you are ordering a wardrobe for my granddaughter – the most improper thing I've ever heard of – and she is doing the same for you,' her grandfather barked.

Jake inclined his head. 'Think of it as a business wager, my lord. She seeks to bolster the reputation of Quimby's, whereas I seek to convince Mrs Quimby that costumes are her *métier*.'

Martha frowned. '*Métier?*'

'An occupation at which you excel,' Cleo said, thinking that French was doing her some good after all.

Martha's chin rose stubbornly into the air. 'I am excellent at costuming actors, and I shall be equally good at costuming polite society. Just look how marvelous my gown looks on Miss Lewis.'

Cleo was wearing her favorite gray gown with its matching spencer. She flashed a look at Jake, warning him not to elaborate on the opinion he expressed earlier.

Of course, he ignored her.

'Miss Lewis looks as if she's wrapped up in gray lichen,' he said. 'Not that I doubt your skill, Mrs Quimby. But as I informed Miss Lewis, if that gown is seen as representative of Quimby's work, no marriageable young maiden will have faith in a Quimby's wardrobe.'

The viscount's white brows drew together. 'My granddaughter is exquisite!'

'No one would argue with that,' Jake said amiably. 'We are discussing only the gown that Mrs Quimby made for her.'

'It is a trifle sad,' Byng put in.

'I didn't make it for Miss Lewis,' Martha clarified. 'An actress at the Drury Lane was supposed to wear it as the evil governess until you, Mr Addison, lured her to a theater in the Americas.'

'Where she will surely become a household

172

name,' he said promptly. 'A romantic heroine is better than an evil governess.'

Cleo took a deep breath. It would serve nothing if she allowed herself to become irritated.

'Now this purple fabric,' Jake said, nodding toward one of the seamstresses, 'would flatter Miss Lewis's hair and skin, rather than making her look sallow.'

The ember of irritation turned into a glowing coal.

'She doesn't look sallow, precisely,' Byng said, squinting at Cleo. 'Though the gray does leach the color from your skin, my dear. If you'll forgive me.'

Cleo took another deep breath and accidentally met Jake's eyes. Which reminded her, as plain as if he'd spoken it aloud, that he found aspects of her jacket – the fit – extremely flattering.

She came to her feet. 'I would prefer that we not discuss my gown, which I adore, by the way, Martha. We came here today to select a wardrobe for Mr Addison.'

Jake turned and picked up the shimmering violet from the seamstress. Stepping toward her, he slung the length of silk around her neck and then tossed it over her shoulder. 'There,' he said with satisfaction.

Cleo looked down, and her fingers curled around the silk. The color was violet that leaned toward blue, with a silvery shimmer to it. It felt like water under her fingers.

'Dear me,' Byng said. 'How interesting.'

'Yes,' her grandfather agreed.

'What?' Cleo asked, turning to them.

'Your hair,' her grandfather said, peering at her. 'It took on an entirely different color. Better.'

'I like my hair as it is,' Cleo said indignantly and not truthfully. She put up her hand and patted the knot at her neck, which seemed to be holding most of her curls back. Perhaps she should have pulled on that turban.

'The color does something for you, miss.' Gussie took Cleo's arm and turned her about to the glass before which Jake had been standing.

Cleo had to admit the truth.

Her hair dampened to copper, a burnished, shimmering color. And her skin looked very nice.

'More like that,' Jake was saying to Martha, off to the side.

Cleo suddenly felt color sweeping into her cheeks. She was standing about like a girl, gawking at her own image. She briskly unwrapped the violet silk and handed it to one of Martha's seamstresses.

'What are you looking at?' she asked, walking over to Jake, trying to look unconcerned. Casual.

'Gowns from Ackermann's *Repository of Arts*,' Martha said.

Byng followed her and took up one of the images. 'That's not bad.'

'It's dated May, almost a year ago,' Cleo pointed

out. 'Perhaps we should find something more current.'

Martha gave her a triumphant smile. 'I have my own arrangement with the journal; they send me all the fashion plates as soon as they're engraved. These will appear in the May issue. I need to be beforehand for the stage, of course. They aren't painted in, but my girls interpret colors as well as anyone working for Mr Ackermann.'

'Excellent,' Cleo said, picking up a sketch of a gentleman wearing a coat fashioned with two lines of large brass buttons down the front and a frothing cravat. 'We must have this coat, in a flamboyant hue. Perhaps with larger lapels.'

'Mrs Andrewes is a dab hand at sketching, so you tell her how you want it to look. Miss Prewitt can paint the drawing any colors you wish, and we'll find the fabric to match,' Martha said. 'Finally, we make the coat to your wishes.'

'Mr Addison's wardrobe should be as unusual as his last name,' Cleo announced. 'Bright colors with variegated lapels, flounced cuffs.' She tapped the illustration she held. 'No black.'

Martha's eyes rounded, and she glanced at Jake.

'I promised to wear whatever Miss Lewis orders,' Jake said, smiling.

'Bring the drawings over here!' the viscount barked from behind them. 'I don't want an American choosing garments that make my granddaughter look like a lightskirt.'

Martha gathered up a handful of illustrations and hurried over to Falconer, accompanied by Jake. Rather to Cleo's surprise, Jake sat down, and the two men began discussing the finer points of ladies' fashion.

'This wouldn't be bad in purple,' Jake said, tapping his finger.

'With touches of cream,' the viscount said, nodding.

Mrs Andrewes began sketching a gown at their direction.

'Not like that!' the viscount said. 'The way he said, rounder at the shoulder.'

Cleo shook her head and turned to Byng. 'I wouldn't have imagined it.'

'Your grandfather is lonely,' Byng said. 'You've given him new life.'

'Yes, but arguing over sartorial details?'

'He's had no one to talk to but me,' Byng pointed out. 'Why not dive into the intricacies of his grand-daughter's wardrobe? On that front, my dear, shall we do the same for Mr Jacob Astor Addison? You do know who Astor is, don't you?'

Cleo nodded. 'A magnate of the fur trade. From bears, apparently. And opium, but Jake is not involved—'

Byng pounced on that. 'Jake!'

'We are friends, as he mentioned,' Cleo said, feeling her cheeks warm again.

Byng snapped his fingers. 'We'd better make him an extraordinary wardrobe, in that case.'

Cleo felt a little misgiving. 'You look like a naughty elf.'

'If I understand you correctly, Mr Astor Addison's wardrobe needs to be spectacularly vulgar, the better to convince polite society that Quimby's is better left to the theatrical sphere?'

'Yes,' Cleo said.

'I am precisely the right person to help,' Byng said with a touch of pride. 'My family has credited me with an uncommon flair for vulgarity ever since I ordered my first garment as a mere lad.'

'Which was?'

'A delightful mustard-yellow coat covered with scallops,' he said reminiscently. 'Ties to match on my knee breeches, worn with a vertically striped waistcoat. Oh, and a tall hat with a red plume. My mother collapsed onto a settee, calling for smelling salts.'

Cleo broke into laughter.

'Over thirty-five years ago now,' Byng told her. 'I am precisely the person to make a dandified American monster out of Mr Astor Addison. I can tell by looking at him that his sartorial imagination is nonexistent.'

'I don't think he cares about clothing,' Cleo agreed.

'We shall begin with fabric,' Byng announced. 'We'll need a monstrous amount of it to cover those shoulders.'

'Excellent,' Jake said from the chairs, where he had apparently been eavesdropping. 'Lord Falconer,

177

if you continue working with the sketches, I shall accompany your granddaughter upstairs to survey Mrs Quimby's fabrics.'

'I shall rest my feet before traipsing upstairs,' Byng said, looking satisfied as he walked over to sit beside the viscount.

'What do you think?' Cleo's grandfather asked him, pointing at the sketch under way.

'Needs to be lower in the bodice,' Byng said.

Cleo rolled her eyes. Luckily, she didn't have to wear the garments for more than a few months.

Jake held out the crook of his arm. 'Miss Lewis?'

There was a look in his eyes that made sensation race down Cleo's spine. Without touching her. Just . . .

She took his arm.

Albeit with the rueful feeling that somewhere up on a fluffy cloud, her mother was applauding. *I can't stand a bracket-faced bluestocking,* Julia crowed. *Go on, darling, prove that you're my daughter!*

Resolutely, Cleo banished her mother.

But not until Julia had a last word.

Those shoulders, dearest . . . Brawny in the best possible way.

CHAPTER FIFTEEN

Jake followed Cleo up the stairs, his eyes fixed on her derrière, reminding himself with each step that he was a gentleman. Gentlemen didn't seduce ladies.

That blasted gray jacket stopped above the waist, and the gown itself was light and floaty. Cleo's rear was –

Generous.

She wouldn't like that word, but he couldn't think of an appropriate compliment. Instead, his eyes kept gobbling up the way her hips swayed. He couldn't look away.

She was taming him like some kind of damned – Cleo swayed her way through the door, and he followed, pouncing on her like the beast he was, and spinning her against the wall.

'Jake,' she chided. But her eyes were shining, and she didn't push him away.

'I haven't thought of a blasted thing other than kissing you since . . . well, since I had my kippers this morning,' he told her.

'Is that a compliment? The kippers beat me out?'

He tucked away a curl that had escaped the large knot at her neck. 'Kippers demand attention. One can't have one's tool at the ready while removing tiny bones from a fish.'

A giggle escaped her, just when he remembered that ladies didn't care to hear about unruly private parts. Cleo didn't seem to mind.

'That's a compliment, if not a refined one,' he said, allowing a finger to trace the graceful line of her jaw. 'You've been on my mind all morning. As well as yesterday. Last night. You're on my mind now. I . . . May I kiss you?'

Their eyes caught and held. 'Yes.'

Baldly put, a businesslike response. No giggling, no flirtatious glance, no pretend hesitation. Just the affirmative.

When he was thinking about how unusual she was, her hand came up to his head and pulled him down to her lips.

So she kissed him first, her tongue darting into his mouth, her fragrance filling the air. Jake's body thudded to attention.

'May I put my arms around you?' he asked hoarsely, a few minutes later. 'Pick you up?'

Cleo's eyes were sultry, the Queen of the Nile in full command of her powers, certain of her beauty and seductiveness. 'Why not, since I have mine around you?' Fingers curled into his hair and one hand slipped down to his neck.

Jake wrapped his arms around her, plucking her up and easing her against the wall so that he could kiss her harder, a needy kiss rather than an exploring one. He stepped closer, pressing against her.

Cleo made a sound in the back of her throat as their bodies met. A needy sound that tightened his body so much that he felt his erection thump against her.

'Not gentlemanly,' he murmured, easing away and kissing her cheek. She had high cheekbones, touched with delicate apricot color.

'Mmmm,' Cleo said, tipping her head back against the wall. His erection throbbed again.

She must be able to feel it. He let his lips slip from her jaw to her neck. Her skin was so –

'Jake.'

He jerked his head up.

'Kiss me,' Cleo whispered, her voice ragged.

He claimed her with that kiss, a primal instinct as desire seared him to the bone. His fingers, his arms, his lips, his whole body had never been this alive.

'You're mine,' he growled, the words coming completely unbidden from his lips.

Her eyes flew open. They had darkened again. He'd probably spend his life trying to figure out the right word. They weren't gray or blue. They were green as bottled glass, the kind that holds the best beer.

He couldn't say that.

Green as wild gooseberries, the ones that are dark and hide among the leaves.

181

'Cleo,' he whispered instead, his voice raw with emotion. 'Mine.'

'I am no man's,' she stated, scowling at him.

'All right,' he said, ignoring his conviction that she was his. Then he kissed her again because he was never any good at words. *I need you*, he said, silently. *I want you.* And far down in the depths of his soul, an alarmed voice: *I may even be falling in love with you.*

She kissed him back, but he didn't know what she was thinking.

The thought was distracting, so he set her on her feet.

'Do you think it's suspicious that no one has come to assist us?' Cleo asked.

Jake was trying to comprehend a language he didn't know, a woman's face. 'Do you regret kissing me?'

'No.'

His chest eased. 'In that case—' His head began to bend back to hers.

'But no more kissing,' Cleo said. Laughter drifted up the stairs. 'What on earth is my grandfather doing downstairs? Martha? Byng?'

'Designing us monstrous wardrobes,' he said, cocking an ear. 'I heard Byng say that he doesn't want me to glimpse the hideous garments he's designing for fear I will run back to America.'

'When we walked in,' Cleo said, looking hesitant, 'I saw your back. Those scars. How did it happen?'

'I happened on a bear with cubs to defend,' he

182

said, wondering if she liked his body or whether it was horrifyingly burly as well as scarred.

'You were clawed?'

He nodded. 'Bitten, actually. One tooth was left embedded in my side. I still have it.'

She shuddered. 'Why?'

'A good luck piece. Some believe that bears can cure themselves, so a bear tooth offers protection and strength.'

'Do you keep yours in your pocket?'

He shook his head. 'I might have put it on a pendant, but I don't see myself wearing a necklace.'

Cleo leaned toward him with a flutter of extravagantly thick eyelashes. 'I don't like to think of you so injured.' Her mouth met his in a sensual collision that sent a flare of heat through Jake's limbs. Somehow his erection swelled even more, making his breeches tent in front.

'We should choose fabrics.' Cleo slid sideways, out of his embrace. She looked as composed as she had while climbing the stairs, whereas he felt unraveled . . . undone.

Changed in some fundamental way.

For the next twenty minutes, Cleo led him from shelf to shelf as he dragged along a stepladder, taking down one hideous fabric after another.

He didn't even bristle.

He was too busy re-sorting his life yet again.

'What do you think of green?' Cleo asked him, eyes bright.

'Certainly,' Jake said, realizing that he'd have to sell all the theaters. He had never cared very much for them anyway. They had been his father's. He could assign his American agent to get rid of them.

'You're not listening,' Cleo protested.

'Fabric is not like kippers.'

Her brows drew together.

'I haven't stopped longing for you because of this.' He waved his hand at the long table, now covered with bolts of cloth, bright, printed: all of it garish. 'There's nothing here to take my mind off you.'

'No?' A smile tucked into the corners of Cleo's lips. Her eyes drifted down below his waist.

Jake's arms went around her again, and he tucked her close so she could feel exactly what he was referring to. 'No,' he whispered, the word coming out a growl.

Someone cleared his throat.

Jake stepped back and pivoted so that the corner of the table covered his middle area.

'Hello, Byng,' Cleo said, looking as serene as if they'd been caught sharing a cup of tea.

'I heard something about kippers as I was climbing the stairs. Are you hungry, Mr Astor Addison?' Mr Byng-Stafford's eyes held a laughing glint.

'Not at the moment, sir,' Jake told him.

'Oh, good. Now you'd better address me as Byng, because that's what all my friends call me, and I have a feeling that you rank in their midst. After all, you have agreed to wear the clothing I am designing. You and I will be virtually the only gentlemen in London stemming the tide of black.'

'The tide?' Cleo asked, looking confused.

'We've been infected in this country by a terribly tedious fellow named Beau Brummell who wears nothing but black,' Byng said. 'Have you heard of him, Mr Astor Addison?'

'I go by Addison,' Jake told him. 'No, I know nothing of the man.'

'Tiresome, very tiresome,' Byng said with a sigh. 'Shall we look at the fabrics you've chosen?' He turned to the long table. 'Just look at this!' He unwrapped a length of chintz patterned with large red tulips.

Jake could scarcely stop himself from shuddering. 'Surely that fabric is meant for a woman's garment?'

'It will make an astonishing coat,' Byng said, ignoring him. 'Dear Cleo, have you seen an orange silk anywhere, perhaps corded? Imagine this fabric with an orange lining. Breeches to match, of course.'

Cleo's face lit up with her dimpled smile. 'I have!' She pulled bolts of cloth to the side, finally coming up with a fabric so bright that it would put a Seville orange to shame.

'Orange breeches?' Jake asked, knowing dismay leaked into his voice.

Cleo sidled over to him and bumped her hip into his. 'Kippers?'

He cracked a laugh. She was right; the image of orange breeches had laid his tool to rest.

'What's all this about kippers?' Byng asked. He had taken out a pencil and was scribbling on a piece of notepaper. 'Now, darling Cleo, I don't want to have all the fun of ordering Addison's clothing. You must do your part.'

'We could choose fabric for your gowns,' Jake suggested. 'Let's make another round of all the shelves, and I will hold bolts up to your hair.'

'Only half-mourning colors,' Cleo reminded him.

Jake had a distinct sense that she had latched on to half mourning as a way of ensuring her crackpot notion of being a wallflower. It wasn't up to him to point out that she glowed, no matter her clothing.

Even in gray.

'Try blue,' Byng said, not looking up as he jotted down more notes. Jake was horrified to see that he had plucked a lilac feather from somewhere and was holding it up to some rose fabric. 'Green is too obvious.'

'Green is not acceptable for half mourning,' Cleo stated.

Jake reached over and stole the lilac feather, poking it into her chignon. It stood up behind her head, waving slightly.

Cleo glanced over at the glass, leaning against the wall, and laughed. 'I think not!'

Byng took the feather back. 'Right idea, but look for violet, rather than lilac.'

186

Jake slipped his hand into Cleo's and led her along the wall. 'What in the hell is the difference between violet and lilac?'

Her fingers curled around his felt like the most erotic handshake he'd experienced in his life. He cursed under his breath, turned and met laughing eyes.

'If you're touching me, I need to put on my damned coat.'

'Well, well,' she said, raising dancing eyes from his waist. From below his waist.

His hand tightened around hers. 'In case you're wondering, this doesn't happen to me. Ever.'

'I'm no expert,' she said, leaning back against the counter.

A swath of fabric just behind her head caught his eyes. It was a pale, clear blue. He pulled it off the shelf.

'Over a cream dress, very simple,' he said. 'There was a sketch downstairs, of a jacket like the one you're wearing.'

She glanced down. 'I thought you loathed this gown.'

'Not all of it.' He held the cloth up to her hair. 'Not the cut.'

'Is blue included in half mourning?'

'With black trim,' he amended.

'Are you horrified by the idea of wearing orange breeches?' she asked in a low voice, as they stood shoulder to shoulder, staring at some purple fabrics and trying to distinguish violet from lavender.

'Yes.'

'Perhaps—' she began.

But Jake shook his head. The game was essential, if not for the reason she imagined. Being decked out in brilliant colors gave him a reason to be at her side. *Every* night, when English gentlemen were trying to win her.

'I shall wear whatever you put before me. I'm looking forward to it.'

Cleo glanced up at him and away, pink washing in her cheeks. There must have been something in his eyes.

'My grandfather is likely exhausted,' she said.

'I'll take a hackney home later,' Byng said. 'This is the most delightful experience I've had in years.' He was standing at the table behind them, squinting at an iridescent green satin he apparently planned to pair with rose-colored silk.

Back downstairs, Cleo returned her grandfather to his litter without a wasted word or gesture. All the men in the room, the grooms and footmen, simply lined up and did her bidding . . . including the viscount.

To his surprise, Lord Falconer looked up at Jake, and one eyelid drooped over amused eyes. 'Fair warning.'

Jake nodded and bowed.

Fair warning?

He knew just what the viscount was implying.

His life would be very different with Cleo than it might have been with biddable Frederica. He had to make an effort to bring his almost-fiancée's face to mind. A rounded chin, he thought.

Now the only chin that mattered was pointed.

'Martha,' Jake said, turning back to the room, 'have you sufficient guidance to begin creating our wardrobes?'

She looked at him, eyes shining. 'Yes, sir. As I understand it, you are staying at Germain's Hotel?'

'I am,' Jake said, feeling grateful that the viscount had left. Cleo's grandfather seemed to think that Jake was an acceptable suitor, but he would not welcome the fact that as of this morning, Jake's possessions had been moved upstairs, into the royal suite across the hallway from Cleo's.

The elderly gentleman in 302 – he who had rejected a piece of warm apple tart – had departed for his home in Lancaster. Moggly had promptly rented the suite on Jake's behalf and would be moving his belongings to the third floor during the day. 'I felt certain that you would wish to avoid donning livery again,' Moggly had said, without further comment.

Jake had never seduced a lady, and he had no intention of beginning now. But Cleo wasn't safe in that hotel, not without *his* grooms – who did not sleep on their feet – guarding the corridor.

'Where would I buy some flowers?' he asked Martha, in a somewhat abrupt turn of topic.

'Covent Garden Market isn't far from here,' she said, blinking at him. 'Though you won't see many gentlemen there. Only a dandy picks out his own flowers, sir.'

'I am soon to be a dandy, am I not?' He grinned at her.

'That's right, sir, you certainly are.'

'I might as well practice.'

Covent Garden Market was a long covered building, stuffed with people selling everything from silkworms to fried eels. 'Primroses, two bundles a penny!' shouted a girl standing by a wheelbarrow. 'Here, you, gentleman, I'll give you sweet violets for only a penny; you won't do better under this roof!'

Jake strolled over and looked at her flowers. The flower girl had sharp eyes and fluffy yellow hair piled on her head, giving her a vague resemblance to a chicken.

'Courting, are you?' she asked. 'I can give you a ribbon for another penny. An' I can deliver a posy every morning iffen you's really serious.'

Jake nodded. 'Is that common?'

'Iffen you's serious,' she repeated. 'All the other gentlemen will send 'em as well, you know.' She looked him up and down. 'You aren't going to win her heart in the usual way of things, are you? You need to go the extra mile.'

Jake couldn't help grinning at her. 'Now why wouldn't I be able to win her heart the normal way?'

'You're too big,' she said. 'You don't speak right, and you – your face isn't the sort to warm a girl's heart, is it?'

Jake burst out laughing.

'Don't you laugh at me. Just look at this,' she said, thrusting a gossip broadsheet at him. 'See him?' She pointed a grubby finger at the depiction of a man wearing a dapper coat and hat. 'That's Reggie Bottleneck, that is. He's a real gentleman and pretty as a picture. I seen him a few times, in real life.'

Jake thought of telling her that he'd not only met Reggie in the flesh, but that he was dispatching him to be a lead actor in New York City, but that news seemed likely to cause dismay. 'Well, I can't compete with him,' Jake said, 'so I'd better have a posy every day. I'll pay for the next two weeks, shall I?'

She frowned at him. 'You're trying to catch me out, aren't you? You'll never still be courting in two weeks. Iffen she's shown you the door, you don't want no flowers going there. You'll have to try another lady.'

'A week, then,' Jake said. 'What shall I send?'

She squinted at the coat that Martha had deplored. 'I'll give you a discount, and if you marry your lady, you can come back and get a flower service. Doing up the house every week.'

'I certainly shall,' he said. He held out his hand. 'My name is Jake Addison, and I'm from America.'

Her face fell. 'So, you'll be going back over the seas?'

'No, I plan to live here,' Jake said, though he hadn't said it aloud until that moment. 'I'll have

191

to sell some businesses I own in America, but the lady I'm courting is British to the bone.'

'That's good,' she said. 'My name's Lulu. I'll find you the right ones, the language of flowers.' She started rooting around in the wheelbarrow. 'The best I've got today, fresh as can be, are snowdrops. They mean hope, which is good because you're hoping, aren't you?'

Jake nodded. 'I am.'

'I have a barra boy, who'll deliver them for me.'

'The lady is Miss Lewis, and she's staying at Germain's Hotel.'

'I know that place.' Lulu darted a glance at him. 'Rich as a platter of gravy, is she? Well, never mind. There's someone for everyone, they say. Why shouldn't an heiress choose you? Tomorrow I'll get some ivy and put it together with lemon blossoms. Them's rare, but I know I can get some. They mean fidelity.'

'Excellent,' Jake said.

'Because she may have all those men after her,' Lulu said, nodding, 'but who's to say if they'll be faithful? Whereas a man like—'

'A man like me?' Jake supplied, choking back a smile because her advice was kindly meant.

'Well, you'll be grateful, won't you? Faithful.'

'I will,' Jake said. 'Be faithful.' He handed over a guinea.

'That's too much.'

'It may take me more than a week to convince her, but I won't be shown the door.'

Lulu looked at him dubiously.

'Trust me,' Jake said.

'What message do you want on the card 'sides your name?'

Nothing came to mind, which didn't surprise Jake. Any bumpkin could do a better job wooing his lady.

'What do you suggest?'

'"You're the queen of my heart,"' Lulu suggested. '"To my heart's gift," or "This little flower conquers time." Or you can compare her to something beautiful. "For a treasure beyond belief," or "Thou art as beautiful as a rose." "Thou" is fancy-like.'

Jake took out one of his cards. He scrawled a message and handed it to her. 'Same message every day.'

Lulu squinted at the card. 'Kipper,' she read slowly. Then, '*You're better than a kipper?*' Her voice rose at the end. 'You mean a kipper, a breakfast kipper?'

'Yes.'

'No!' she said, dropping the card into the wheelbarrow and putting her hands on her hips. 'You can't do that. You're handicapping yerself, just like a race. You'll never win her with something so . . . so smelly!'

'I have to be myself,' Jake said.

Lulu sighed. 'I oughtn't to take your money. It's stealing from the simpleminded, that's what it is. No one's going to believe this.' She mournfully tied a ribbon around the snowdrops. 'An American who compares an English lady to a kipper. Couldn't you just say, "You're prettier than a posy"?'

Jake plucked the card back out of the barrow. 'For Miss Lewis, at Germain's Hotel.'

'When she boots you out, you come back here and I'll give you what money's left,' Lulu said. 'It don't sit right with me not to.'

Jake grinned at her, and then bowed. 'Miss Lulu, you'll be doing flowers for our wedding.'

'Pride goeth before a fall, Mr American!' she shouted after him.

CHAPTER SIXTEEN

Grosvenor Square, London
Lord and Lady Overbury's townhouse
A ball in honor of their daughter, Penelope
Ten days later

Cleo strolled into her grandfather's drawing room, ready for her debut into polite society, feeling a strange mixture of excitement and nerves. She kept reminding herself that she planned to be a wallflower, and the last thing she wanted was a cluster of suitors.

Martha's gown was unlikely to support her wallflower ambitions.

'That boy did you proud when he ordered that gown,' the viscount exclaimed, struggling up from his chair.

'Addison is no boy,' Byng said. 'Turn around my dear. Allow me to relish every detail.' He nodded as Cleo twirled in front of him. 'Exquisite.'

Her narrow gown was made from the shimmering violet fabric that Cleo had first seen slung over Jake's shoulder. It cinched under her bosom, and a transparent overskirt billowed over it, with an elaborate hem made from bunches of the violet fabric. The extra weight made the overskirt dance around her ankles whenever she moved.

She wasn't going to be a wallflower, not in this gown. Somehow she couldn't make herself care.

Byng was grinning. 'It would be impertinent of me to mention the bodice, but I shall, anyway. Delightful!'

'Hush,' her grandfather scolded.

Cleo's bodice was indeed low, though nothing akin to what her mother had regularly worn. Puffs of transparent gauze pretended to be sleeves, leaving the tops of her shoulders bare.

'In truth, the bodice is practically puritanical,' Byng said. 'At the opera last night two ladies balanced their bosoms on the edge of their box for all to view.'

'Naked as the day they were born,' Falconer agreed.

'Nipples staring at the audience like fisheyes,' Byng supplemented.

'Let's make our way to the carriage,' Falconer said. 'I'm introducing my granddaughter to polite society. I don't want to miss a moment!'

Cleo tweaked her elbow-length gloves and took his arm.

'I'll open the door since Ponder is unaccountably missing,' Byng said, trotting ahead of them.

'Pay particular attention when I introduce you to the Earl of Lilford,' Falconer told Cleo. No matter how many times she insisted that she didn't wish to marry, her grandfather had taken on the role of matchmaker with gusto. 'He's a reasonable age, doesn't leer at women – and he has all his teeth.'

'An inducement to marriage,' Cleo murmured.

Her grandfather nudged her with his elbow. 'Many a gentleman's missing his teeth. Not to mention, most of them are lecherous as monkeys.'

That was information Cleo already knew; life with Julia had made it very clear just how eagerly a seducer eyes his prey.

Though to be fair, Julia often did the eyeing.

They walked into the Overburys' grand ball-room, pausing just long enough for the butler to bellow, 'Viscount Falconer; his granddaughter, Miss Lewis; Mr Byng-Stafford.' Cleo didn't feel even a tingle of nerves.

Why should she?

She had no interest in polite society or in marriage.

Yet when every head in the room swiveled toward them, eyes shining with avid curiosity, her gloved hand instinctively tightened on her grandfather's arm. A flock of gentlemen started toward them, as evidenced by black coats needling through colorful gowns, heading in their direction.

Jake's dress had done its work; Martha would be so pleased. Equally likely, the news of Cleo's fortune had spread. Her man of business had informed her yesterday that wealthy Londoners were haranguing him daily because they wanted

Lewis Commodes installed in their mansions before their neighbors could acquire them.

'Steady as she goes,' her grandfather murmured, tapping the step below him with his cane. In the last week, his gout had improved remarkably, and he hadn't taken the litter in two days.

Byng was chuckling on the viscount's other side.

'I planned to be a wallflower, Grandfather,' Cleo whispered.

He gave her a tender smile. 'There's nothing I can do to stop them, dear. Your mother was the same.'

I taught you well, Julie supplied.

Julia's voice had faded in the last few days, rarely popping up to offer irreverent comments, but Cleo had spent years of her life watching her mother's entrance into a room electrify any men in the vicinity.

Indeed, this felt familiar.

'I must hunt down Addison,' Byng said. 'I can't wait to see the splendor of a suit I designed.'

He wandered off, and Cleo's grandfather began nimbly introducing her to the men clustered before them.

'The Honorable Patrick de Grey,' he said, scarcely allowing her time to curtsy before he moved on to the next. 'Giles Renwick, the Earl of Lilford. Louis Pettigrew, Viscount Loring. The Honorable Algernon Dunlap.'

Cleo curtsied and smiled, and smiled, and smiled. Jake did not join them. Perhaps he hadn't arrived yet. Perhaps he'd lost his nerve. Or perhaps he simply didn't want to dance attendance on her.

Her smile cooled at the thought, and Algernon Dunlap (the Honorable) rushed into an explanation of the fact that he'd asked her for a waltz, although he knew perfectly well that she oughtn't to waltz, not having been approved by the patronesses—

Cleo cut him off. 'Of course, I'll waltz with you. Don't be silly.'

'Your eyes are like violets drenched with rain, Miss Lewis,' he breathed.

She barely caught back a stronger word than 'silly.' 'It's merely my gown,' she told him, turning gratefully to the Earl of Lilford, who had requested the first dance. At least he was old enough to be self-possessed.

As he escorted her onto the dance floor, Cleo noted that Lilford was tall and broad-shouldered, if not quite as powerful as Jake. He was definitely more quiet, appearing perfectly content to circle the floor without wasting words.

It was restful, she told herself.

I disagree, her mother piped up. *A silent man, like silent waters, can run deep and dangerous. Although he has a nice chest.*

Cleo gave Lilford her most enchanting smile. That spurred a reaction: he raised an eyebrow and finally spoke. 'Have we met before?'

'My grandfather only just introduced you to me,' she pointed out.

'Your smile—' He shook his head. 'Perhaps we met as children.'

'I doubt it,' Cleo said. She had a sudden, uncomfortable idea that perhaps he had met her mother. And if he had met Julia . . . He was precisely the type whom her mother preferred, and moreover he had to be thirty years of age, which gave him a good decade to have crossed Julia's path. 'Perhaps you met my mother, Mrs Julia Lewis.'

'I have not had that pleasure.' As the music ended, he drew her to the side of the room. 'May I have the next dance, Miss Lewis?'

'No, thank you,' she said.

The earl blinked. 'The supper dance?'

'No, thank you,' she repeated.

He stared bemusedly at her; it seemed that the Earl of Lilford was accustomed to getting what he wanted. Cleo gave him a kindly smile and walked away. She was tired of dancing – and since that was her first turn around the ballroom, it didn't bode well for her grandfather's marital scheme.

She should have been more adamant about her dreams of being a wallflower.

Slipping between eagerly chattering guests, she decided to look for a glass of wine. Everywhere she looked, ladies seemed to be sipping lemonade, which was not to her taste. She hadn't walked two steps before Algernon popped out of the crowd, followed by three other young men who flocked around her like baby crows.

They took her to an adjoining chamber holding

round tables, with plates of dainties laid out on a sideboard. Algernon escorted her to a chair, and then they all stampeded toward the cakes.

'I merely wish for a drink,' she began to say, but they were gone.

Somewhat amused, she glanced around the room – and discovered Jake, surrounded by ladies. His garments were easily as colorful as theirs, but his height meant he was readily spotted.

A germ of happiness made itself known. She adored her grandfather and Byng, of course. But she'd lost them somewhere in the fray, and it was nice to see a friend. She didn't watch for more than a moment before deciding that Jake's plan to thwart her expansion of Quimby's into polite society by costuming himself as an American clown had failed. His broad shoulders, clad in that unusual flowered chintz lined with orange, didn't make him look clownish.

He was even more manly. Just like a silent (but very deep) stream, his chiseled features lent a dangerous air to the ensemble. Algernon would have looked absurd; Jake looked like a warlord.

Perhaps that was a consequence of his forbidding expression. If she had to guess, she'd say that Jake disliked being at the ball even more than she did.

A lady plucked his sleeve, so he turned and caught sight of Cleo. His head jerked up. That wasn't a plea in his eyes: it might have been a threat.

Cleo suddenly felt more cheerful than she had all evening. She grinned, putting her elbow on the table and propping up her chin the better to watch. 'Better than a play,' she mouthed, waggling her eyebrows.

His eyes sharpened, threatening her with all manner of punishment, she'd guess. From dismemberment to . . .

Algernon hurled himself into the chair next to her, causing a few drops to spill from the glass of lemonade he carried. All her swains flocked back, carrying plates of sweet desserts for her – and wine for themselves.

'I haven't met any ladies other than our hostess,' Cleo said, glancing around at her escorts. She couldn't remember the names of Algernon's friends.

Algernon's brows drew together. They were high and as perfectly arched as Westminster Bridge. 'Peters, fetch your sister, why don't you?'

'She'll be sitting with the other wallflowers,' Peters replied, a distinct whine in his voice.

He was seated to her right, so Cleo gave him a direct look. 'Your sister sounds like just the sort of lady whom I would enjoy meeting.'

Peters responded to her tone of voice just as recalcitrant plumbers did, getting up and scuttling away.

'Miss Lewis, what a pleasure to see you.' Bowing briskly, Jake pulled out Peters's chair and dropped into it without waiting for her to rise and curtsy.

All her gentlemen jumped up and milled about, a consequence of the ladies who had trailed Jake across the room.

'Lemonade?' Jake asked, picking up her glass and sniffing it.

'Alas.' Cleo couldn't help it. Happiness was swelling up in her chest. These boys were silly, and she was bored. She *hated* being bored.

Almost as much as she hated lemonade.

Jake nodded at a footman, who leapt to his side. 'Two empty glasses, if you please.'

The footman blinked but complied. Jake plucked a slender flask from an inside pocket, screwing it open. The apple flavor of the French cognac drifted into the air.

'Good evening,' called a laughing voice.

'Lady Yasmin!' Cleo cried, looking up. 'Do join us, please.'

Yasmin paused with a hand on Cleo's chair and leaned down to brush her cheek with a kiss – which meant that Cleo had a direct view of five lads come close to swooning, while the young ladies started fluttering their fans under widened, innocent eyes. Yasmin's bodice could not be called modest. Moreover, her skirts were surely dampened, given the way they clung to her slender legs.

Jake rose to his feet. 'Lady Yasmin.'

She dropped a curtsy. 'Mr Addison.' She tapped the shoulder of the young lady sitting on Jake's other side. '*Chérie*, your mother is looking for you.'

The maiden's eyes filled with horror, and she rushed from the room.

'How are you?' Cleo asked, smiling.

'I am filled with ennui,' Yasmin said, seating

herself. 'I shall improve, Mr Addison, when you offer me some of that marvelous concoction. I do like a man who comes prepared.'

The footman brought another empty glass. Jake poured Yasmin some brandy and seated himself again.

Cleo gave Jake a little push. 'Do move back so that I can see Lady Yasmin around your bulk.'

His chair audibly groaned as he shifted it backward.

'This brandy is marvelous,' Yasmin said, turning to Jake, her eyes frankly appreciative.

'French,' Jake said.

'*Mais bien sûr*,' Yasmin said. 'Calvados, isn't it? From Normandy.' She looked around the table and suddenly flapped her hands. 'All of you, shoo, shoo! *Allons-y!*'

Algernon gaped at her, and the rest stopped chattering. 'Well, I *never*,' one of the ladies snapped, and the table emptied itself.

'That's better,' Yasmin said, stretching out her legs and crossing exquisite silk slippers. 'I didn't realize when we met earlier this evening that you were so interesting, Mr Addison. Everyone is twittering about "the American's' clothing. I noticed your coat, of course, but I hadn't understood they consider your sartorial excess akin to a national flag."

Cleo was conscious of a prickling feeling in her spine at the way Yasmin was smiling. Not that Jake was Cleo's property.

'I am that American,' Jake drawled, his accent more pronounced than it had ever been.

Somewhat to her relief, Cleo realized that he wasn't pleased. She would think less of him if he transferred his attention.

Yet how could he not admire Yasmin? She was exquisite.

Just so had her mother described a hundred indiscretions. How could she *not* move on to the next handsome actor?

'Don't be such a twig in the mud,' Yasmin told Jake. 'No, *stick* in the mud. That phrase is American. Did I use it properly?'

'Yes,' Jake said. 'Have you been to my country?'

'Alas, no, I grew up in the French court,' Yasmin said. 'Americans made their way there, which is how I learned some of your amusing phrases. One of my favorites is "some pumpkins."'

'Which means?' Cleo asked, pushing away memories of her mother's conquests.

'*Ooh, là, là,*' Yasmin said, sounding very French. 'You use it toward someone who thinks that they are very special indeed. As in, the English ladies seem to think that Mr Addison is "some pumpkins." Surprising, given that he is not in the usual style.' She gave him a beaming smile. 'One could describe your coat, Mr Addison, as a "lally-cooler." A big success,' she told Cleo.

'Your brandy is "some pumpkins,"' Cleo told Jake, saluting him with her glass.

'I miss brandy, in this misbegotten country

where everyone thinks young ladies should drink lemonade, morning, noon, and night,' Yasmin said. 'We French don't consider sour juice mixed with sugar to be an appropriate drink, even for children.'

Jake shifted, and his chair gave another warning creak, as if it were about to give way. 'I believe you promised me the next dance, Cleo.'

One of Yasmin's eyebrows flew up at this familiarity.

'We're merely friends,' Cleo said to her, hastily. 'Please do call me Cleo as well.'

'I would be honored,' Yasmin said. She raised her glass with a twinkling smile. 'We shall meet again later.'

Cleo was somewhat amused to find that the moment she entered the ballroom with Jake, every head swiveled toward them.

They faced each other as the strains of a waltz began.

Jake's hand settled on her back, making her body flare to life. Meeting his eyes, she saw the same awareness in his gaze. His fingers tightened, blazing five imprints through his gloves and the frail silk of her gown.

'I suspect that your Quimby's wardrobe is a success,' Cleo said, rushing into speech. 'Have you been sharing the provenance of your coat with all who ask?'

'No. A few fellows have cast me pitying looks. Any

man in his right mind who saw a fellow wearing this coat would run in the opposite direction. Have you noticed my gloves?'

She smiled. 'How could I not?'

'Pink,' he said with disgust. '*Pink!* Martha Quimby insisted.'

'The ladies are clearly not running away,' Cleo observed, with a gurgle of laughter. 'Whether or not my gown garners orders for Quimby's, I feel beautiful in it, Jake. Thank you.'

Jake's hand tightened again, and Cleo felt a wild need race through her, so much so that she drew in a shuddering breath. His eyes didn't leave hers; they burned with a hungry possessiveness.

They were nearing the end of the long, narrow ballroom.

'You dance very well,' he said.

'My mother didn't care for governesses, but she rather liked dancing masters.'

'In that case . . .' With a glint in his eyes, Jake tightened his grip and began turning her in a series of rapid circles. The other dancers flashed by, their curious gazes blurring together.

'I'm damned hungry,' Jake breathed into her ear. He was necessarily holding her close; her gauze skirts were wrapping around his legs and billowing free. A shiver made its way down Cleo's back as his thigh pressed to her own.

She pulled herself together. 'There will be a supper served at two in the morning.'

He slowed and began making his way more decorously up the length of the room. 'I shan't survive until two a.m. I'm not hungry for food.'

Cleo almost smiled, but caught the censorious eyes of a matron. There was scarcely candlelight between their bodies, so she eased away. 'You're a marvelous dancer, Mr Addison.'

'My mother enjoys it. And Frederica—' He stopped.

Cleo looked up at him. 'Frederica?'

'A young cousin of my friend, the Duchess of Trent. Merry is like a member of my family. She couldn't be here tonight, but she looks forward to meeting you.'

Cleo didn't know what that information meant, but he didn't give her time for reflection. Their eyes met again, and she drew in a rough breath. 'You mustn't,' she whispered.

'Look at you?' his voice was low and harsh. 'I can't not. You're so damned . . .'

Cleo had never prompted a compliment in her life. Foster, her former fiancé, had burbled with praise like a fountain, so she knew how false compliments were, how easily they were given. But her eyes asked, anyway.

'*More.* More than kippers,' he added.

Just like that, the aching tension between them eased.

'Kippers!' she cried. 'I'll have you know that Gussie is horrified by those cards you've sent. The snowdrops were bad enough, but the lemon flowers, and then the lovely forget-me-nots, lilies, and the rest, all of them mentioning fish. She has begun threatening to throw your posies in the rubbish.'

'I like to picture them next your bed,' he said with a smile that Cleo felt down her backbone – not because it was erotic, but because it was affectionate.

The waltz drew to a close.

'Thank you, Mr Addison,' Cleo said, dropping a curtsy. She felt as if every single head in the ballroom had turned in their direction, so she drew on years of keeping her composure in embarrassing situations.

'American,' she heard. She glanced over and saw a lady fluttering her fan and ogling Jake as he bowed. The lady's eyes widened as she frankly surveyed his rear.

The Earl of Lilford appeared at her side. 'Miss Lewis, may I have the honor of this dance?'

He certainly was persistent. Cleo gave him a warmer smile than she might have, if only to halt any gossip about the intimacy of the dance she had shared with Jake, and dropped into a curtsy. 'I would be enchanted.'

She didn't see Jake again until two hours later, when he escorted her onto the floor for a sedate minuet, in which no whirling – and little speaking – was possible. 'Your coat is a tremendous success,' she said, during one of the intervals when he held her hand and she revolved in a circle about him. 'Everyone is talking about it.'

Jake shrugged. 'I am leaving after this dance; I've had enough of peacocking around crowded rooms. Germain's gave me a proper-sized suite, and I've been enjoying having enough space to stretch my legs.'

The dance separated them and brought them back together before Cleo could figure out her response.

'My own dining room, just like yours,' Jake said, his American accent deepening.

She narrowed her eyes. Her lips scarcely moving so that no one could overhear, she asked. 'On what floor?'

Jake's smile widened. It should be outlawed, that smile. She would never have imagined that his face, so somber and unfriendly in repose, could transform into –

She wasn't sure how to describe it. His eyes were burning but laughing too.

'The third.'

'No,' she ordered, suddenly realizing that she had to gain control over this situation. Living on the same floor, it would be far too easy to agree to improprieties.

'I'm afraid the deed is done,' he said. Their hands were linked as the dance required, but his thumb rubbed her palm in an entirely inappropriate fashion. 'I moved in ten days ago.'

'There will be *no* brandy and conversations about money or anything else.'

'Certainly not,' Jake said, his eyes shocked. 'I wouldn't dream of such a thing. Never.'

'No kisses.'

'Absolutely not!'

The dance ended and she just caught herself before poking him in the chest. 'No knocking on my door.'

He bowed. 'Your wish is my command.'

CHAPTER SEVENTEEN

He didn't knock.

One moment Cleo was nibbling on a piece of buttered toast and instructing herself not to think about Jake, especially not about the way they had danced together the night before, or the way his legs looked in taut breeches, or the way his eyes –

The next moment the door to her dining room was open, and the man himself was striding in.

Cleo looked up.

'Contracts to discuss,' he said briskly. Sure enough, he had a sheaf of papers tucked under his arm. But in his hand . . .

'Are those kippers?' she asked, knowing the answer, because who could mistake that smell?

'Yup,' he said, sounding insufferably American. He pulled up a chair and put the kippers on the table between them. 'Once I realized that you'd never tried them, I couldn't allow that pitiful situation to continue. As a friend. Though my valet had to offer the chef a handsome bribe; I gather his French sensibilities were offended.'

Robbins was hovering beside the door. 'Miss Lewis?'

'It's all right,' she said resignedly. 'Mr Addison is a business acquaintance. I suppose I shall allow him to share my breakfast. You may return to the corridor.'

'Actually, I'd be grateful if you would run down and ask the kitchen to brew my morning coffee,' Jake said. 'A pot, if you would.'

'Very well,' Cleo said, nodding to Robbins.

He left, and Jake turned back to Cleo. 'Kippers and coffee were made by the Almighty to go together.'

Cleo wrinkled her nose. 'Fusty beans and oily fish.'

'American drink, and British breakfast,' he said, his eyes glinting. 'As I said, made by the Almighty to—'

'Never mind that,' Cleo said hastily. 'What are you doing here, Jake?'

'I've decided to acquire a factory, but the process of title registration of the deed is unfamiliar to me, as it's spelled out in the principles of property and succession. I was hoping you could help.'

Cleo brightened. She had been reading contracts since her father passed her the first one at the age of twelve. 'Of course!'

'Excellent,' Jake said. He began cutting the kipper into pieces.

'I might try one bite,' Cleo told him, wrinkling her nose again. 'It smells.'

'Smoky and delicious,' Jake said.

'When it comes to *kippers*, you can find adjectives?'

'Mouthwatering comes to mind.' He eyed her, and just like that, desire quivered in the air between them.

'Jake,' she said warningly, putting down her fork.

He sighed. 'No kissing. No brandy.'

'Exactly,' Cleo said. 'This is dangerous enough, the two of us eating breakfast without a chaperone.'

'You don't care about your reputation, and besides, Germain's prides itself on allowing no gossip to escape their front door. I have the feeling that adultery accounts for a good portion of their profits.'

'My grandfather cares,' Cleo said. She gave Jake a wry smile. 'It's become increasingly clear to me that my mother's rash behavior hurt my grandfather deeply. Likewise, my grandmother, when she was alive.'

Jake nodded. She watched as he plucked a piece of toast from the rack, cut off a square, buttered it, and piled a piece of kipper on top.

'That is remarkably ill-mannered,' Cleo informed him.

'As ill-mannered as when you put your elbow on the table last night?' he retorted.

She almost put out her tongue but recollected her dignity just in time. 'Not in the same category as piling fish on top of bread.'

Jake held out the square of buttered toast and kipper. 'Taste.'

Cleo bit her lip, feeling very certain that the last thing she wanted was fish.

His dark gaze went to her mouth and then quickly back to her eyes. 'Please?' His voice had a raspy note that sent flickers over her skin.

She didn't need her mother's prompting – the mother who had gone almost entirely silent, just when maternal advice might be welcome! – to know that she was in precarious waters. 'All right,' Cleo said reluctantly. 'But then you must return to your suite, Jake. If we did cause a scandal, I would refuse to marry you, and my grandfather would be embarrassed and, I daresay, deeply hurt.'

He nodded and held up the square of bread.

Cleo opened her mouth, and he popped it inside. To her surprise, her mouth sang with happiness. The kipper was smoky, salty, and fatty. What's more, the bread tasted fresh, as if it had been toasted that moment over a fire, rather than being trundled up from the depths of the hotel.

A satisfied look spread over Jake's face. 'When you find yourself missing your mother, if you eat enough kippers, the ache of it will go away.'

He held out another square, and Cleo obediently opened her mouth. 'Kippers are a panacea for grief?' she asked, after she swallowed.

'My father died unexpectedly. Kippers helped.'

She smiled faintly. 'I wish I'd known that when my own father died. What happened to yours?'

He hesitated.

'You needn't tell me,' she said, seeing that his jaw had hardened.

'He became addicted to opium,' Jake said flatly, looking up. 'Doctors had given it to him for an injured shoulder.'

'That's why you changed your name,' Cleo guessed. She reached out and picked up a piece of kipper on toast. 'Here.'

He opened his mouth. He had beautiful lips. Cleo swallowed hard and then leaned in, trying to pop the toast in his mouth without touching his lips. They closed around her fingers, and his tongue licked a caress before he let her free.

'I . . .' Cleo began, with no idea what she would say.

At least the dark look in Jake's eyes was gone. 'Better than kippers,' he said huskily.

'I'm sorry about your father's death,' Cleo said, trying to ignore the tight feeling in her chest. 'I gather you became an Addison after you lost him?'

'I refuse to be associated with the opium trade,' Jake said. 'There are other addictive substances.' His eyes searched hers. 'You, for example.'

Panic made Cleo's heart speed up. She wasn't ready for . . . for whatever this was. 'I miss my mother less than I did a few months ago,' she found herself saying. 'She used to talk to me in my head every hour or so. But now her voice is silent, and I miss *that*, as if I've lost another part of her.'

216

Smiling faintly, Jake held up a piece of toast. 'Eat,' he said, simply.

The door opened, and Robbins entered with a steaming pot of coffee.

'Thank you,' Cleo said. She nodded at the footman, and he backed out the door.

She wasn't feeling sadness; instead, a mild terror was rolling around in her stomach. What would become of this *friendship* with a huge American man with unpolished manners and the tendency to blurt out raw truths?

'I want to kiss you again,' Jake announced, proving her point.

'I am not available for casual busses,' Cleo stated.

'Why not?'

She frowned at him. 'Why not? What we shared was no mere kiss, Jake. If we continue in that vein, we shall find ourselves in bed. I hope you don't expect me to shilly-shally around the subject.'

He nodded, chewing meditatively. 'That's true.'

'I don't care to have an *affaire* with you, and I'm uninterested in marriage.'

'So you said. I am growing curious about your mother.'

Cleo sighed. If they were to be friends, then he might as well know the truth. 'My mother enjoyed the company of men.'

He didn't show any signs of shock. 'I see.' Jake held a square of kipper toast to her lips. 'Eat.'

Somehow she found her mouth opening.

It *was* strangely comforting.

'When Mother and I traveled with a theater company, they would often cook meals by the side of the road,' she told him, after she swallowed. 'I believe that kippers were a daily meal.'

'Not for you?'

'We never ate with the company. Mother preferred to stay in the best inn in the vicinity. We would often travel more slowly than the company, staying in the Olde Starre Inn in York, for example. We might miss the opening night, but we'd be there for the second night.'

Jake shook his head. 'I had no idea that devoted theatergoers accompanied players.'

'They don't,' Cleo said bluntly. 'My mother was unusual. In many ways.'

CHAPTER EIGHTEEN

Jake had never been so curious in his life. He wanted to know everything about Cleo, every detail of her childhood, right up to the fellow she'd mentioned once, who tried to compromise her.

He meant to punch the man in the face if they ever met.

It had made her wary – of him and of men in general. She had meant it when she said she didn't want to marry. Why?

He had the feeling that she knew, even if she wouldn't admit it, that he wasn't sending her daily posies as part of a campaign to steal Quimby's. But she wouldn't allow herself to entertain the possibility that he was courting her.

'Will you tell me more about your mother?' he asked.

Cleo's smile was small but sweet. 'Julia had tempestuous passions: for people, for plays, for clothing . . . She loved to dress up like a queen and stroll down the main street of a town where the company would be performing that night. Passersby would occasionally think she *was* the queen, which she found delightful. Or the lead actress, which she also enjoyed.'

'Where were you?' Jake asked.

'When?'

'When your mother was parading down the street?'

'Oh, I played lady-in-waiting,' Cleo said. 'Or I stayed in the caravan. I loved our little wagon, but my mother viewed it merely as a vehicle that took her from performance to performance. Now that it's mine, I plan to travel around England, staying *in* the wagon.'

'So, you still have it?'

'Absolutely! I rented a stable in the Kensington Mews to house my horses and the wagon. I could show it to you sometime.'

Jake watched the color deepen in Cleo's cheeks and wondered if she'd ever been able to keep a friend, given all that traipsing around the country. 'I would love to see it. When you say that your mother enjoyed the company of men, what exactly do you mean?'

She paused and fiddled with her fork before squaring her shoulders and looking up. 'My mother could not help herself when it came to a handsome leading man.'

Jake nodded, though he didn't really understand.

'One after another,' Cleo said, her clear eyes on his. 'You might as well understand that, since we've broached the topic. She was extraordinarily beautiful, and they generally didn't resist her, even if they were married.'

'I see.'

Cleo smiled faintly. 'I don't expect you really do; we think of men as libertines, not women.'

'You'd be surprised,' Jake said dryly. 'Was that difficult for you?'

'There were embarrassing moments,' Cleo said, flipping her fork over and over once again. 'Not the fact of it, so much. By the time I understood, it felt customary. But we were occasionally confronted by men who had their hearts broken.'

'After one night?' His voice was incredulous.

'Sometimes she kept them for a week or more.'

'You make her sound like a cat toying with mice,' Jake said.

'A fair assessment. She would often move on to the next mouse, without informing her current lover. When I was younger, I found it horrifyingly embarrassing.'

'She was wrong to do that,' Jake stated.

Cleo shrugged. 'Right and wrong are subjective values. Julia did many things that society found wrong: she slept with married men, for example. But she never beat anyone, woman or child. She didn't steal.'

'Married men?' Jake's eyebrow crooked.

'They chose to leave their wives, whether for a night or a week.' She kept fiddling with her fork, poking the tines into the tablecloth. 'Julia wasn't entirely honest with them, because she invariably expressed her emotions so lavishly.'

'How so?'

221

'The first time she would feel *so much*. She spun descriptions of the two of them together forever, married. You remember how Romeo was in love with a lady called Rosaline before he caught sight of Juliet at a ball? My mother was the same. She had an endless ability to fall in love with someone new.'

He nodded. 'Leaving a string of broken hearts behind her.'

'Some men were content with one night, counting themselves lucky. She could light up an entire room. When she was sad, the world wept with her. I adored her.'

Jake's right hand curled into a fist, thinking of a young girl buffeted by her mother's tempestuous disposition, but he kept his expression even.

'She loved me,' Cleo said. 'The men came and went; she worshipped them for a day or a week, or even a month, but never longer.'

She caught the expression in his eyes.

'We don't think badly of men who do the same,' she said tartly. 'Or at the least, we merely tarnish them with half-admiring labels such as "rakish."'

'True.' Jake frowned, trying to stop himself from being critical of the mother of a young Cleo. 'Were you ever frightened? Or in danger?'

'Oh, no, never. Irritated, amused, bored . . . acutely embarrassed when I was the one to inform a man that he had been passed by. Especially if they wept. By the time I was seventeen, I couldn't imagine how she could be interested in yet another

Hamlet, striding across the stage in a melancholy fit of humors. But she invariably was.'

'Meaning?'

'The man in question didn't have to be tall and handsome,' she explained. 'Hamlet, after all, was described by his mother as "fat and short of breath." My mother found acting ability enchanting. She loved the idea that a man could be himself and the next moment, someone else.'

'I'm not sure that actors always know who they are,' Jake said, thinking of his father and his lifelong wish to be on the stage. 'The temptation to play a role is very great. Like your mother playing queen?'

'Exactly!' Cleo said, smiling at him.

He drew in a slow breath because he wanted to skirt the table and kiss her senseless, but that wouldn't be appropriate. Gentlemanly behavior seemed harder and harder to maintain. 'So, your mother played queen, and her lovers played princes? Kings?'

'Until she got to know them as men,' Cleo said. She started fiddling with her toast. 'It was a bit sad, really. She adored the king, but the man underneath, the man who didn't have Shakespeare's lines to recite, was never as appealing.'

Jake phrased his next question carefully. 'Was the man who attempted to force you to marry him part of a theater company?'

She shot him a wry smile. 'Yes. He is a terrible actor, so my mother couldn't abide him for that reason.'

'Is this blackguard still in the same company?'

'I have no idea,' she said. 'The question is irrelevant, Jake. We were betrothed, but I broke it off. And his attempt to compromise me with a public kiss failed as well, since I found the notion of marrying someone for that reason laughable.'

The words hit his gut like a rock. 'You were betrothed!' He could have met her, only to find out that she was married – to a despicable man.

'Briefly. All of two months,' she said lightly.

Robbins entered the room with a silver platter holding a vase of flowers.

Jake scowled. He was starting to feel like a monster, driven to find Cleo's former fiancé and beat him to smithereens. Leave him on the floor, driveling apologies.

The footman placed a small vase in the middle of the table. 'Snowdrops today,' he observed. 'Would you like me to read the card, Miss Lewis?' He offered it to her on a small silver salver.

'No, thank you,' Cleo said. 'I believe I know the wording.'

Robbins bowed and retired. Jake was pretty sure that the entire hotel knew the wording of his card.

'Wait until they hear that you brought kippers to my breakfast table,' Cleo said wryly.

'We are likely of great interest,' Jake acknowledged. 'My valet tells me that curiosity has grown since I moved to the suite across the corridor.'

Cleo shrugged and looked at the cup of coffee he placed before her. The smell of roasted beans swirled in the air between them. 'I will reluctantly admit that kippers are agreeable, but I don't think I'll ever like that brew.'

Jake tipped some cream into his coffee and followed it with a teaspoon of sugar. 'I spent a month of my life near to death. In the darkest days, I remember thinking that as long as there was coffee to wake up to, I might as well keep living.'

She looked up suddenly. 'Was your illness connected to those ferocious scars on your back from the bear's attack?'

'The wound became infected,' Jake said, nodding. 'You may hanker after the experience of cooking by the side of the road, but I found it difficult to brew proper coffee over a fire. The twigs would go out, or a wind would collapse my tripod.'

'I can imagine you in the wilderness,' Cleo said. She smiled – and his body responded just as it did to the smell of coffee in the morning.

With urgency, desire, and utter conviction.

'Damn, you're beautiful,' he said, the words unbidden.

A teacup filled with coffee paused at her lips, and her eyes widened. 'A compliment, a genuine compliment!'

'What's more, with kippers in front of me.' He waited until understanding filled her eyes. 'Cleo, I am no longer interested in Quimby's.'

She put the coffee down without tasting it. 'I see. Is that why you are dressed in black this morning?'

'Am I supposed to wear colors in the daytime as well?' He felt a thump of alarm. It had been a relief to put on clothing that fit his shoulders without making an exhibition of them. 'I shall be wearing buttercup yellow tonight, while escorting Merry to Vauxhall Gardens.'

'I shall look forward to seeing that. My grandfather, Byng, and I shall dine with some friends, and attend afterwards,' Cleo said.

Jake narrowed his eyes. 'Which friends?'

'The Earl of Lilford and his sister, Lady Lydia. Oh, and Lady Yasmin, whom you met last night. I had a delightful conversation with her over supper, but you had already left by then.'

'Martha Quimby's breeches were so tight in the arse that I was afraid they would split up the rear,' Jake said. 'The coat as well.' He moved his shoulders, remembering. 'Not to mention that neck cloth frothing around my neck and scratching my chin.'

Cleo burst out laughing. 'I see that you're wearing a narrow cravat this morning. I can see a stripe of your neck. Gussie would be horrified.'

'Do try the coffee while it's hot.' He watched as she sipped the drink.

She wrinkled her nose. 'I like the smell but not the taste.'

'Too bitter?'

She nodded. He leaned over and put a spoonful of sugar in the cup. 'Try again.' Then he watched as she drank. Cleo put it down.

'It's different from tea,' she said cautiously.

'Exhilarating, where tea is comforting,' Jake said. 'When the temperature in the mountains fell to the point at which air bit at our exposed skin, I would brew coffee and my men would cheer.'

'Tell me about your travels,' she said, her eyes on his.

Jake felt like an adolescent again, his body obsessed by one thing, his cock in control and his mind a distant second. He picked up his cup of coffee and stood.

'Could we move to the settee? Cooling kippers are an incentive to eat quickly and leave the table.'

She poked at the curling edge of the kipper with her fork. 'I see.'

He walked around the table and offered his arm. Cleo looked at him without pretense from under those wanton lashes of hers. 'No kissing,' she commanded. 'I don't mind if the entire hotel gossips, as long as *I* know my behavior is above reproach.'

Jake nodded. He was fairly sure that the erotic tension in his eyes was masked by gentlemanly courtesy. Cleo didn't show any sign of guessing that inside he was a ravaging beast who wanted to . . .

All those things that he wouldn't do because, damn it, he *was* a gentleman. He wouldn't touch her here, in her breakfast room. She might order him to never enter the room again.

The morning wore into afternoon as they talked.

And laughed. At some point, Jake grabbed the curling sheaf of papers, the contract he brought with him.

Cleo read it far more quickly than he had, noting three immediate problems, two things he might wish to negotiate, and a legal query for his solicitor.

In a triumph of mind over body, Jake didn't kiss her. He battled for control of his body and won.

He didn't even touch her. They sat at their respective ends of the settee as one subject led to the next. His solicitor probably knocked on the door of his suite and left, not knowing where to find him. Jake remembered the appointment – and ignored it. He was negotiating for a house, a mansion, really. It was a townhouse that a man buys when he's putting down roots, planning to marry, planning for children. In Davies Street, a short walk from her grandfather.

All of which depended on Cleo.

Everything depended on Cleo.

Years later, he could still remember how difficult it was to leave in the late afternoon, knowing that she would be having dinner with an eligible earl, while he dressed like a candelabra shined to a fine polish to dine with Merry.

But he was used to games of strategy.

Bowing over her hand, brushing a kiss with his lips, bidding a cheerful goodbye . . .

Strategy.

Cleo was like no other woman he'd met: independent, comfortable in her own skin. She didn't ask for reassurances that she was beautiful or charming, the way other women had to this date.

It was one of the things he had liked about Frederica, actually. She hadn't tried to coerce or coax him into making compliments.

Even thinking about Frederica felt wrong now. She was weak tea to Cleo's strong coffee.

Frederica was peaceful, and he would have had a serene, boring marriage. Cleo was the strongest coffee of his life: energizing, independent, free.

'I am looking forward to introducing you to Merry tonight at Vauxhall,' he said, in place of the hundred inappropriate sentences that came to mind. 'The Duchess of Trent is one of my oldest friends.'

He liked the way Cleo's gaze drifted over his shoulders. He hung on to that. She liked his kisses. She liked his size. She liked him.

Surely, that would be enough to hold off the Earl of Limbow, or whatever the fellow's name was.

'No bringing brandy to my door tonight,' she said, just as he was taking his leave.

'I know,' he said regretfully. He had done enough, moving to the suite across the corridor.

'Why did you move to this floor? Did you think that I would invite you to my chambers?'

'No,' he said, truthfully. 'You are not safe. Your footman was asleep when I visited you the other night. My grooms are not so lax. As of ten days ago, no one may enter this floor unless they are genuine employees of the hotel.'

'That's very presumptive of you!'

The words flew out of his mouth. 'I take care of my own, Cleo.'

Having said that, he broke his own rules and brushed a kiss on her astonished mouth before he left.

CHAPTER NINETEEN

Later that evening

'We need to leave for Vauxhall,' Merry announced after dinner. 'Goodness me! I hadn't noticed, Jake, but you look as pretty as a spring bouquet!'

Jake did not look down at the lavender scallops adorning his coat and waistcoat, because he was trying hard to forget that they existed.

'I vow I cannot wait to meet this paragon of yours,' Merry continued. 'I must say that I am so happy you are no longer planning to marry Frederica.'

'As am I,' Jake said with a wry nod.

'But I regret the fact that I wrote your mother about that opal ring,' Merry confessed.

Jake scowled at that. 'You did ask me first.' He could hear repentance in her voice, but bone-deep irritation made him jam his hands into the pockets of his wretched satin coat.

His mother could no more resist the temptation to meddle than . . . than Cleo's grandfather could stop himself from matchmaking. Back in New York, she'd be dropping hints, and poor Frederica would listen and believe.

'There was no talk of rings between me and Frederica,' Jake said. 'I hadn't even kissed her.'

Merry put a hand on his arm. 'I am sorry, Jake. I'll write to Mrs Astor immediately, shall I?'

'What will you say? If you mention Cleo, my mother will board a packet the next day and sail for London. They have clippers that cross the ocean in just over a fortnight. I need time to woo.'

'Mrs Astor does have a commanding manner,' Merry allowed.

'She's become more forceful than you remember,' he said grimly. 'Since my father's death, she has directed her considerable energy toward the family. She married my sister off a mere nine months later, thankfully to a good man, which leaves Mother no one to concentrate on but me.'

'I won't mention Cleo,' Merry promised. 'What if I write that I misinterpreted the purchase, and you have given the ring to me in respect of our long friendship?' She grinned. 'You'll have to give me the opal, of course. It *was* exquisite.'

'What will your husband think of your accepting jewels from a man?'

She laughed. 'If Trent returns while you are wearing that scalloped coat, you could give me the contents of the queen's vault, and he wouldn't believe you tempted me into an *affaire*.'

'Fine. You may have the opal. My breeches might well split when we dance. I'm just warning you.'

'Something to look forward to,' Merry said brightly.

Viscount Falconer's party dawdled over their meal and arrived at Vauxhall Gardens an hour after they were bid by the Duchess of Trent's invitation to a private event in the rotunda. Cleo didn't want to admit it, but though Byng and Yasmin made her laugh during supper, and the Earl of Lilford's grave compliments were a pleasure, and her grandfather's warm gaze made her happy . . .

She couldn't wait to see Jake.

She kept thinking about him, her heart speeding along in her chest, a flush rising in her cheeks – and then she forcibly reminded herself that infatuation had never done anyone any good.

She was no better than her mother, hungering for a man.

The very thought made her give Lilford a charming smile as they climbed into his carriage to travel to Vauxhall.

Cleo had heard of the gardens, of course, but even so, she was dazzled by the thousands of lanterns that hung from the trees. Her grandfather and Madame Dubois unerringly threaded their way through avenues crisscrossed with rosy garlands; Byng had a headache and had remained home.

'Do you like him?' Yasmin whispered, as they strolled down the main avenue, following the Earl of Lilford and his sister.

'Who?'

'The hidebound earl.'

'Hidebound?'

'Conventional, unable to change, rigid as a lamp-post,' Yasmin replied. 'What's your word of the day?'

Lilford glanced back at them.

'He heard you,' Cleo observed. 'The word of the day is "high-blown."'

'What does that mean?' Yasmin asked.

'Swelled with wind, prideful.'

Yasmin giggled. 'How extraordinarily appropriate. *A certain earl is high-blown due to being so highborn that he thinks he is high-flown as a king, but a high-minded fool will always—*' She broke off as Lilford snapped around his head around and gave her a cold stare.

'We're merely practicing the English language,' she called to him. 'How do you choose your words?' she asked Cleo, after the earl looked away.

'I open a page of Samuel Johnson's *Dictionary of the English Language*, find an interesting word, and try to use it that day.'

'I should buy a copy to improve my English vocabulary. I forgot to use *high-stomached* . . . which means obstinate or lofty.'

'Your English is very good,' Cleo said.

Yasmin shrugged. 'To be honest, there's not

much to do when one's mother is entertaining an emperor. Not to mention I've found myself in many a drawing room, thrown into company with Englishmen waiting to talk to Napoleon. Better to talk to them than with ladies who have no fondness for my mother, due to their loyalty to the empress.'

Cleo squeezed her arm. 'I'm sorry.' One of the reasons that their wagon never traveled with the theater company caravans was the inevitable animosity from leading men's wives.

They left the main avenue and walked toward a grand rotunda, a structure fashioned from open pillars decorated with floral garlands, the roof hung with candelabras. Exquisitely dressed guests leaned against the marble pillars or sat at small tables and sipped champagne, while in the innermost circle couples whirled to a waltz performed by a small orchestra.

Cleo was inured to glamour by years of theatergoing, but she had to admit to a touch of awe.

'Look!' Yasmin said, nodding.

A lady was advancing down the steps from the pavilion. She had a white satin train and a green wreath on her head that seemed to sparkle in the light.

'Princess Charlotte,' Yasmin whispered. 'From what I hear, she is desperate to marry, but her father can't settle on the right prince. She's wearing a Vittoria Fête dress. All the gossip columns are saying that they should be worn as a gesture of support, to suggest that England will defeat Napoleon once again.'

Cleo knit her brow. 'I don't understand.'

'They were originally worn to celebrate the English victory at the Battle of Vittoria a couple of years ago,' Yasmin explained.

'I can only see the train,' Cleo said.

Yasmin flipped open her fan and pointed behind its shelter. 'The Duchess of Trent is there, to the left, wearing a fête dress as well. See how the veil falls from the back and is worn over the arm as drapery?' They had reached the shallow steps leading up to the rotunda; Cleo's grandfather was speaking to a majordomo flourishing a guest list.

Her Grace was a sweet-faced, exquisitely dressed beauty – who came up on her tiptoes to kiss Jake on the cheek as they watched. Cleo instinctively halted before the steps. '*She* is the Duchess of Trent?' she whispered.

Merry, Jake's oldest friend. The lady put a gloved hand on his cheek, and he smiled down at her . . .

'Happily married,' Yasmin stated. 'You need fear nothing from her.'

Cleo nodded.

'I heard that Addison planned to marry her when she debuted, you understand, but something happened, an accident or some such, and by the time he returned from the wildernesses of America, she was already betrothed. Or perhaps she had left for England, where she met the duke. I am not sure.'

'How on earth do you learn so much gossip?' Cleo asked.

'I find people interesting,' Yasmin said. 'I forget how the story went. Some sort of Romeo and Juliet love affair, I believe, but when he didn't return from the West, they thought he was dead, and she married another.'

Cleo swallowed. The Duchess of Trent was laughing at something Jake told her.

'As I said, it was years ago,' Yasmin said. 'Do not think twice about it. For example, although he resides in the ducal townhouse in the absence of His Grace, no one has bothered to imagine that they are having an *affaire*.'

Jake wasn't residing in the ducal townhouse, but there was no point in revealing the fact, which she definitely oughtn't to know.

'Addison is not a duke, and that jaw . . .' Yasmin shook her head. 'He does have sartorial flair though, doesn't he? Ice blue with lavender scallops is most unusual in a man's coat, but it suits him.'

'True,' Cleo said, dropping Yasmin's arm so that she could pick up her skirts and climb the steps. The rest of their party had already gathered at one of the small round tables positioned between marble pillars.

Cleo felt very peculiar. Of course, Jake had a life before they met, and it wasn't as if she had any claim to him.

True, they had kissed. And eaten breakfast together. Spent a day together, for that matter.

The moment she and Yasmin seated themselves, a flock of men clustered around their table like sparrows looking for crumbs. But even as Cleo chatted with Algernon Dunlap, she kept turning over her reaction to seeing Jake's best friend.

Jake had told her without a shred of self-consciousness that he was escorting the Duchess of Trent to Vauxhall. Everything Cleo had ever heard about Her Grace implied that she adored her husband.

Clearly, Merry adored Jake as well.

That's what Cleo didn't like.

A waltz began and Jake swept Her Grace onto the dance floor. He was dancing with Merry the way he had with Cleo, turning her in sweeping circles. The other dancers drew back, watching as if the two were lead actors on the stage, Romeo and Juliet at the ball.

The Duchess of Trent was tall for a woman, and she matched every one of Jake's steps with ease, likely because they had danced together for years. Cleo couldn't stop watching as the dance drew to a close, and Jake escorted his friend to a table on the other side of the rotunda.

Women closed in on his table the moment he sat down, approaching him without pretense. Jake didn't appear to notice; he was leaning forward, tucking a stray lock of hair into the silver band the duchess wore to hold her hair in place.

She had a lot of hair. Cleo had never realized that she disliked chestnut-colored hair. As well as women with large bosoms and the habit of waving their hands around as they spoke.

'People gossip about the Vauxhall masquerades because a woman is free to act upon her own initiative here,' Yasmin said in her ear. 'Do you see how the ladies are besieging your American?'

'Yes,' Cleo said. The duchess was leaning forward, tapping Jake on the shoulder with her fan, laughing again.

'He doesn't know we have arrived,' Yasmin said. 'Summon him.'

'No.'

As they watched, Jake turned to look around the rotunda, but she was slightly behind a pillar. He would only be able to see her skirts.

Yasmin sighed, then stood up. In a movement so swift that Cleo almost didn't catch it, she put two fingers in her mouth and whistled. The low sound cut through the music, and Jake's head jerked up. He came to his feet instantly.

Cleo looked away. Jake wanted her. She knew it with every bone in her body. That wasn't the problem.

'That's how you summon a man,' Yasmin said with satisfaction, sitting back down.

'Why did you *summon* Mr Addison?' the Earl of Lilford asked, a distinctly unfriendly tone in his voice.

Yasmin shrugged in a manner that made the already low bodice of her gown slide even lower. 'He is so delicious. A man, a true man, is so

239

exhilarating. There is a touch of the wilderness about him, don't you agree?'

Cleo kicked her under the table. Lilford's eyes looked like chips of ice. She leaned toward the earl, interrupting the battle.

She gave him a smile. *The* smile.

He blinked. Cleo didn't often bring out her mother's weapons, but she held them in reserve.

Yasmin began chuckling. 'Of course, there are tools other than a whistle.'

'May I have the honor of this dance?' Lilford asked, coming to his feet.

'Yes, thank you,' Cleo said, taking his hand.

They slid seamlessly among the waltzing couples. The earl was a remarkably competent man. Jake's boisterous circles were not for him.

'He has seated himself,' Lilford stated, after they circled the rotunda twice in silence.

Cleo looked at him, surprised. They had danced together several times since they first met, and Lilford had never spoken.

'I assume that you wish to avoid Addison,' he added.

'I have no need to avoid anyone,' Cleo said, tipping up her nose.

'Ah, then this dance is meant to prompt jealousy?' With a smooth movement, the earl pulled her closer, turning in a circle, just slow enough so that anyone could tell their legs were brushing.

'Stop that,' Cleo hissed.

'I am an actor ignorant of his role,' Lilford said.

240

To her surprise, there was a hint of dark humor in his eyes.

Cleo opened her mouth, but she couldn't think what to say.

'British can dance as extravagantly as Americans,' Lilford added. Before she could respond, he drew her even closer and began to turn, weaving with extraordinary grace between the revolving couples around them. Her skirts flew out and fell back; the music felt as if it were in her bones, as if they were a couple revolving atop a music box.

She found herself laughing, unable to resist the glint in his eye. Just as with Jake and the duchess, the other dancers drew to the side, allowing Lilford to spin her through the open dance floor, the two of them spiraling like falling maple leaves in autumn.

Throughout, a prickling in her shoulders suggested that Jake was watching. She edged closer to Lilford until her bosom was touching his coat. Just as the duchess's had touched Jake's.

The music ended when they were on the opposite side of the rotunda from her grandfather's table.

'Thank you,' Cleo said, shaking her skirts. Her cheeks were pink, and a few curls had broken free from the intricate arrangement Gussie had worked on for over an hour, braiding silver trim into her curls. 'I didn't imagine . . .'

'You thought I was too *high-blown* and *highborn* for dancing?' Lilford asked, quoting Yasmin's earlier judgment.

Cleo cleared her throat. 'Of course not.'

'Shall we stroll down the avenue?' He raised an eyebrow and then added, silkily, 'Your back is turned to your grandfather's table, but it does seem that our dance gained everyone's attention. You'd be doing me a favor, because I am quite certain that Lady Yasmin will offer an acerbic review of my dancing skills.'

The avenue leading from the rotunda was brightly lit, unlike the avenues reputed to be shady and dangerous.

'The Duchess of Trent has joined our table,' Lilford added.

Cleo frowned. 'You see a good deal more than you let on, don't you?'

His mouth flattened. 'Silence doesn't equate to idiocy, Miss Lewis. I do not care to chatter like a mob of sparrows.'

'Yes, I should like to go for a stroll with you,' Cleo said.

She felt pricklingly embarrassed that he guessed she wished to avoid the duchess; yet another part of her felt strangely comforted. She wasn't the only person who had noticed the unusual closeness between Jake and his best friend.

Lilford took her arm as they walked down the steps, and as if the statement didn't come from the blue, he said, 'Mr Addison is fond of the duchess, but no more. The Duke of Trent is a close friend, and I can assure you that his duchess is *his* and his alone, whether His Grace is in London or not. There is no adultery.'

'I would never suggest that!' Cleo cried. 'How . . . how bold of you to venture into the subject.'

He glanced down at her, his face impervious. 'I am bored by trivial chatter.'

'No wonder you and Lady Yasmin are not friendly,' Cleo said, before she thought better.

His jaw hardened. 'Speech with Lady Yasmin is like drowning in trivialities.'

She opened her mouth, but he shook his head. 'Undoubtedly, she has inestimable qualities, but when she starts chattering like a metal clapper, it's all I can do not to leave the room.'

'I didn't know you felt so much emotion about the matter.'

His eyes flickered. 'I do not.'

'At any rate, I never thought for a moment that Mr Addison and Her Grace were more than friends.'

They walked a bit farther, the music fading behind them.

'I want to be first,' Cleo found herself saying impulsively. 'First choice.'

'I can understand that.'

'From what I've seen, Lord Lilford, the physical act of adultery is as harmful as the emotional truth that one's spouse has had to settle for you.'

'I have given it no thought,' Lilford said.

Cleo kept talking because she was working it out in her head. 'I have no strong desire to marry, but if I did agree to such a relationship, I wouldn't want my partner to secretly long for anyone else

243

or decide that novelty was – was—' She broke off, unable to express her feelings.

Lilford looked down at her. His eyes glinted near silver in the flaring torches. 'No man in his right mind would leave you for another.'

Cleo blinked at him, thinking that her plan to become a wallflower was a definite failure. Lilford drew her to the side of the path as quick footsteps came up behind them. Was he going to kiss her? She could have sworn –

A large hand curled around her waist and the light citrus scent of the earl's soap was eclipsed by a deeper, wilder scent: cognac and coffee. Jake's voice rumbled in her ear, 'I've been looking for you, Cleo. Evening, Lilford.'

The earl never smiled, or at least, Cleo had never seen him in a good humor. He fell back a step and bowed, but she could have sworn that his mouth tilted just a small amount. 'Mr Addison.'

'I'll see Miss Lewis back to safety.'

'Miss Lewis.' Lilford bowed again and left without a backward look.

So much for that near kiss.

Cleo frowned. She didn't believe that – She dismissed the thought because although she wasn't certain about Lilford's feelings, there was no mistaking Jake's. He was staring down at her, his eyes frosty and possessive. Territorial.

Cleo moved out of his grasp and put her hands on her hips. 'Why are you glaring at me?'

244

'I've been looking for you.' His mouth smiled but his eyes didn't. 'I looked for you all evening. Imagine my surprise when I find you dancing with that British popinjay!'

'Popinjay?' She deliberately looked Jake up and down. 'He looks like a crow in comparison to you.'

His mouth curled. 'His hair glistened in the torchlight as I chased you down this alley.'

'Avenue.'

'More to the point, why in the hell was I having to chase you?' he growled, both hands catching her around the waist this time.

'Don't look at me like that!'

'Like what?' His breath warmed her face as he kissed her forehead.

'As if you own me,' Cleo said, pushing at his chest. 'You don't. I've been doing some thinking, Jake, and I believe that we should end things right now.'

He froze for a moment and then leaned in and kissed her lips. 'Things? What things?'

'*Things*,' Cleo said, her voice rising despite her desperate wish to stay calm. 'Us. Whatever this thing is.'

'You want to end the two of us?' His voice was as far from the elegant cadence of a gentleman as she could imagine, closer to a snarl.

Cleo frowned at him. 'There *is* no us! I'm not your fiancée or your – your friend, or your lover. We merely kissed.'

'And shared breakfast.' He had managed to pull her close, and his erection throbbed against her, though he didn't push.

'It's not enough,' Cleo said stubbornly, hanging on to the important realization she'd had by a slender thread. 'I want more.'

'So do I,' he said instantly.

'Not from you.'

He went still again. She couldn't see his face, but his hands fell away from her, and he stepped back. 'From Lilford?'

'No.' It would be easy to let Jake think that, but it wouldn't be fair. 'I don't mean *more*, as in marriage or a title.'

'Then?' Jake's body was tight as a kite string, not with rage but with some other emotion she couldn't name. 'Whatever you want, I'll give it to you. Except a title. Though I believe I could buy one of those.'

'You can't.'

'The hell I can't. I'll give you anything you want, Cleo.'

Cleo felt a wave of panic. Jake's voice had a dark, liquid confidence in his own abilities that made her want to give in. But she had decided long ago that she deserved *more* than her mother ever gave – or her father ever got.

Jake wanted her, but he *loved* Merry. The duchess whom he had meant to marry if a bear hadn't felled him.

If fate hadn't intervened.

246

'I want to be the only one,' she said.

Jake's face softened. 'There hasn't been anyone else for me since the moment I saw you.'

Cleo's heart sank, and she bit her lip. She had replaced Merry, at least to some extent. 'That's exactly what I'm saying.'

'I don't know what you're saying.' Jake reached out and rubbed her lower lip with his thumb. 'I saw you in Quimby's, and I moved to Germain's the next day, Cleo. I loathed your turban, but I had to be near you.'

She blinked, registering the set of his jaw, the intensity in his eyes. 'You were buying Quimby's, not me.'

'I saw you,' he repeated.

'Now I feel like a piece of china.'

He pulled her into his arms. 'I understand if you want more than me, Cleo. Better. Titled. British. Fancy, like Lilford.'

She wrinkled her nose. 'I don't want fancy.'

'Perhaps I put you off with the kippers.' His voice was confident, but his eyes searched hers. 'I can give them up. Believe me: no woman has entered my mind since I met you.'

'I do believe you.'

His tongue licked her bottom lip, making a shiver run down her legs. 'Good.'

'I saw you and the duchess together,' she blurted out.

'So?'

'You wanted to marry her, except you were

247

trapped in the wilderness, and she married before you could get to her, and now you're just friends – and I *believe* that, I really do. But I want more.'

'I want more, too.'

His lips caressed hers, and Cleo gave in with a little moan. Jake's kiss was greedy, licking into her mouth as if he wanted to drink her in. They didn't stop kissing until she was wound tight in his arms, her body shaking, her breath ragged.

Jake pulled away and rumbled into her ear, 'Tell me what you want, Cleo. I'll give it to you.'

She looked up at him. She never cried. Ever. But her eyes felt hot.

'Darling.' His voice dropped even lower.

'I want the way you look at the duchess,' Cleo whispered, feeling acute embarrassment. 'To be the person you wanted to marry then.'

'I didn't come back when Merry debuted because I didn't care enough.'

'You were injured—'

'The following year,' he interrupted. 'By then, she'd been making scandals up and down New England. Did all that gossip tell you that one of Merry's fiancés sued her for breach of promise?'

Cleo shook her head.

'Ask her about the rubbishing fellows she tied herself to before she came over to London and met Trent on a balcony. Mind you, she was betrothed to his brother at the time. Betrothal three or four. I lost count.'

Cleo's eyes widened.

'Merry had a bad habit of accepting proposals from the wrong men. But trust me, Cleo, if there had been a moment when she and I wanted to marry each other, we would have done it, and not one of her fiancés could have stopped us.'

'You danced with her.' His words were sinking in, but the anxiety twisting in Cleo's stomach hadn't gone away.

'While waiting for you to come. You were late. Merry kept teasing me, damn her, about the way I couldn't stop looking for you. And then when I finally saw you, you were dancing with that – that *Englishman*.'

Cleo's heart clenched. 'You loved her first, and maybe you'll always love her, and you were dancing with her, and she's so *beautiful*.'

'Not the way you are.'

'I'm not beautiful. You said I was witchy, remember?'

His kiss was hard. 'You're gorgeous,' he rasped. 'Witchy because you obviously fucking be-witched me.'

Cleo smiled. 'You shouldn't swear in the pres-ence of a lady.'

'You did. When we first met. I told Merry that you couldn't possibly be a lady, and then you turned out to be the granddaughter of a viscount, because you're the most surprising woman I've ever met. There's no one like you.'

Cleo hitched up one side of her mouth. 'Are you certain you never wished to marry the duchess?'

'You think I'm nurturing a broken heart? *Me?*'
He stared down at her, eyebrow raised, his hair
rumpled from her hands, looking male and
surprised and slightly outraged.

'You could be,' she said defensively. 'She's your
best friend.'

'Actually, I have the feeling you may be. Merry
and I don't share interests; we share memories.
Our childhood.'

The words hung on the evening air like a promise.

'Oh,' Cleo said.

'You both live in England. I need to get used to
rain.'

Cleo shook her head, a wave of panic washing
over her. 'Don't assume that I – I'm not ready for
– No. I was – No.'

He broke into laughter. 'We're invited to dinner
with Merry at the end of the week, and then you'll
see right away that she is a sister to me.'

'We should return to the rotunda, and I'll meet
her now.'

'I told your grandfather that I would bring you
home. That silly girl Lydia, Lilford's sister, fell
down the steps in a flurry of petticoats, then she
burst into tears and insisted on being taken
home.'

'Was she injured? You didn't tell him!'

'No injury except to her pride. A great many
people had a clear view of her undergarments, so
she had hysterics.'

'Poor Lydia,' Cleo said.

'Yes, well, Merry invited the entire table to an intimate dinner on Friday. Now I am escorting you home because I promised your grandfather I would. Lilford has to take his sister straight home, and your grandfather chose to leave with him.'

Cleo frowned at him. 'I fully meant to break off our connection. What if I had?'

Jake looked down at her, his eyes crinkling with a smile that didn't show on his lips. 'I would have convinced you otherwise.'

'But what if you couldn't? What if you had intended to make Merry your bride? What if you—'

His thumb rubbed over her lips. 'You need to trust me, Cleo. I'm not your mother, moving from one lover to another without thought. I've never wanted anyone the way I want you. Which doesn't mean I'm going to push you into something you're not ready for.'

Cleo managed a wavering smile. 'I don't know why I feel so shaken. I'm very independent.'

'You are independent and confident, and I love that.' His kiss was so deep and searching that she found herself leaning against him, legs trembling.

But she shook her head. 'No.'

'No kisses?'

'Not that.' Cleo sighed, leaning her head against his absurd coat, loving the strong beat of his heart. 'Kisses are meaningless. No one knows that better than I do. No more kissing, Jake. If we are to get to know each other, this feeling shouldn't be a part of it.'

'I have a word of the day for you,' he growled. '"Carnal."'

'That's what we should avoid,' she pointed out. 'Carnal kisses are meaningless.'

'Mine aren't,' Jake growled.

He kissed her in the carriage all the way back to Germain's to prove his point, and then left at her door with a final kiss that ended with a nip of her lower lip and a muttered comment about her being a witch.

Cleo closed the door and leaned against it, smiling at the ceiling. Her blood felt like warm honey, and her knees were weak.

Through the door she heard a growling voice.

'Tomorrow morning. Kippers. Coffee.'

'No kisses,' she ordered.

His throaty groan made her think about him. Carnal mouth. Carnal cheekbones. Carnal . . . Could forearms be carnal?

She had the feeling that Samuel Johnson hadn't included that word in his dictionary.

CHAPTER TWENTY

7, Cavendish Square, London
Residence of the Duke of Trent
An Intimate Dinner

'The Earl of Lilford and Lady Lydia Renwick.' Jake grimaced, disappointed that it wasn't Cleo. She had insisted on attending Merry's dinner with her grandfather and Byng.

'Why in the hell did you invite Lilford?' he asked, dropping his voice because he was escorting Merry across the drawing room to greet her guests.

'Lady Lydia needs practice in society, as her mother is no longer with us. If she is not careful, her reputation will be ruined.'

Jake grunted.

'You know how much I hate the way gossip can mar a lady's reputation. I have already heard blather suggesting that she is a hoyden who deliberately showed her petticoats at Vauxhall.'

Merry tended to share uncomfortable truths, though people who loved her didn't care.

'What's more, her brother is a pleasure to look

253

at,' Merry added with a chuckle. 'He never conde-scends to me. Lilford is a good man, Jake. You'd like him. My husband thinks a great deal of him.'

Having seen the way the earl looked at Cleo, Jake was damned sure that he would never like Lilford. They arrived at the drawing room door just in time for the butler to announce Viscount Falconer, Miss Lewis, and Mr Byng-Stafford.

If Jake hated the clothing that Martha had made for him, he had no such objections to Cleo's ward-robe. This evening, she was wearing a dinner dress that her grandfather and he had designed together. The silk was a soft violet-blue color, with a bodice that clasped by a jet brooch, as was proper for half mourning. But the way that brooch drew attention to Cleo's bosom?

Which was, admittedly, magnificent?

Jake watched Lilford bow over Cleo's hand and realized that he'd made a tactical error. Yes, the clothing he selected would bring Martha's skills as a modiste to society's attention.

But they also brought that same attention to Cleo.

Merry's eyes were dancing with delight at what-ever Cleo had just said to her. A sense of rightness settled over him again as he watched the two women he loved most in the world laughing together. He'd come to London for business, but it had been the best decision of his life.

He nodded thank you in the direction of heaven and moved forward.

'Here's Jake,' Merry said, turning to him.

Jake bowed. 'Good evening, Miss Lewis.'

Cleo dropped a curtsy. Puffed sleeves caressed her upper arms just where he would like to put his hands and draw her toward him for a kiss, rather than drop a kiss on her gloved hand. In the last three days, she'd allowed him to join her for breakfast, but without kissing. To get to know each other, she said. She spent the evenings with her grandfather.

Bloody hell.

It was going to be a long dinner.

Damned if Lilford's eyes didn't glitter with amusement when he looked over Jake's coat. But he kept his mouth shut, thank God, and simply wished him good evening.

'Good evening, Lady Lydia,' Jake said to the earl's sister. The girl looked as if she were around twelve years old, with curly yellow hair tied on top of her head. She had a nervy look about her, like a horse that would invariably leap from the starting gate before the flag dropped.

'Good evening,' she squeaked. Her gaze rested on his jaw with some dismay, and she curtsied so deeply that he half expected her to sprawl on the floor. Surely he wasn't so terrifying? Particularly given that his coat was carrot-colored with purple trimming?

Viscount Falconer signaled his willingness to be greeted by thumping his stick on the floor so Jake moved toward him and swept a deep bow; he might be an American, but he had been well-trained by a British nanny. 'Good evening, Your Lordship.'

Falconer looked him up and down. 'Byng ought to be drawn and quartered.'

Jake made a sound in his throat that managed to agree without discourtesy.

'Nonsense!' Byng cried. 'I heard that, Falconer. Mr Addison looks delightful.'

'I agree,' Merry put in, her face alive with mischief.

'No man wants to look delightful,' the viscount retorted. He thumped his stick on the floor again. 'It is time to end this folly. Granddaughter, the man has paid his dues by wearing those wretched garments. He looks like a veritable peacock.'

'My primary complaint is that the garments aren't comfortable,' Jake said, shifting his shoulders or rather, attempting to shift them.

'Because they actually fit you,' Byng pointed out. 'I will admit that the swallowtail design of this particular coat might have been a trifle high-spirited, especially in the rear.'

'You feel imprisoned?' Cleo asked Jake with a distinctly unsympathetic air.

'Yes.'

'A corset is far worse,' she told him. 'Imagine our female ancestors, forced to wear side bustles that made it difficult to edge into a room. You have scarcely experienced the torments of fashion.'

'I find shoes very unpleasant,' Lady Lydia said,

256

with the air of someone announcing an interesting discovery.

Lilford held out his arm to Cleo while his sister monologued on the possibility of treading on a garden worm while barefoot.

By the time Jake made it to the other end of the room, where sherry was being served, Cleo was seated with Merry on one side and Lilford on the other. He sat down beside Viscount Falconer, nursing his glass of sweet sherry.

He had to instruct Trent to acquire better wine, once the duke returned to London.

'You'll never catch my granddaughter if you don't get out of those clown suits,' the viscount said dispassionately.

Jake startled.

'You want her, don't you?'

'Yes,' Jake said, putting it as baldly as Falconer had.

'You'll have to move to this country.'

From Jake's point of view, he didn't *have* to do anything. But the truth was that for Cleo, he *would* do anything.

'I am buying a townhouse in Davies Street, around the corner from you.'

'That'll do,' the viscount said, satisfied. 'How are you planning to talk her into it? Making a game of yourself by wearing those garments is not the way to a girl's heart.'

Jake shot him a disbelieving glance. 'She designed them. I'll wear them.'

'*Byng* designed them. You're not talking of marrying Byng.'

'No.'

'I see that I'm going to have to help,' the viscount said with a sigh. 'I thought it was enough to introduce my granddaughter to polite society, but now I see that one's work is never done.'

'Are you playing Cupid?' Jake was torn between a wish to laugh and the horrified realization that the viscount and his mother were likely to meet some day. Sooner rather than later, if he managed to talk Cleo into accepting his proposal. He hadn't been jesting when he told Merry that his mother would catch a packet to cross the ocean if she heard the faintest rumor that he was courting a lady.

'I suspect I am,' the viscount said. 'And fair warning: I have advice for child rearing, based on my own failures.'

'We're running ahead of ourselves.' Jake glanced at Cleo, who seemed to have Lilford enthralled. 'I will do my best, but she may choose someone else. Merry tells me that earl is "pretty."'

'My granddaughter doesn't care for pretty ornaments, luckily for you,' the viscount said, finishing his glass of sherry and turning to Merry. 'Your Grace, what on earth is your husband doing, keeping sweet sherry in his cellars?'

'Trent loathes the drink,' Merry said cheerfully. 'But since he's not here, I ordered the libation of *my* choice. Those of you with excellent palates will simply have to suffer. I promise that the dinner

258

wines were chosen by our butler and will have august pedigrees and the rest of it.'

Cleo saluted her with her glass. 'I admire you, Your Grace. I shall serve no ratafia and no lemonade when I have a household of my own.'

'When you have that household, you'll learn that one's butler is the king,' Merry told her. 'Mine is nodding at us, which means that we must make our way to the table.'

'This sherry is perfectly peppery. I adore it!' Lydia exclaimed.

Jake blinked at her. If there was one word that didn't describe sweet sherry, it was peppery.

'Peppery means absolutely delicious,' Lady Lydia told him. 'I know it's challenging for older people to keep up with the latest verbiage. My brother is often confused.' She hopped to her feet.

Jake caught Cleo's eye; her mouth was quivering with laughter.

'Mr Addison, do bring Lady Lydia into dinner,' Merry told him. She had bent down next to Viscount Falconer and was steadying him as he clambered to his feet.

Cleo rose and slipped her arm into the Earl of Lilford's elbow; Byng instantly claimed her other arm.

'You're scowling,' Lady Lydia whispered as they trailed after the others into dinner.

Jake grimaced. His mother would be appalled by his ill manners. 'Have you been presented at court, Lady Lydia?'

'Not yet, Mr Astor Addison. My brother will escort me to the queen's drawing room next week.'

'Just Addison will do.' He pulled out a chair for her, as directed by the butler's nod.

'Mr Addison, then,' she said, as he seated himself beside her. Thankfully, Merry had placed Cleo on his other side, with Lilford beside her.

Once they were all seated, Lady Lydia began telling him a long tale about a young lady last Season who had been stung by a bee just before her reception by the queen. 'She could only see out of one eye,' she said with a portentous gasp.

'Unfortunate,' Jake remarked.

'Do you have a sister?'

He nodded.

'Was she presented?' the girl asked.

Jake schooled himself to patience. 'That would be impossible, since America does not have a queen.'

'What a shame!' Lady Lydia cried. 'Don't you wish you could turn back the clock? Just think how happy it would make all the young ladies to make their curtsy before Her Majesty. Why, one can hardly consider oneself a true lady without that!'

Jake was under the impression that a debut resembled a line of woolly sheep being paraded before a buyer, but probably the observation wouldn't be welcome. He certainly wasn't interested in discussing the concepts that lay behind democracy.

At the head of the table, Merry finally turned

from the viscount to Byng, and all around the table, heads turned like clockwork to the other side.

Which meant he was able to talk to Cleo.

'Do you have any American cant to share?' Cleo asked him, rather unexpectedly.

He raised an eyebrow. 'Cant?'

'Unconventional words, like those Lady Yasmin was using at the ball: "some potatoes," for example. My mother adored knowing such phrases; since young people make up most of them, she felt it kept her young.'

Jake nodded, storing that detail about her mother away to think about later. He was fast thinking that the main obstacle between marriage and Cleo was Julia Lewis. 'The term is "some pumpkins."'

She dimpled at him, and warmth glowed in his stomach. 'May I bring you some decent sherry later?' he asked in a low voice.

'Absolutely not.'

'I thought perhaps I could bribe you to allow me to wear regular clothing tomorrow.' He glanced down. 'I am planning to go to Tattersall's auction on Hyde Park Corner. Any buyer seeing me stroll into the building will raise the reserve price for even a broken-back steed by a hundred pounds.'

Her eyes twinkled. 'Tattersall's is exactly where you *should* wear Martha's clothing. At a ball, you are so surrounded by ladies that the gentlemen can't make their way to you and ask who tailored your clothing. No, I am sorry, Mr Addison. What does your valet have planned for tomorrow?'

He groaned. 'Pale blue breeches with a green coat. A spotted scarf, so starched that I shan't be able to see my own feet. My valet is enjoying himself greatly, though he regularly informs me that if his colleagues in New York or Boston could see me, he would die of mortification.'

'I am certain that you will garner much attention at the auction,' Cleo said in a silken tone that told him just how much she was enjoying the thought of his mortification.

'It isn't even the color so much as the fit,' he replied. He glanced down at the thick linen napkin covering his legs. His tool felt as if it was strapped to his leg.

Did British gentlemen not get erections at awkward times? Perhaps not. He couldn't adjust himself without going to a retiring room and unbuttoning the tiresome double fall. What was he supposed to do now? Pray that Cleo's bosom didn't catch his attention again?

With her, it wasn't a matter of body parts. He had inappropriate reactions to the sound of her laughter, the way her eyelashes lay on her cheek, the way she managed to sound wry when talking of accomplishments that no other woman of his acquaintance had attempted, not to mention achieved.

Real irritation likely shone in his eyes, but instead of getting wary or even frightened, the way ladies often did when someone with his forbidding visage was displeased, Cleo just laughed.

And glanced at his mouth, he noticed.

She liked kissing him, for all she'd forbidden the practice. Something eased in the area of his chest.

'Your breeches are uncomfortable?' she inquired in a politely solicitous tone.

'Very.' He kept it short because he couldn't go into detail.

To his shock, the next thing he felt was a whisper-soft sensation as slender fingers touched his thigh. 'May I?' Cleo whispered.

He coughed to cover up the exclamation that almost left his mouth. 'Yes,' he managed. He reached out and snatched up his glass of red wine.

'Dear me,' she said. 'This fabric is rather tight.' Cleo tried to pluck the silk, but of course she couldn't.

At this exact moment his tool was trying to break free from the other side and being strangled instead.

'Damned right.' He took a large swig of wine.

Lady Lydia turned her head and gave him an admonishing glance before returning to her conversation.

'Apologies,' he muttered.

Cleo's fingers spread until she was lightly gripping his thigh. Or at least the top part of it, because her hands were absurdly small compared to his legs.

'I believe your discomfort stems from the fact the fabric was designed for a gown,' she told him, looking at him as innocently as if she hadn't a

263

hand on his leg. If his cock had been trapped on the left rather than the right side, she'd be touching it.

He tried to drag air into his lungs. 'I – I see.'

'Therefore, it causes you discomfort.'

That light in her eyes? It should be banned. Outlawed.

Her fingers tightened, strong for a woman, and warmth spread through him. When her hand slipped away, he felt the loss through his body. He took another gulp of red wine and muttered a curse between clenched teeth.

'Did you say something, Mr Addison?' Cleo asked.

He took a breath and got himself back under control. *All* of him, damn it. He wasn't an adolescent. 'Nothing important.' He sounded furious and he knew it.

'You're terrifying the children,' Cleo said. There was nothing in her eyes but mockery. Warm mockery. She turned away to speak to Lilford. To his right, Lady Lydia was staring at him with concern.

'Forgive me,' he said. 'I am—'

'You look like someone suffering from digestive difficulties,' Lady Lydia said, adding insult to injury by patting his hand. 'I suffer from nerves, and my stomach clenches as a result.'

Jake watched her gloved fingers touch his and thought about how bewildering the world was. Cleo touched him with a fingertip and the hairs on his body stood up, begging for more. Her every touch was a caress.

Lydia's touch just annoyed him.

With one hasty look at his face, the girl tucked her hand away, showing that she wasn't quite as obtuse as she appeared.

He searched his brain for something to say, but young ladies weren't his forte. In fact, he recognized now that he'd almost proposed to Frederica because she monologued. A gentle burble, like a mountain stream.

All about cows.

'You described the young lady with the swollen eye at her debut,' he said. 'Are you worried about your debut?'

Lady Lydia's eyes dropped, and she fidgeted with her fork. 'No, certainly not. It will be marvelous, of course.'

'I'm American,' he said. 'I don't gossip, and I don't care about the court.'

'I know that!'

'So, you needn't pretend. Are you worried that the queen will belch?'

She broke into a startled laugh. Jake caught her brother's eyes across the table and for the first time, Lilford's gaze held something other than dispassionate indifference. He was worried about his sister.

'I'm afraid that I will trip,' she admitted. 'When I'm nervous . . .'

CHAPTER TWENTY-ONE

Throughout four removes and two rounds of sweets – because as the duchess blithely informed the table, in her husband's absence, she had ordered twice the normal number of desserts, most of them chocolate – Cleo kept going over the moment when she had touched Jake's leg.

Temporary insanity was the only explanation.

She touched his thigh!

True, he had assented, but his jaw had tightened.

More to the point, ladies didn't do that. Ever. Not even her mother. She thought about it and changed her mind. Julia probably did grab men's legs under the tablecloth.

The idea made her queasy.

'I'm for my bed,' her grandfather said, coming to his feet. She hurried to his side, but Byng was there already.

'Of course, you must stay for tea,' her grandfather ordered. 'Addison!'

Jake was standing, talking to Merry.

'Yes, sir,' he said, turning to bow.

'See my granddaughter safely home, won't you?' the viscount said.

Did Falconer have any idea that Jake was staying in the same hotel as she? Surely not. Her grandfather was tottering toward their hostess. Cleo narrowed her eyes. Falconer had a way of suddenly appearing frail when he wished.

She was getting the distinct impression that her mother had learned her uncanny ability to get her way at her father's knee.

'Certainly,' Jake said. 'Good night, sir.' He bowed again and turned to Cleo. 'May I escort you to the drawing room, Miss Lewis?'

It was a good hour before tea was consumed and Cleo found herself seated opposite Jake in the carriage. 'This is a different vehicle than you had the other night,' she said, patting the blue velvet that lined the walls. She was trying to avoid his eyes, so she didn't embarrass herself by flinging herself into his arms.

'Just delivered,' Jake said. 'I needed my own carriage. I wouldn't have chosen blue velvet myself, but I didn't want to wait for a design to my own specifications. This conveyance was ordered by a nobleman who couldn't afford his own good taste.'

'The lampshades are silk in the same shade of blue,' Cleo observed, trying to make polite conversation.

'The vehicle cost four hundred and fifty pounds.'

'Robbery!' Cleo cried. 'The price was due to your American accent. Though I might mention that it's considered uncouth to share the cost of purchases.'

'We'll have to keep a running total of uncivilized gestures,' Jake said, grinning at her. He began ticking off on his fingers. 'Which is the most egregious? Informing you of the price of a carriage, putting one's elbows on the table at breakfast, discussing water closets, snorting—'

'You, not me!' Cleo cried.

He shook his head. '*You*, Miss Cleopatra Lewis. You snorted at me, and while I might have deserved it, the gesture definitely goes on the list. Not to mention the fact that during the meal we just shared, you—'

'I apologize,' Cleo interrupted.

His mouth curled into a smile. 'Best thing that's happened to me in days.'

'Oh.' The vehicle swayed as they rounded a corner. 'Your vehicle's undercarriage is very smooth.'

His eyes glinted with amusement, but he followed her lead. 'Would you like to see some of the more creative aspects of this overpriced vehicle?'

Cleo nodded.

Jake flipped up the seat next to him. She might have expected to see a few blankets, or a bag of sand for the wheels, perhaps some tools. Instead, he pulled a lever, and a silver platter slowly emerged, holding several empty glass decanters and some crystal glasses.

'My traveling wagon has something quite different,' Cleo said. She glanced at the seat beside her.

'A commode! You're seated on top of mine. I'm disappointed that I haven't surprised you.'

'Lewis Commodes embarked on the carriage trade three years ago,' she told him.

'I'm certain that I can still shock you.' Jake's eyes were alight with mischief. 'Look up.'

The roof was covered in shimmering blue silk that resembled the top of a canopy bed, twisted into a center medallion.

'Interesting,' Cleo said, thinking that it was a terrible waste of money. The silk would quickly mildew if moths didn't eat it first.

Jake grinned at her. 'Watch.' He reached up and twisted the medallion. It came free – and so did the silk, which split and fell to the front and back, draping itself on top of Cleo's headdress before she pushed it free of her shoulders.

'Why on earth,' she began – and stopped, her mouth falling inelegantly open. The ceiling of the carriage was covered in mirrored glass, diamond shapes so beautifully pieced together that she could see their reflections with almost no distortion. 'Why would anyone want a mirrored ceiling?'

'An interesting question,' Jake said. 'We'll have to discuss it sometime, but at the moment, we have arrived at Germain's.' He pushed the door open and leapt out before offering his hand to Cleo.

With a final glance upward, she stepped down to the street.

Her traveling wagon had been made by the very

best French artisans, but the ceiling was a beautiful red leather. Not mirrored glass.

'What if the carriage toppled?' she asked, shaking out her skirts. 'Those splinters of glass might injure the passengers.'

Jake burst into laughter. 'Practically minded, aren't you?'

'Of course I am,' Cleo said, somewhat crossly. 'I would have asked the cartwright to replace that glass with an excellent cowhide.'

He held out his elbow. 'May I?'

'If my grandfather knew where you are dwelling,' Cleo remarked, as they mounted the steps leading to the hotel, 'I daresay he would never have asked you to escort me home.'

'Imagine if he knew the proximity of our suites,' Jake agreed.

Cleo gave him a direct look. 'He would find it dismaying, and since we are both adults with no intention to engage in improper behavior, the fact is irrelevant.'

Jake agreed, but once they were in the corridor outside her door, he seemed to forget. First he kissed the tip of her nose, which wasn't worth complaining about. But before she could say anything, he brushed a kiss on her lips.

Cleo found her hands gripping the lapels of his greatcoat, and he must have taken that as encouragement, because his next kiss was searching, and she couldn't stop herself from answering silently.

270

Five minutes later, they hadn't moved, one deep kiss following another, and then another. Cleo's brain blurred, and for the first time in her life, her body was in command rather than her mind. Under her fingers, Jake's chest was rising and falling quickly, his urgency matching hers, though neither of them moved.

When he finally drew back, Cleo said, 'We must look like those kissing statues they have in Italy.'

His brows drew together. 'Aren't those generally unclothed, or wearing merely a swatch of fabric? Not that I think it's a bad idea if accuracy demands we disrobe.' He touched her lips lightly with one finger. 'You look well-kissed, and I've never seen a statue with that look in her eyes.'

'No disrobing,' Cleo told him, the huskiness of her own voice a surprise.

'Brandy?' Jake asked. His finger had wandered to her cheekbone and began tracing a caress that felt like a heart. 'I bought something that you'd like today. Napoleon's favorite, Courvoisier cognac. He is rumored to have sent crates to his soldiers to drink with their daily rations.'

'We'll have to ask Yasmin if that's true.' Cleo looked at her fingers, holding firmly to the lapels of Jake's coat. Merely telling herself to retreat to her suite didn't seem to be working.

'May I offer you a sip?'

His voice wound around her like the proverbial siren's song, crowding her head with images of the two of them . . .

271

Her head swung up with a gasp. 'The mirrored ceiling!'

Jake's face transformed from an intense gaze that she associated with desire into wicked, laughing mischief. 'Realized something, darling?'

'That's so improper,' Cleo concluded, thinking it over.

Knowing that she would rather like to look over Jake's shoulder and see his . . . see him. From the rear.

'Someday,' Jake promised in a low rasp.

A tightness in her throat stopped Cleo's response. She looked up at him, cataloguing what she saw: somber eyes – no, *longing* eyes. A strong nose. A stronger jaw. An American air to him, imperceptible but intrinsic.

The air of a man who would change his last name because his uncle had soiled it.

'Jake,' she whispered.

'You're not ready for us,' he said, dropping a kiss on her lips. 'But when you are, the carriage awaits.'

She could feel herself reddening. 'It's time for bed.' And quickly added, 'Separately, if that needs to be said. Because we're not having an *affaire*, remember?'

'I do remember,' Jake said. His finger rubbed her lip again.

'You shouldn't speak to me that way,' Cleo answered, her voice shaky.

'What way?' He smiled down at her.

'Tenderly,' she managed.

His smile . . .

She'd never seen one like it.

'Even a queen can't have everything she wants,' Jake said, his hand curving around the back of her head. 'Kiss me once more, Cleo. Take me through the night.'

CHAPTER TWENTY-TWO

After the duchess's informal dinner, Cleo's life rearranged itself into a pattern. Jake appeared every morning with a plate of kippers. He'd found someplace in London that sold him a cranking mechanism for grinding beans, and fifteen minutes later, her dining room would be fragrant with freshly brewed coffee.

Cleo began every morning with India tea, but ended the meal with a hand-brewed drink. Not because she liked coffee, but because she liked Jake: the man who would lean toward her, plunking contracts down on the table and demanding her opinion of the eighth page, because he was sure that a blackguard was trying to rook him.

After the meal, they would separate, she to her plumbing contracts, her French studies, her philosophy essays, and he to . . . whatever he was doing.

For the life of her, Cleo wasn't quite certain.

He liked to acquire companies and challenge her to figure out how to make them better. For example, he became interested in Flemish lace, but when he tried to buy the company, the lace turned out to have been made by a convent of nuns. They were glad to sell him their lace, but not their convent. On Cleo's suggestion, he offered them apprentices, who would form the core of a new lace company in a few years.

Meanwhile, Quimby's was doing so well that Martha hired four more seamstresses. Every evening Cleo would don one of Martha's gowns. They had a certain look to them, she was realizing. Like any modiste, Quimby's had carved out a specialty, a niche.

Their niche?

Gowns that would look well under theater lights. Gowns that would make an entire audience full of men – and women – fall in love with the actress lucky enough to wear them. Half mourning or not, Martha's gowns sparkled, and even if Cleo protested in a fitting that she didn't need quite so many jet beads sewn onto her hem, she never won an argument.

In the evening, Jake would escort her to her grandfather's for dinner, or to a society event. Later, in the corridor reserved for the two of them, they would kiss for an hour, the very air vibrating with desire.

He never asked for more. He would lean over her, one arm braced against the wall above her head, and just kiss her. Cleo had never imagined that such erotic sounds could come from her own throat, but they did.

She couldn't lie to herself. She clung to him, whimpered when he turned aside to kiss her eyes or jaw. It was in those moments that her mind would focus with utter clarity on one fact: she felt as if she would die if they never made love.

After years of silently criticizing her mother's passions, she was consumed by one greater than Julia had ever experienced. The odd leading actor, after all, had been married or easily distracted. Julia would shrug and drift off to another man.

For Cleo, there would be no drifting to another. Each day her understanding of that fact grew. Every kiss, every word, every touch knit her closer to him.

Made her –

Made her love him, if truth be told.

More than tea. More than Lewis Commodes. More than . . . more than anything or anyone in the world.

Three weeks had passed since their first shared breakfast. Thankfully, no hint of scandal had leaked from the hotel; Germain's boasts regarding their guests' privacy appeared to be accurate.

This evening Jake would escort her to a midnight soirée, a newly fashionable entertainment. Merry would come as well, chaperoning Lady Lydia, which was something of a jest as Merry was such a wild spirit. But she *was* married, and she *was* a duchess . . . .

Cleo nibbled a light supper while Gussie wound her curls into a knot high on her head, weaving ribbons sewn with jet beads throughout. Her gown for the night was deep purple with a low bodice and sleeves that didn't begin until halfway to her elbow.

'You must remember all the details of Lady Yasmin's ensemble,' Gussie ordered. 'Martha says as how her gowns all come from Paris, and the designs can't be found anywhere, for love or money. There's a French magazine that Martha just found, *Galeries des* . . . something, but Lady Yasmin's gowns are a step above.'

'I'll remember,' Cleo said. She finished a ham croquette.

'You've got your appetite back,' Gussie said, sticking in a few last pins for good measure. She winked at Cleo in the glass. 'Not the French chef who's responsible for it either.'

'His cooking is quite good,' Cleo said, avoiding the subject.

Life with her mother had been tempestuous, driven by Julia's passions and her energy. At the same time, Cleo always knew what they were doing next, because Julia was dependably erratic. Her mother would visit a new theater, fall in love, start an *affaire*. There were variations on the theme – Julia might discard Hamlet and choose Macbeth – but life had regularity.

Now every day was all new.

What was she doing? She wasn't stupid. Or naïve. Every kipper, every posy (all with the same message), every smile, every waltz, every shared kiss drew them closer.

'Perhaps tonight's the night,' Gussie said, wading into the unspoken subject.

Cleo scowled at her. For a second, she waited for her mother to chime in on the possibility of a proposal, but Julia was silent.

'Mr Addison is going to ask you to marry him, you know he is,' her dresser said impudently. 'We're all just waiting for the moment when you come back from one of these evenings with a sparkler on your finger.'

Gussie's face was alive with excitement. She knew something. Perhaps about a ring, given that she and Jake's valet spent hours together downstairs, washing, sponging, and ironing garments. 'Do you want to know a secret?' she asked.

'No,' Cleo said quickly.

'It's an opal,' Gussie whispered, unable to contain herself. 'He bought it here in London. It used to be in Mr Addison's bedside table, but it's gone. It must be in his pocket because Mr Moggly hasn't seen it lately! Mr Addison is waiting for the right moment.' She heaved a sigh. 'Just like that last scene in *Love Conquers All*, when the prince offers the dairymaid a diamond.'

Cleo's heart skipped a beat. 'I don't know what you're talking about, and I don't want to know.'

'Are you certain? Forewarned is forearmed, or so my da used to say.'

Cleo shook her head. Every day, she felt a growing sense of certainty, a kind of delicious trust.

But she wasn't ready. She wasn't quite there.

Her father's silent, dogged faithfulness to her mother had been a daily lesson in the importance of marital choices. Her mother had not mourned his death; she was back at the theater a few days later. She hadn't been cruel: it simply wasn't *in* her.

Julia had moved from man to man, the one who was in front of her at any given moment being the most important. If there was anything that Cleo wanted to avoid, it was that.

But Jake showed no potential for disloyalty. He appeared every morning, arriving before his flowers, but with the same sentiment in hand. To him, she was more important than kippers.

It wasn't a romantic statement, but the hard-headed businesswoman in Cleo adored it. Her mother would coo over a man's chiseled features and forget about him by breakfast the next morning.

Men don't forget about kippers. At least, not men who love fish as much as Jake did.

'I'll be taking myself off downstairs,' Gussie said, after a last look. 'Your gloves are on the table, along with the furred pelisse, as it's a chilly evening.'

Cleo glanced over. 'No fan?'

'You don't need to protect yourself, not with him,' Gussie said. 'No one would dare to attack Mr Addison. He's that large and anyone can tell he's dangerous.'

Famous last words, as it turned out.

CHAPTER TWENTY-THREE

Jake stopped by Covent Garden to pick up a special posy from Lulu, who was growing cautiously optimistic that he might actually win the heiress.

'Your new clothing might do it,' she said, eyeing him. 'You're pretty as a new penny tonight. For good luck.' She tucked a marigold into his button-hole. 'This here's a button-ear, and all the best gents wear them.'

Jake had never worn a flower in his life. But he'd never imagined himself in a yellow coat, or marrying an Englishwoman, for that matter. He'd never wanted a woman as much as he wanted Cleo. He went to bed every night with aching balls, his body thrumming with need that his hand never relieved.

He was strolling along the street wondering whether kisses could be addictive when two bruisers lunged from an alley.

He spun around with instincts built from years in Oregon Country, got hold of one of them and hurled him to the side. Annoyingly, a seam on his coat audibly ripped, followed by a thunk as the fellow's head struck the brick wall.

Jake was leaning over his assailant to make sure the man was still breathing when his arm burned with sudden fire. He swung about with a curse.

Assaulting a fool wearing cloth of gold with a fluffy flower in his buttonhole was one thing. A dandy practically deserved to give up his money, to Jake's mind.

But bringing a knife to the business? That put the offense in a different category.

The man who had slashed his sleeve, nicking his arm, was short but strong, with piggish eyes and a knife in his right hand. He snarled something as his eyes raked over Jake's golden coat – embellished with large brass buttons and gold twist.

Jake could interpret a British snarl just as well as a bear's. 'Back away,' he ordered, slipping a knife from his boots.

The man opposite him showed no reaction to the appearance of Jake's weapon, other than a flicker of his eyelids.

'Knives bring death to the table,' Jake pointed out. He flexed his biceps and rolled his shoulders, testing his balance by bouncing slightly on bent knees. Damned if the rear seam in his breeches didn't start to give way. He'd be fighting naked in a moment.

Not that he didn't do as much in Gentleman Jackson's Boxing Academy every Thursday.

'I'll lick you, you jack whore!'

'As it happens, my name is Jake not Jack.' He began casually circling to the right. Sure enough his assailant edged right as well, keeping them face-to-face.

'Don't give a bloody damn what your name is,' the man growled.

'Tsk, tsk,' Jake said, taking two more steps sideways until he had his back to the brick wall. He didn't care to seriously damage the man. He had plans for the night, and they didn't include explaining himself to a Bow Street Runner.

'Fight!' a woman's voice shrieked.

With any luck a Runner would come along before the fool lunged at him.

But no.

Blatantly signaling his intentions by shifting his weight and lowering one shoulder, the man charged at Jake, who fell back as if frightened – waited – and leapt to the side. His assailant slammed into the wall with the same force as had his mate, crumpling to the ground.

Jake kicked away the knife that fell from his limp hand.

'You rang his bell,' a man observed, stepping from the gathering crowd.

'He deserved it for damaging my flower,' Jake said, fluffing up the poor marigold. He could feel a trickle of blood down his arm, but nothing serious.

'Damned right!' the man retorted. 'American?'

'You're bleeding!' the woman cried.

'Yup,' Jake said. 'I need to return to my hotel. Will you watch over these two until a constable

282

arrives?' He wiped the blood off the back of his hand on his breeches: this suit would never convince anyone to buy from Quimby's. It had fallen apart at the first sign of action.

The bystander picked up the first ruffian's knife. 'They'll be put in gaol for this. For a man like yourself, you comported yourself well. I wouldn't have thought it.' He waved his hand at Jake's attire.

Jake gave him a wry smile. 'A true compliment. I thank you.'

When he entered his suite, Moggly pivoted and scowled. 'What in the devil happened to you, sir?'

'Dustup,' Jake said.

'Your sleeve is slashed, sir! Your breeches . . .' The valet's voice rose. 'Is that blood on your hand?'

'A couple of bruisers thought that I was an easy mark, given my clothing,' Jake replied. His coat sleeve was torn from the shoulder, and the white lace cuff on his left hand was soaked in dried blood. 'It's already stopped bleeding.'

Moggly walked around Jake like a horse breeder at Tattersall's. 'You seem relatively uninjured.'

'My knuckles took a rap or two.'

A cunning look crossed his valet's face. 'We must prevent infection,' he said earnestly. 'Nothing better than a woman's touch, sir. I suggest you knock on Miss Lewis's door and ask her to sponge off that blood.'

Jake raised an eyebrow. 'Matchmaking?'

'You just need to talk her into it, like. Miss

283

Daffodil thinks as her young lady is halfway in love with you already. Maybe even more.'

Jake wasn't so sure, but he was nothing if not patient.

'You could collapse at her feet,' Moggly suggested. 'With your hand outstretched so she can see those bloodstains. Women love to play ministering angel.'

'She might faint,' Jake said – and shook his head. Cleo wasn't the fainting sort. Still, it wasn't a bad idea to knock on her door. For one thing, if they were still to attend the midnight soirée, he would need a change of clothing. The remnants of Martha's garments were draped around his body like golden rags.

'Take this,' Moggly said, thrusting the decanter of French brandy into his hand. 'You don't want infection, after all.'

Out in the corridor, Jake glanced at his footman and Cleo's. The pair were far away, next to the stairs, talking so busily that they didn't notice his door open, let alone Cleo's door close behind him.

He had become accustomed to walking into Cleo's dining room for breakfast and again later in the evening, announcing himself as he entered her sitting room. But she was not in either room, though outer garments waited for her on the sideboard.

Jake hesitated and then rapped on the door that led to her bedchamber.

'Gussie, I—' Cleo called. She opened the door and stopped. 'It's you!'

Jake was wrestling with a critical voice that told him that red-blooded, grown men don't *ache* to take women into their arms.

Before he could succumb to that impulse, she took in his destroyed coat and bloodstained cuff. She didn't faint.

Her eyes widened slightly. 'Does anything hurt?'

'No,' he said, smiling.

'The blood on your hand is dry,' she said, picking it up and turning it over. 'Your arm, I presume? I have honey and warm water.'

He raised his uninjured hand. 'I have brandy.' He followed her into a palatial bedchamber that precisely matched his, from the canopied bed to the seating arrangement by the window. She had the same inlaid walnut cabinet to the side, topped with a porcelain bowl and pitcher.

But where his was bare but for his shaving brushes, hers was scattered with ribbons, bottles, and feminine trifles. He would like to see his brushes surrounded by those pretty fripperies.

'Take off your coat,' Cleo said. 'Gussie has disappeared into the bowels of the hotel, but I can summon help.'

'There's no need,' Jake said, shrugging off his yellow coat. He gave a tug on the linen sleeve of his shirt, but it was one of his own garments – not Martha's – and made of sturdy stuff.

'I'll do it,' Cleo said. Before he could respond, she began slashing the cloth just below his shoulder.

'Is that a pocketknife?' he asked, craning to see over his own shoulder.

Cleo's head was bent as she carefully pulled the fabric away before cutting it. 'Yes, it is. There, that's good enough.' She put down the knife, grasped the fabric in both hands, and ripped the sleeve free.

Jake cleared his throat. 'I could have just removed it.'

'Nonsense,' she said, holding his arm and turning it to the light. 'The fabric was already slashed. The wound doesn't appear to be too deep.' She put down the pearl-handled knife and turned away to wring out a cloth in water. Her hair was piled on top of her head, which left the gentle slope of her neck free as she bent over the basin.

Desire settled into Jake's bones like a familiar visitor. He had an overwhelming wish to kiss her nape. To bury his nose in the delicate silk of her skin, pulling her against him and winding his arms around her.

Instead, he kept himself contained, not moving a muscle as she carefully dabbed dried blood from the shallow cut.

'Does it hurt?' She lifted her face to his and he couldn't stop himself from kissing her, a kiss as light as the brush of wings.

'No,' he said. 'It's nothing, Cleo.'

'It's *not* nothing,' she said. 'Men have died for less.' He didn't respond. 'I suspect you are thinking that a glancing wound is nothing compared to a bear's tooth?'

'Something like that,' he admitted. It wasn't true.

The only thing in his mind was her. He reminded himself again that he was playing a long game. He couldn't blurt out a proposal of marriage. He didn't even have a ring, now that Merry had taken possession of his opal. The jewelers were taking an unaccountably long time fashioning the new ring he'd commissioned.

'The bear nearly had me,' he admitted, watching as Cleo poured out brandy and washed his wound.

'Because of the infection?' She patted the wound dry and began dripping honey on it.

'Yes. I don't remember much. My men strapped me down and carted me over a mountain to see a doctor.'

'Good for them.' Cleo picked up a length of snowy white cotton and wound it around his arm, tucking the end beneath. 'You'll need to change this bandage morning and evening. Wash the wound with soap, disinfect it with brandy, and add honey for healing.'

'You are remarkably unperturbed,' he ventured. 'Surely many ladies faint and call for assistance? If not swoon from the mere presence of a man in their bedchamber?'

'Would they?' She glanced up at him with a wry smile, before testing the tightness of the bandage. 'Most gentlemen would be aggravated, if not terrified. You appear to be imperturbable. Besides, I'm not a lady.'

'Why would you say that?'

'Among other things, the most obvious: I'm my mother's daughter, and she rarely saw a leading actor whom she didn't welcome to her bedchamber. 'Twas not a ladylike habit.'

His eyes locked with hers. 'You, Cleo, are not your mother.' He knew that to his bone marrow. 'The man who marries you will never worry that you'll run around to ogle Romeo at the stage door.'

'My mother never lowered herself to the stage door,' Cleo said, dimpling at him.

He bent his head and kissed her. 'She smiled at them from the front row instead?'

'How did you know that?'

'Because if she resembled you, and you were in the front row, I would jump off the stage and sit beside you.'

'Jake.' Her eyes searched his. 'I'm afraid to marry.'

'We don't need to talk about it now.'

'As a married woman, I would lose my financial right to Lewis Commodes.'

'I shall give it back directly,' Jake stated.

'It's more than that. I've spent my life, my whole life, at my mother's behest,' Cleo said, tumbling into words. 'Her moods would change in a moment. She was in love and out of love. A Romeo would be marvelous, but if she happened to see *Julius Caesar* the next night . . .'

'Are you afraid that you are like her? Because you are not.'

She shook her head. 'I take after my father, but it made me wary. Mother would simply forget one man, moving on to the next.' She swallowed hard. 'I . . . I was an afterthought in her life.'

'You would never be an afterthought for me. I think about you all the bloody time. It's enraging.'

He saw a smile in her eyes, so he kept talking. 'It's gone beyond kippers, Cleo. I think about you in the bath. While dressing. I accompanied Merry to church last Sunday, and the Almighty would have been very dismayed if he could see the object of my worship. In short: I'm bloody well in love with you.'

'Romantic,' she said, a tinge of irony in her tone. 'You need to practice.'

'I've never had to.'

'Practice?'

'Never wanted to.'

'No Juliets? Because I've seen that in the theater world. Theater owners sometimes look at young actresses—'

'I don't.' He shook his head. 'Never. I inherited the theaters from my father. He would have loved to be an actor, but an Astor can't perform on the common stage, so he bought theaters instead and then gave himself over into opium dreams where he ruled the stage as lead actor. I have tried my damnedest to make a go of them. For him.'

'I wondered,' Cleo said. 'In London, actors often

289

hold shares in their own theater. Even the impresarios have theatrical backgrounds. Whereas you seemed to have no real interest in the dramatic arts.'

'May I sit down?'

Dismay filled her eyes. 'I've kept you standing when you have an injury!'

Jake snorted and picked her up into his arms.

'Oh.'

'It's nothing, Cleo.' He bent his head and nuzzled her nose. '*Nothing*.' He headed toward an oversized plush chair to the side of the room. 'Do notice how proper I am. I'm not heading for the bed.'

'I should hope not!'

He heard a distinct ripping sound as he sat down. 'My breeches,' he told her. 'It's not meant as a criticism of Martha's sewing skills, but no actor playing Hamlet could get through the sword-fighting scenes without causing a scandal.'

'That's my fault!' Cleo exclaimed. 'I told Martha that she needn't double stitch the garments she made for you. In my defense, very few gentlemen engage in vigorous exercise of any kind. Which reminds me that you didn't tell me how you received today's wound.'

'A couple of fools thought my marigold buttonhole signaled that I was an easy target.'

She leaned her head against his chest, her weight settling into his lap with all the rightness of a puzzle piece linking to its match. She ran her hand up his bare arm. 'I've only seen a man's arm bared on stage.'

290

'Those productions must be more daring than American ones,' Jake said. He was ordering his tool to settle down and not insult Cleo by throbbing against her bottom. Her delicious, rounded –

It was useless.

'*Julius Caesar*,' Cleo supplied. 'Togas, remember?'

He reached out and grabbed the brandy decanter. He held it to her lips. 'A taste?'

'No, thank you. Mother and I saw John Philip Kemble's famous production a few years ago.'

'He was wearing a toga, I presume?'

She nodded. 'So short that his knees were visible.'

'Men's knees are uninteresting,' Jake said. He took a swig of brandy. The brawl had been nothing, but his nerves were on edge.

Cleo seemed to understand; she looped an arm around his neck and rubbed her hair on his shoulder. 'I like men's knees. Have you ever been to a revue?'

He frowned. 'Perhaps the word means different things on different continents.'

She gave him an impish smile. 'On the day I turned eighteen, my mother took me to a Greek and Roman revue held in a brothel that catered to women. A parade of good-looking men in togas were available for bedding at a price.'

'Did you?' His heart was thudding because if she *had* welcomed a man to her bed . . . well, then, perhaps she would –

'No.' She blinked at him and then sat up. 'You're disappointed! I thought men *wanted* their wives to be unpracticed in such matters. That is, if you . . .'

'Oh, I want to marry you,' Jake said, the truth of it coming out comfortably. His arms tightened in case she wanted to make a run for it at the very idea. He pulled her back against his chest.

Cleo being Cleo, she brushed the statement aside in search of clarification. 'Men like their brides to be virgins.' She waved her hand. 'Along with silent, obedient, docile, all the rest of it.'

A pang went through Jake: she was describing his stupidity before he got to know her. 'Until those men learn better. Until they meet someone who will be a partner in every way. Who is annoying and challenging and just damned perfect. After that, a man doesn't give a damn whether his chosen is a virgin or not.'

She was smiling up at him, so he tried to say it all over again with a kiss. Every time they stopped to breathe, he would kiss her again, unable to stop, or she would nibble on his lower lip, and desire would blaze up between them. His right hand entwined with her hair and pins scattered, causing silky ringlets to fall below her shoulders.

At some point, Jake realized that his fingers were trembling, and his heart was racing. Cleo's fingers had slid under the ripped remnants of his sleeve, caressing his biceps. 'To return to the question of the revue,' he said, somewhat unnerved to discover that his voice had turned rough and low, 'a man *might* hope that the woman he met was experienced, because she might be more willing to admire his knees.'

Lust was pouring through his veins, fueling an unspoken addendum to his question. Jake's right hand tightened on her hip as he forced his fingers to stay still. He wanted to explore her curves. He tingled with the elemental impulse to caress every inch of her body.

Cleo's breath was as ragged as his, but she crooked an eyebrow. 'Euphemistic, Mr Addison.' She leaned back against his shoulder. 'That's my word of the day, and I do believe I used it correctly.'

'I need a word of the day too.' He kissed her nose, letting his hand slide up to her narrow waist. '"Inamorata." Do you need me to explain?'

She shook her head.

Something in Cleo's eyes told him to back away and not mention marriage again. 'You like my muscles, even though they are ungentlemanly,' he said, instead of the proposal that hovered on his tongue.

Cleo eased into a smile. 'Yes.' Her lips had turned rosy red. He couldn't help himself from sinking into another urgent kiss. No woman had ever made him feel so wild, as if kissing her was as important as breath and life.

After a minute or so, she said, 'Those Roman skirts at the revue were constructed of flaps. I was

293

rather surprised to find that nothing was worn beneath. Each movement revealed *everything*.'

'I could rip what's left of my breeches into strips if you wish,' Jake said agreeably.

'Martha would be horrified,' Cleo said with a giggle. And then: 'All right.'

'As my lady commands.' With a smooth motion, he slipped a hand under her legs and picked her up an inch or two, just enough so that he could give his breeches a wrench with his other hand. Sure enough, the fabric came away from the waistband with an exuberant ripping sound and slipped down his right leg. He promptly wrenched down the left one as well.

'Jake!' Cleo protested.

'I'm turning my breeches into a toga,' he replied, aiming at a reasonable tone. 'So that you can enjoy my legs as much as you did those of the fellows at the revue.'

He pushed the ripped silk over his knees and settled her back in his lap, snuggling her round bottom against his drawers. 'Moreover, my legs were being strangled. The truth is that my body isn't elegant enough for such clinging attire.'

Cleo was gaping at him, but his cock throbbed against her rear, and her mouth snapped shut.

'I apologize,' he said. 'It's not under my control. Perhaps the gentlemen at the brothel were more discreet.'

'As I recall, they were,' Cleo said, one side of her mouth tipping upward.

'More like this?' He crooked his forefinger and let it hang, wiggling it side to side.

She started laughing. 'How can you jest while . . . while we . . . this is going on?'

'I like imagining you as a girl, eyes wide, watching a line of men with brewer's droop parade around a stage.'

'Brewer's droop?'

'A reference to the ill effects of drinking too much beer. I have another one: you were ogling sleeping beauties in togas.'

'I found it embarrassing,' Cleo said. 'I might add that my mother had no intention of hiring an escort for the evening for herself or me.'

'No?'

She smiled faintly. 'In my mother's world, men were there for the having, with no need to pay for them. She merely thought that I should know what an unclothed man looked like. She felt I was sadly prudish.'

'She ran the risk that you would define men by their limp accoutrements.' Jake couldn't stop himself from nudging his hips upward. 'I never have that problem around you. Actually, just touching you makes me fly the flag.'

'What?'

'Think flagpole. Makes me pitch a tent.' His hand slid up to her breast as he choked back a throaty groan. 'I adore your curves.'

'I thought you were a man of simple words,' Cleo said, a giggle escaping her throat. 'It turns out that you have quite a command of metaphor.'

Brief statements ranged themselves up in his head, wanting to make their way out of his mouth.

Marry me.

Love me.

Be mine.

He bent his head to kiss her instead.

CHAPTER TWENTY-FOUR

Cleo had never given much thought to the effects of desire on the male body, but it was disconcerting to realize that *her* body was in the grip of an all-consuming sensation that was making her fingers tremble and her blood simmer.

The part of her mind that made her *Cleo*, and not her mother, was still clearheaded, observing as Jake stretched out his leg and flexed his muscles. His thigh rippled beneath her bottom, sending a pulse of raw hunger up her body.

'Do you approve?' Jake asked, dancing laughter in his eyes as he gestured toward his leg.

This evening was going to end in her bed. She was honest enough to admit it to herself. Yet the evening wasn't about marriage.

It was about desire. She would never allow herself and her future to be defined by that. Lust was simply another emotion.

Even though she had a strong suspicion that she might lust for Jake's legs for the rest of her life.

Jake toed off one boot and then the other. He was as akin to the men in that Greek and Roman revue as an oak to a sapling. They had been slender, graceful, shaped like ideal noblemen. Jake was not.

Cleo shifted restlessly, desire pooling in her belly. 'Am I too heavy for your injured arm?'

Jake brushed his mouth over hers. 'If I was in pain, I couldn't maintain an erection, to be blunt.'

'You always *are* blunt,' Cleo replied, with a hiccup of a laugh.

'I won't change, Cleo. I wish I could promise that, but I think it's bred deep in my bones. My mother reports that my first sentence was discourteous.'

She laughed. 'What was it?'

He kissed her again, a bit harder. Their faces were so close that she could see the evening blue of his eyes – and the expression in them made her gasp, 'Jake.'

This time they didn't stop kissing until they were both out of breath again. One of Cleo's arms was around his neck, but her other hand was under his loose shirt, roaming over taut muscles.

Jake cleared his throat. 'I didn't speak for my first two years, at which point I broke into full sentences.'

'Oh.' Cleo couldn't stop looking at his lips.

'My first sentence was an observation.'

'Hmm?' she murmured. She pulled her hand from under Jake's shirt and ran both hands over his forehead and down the planes of his cheeks. Some women might not consider him handsome, but to her, the raw masculine strength in his chin, cheekbones, and nose was devastating.

He smiled at her, a spark deep in his eyes. 'It was a loving comment.'

'Yes?'

'After all, a woman might not have noticed that she'd gained a great deal of weight.'

Cleo drew back. 'Oh, I'd say that the chances of that are fairly slim.'

'Luckily, in my mother's case, she had a son willing to point out that she had grown, shall we say, larger?'

'Oh, dear.'

'My first sentence has been reported as, "Mama, did you know that your stomach is as big as your bottom?"'

Cleo burst into laughter. 'What a dreadful little boy you were!'

'I prefer observant and helpful. I had realized that my mother couldn't see behind her. Though I hadn't known she was wearing a bum-roll under her gown, nor did I realize that she was carrying my little sister.'

'Indelicate,' Cleo murmured, tracing his bottom lip with a finger.

He opened his mouth and lapped it with his tongue. 'I speak too quickly and bluntly. You might not like that in the long run.'

'I'm truly disinclined to marry.' Their eyes met. 'If it means I give up Lewis Commodes. Quimby's.'

'With me, you keep them all.' He lowered his head, so his breath feathered over her lips. 'But if you don't want to marry me, Cleo, I'll just keep loving you from across the corridor. Wherever you go: Paris, Moscow—'

She pulled back. 'Moscow!'

'I read in the *Times* yesterday that Russian castles reek of sewage when the wind turns. They need you. And where you go, Cleo, I will go.'

His kiss was demanding and tender at once. His right hand stroked a burning path from her neck to her collarbone . . . and paused, presumably because she was gazing at him. 'Cleo?'

'I may not have learned French, but I did learn the Bible. I can recognize a shortened quote from the book of Ruth.'

'Whither thou goest, I will go,' Jake said, his tone growly but solemn. 'Where thou lodgest, I will lodge, even if you make me live across the corridor. Thy people will be my people. Thy country will be my country.'

Cleo blinked up at him. 'My country?'

'I'll never be a real Brit, you know that, right?'

'I would never want you to be.'

'I'm not an idiot, Cleo. You didn't have to travel with your mother. You were already running Lewis Commodes, for goodness' sake.'

'Someone had to look after her,' Cleo objected.

He kissed her. 'You love the country roads of England, and there's nothing wrong with that.'

'Don't you love America?'

'Not the same way. Not the way I love you.'

The words trembled in the air between them.

'Oh,' Cleo breathed.

The seriousness in his eyes faded to amusement. 'Fair warning: I mean to make you love me too, with all my faults. I have a strategy, a plan.'

'You do?' Cleo whispered.

'I always have a plan.' He lowered his head. 'It doesn't include seducing you, as that would be ungentlemanly. I promise to share all the details, to make it fair.'

She took a deep breath. 'Would it . . . would it allow for being seduced?'

He gave a husky laugh. 'Yes.'

Cleo stood up, unsurprised to discover that her legs had a wobbly, loose sense of freedom, as if they would gladly do unladylike things. Splay open, curve around a man's hips . . . She turned to face him. 'I am not agreeing to marry you.'

It felt terrifically important that he realized that.

'I understand,' he said, coming to his feet. 'Once I have implemented my strategy, I hope to change your mind. Just so you know.'

'Does this plan include kippers and coffee?'

'Yes.'

'You have already—' She broke off.

'Yes.' His eyes were at half-mast, gleaming at her. His shirt was ripped away from one sleeve, and he wore nothing below the waist but his drawers, which did nothing to hide the middle of him. That part.

'I couldn't bear to be forgotten,' she blurted out. 'But I don't want to tie anyone to me with a ring either. My father . . .'

301

She paused, expecting to hear her mother's voice announce that it wasn't her business, but Julia's voice was as silent as a stone.

'My father was faithful to his marriage, though Julia forgot him. I couldn't bear that.'

His voice was warm and firm. 'No one could forget you, Cleo, and I certainly wouldn't want to.'

'My mother would sleep with the handsomest man in London one night and forget him the next.'

'You are not the most beautiful woman in the country,' Jake said, taking a step toward her. 'Your chin is sharp and a bit witchy. Your eyes are too big for your face. There are people who don't like red hair, nor the freckles that come with it.'

Cleo couldn't stop herself from smiling. 'You aren't one of them.'

'No, but I'm listing all the reasons why you are not a leading lady, to be loved and left. I'm not looking for beauty, Cleo. If I were, I'd be chasing after your friend Yasmin, who is arguably one of the loveliest women I've ever seen in my life.'

Cleo smiled again. 'She is, isn't she?'

'She would drive me mad in an afternoon,' he said dispassionately. 'She's caviar and you're kippers.'

Cleo scowled at him. 'You need to memorize a few compliments.'

'I love kippers. I love you.'

If she said the same . . . If she told him that she loved him . . . Panic rose in her chest. She knew all too well what it was to be vulnerable to someone. A child has no choice when it comes to loving one's mother, but a woman has a choice when it comes to a man.

Yet a sinking feeling in her chest suggested that she'd made the choice already. The choice had been made in a moment she hadn't noticed, between a bite of kipper and a sip of coffee, between a shared contract and a whirling dance.

'You haven't been introduced to my strategy yet, so there's no need to worry about it,' Jake said gently, tipping up her chin. He had registered her panic. 'There's no rush.'

'When are you going to tell me the details?' she managed.

'When the time is right. This is love and war, Cleo. We've already had the war.'

She felt a desperate need to be in control of the moment. She took a shuddering breath just as Jake turned away.

'It's time for me to return to my chambers,' he said. 'I think that the midnight gardens are likely closed by now. Merry and Yasmin will have enjoyed themselves without us.'

Cleo couldn't help her gaze: it went straight to his rear end. She came up behind him. He tensed; she had the feeling that Jake always knew what was happening behind his back.

Another step and she wrapped her arms around him, flattening her breasts against his back. 'I'm not as good as you are at understanding my own feelings.'

Jake let out a strangled groan. Cleo's hands slid down his stomach ridges, flattening his linen shirt against the bulges and valleys of his body, going lower.

She stopped, feeling the way his shaft throbbed against her palm.

'Fascinating,' she whispered.

'May I turn around?' His voice rumbled in his throat.

'Not yet,' she whispered.

'All right.' He understood; she heard in his voice that he knew how important it was to her that –

'I'm not like my mother, am I?' she asked. 'Approaching you without—' She pulled her hands away.

'I'm at your feet,' Jake answered, his large hands capturing hers, though he didn't turn.

'It's just that men in her presence forgot their wives,' Cleo said, rubbing her cheek against his warm back. 'I can't explain it.'

'I don't have a wife to forget. I only have you.' His hands curled around hers. 'May I?'

She dropped a kiss on his back by way of answer.

He bought their hands against his body slowly. When her fingers instinctively curled around his shaft, his head tipped back, and a rasping sound broke from his throat. His hands remained still, cupped over hers, allowing both of them to feel his body tremble.

'It's not the caress, Cleo,' Jake said. 'It's that *you* are touching me.'

304

Was that part of his strategy? She didn't care. 'I'd like to touch you without your shirt.' She gently pulled her hands free and walked around him until she stood before him.

'Are you all right, darling?' he asked. His cheeks were flushed but his eyes were not impatient or lustful. He looked at her –

She found herself smiling. 'I won't be able to get out of this gown by myself,' she announced. 'Martha sewed any number of tiny buttons inside to make it fit my bosom the way it does.'

'It's a bloody miracle, that bodice,' Jake said, looking at her breasts.

'You could take your shirt off,' she suggested.

He put his hands on the hem and wrenched it over his head without wincing or otherwise appearing to notice the bandage around his arm. His hands settled back on his waistband. 'Rags next?'

Cleo's palm was still tingling from the press of his shaft. She knew the shape of it, and the strength of it. 'You could have been shipwrecked on an island, like the opening of *The Tempest*,' she said, looking at the rise and fall of his burly chest.

'I agree,' he said, rather surprisingly. 'I came to England's shores and shipwrecked on my first glimpse of you.'

'Not the first!' she said, laughing. 'Not in my turban.'

'I went back to Merry's that night and told her that I was moving to Germain's Hotel.'

'Only because you wanted to win Quimby's!'

He shook his head. 'I wanted to win you. I didn't know yet, but that's the truth of it.'

It was an interesting point, but Cleo couldn't stop looking at him. Her blood was past a simmer now; it was making itself known in ways that she hadn't expected. Her nipples, for example . . . She glanced down, and sure enough, they were standing out against the light fabric of her gown.

'I do love a short corset,' Jake said, his voice sliding lower. He didn't move, though.

She didn't want him to be undressed, completely undressed, while she remained clothed. It was too much like that brothel, with men in Greek togas and come-hither eyes, and elegantly gowned ladies languidly sipping glasses of sherry.

Cleo turned around. 'It's easiest if you unbutton from the top.'

He didn't say a word, but he managed to undo her gown in a quarter of the time that Gussie took. When Cleo felt the last buttons open, she slid it off her shoulders and stepped out of it, turning.

Her short corset was French, made of pale pink material embroidered with rosebuds, and her chemise matched. The corset laced in front, the better to support her breasts, so she untied it. Loosened, it fell to the floor, and she stepped sideways again.

Now they were opposite each other, she in a transparent chemise and he in a pair of drawers, with a yellow silk waistband on top.

'Cleo?' he said. 'You needn't.'

She was watching the way his chest flexed as he shifted his weight but she looked up. 'Yes, I do,' she said simply. 'You and I – whatever we are – this has been coming since the first day you stole into my room with a decanter of brandy.'

His eyes glittered at her from under heavy lids. 'May I remove my clothing?'

'Yes,' she said. The tremor in her voice was excitement more than nerves, and when his hands went to his waist, she pulled her chemise over her head.

CHAPTER TWENTY-FIVE

Unlike many maidens, Cleo knew exactly what was expected of her during intimate acts. She owned a box of ribboned condoms, given to her by her mother. She could visualize everything, thanks to advice handed out over cups of tea.

At the moment she couldn't remember anything, and Julia's commentary had disappeared.

Jake picked her up in his arms and set her gently on the bed, while she – she, who could always think of something to say! – watched his face mutely. He stretched out next to her, head propped on his elbow, so she moved to her side as well.

The look in his eyes? No man had ever looked at her mother that way, including her father. Cleo found herself holding her breath, wanting to capture the moment. But Jake's gaze fell to the curve of her hip, and thick lashes veiled his expression.

Still, she knew what she'd seen: love and possession, not just desire.

So, they *would* marry.

She would allow him to go to his knees and

produce that opal. She'd also require him to sign over Quimby's and Lewis Commodes to her one minute after their vows, but he'd already agreed to that.

Crucially, she trusted him. The guard she held over her heart – the one that developed after she nearly married a thieving fellow with a nice profile – eased.

Perhaps even dissolved.

Jake reached out a hand and trailed a caress over her hip, sending jolts of heat through her body. She followed his gaze down to the heavy curve of her breasts.

'The sight of you naked is enough to make me die happy,' Jake said, his hand sweeping over her curves again.

'I'd rather you didn't die,' Cleo said primly. All her mother's advice flooded back into her head. 'This likely won't go well the first time. It might hurt.' She knit her brow, gazing at his erect shaft. 'Also, we may not be immediately compatible, but I have been assured—'

He leaned in and brushed her lips with his, and she stopped abruptly. 'We're both new to this, Cleo. I've had intercourse, but I've never made love.'

She smiled.

'We can take our time. Get to know each other.' He ran a hand down her arm. 'Your skin feels like petals, rose petals, the way they feel if you pinch them between two fingers.'

'Surprisingly romantic.'

'I told you I'm an observer.' He leaned closer until his lips drifted over her forehead, down her temples, nipped her earlobe, making her shiver. 'You smell like May sunshine. Enticing, sweet, with a touch of the first jasmine flowers, the kind that bloom in a hedge.'

'Jake,' Cleo whispered.

'I'm not good at fancy adjectives.' His lips pressed against hers and she instantly opened, welcoming him, rolling to her back. He followed her, and as his hands settled on her breasts, they groaned at the same moment. One thumb rubbed over a nipple, and Cleo arched instinctively into his warm grip.

'You like that,' Jake murmured, looking at her with hooded eyes.

'Obviously,' Cleo managed. She ran her hands down his back, loving the ripples of muscle as his shoulders flexed. She wasn't quite sure of the etiquette. Would it be proper for her to touch his arse?

'I adore your breasts,' Jake said, replacing his hand with his tongue. 'Your nipples are like raspberries.'

Feelings torched through her, and Cleo abandoned thoughts of propriety. She pulled him closer, wound her legs around his hips, instinctively pushing up, and gave a faint scream as sensation blazed higher. 'That – that—' No words came to mind.

Jake's unruly hair brushed her chin as he eased away from her breast.

'Stay!' she commanded, clutching his shoulders.

He kissed her. 'I need you to want me, Cleo.'

'I do,' she promised.

His laugh was more like a growl. 'Not yet, not enough.' He moved down on the bed, pushing her legs apart. 'Lovely,' he breathed. 'More rose petals to caress—'

He brought his tongue to bear, and Cleo gave a startled cry. She lost her mind, sensation lashing her body. When he brought his hand into play, her toes curled and every muscle in her body knotted, pleasure spilling from his warm tongue down her arms and legs. She screamed aloud, her hands clutching his hair, holding him in place.

'That's wonderful,' she murmured a moment later.

Jake grunted and came up over her, braced on his forearms. 'I did gather that you found it pleasant.'

'It was bottled joy,' Cleo said dreamily. 'Through my whole body, like French brandy but so much better.'

His mouth eased into a smile, and she traced his bottom lip with a finger. 'I want to kiss you all the time,' she said, hearing the huskiness in her own voice with faint surprise. Not to mention the truths slipping out of her mouth. 'When you're talking about contracts, or kippers, or when we're waltzing.' A feeling of faint anxiety rolled over her.

'Do you suppose that now I'll be thinking about *this* all the time?'

He grinned down at her. 'I damned well hope so, Cleo. I already do.' He ran a hand down the side of her body, and pleasure thrummed under her skin. She shivered, looping her arms around his neck.

'For tonight, would you like to stop here?' he asked, leaning down to nuzzle her neck.

She laughed. 'You don't understand, Jake.'

He raised an eyebrow.

'I *am* my mother's daughter, and for the first time, I don't mind admitting it. I want more. All of it.' She reached down and ran her fingers over his erection, exploring its velvety hardness, watching the way Jake's eyes darkened and his muscles tensed.

'I can oblige.' His voice was low and hungry.

Cleo let her fingers curl around him. She wanted to explore him, the way he had her. 'I plan to savor you,' she whispered. 'The way you did me. All of you.' She dipped her fingers below to caress one of his balls. A groan broke from his throat.

Urgency was building in her blood again. She closed her fingers around his shaft, loving how it throbbed against her palm.

'May I?' Jake had never sounded so American, all his rough masculinity bound in a throaty question.

'We need a condom.'

'I don't have one here, but I won't spill inside you,' Jake said in her ear. His voice was strained.

Her mother had told her never to trust a man who made such promises. But Jake . . . She could trust Jake. Plus she had to admit that she wasn't entirely sure where the box of condoms –

She turned her head and realized that the box was sitting squarely on her bedside table. She smiled ruefully. 'It appears that Gussie felt I should be prepared in the event that you visited my bedchamber.'

A moment later, Jake had smoothed one onto his shaft.

Cleo smiled at him and then arched up, rubbing him against her core. 'That feels so good!'

He leaned down to kiss her, and then she felt him breach her. Raw feeling coursed through her, not pleasure nor pain.

Jake took a deep breath. 'All right?'

Cleo wiggled. 'I feel as if I'm a worm on a hook.'

He let out a ragged laugh and bent to rub their noses together. 'Who's the unromantic one now?' He pulled back and then eased forward again. Her hands curled tightly around his forearms.

It was new, and slightly frightening, but his arms felt like a cradle, surrounding her with strength and protection. He withdrew again, making her gasp, then pushed back, slightly farther.

'How is it?' he asked, his voice deep.

'Not terribly pleasant,' she admitted.

'Does it hurt?'

'Twinges.' She curled her hands tighter around his arms and rocked slightly. 'Oh!' She knitted her

313

brow. It wasn't agonizing. It was just strange and new.

'Ready for more?' He eased farther into her, then kissed her until her senses swam, and Cleo couldn't help bucking against him. 'More,' she ordered.

'Your wish – my command,' Jake growled.

'More' didn't turn out to be a good idea. 'Kiss me again, Jake,' Cleo whispered.

He instantly complied. 'Do you feel gutted, darling?'

She couldn't help a burble of laughter. 'Did you just describe making love as a "gutting"?'

'I'm trying to imagine it from your point of view,' he said, his voice strained. 'I'm not a small man.'

Cleo wiggled, trying to get comfortable. '"Gutted" might actually apply.'

A groan broke from Jake's lips.

'Does it hurt if I move like that?' she asked, stilling.

'The opposite.'

'Some pumpkins?' she asked teasingly, wiggling some more. Her flesh was easing around him, making some of the discomfort sparking from their connection disappear.

'Hell, no,' Jake said hoarsely.

Desire fluttered through her again, not as a gripping force, but a promise. 'It's not too bad,' she said, experimenting with moving her hips upward. 'I suppose you fit.'

His lips opened but no sound emerged. His hair

was deliciously tumbled over his forehead, and his jaw was set.

Pain faded, leaving discomfort. Cleo started moving slowly, nudging up with her hips, creating her own rhythm. Jake was braced on his elbows on either side of her head, his lips dusting her forehead with kisses, his hips steady.

She arched her neck and caught his mouth.

One of his hands came and slipped under her bottom, lifting her slightly as he thrust forward for the first time.

This kiss felt different, perhaps because their bodies were connected, snug against each other. 'You feel so damned good,' he said into her mouth, a while later.

'You swear too much,' Cleo said cheerfully. The pain had diminished, and although she wouldn't describe intimacy as the best thing she'd ever felt, it wasn't terrible.

'Cleo,' Jake said, the sound strangled. 'May I continue?'

'Yes, of course,' Cleo said, thinking that she was offering a very odd form of hospitality. Not entirely comfortable. One could see it as an exchange. Pleasure for pleasure, just not experienced at the same time.

Jake groaned. Then, to her surprise, he pulled away and came back on his heels. Cleo's eyes widened, looking at his erection. It seemed even larger than it had earlier in the evening.

'Enough for a first try?' Jake asked.

Cleo's blood thrummed at the sight. She cleared her throat. 'We did fit.' She sounded ridiculously prim.

'Hmm,' Jake said. He lay back on his side next to her, as if they were finished.

'Not yet,' Cleo said firmly, twining her hands into his hair and giving him a tug. A shudder went through her whole body as his weight settled back on top of hers. Without another word, he bent his head and took her mouth.

She tried inarticulate sounds to coax him, but Jake seemed content to simply lie against her, kissing her over and over. She ran a hand down his bare back, loving the taut power in those swelling muscles.

Jake's kisses were incendiary, but he never stirred under her caress, his powerful muscles quiescent.

Until she snapped.

'Enough!' she gasped.

'Of course.' He instantly pulled away.

'I didn't mean that,' Cleo said. She managed to shift beneath him so that she could bend her knees, cradling him where she wanted. Sensation burst through her, scorching down her legs. 'Try again, Jake,' she gasped. 'Try again. Please. I want more of it . . . more of you.'

'Perhaps tomorrow?' He brushed her lips with his, his eyes gleaming under heavy lids.

'*Now.*'

'I don't want to hurt you,' he whispered.

'I'm aching,' Cleo said bluntly. She gave up on

the question of etiquette and slid her hands down to his powerful arse. A throaty sound broke from her lips.

'Can't have that,' Jake muttered, putting himself where she wanted him.

'Better,' Cleo whispered. Her fingers curled around his shoulders. 'More.' He slid farther into her, easier now, sparkling sensation throughout her body.

Finally, with a deep groan, he came to her all the way. Cleo had a strange feeling in her chest, as if she couldn't catch a breath, as if urgency had replaced all the air in her body. Jake seemed to know instinctively; his body gathered, and he thrust forward.

This time, it was the opposite of uncomfortable. Cleo gave a little shriek, her hands sliding up his back and tightening on his shoulders. He made a sound, something between a chuckle and a groan . . . pulled back.

There was a rhythm to making love. Cleo was dimly aware that she was proving a natural. Within a few minutes, her legs were curled around Jake's hips, her body meeting his urgently, sensation spilling from their joining down to her very toes.

Jake seemed as dazed as she was, kissing her between gasps, sweat gleaming on his shoulders. Desire fizzed in Cleo's veins. When he cupped one of her plump breasts in a hand and rubbed his thumb over her nipple, she cried out. He laughed.

'You're not supposed to laugh during intimacies,' she managed.

Jake's callused thumb rubbed slowly again, and she opened her mouth but managed to choke back a cry.

'I laughed because I love you,' he said, eyes slumberous, serious.

She couldn't respond; his rough caress had stolen words and left only desire, and when he took up a rhythm that seemed to inflame her more with every movement she started gasping, her legs tightening around his hips, her head thrown back.

'You are amazing,' Jake whispered, kissing her neck. He pulled up one of her legs and settled her into a slightly different position before he surged forward. Her eyes widened, and a cry broke from her lips.

No laugh, this time.

Jake's breathless groan burst from his throat. 'That's it, darling. Now.'

Now?

What was he thinking . . .

Sensation rolled over her like a wave of the sea, tossing her underwater, blinded, breathless, urgency rolling through her again and again.

Jake wasn't the sort of man who reconsidered intimate activities after participating in them. The women with whom he'd shared a bed had been convivial and pleasure-seeking. They generally rolled away from each other with mutual relief, as

318

he was careful to avoid young women or anyone who might have delusions that he would fall in love with her.

But this?

He lay on top of Cleo, his body shaking, unable to catch his breath, feeling as if he wasn't the same man. As if intimacies could change someone at a profound level.

Slowly he moved, shifting his weight so she could breathe, their bodies separating with obvious reluctance.

'Sweat,' Cleo said, wrinkling her nose. She reached out and touched a drop running through his smattering of chest hair. 'I can't imagine why . . .' Without finishing the sentence, she leaned over and lapped it up.

The feeling of her tongue on his chest made hunger wash over Jake. His shaft swelled, desperate to unite again, fever burning in his blood.

They couldn't do it again. Not until she healed.

Making love to Cleo felt completely different from anything in his experience.

Their eyes met.

He was in love with her. Loved her. Would always love her. His mouth opened to say as much, but she was caressing his stomach, fingers trailing lower.

'Wait,' he said, the word bursting from his chest. He knifed off the bed and disposed of the condom, poured fresh water into the basin, and then came back to gently wash her.

Cleo lay back like the queen she was, her body shivering slightly from his touch.

He cleared his throat. 'Are you sore?'

'No,' she said, with a distinct note of satisfaction. 'I feel different. Tired.' Her eyes caught on his movements as he washed himself. 'Not so terribly tired. I thought you would . . .' She crooked one of her fingers down, just as he had done earlier in the evening discussing limp phalluses.

'I would. I did. Normally, I would.' He stumbled around the words wondering if it was the right moment to tell her that he desperately wanted to marry her. That living across the corridor would never be enough.

But then she reached out, closing her fingers around his shaft, and edged closer. Her lips were swollen, cherry red from his kisses rather than their normal pink.

'May I kiss you as you did me?'

His stomach muscles contracted from shock. 'Ladies don't—' he said, before he could stop himself.

Wicked laughter shone in Cleo's eyes. 'I keep telling you, Jake. I'm not a lady.'

And then she proved it.

CHAPTER TWENTY-SIX

Cleo slept late the next morning. Gussie had only just ushered her into the dining room when Jake's knock heralded the arrival of kippers and coffee. Scorching embarrassment suddenly swept over Cleo. Hectic heat rushed into her cheeks.

Jake had returned to his bedchamber in the middle of the night. Gussie had woken her with chatter and a cup of tea, and Cleo had hardly a chance to breathe, let alone think about the previous night.

With him.

The things they . . .

Jake grinned at her, his eyes sparking with amusement. Of course, he would have had other breakfasts like this, meals shared with a woman whose body he had intimately caressed. Gussie whisked out of the room, a naughty smile on her face.

Gussie had instantly known what happened last night – not just because the sheets were marked, but also because Cleo's hips showed a faint imprint of fingers. Cleo thought that was due to the third time they made love, when she found herself sitting up in a scandalously revealing position that –

That she really liked.

In fact, she'd liked all of it. Which made her feel queasy.

Her mother liked all of it too, but pleasure never made her stay with anyone.

'I brought you a present,' he said, as soon as the footman left the room.

The opal.

It had to be the opal ring. Cleo's lips curled into a smile. She still wasn't certain, but she wanted . . .

She wanted the promise of a promise. That's what a betrothal ring was, after all. A promise.

Jake stood up and walked around to her, then crouched down next to her chair. Cleo could feel her heart pounding in her chest. The memory of her previous fiancé, Foster, kneeling before her, a velvet box in his hand, came to mind. Foster's face had been reverent, head bowed as if she were far superior, a lady on a pedestal. As if he were besotted.

Jake sat back on his heels, his eyes laughing, holding out a small velvet box. He didn't seem inclined to ask the requisite question, so she reached for it.

The box came from Rundell & Bridges, Jewelers. She didn't bother much with jewels, but even she knew their reputation.

'This isn't—' She stopped and cleared her throat. 'This isn't because of last night, is it?'

He looked surprised. 'No, no, I commissioned it weeks ago, after—'

Cleo met his eyes. 'After?'

'After the morning when we met in Quimby's the second time, to order clothing.'

She couldn't stop herself from smiling as she unpicked the knot. Of course, they *had* kissed upstairs at Quimby's. But she wouldn't have thought –

'I hope you like emeralds,' Jake said.

Not opals? She did like emeralds far more than opals, as it happened. Cleo shook the ribbon free and smiled at him. 'I love emeralds.' She tipped open the elegant box.

Her mouth fell open.

'You needn't wear it,' Jake said when she didn't speak. He reached out and ran a finger down the smooth curve of the bear's tooth. 'They did a good job of turning it into a pendant, didn't they?'

Cleo found her voice. 'Absolutely. Thank you.'

The tooth was curved and wickedly sharp; the jeweler had circled the top with an elaborately braided gold wire and hung it from a golden chain. Green stones studded the top of the tooth, poking out between twists of gold.

'Is this the real tooth, the one from the bear that attacked you?'

'Yes,' Jake said cheerfully. 'I've kept it around for good luck, but I thought I'd give it to you instead.' He bent toward her, captured her head in his

323

hands and kissed her, a sensual, casual kiss that made Cleo's mind spin.

'You're my good luck now,' he said, standing up and moving back around to his side of the table. 'Besides, as I told you, it offers protection. The bear can protect you whenever I'm not at your side.'

Cleo watched him go, belatedly snapping her mouth shut. It wasn't an opal ring, but it was something. Her finger touched the cruel tip of the bear tooth, and she found herself shuddering. It was as long as a knife blade and could easily have pierced an organ that Jake could not survive without.

'You really could have died,' she said, clicking the box shut.

'Yup,' Jake said. 'If the thought bothers you, just throw it away.' He cocked his head. 'Perhaps strip the jewels first. I asked for a wire around it, but Rundell convinced me that no lady would wear such a thing unadorned.'

Cleo's fingers closed around the box defensively. Even if it wasn't a ring, he'd had it made for her. 'I will wear it.'

'You could pair it with a scarlet dress, once you're out of mourning,' Jake said, deftly cutting up toast into the small squares he favored. 'You'll look like Lady Macbeth, ready to murder any man who stands in her way.'

'That seems an unfair characterization of the lady.'

Jake shrugged. 'I haven't seen the play, but she's famously bloodthirsty.'

'She does urge her husband to kill the king,' Cleo said. She took a drink of tea. Why was she so unnerved? The opal ring would make its appearance at some point.

In fact, Jake was being quite sensitive. If he'd asked her to marry him this morning, it would feel as if she had traded her virginity for the ring. Or as if his proposal was dependent on their successful union.

She could feel herself growing pink again. Their union had been successful. In fact . . .

'Don't look like that,' Jake growled.

Her eyes flew from his chest to his face.

'Unless you want me to pick you up and set you on your back on the breakfast table and take you right here.'

'Certainly not!' she said quickly, perfectly aware that she was turning even pinker. She *did* want that, albeit without the fish. She shifted restlessly in her seat.

'The bedchamber would be fine too,' Jake said, his voice dropping to a deeper note. 'I live to serve.'

'Hush.' Cleo cleared her throat. 'How can you not have seen *Macbeth*? It's a staple in every repertoire.'

'I don't like going to the theater.'

'You don't? Then why on earth haven't you just sold the theaters?'

'My father loved them so much.' He gave her a wry smile. 'I was a terrible disappointment to him.'

'I know that experience,' Cleo said. 'My mother wanted me to have the same *joie de vivre* as she had, to be a partner in . . . in crime, though that isn't the right word. I just couldn't do it.'

'She wanted you to be a friend, not a daughter?'

Cleo nodded. 'Even when I was very young, perhaps ten years old, she needed a confidante. Her moods were so volatile, you see. She would be tempestuously in love, and then thrown into the depths of misery or hideously bored. The poor men wouldn't know what happened to them.'

'But you were always there.'

'Yes.' She turned back to her plate. She ate one piece of kipper every morning to be polite, but the truth was that she vastly preferred eggs.

'My father was not volatile.' Jake started turning the crank on his coffee bean grinder, and the smell spread through the room. 'He was steady in his true love for the theater.'

'It's odd that both our parents had such a passion for the theater. My mother did love plays, as well as actors.'

'The odder part is that you are the first person I've met who was more interested in the business side of the profession. *That*, my dear Miss Lewis, is the truly astonishing part of this odd coincidence.'

His mouth curved into a smile, and Cleo felt another stab of desire.

'But to be truly precise, the best aspect of all this is what happened last night.'

'I'm not sure that should happen again,' Cleo said. Little prickles of anxiety kept going through her. Her grandfather would be so disappointed if he knew that she was taking after her mother, sleeping with a man out of pure desire, scandalously unmarried.

'It will happen,' Jake said, pouring hot water over his ground beans.

'Is that a stocking?' she asked, looking closely at what he was doing for the first time.

'Yes. I used to use a sock, but silk stockings are far better,' he said. 'Don't worry; it is unworn. But more importantly, Cleo, you and I are together. However you want to term it or label us. Our servants know. We know. It only remains to tell your family and mine.'

Cleo couldn't help it: the opal ring went through her head again. If they were *together*, why hadn't he gone down on one knee? Why a bear tooth rather than a ring?

But she forgot all about the question.

Jake's plans for the evening were so detailed that he managed to talk her into practicing some of them immediately.

CHAPTER TWENTY-SEVEN

'I don't feel like going to dinner tonight,' Cleo told Jake two weeks later. They were lingering over breakfast, the way they often did these days. Rather than schedule meetings in the morning, as she normally did, she had taken to pushing everything to the afternoon.

The evenings? The *nights*?

All Jake.

They talked constantly, never seeming to run out of subjects for conversation.

'But Merry is excited to introduce you to her husband,' Jake said, unnecessarily. 'We can't miss it. She invited Yasmin and Lilford, although have you noticed that they don't speak any longer?'

Cleo rolled over on her back and stared up at the ceiling. Jake had lured her from the breakfast table to the bed, and she was still catching her breath. 'I believe Yasmin was enticed by his profile, but something happened and now they don't speak.'

'I never liked him,' Jake said comfortably.

'That's just because my grandfather wanted me to marry him!'

'No, because he wanted to marry you. Your grandfather wants you to marry *me*,' Jake said, with evident satisfaction. He reached his arms above his head and stretched.

Can't do that if you don't ask, Cleo thought, but she kept her mouth shut. She was learning about Jake. He went his own way, at his own speed.

It was entirely her fault that she found herself in the grip of trepidation, waiting for the moment when he lost interest and forgot about her. The fact that he occasionally mentioned how he instantly moved to the hotel after meeting her at Quimby's didn't help.

It was too much like something her mother would have done.

Julia's desires were instantaneous. She would do anything to obtain the man she fancied. Her voice seemed to be permanently silenced in Cleo's head, but she knew her mother would approve of Jake.

Jake bounded out of bed. Making love in the morning relaxed Cleo, as if honey slid through her veins. It energized him, sending him charging out into London seeking business opportunities.

'I'll have the carriage brought around at noon,' he said. 'I want to take you on a picnic. And before you ask, Gussie told me that your schedule is clear.' With a last kiss, the door clicked behind him as he headed across the corridor.

Cleo stayed where she was.

It was absurd that she worried about Jake. They

were so close that she couldn't imagine loving another man the same way.

Gussie bustled in sometime later, undoubtedly warned by the hotel's gossip circuit that Jake was back in his suite. Her eyes darted to Cleo's hand, but they had stopped discussing it.

The subject felt old. Odd. Embarrassing.

'Your new gowns have arrived,' Gussie said briskly. People in society were making their way to Quimby's, inspired by the beautiful garments that Jake wore, not to mention the glittering half-mourning gowns that Martha had perfected. At this rate, Martha would have to hire even more seamstresses.

Martha had not turned Cleo into a wallflower.

'Tonight you will wear the first evening gown that is not in half mourning,' Gussie announced, holding up a gown that looked like a narrow swath of pale blue silk. 'There's a sheen to the fabric, see?' It shimmered as she held it up. 'Martha used strings of pearls on the bodice. Not real pearls, obviously, but aren't they pretty?'

'I'm not sure that strip of fabric qualifies as a bodice,' Cleo said dryly.

She hoisted herself up against the back of the bed. She was tired. Perhaps she should tell Jake that she needed a night by herself. To merely sleep, the way she used to, like a starfish in the middle of the bed, rather than with a huge, protective male curled around her.

This was absurd. She was waiting for an opal

ring as if she were a damsel on the marriage mart, pushed by her family to make the best match. Even worse, she was afraid that Jake was *becoming* her family.

She was in love with him, which gave him power over her.

By noon, when Cleo strolled down the front steps of the hotel, she felt more herself. She didn't care about a ring, or about marriage. Why should she? Her man of business had informed her this morning that the royal residence Carlton House had asked to have Lewis Commodes fitted from attics to basements. They would now be able to emblazon their products with *By Appointment to the Prince Regent*.

Huzzah!

Jake leapt out of his carriage as she approached, kissed her hand, and steadied her as she stepped onto the mounting box and into the vehicle.

'Where are we going?' she inquired, as the carriage took off at a good clip.

'Green Park.'

'Isn't that home to highwaymen?'

Jake chuckled. 'Not during the day.'

'Robert Walpole himself was robbed in Green Park!' Cleo remembered.

'Who's that?'

'One of our prime ministers.'

'No one has approached me,' Jake said, shrugging. 'The tall trees remind me of American forests. And it's not fashionable.'

Cleo smiled at him. 'That's the lure?'

'It means that I don't have to dress like a fop,' Jake said dryly.

She let her eyes travel over him slowly. Given the warm weather, he wasn't wearing a greatcoat. His clothing wasn't orange, purple, or flowered. It wasn't overly tight. It didn't shimmer or glisten. Instead, he was wearing a gentleman's frock coat, the kind that is designed to indicate status, but also allow for movement.

'I suppose you'll be able to fight off those highwaymen,' she murmured, shifting in her seat because . . .

Because.

His eyes gleamed at her. 'I'll do my best.'

Green Park turned out to be near wilderness, with just a winding road running through it. She looked through the carriage windows, entranced. She'd never seen the great forests of the North, nor even Epping Forest. Tall trees crowded up to the road.

'Oh, look!' she breathed.

He slid over.

'I saw a bluebell meadow through a gap in the trees . . . You missed it.'

'The park includes forty acres of mature trees, with a few meadows sprinkled here or there. They're talking of landscaping it,' Jake said, his voice dropping to a growl. 'I'm stopping that.'

'You are?'

'Got hold of the fellow they contracted,' Jake

said, with satisfaction. 'Name of John Nash. I'm fairly sure that he sees it my way. London is full of sculpted parks with rows of flowers. This one should remain wild.'

'I didn't know you were interested in parks,' Cleo exclaimed.

'I've been coming here whenever I need to stretch my legs and breathe.'

Before Cleo could respond, the carriage rumbled to a stop, and Jake jumped out. A rush of air came in the open doorway, not the neat flowery smell of English hedgerows, but something fresher. Cleo stepped out, just in time to see the coachman and footman disengage the horses and lead them away.

'Where on earth are they going?' she asked, as Jake kicked a stone more securely under one of the front wheels and came around to her.

'To water the horses.' He slung an arm around her shoulder. 'Can you hear anything?'

She cocked her head. 'Starlings.'

'Fighting,' Jake said, nodding. 'They're city birds, but give them a chance and they'll make their way out here and brawl on the treetops.'

'I can't hear anything else,' Cleo said, wonderingly.

'The road stops here, so no one comes this way,' Jake said.

'How did you discover it?'

'I lope around for exercise,' he said, looking slightly uncomfortable. 'Not gentlemanly, but I seem to require more movement than most. I certainly couldn't do it in Hyde Park.'

Cleo blinked, thinking about his expression, and then: 'You don't wear clothing!'

'I wear some clothing,' Jake said, his eyes crinkling at the corners. 'Breeches, but they're made from cotton and not fashionable.'

She smiled and ran her hands around his middle. 'High-waisted?'

'Not particularly,' he said, lowering his head to drop kisses on her forehead.

'I should like to see you running about,' Cleo said, running her hands up his back and then stepping closer to his warmth.

'Any time you wish. Are you hungry?'

Cleo thought. 'A bit. But it's chilly for a picnic.'

'We'll eat in the carriage. Wait a minute.' Jake leaned back in the door. The elms were so tall they seemed to be touching the skies, only hazy rays slanting through their leaves. Their pale pink flowers littered the ground all around them like hearts.

Cleo felt a kind of joy that she hadn't known before, so she took a moment to catalogue it. The forest, the silence, the birds singing now, the . . .

The man.

Jake was leaning in the doorway of his carriage, shoulders braced as he pulled at a mechanism inside the vehicle that was proving recalcitrant. It wouldn't be proper to come behind and wrap her arms around his waist. Or daringly put her hands on his arse.

'*There*,' he growled a moment later, while Cleo was still debating the question.

'What?' she asked.

He turned around with a grin. 'The vehicle is transformed.'

Cleo looked in to find that the bottom part of one of the seats had swung up and the cushion unfolded to create a . . .

'Bed?' she asked in disbelief.

'Look there,' Jake said, a thread of pride in his voice.

'The back of the seat folded down?'

'And slid forward, allowing the legs of the travelers to stretch out during night travel.'

'That is far more restful than my wagon,' Cleo admitted.

Jake picked her up in his arms with one smooth movement and put her inside.

'It's quite comfortable,' Cleo said, pulling her skirts to the side so she could crawl farther inside.

'The mattress is padded with cotton,' Jake said. The light in his eyes said a great deal without words. 'I'm leaving my boots outside the door.'

'I'm hungry,' Cleo said, handing him her slippers.

'I'll feed you.'

He opened a basket that had been strapped to the back of the vehicle and turned out to hold chicken tartlets and sparkling wine. Somehow, bite by bite, Cleo's clothing ended up to the side.

'Now you,' she ordered, when she was down to her chemise.

Jake tore off his shirt and coat, falling back to wrench off his breeches and stockings. He rose on his knees, his erection thumping against his stomach.

Cleo smiled, reaching out. 'I love this part of your body.' Her fingers ran over the lean muscle of his sides, from his arms down to his hips.

Jake frowned, looking down. 'Why?'

'You're so warm under my fingertips, and I can feel muscle just under the skin.' She ran her hands up his sides again. 'I can't explain it, but . . .' She swayed closer and kissed his lips.

'No need to explain,' Jake said, his hands closing around her sides and sliding down her hips, the translucent fabric of her chemise caressing her skin. 'I could never get enough of this curve.' His eyes shone with need and hunger as he began pulling the chemise up her legs.

Cleo smiled as she fell backward onto the padded mattress. She smiled when her chemise disappeared.

But she laughed when Jake reached up and unscrewed the silk roof covering. The mirror glinted in the sunshine coming in the open door. There they were, slightly refracted by the mirrored segments. They lay next to each other staring up at the ceiling.

'If I move quickly to the side, my chin looks even more witchy than you thought when you first met me,' Cleo said, experimenting.

'I don't think that,' Jake said, rolling on his side next to her.

'Well, you did think so. You told me.'

She rolled her head quickly, and his lips missed her cheek and kissed her ear instead.

'I love your chin,' Jake said, rolling on top of her. 'And your eyes, nose, ears, cheekbones, fore-head.' He punctuated every word with a kiss. 'The truth is that I said that about your chin, but I admired it anyway. And your breasts.'

He shifted down so that he could kiss her breast, lavishing attention on her right nipple. Cleo watched the ceiling though she couldn't help a wiggle and a gasp.

'Your chin was an omen, and you bewitched me. Because I love your chin, almost as much as I love your breasts.'

'I love your arse,' Cleo said, still looking up at the roof. 'It's so . . . tight.'

Jake laughed, a chuckle that bounced around the small carriage. But when her hands slid down his back and caressed his rear, amusement dis-appeared from his face. 'If you bewitched me, I accept,' he said, reaching down to shift her legs apart.

Cleo gasped and shivered as his caress slid up her thigh. 'I didn't,' she managed, biting back a moan. Heat torched through her at the touch of his callused, tender fingers.

'I do love your chin,' Jake said, his voice a low growl. He shifted down, kissing it. 'Your neck.

337

Collarbone. Breasts . . . Did I mention breasts?' He moved again, the better to kiss her there.

'Yes,' Cleo whispered. 'You're listing body parts again.'

He said something inarticulate and moved still further down her body. Her heart was beating frantically even before his lips joined his fingers, plying a kind of magic that made her whimper and cry out.

On the ceiling, if she squinted so that her face came together . . . She squeezed her eyes shut. She couldn't feel *that*. Not what she saw on her face. Her body stilled.

Jake added another finger, and the thought slipped from her mind.

Neither of them spoke again until she had stopped shaking and was trying to catch her breath, trying to catch the sensual pleasure spiraling through her body. Opening her eyes again.

'You enchanted me,' Jake rumbled, reaching to a side pocket in the carriage and pulling out a French letter.

'It was mutual,' Cleo whispered. She watched the reflection of his tousled head, the shifting powerful shoulders, his muscled arse.

His hard, thick length slid into her as they came together with as much fierce energy as any wild animal in the park that day.

Finally, they fell asleep together, in a spray of dappled sunshine, and woke to find the light fading. 'We should go back,' Cleo said sleepily. 'Dinner tonight with Merry.'

'There's just enough time,' Jake said. He hunched over her, his lips at her breast.

Cleo looked at the roof, admiring the view. 'I like your carriage.'

She felt Jake's lip curl into a smile against her skin. 'Good.'

CHAPTER TWENTY-EIGHT

Cleo walked into her hotel suite in the late afternoon to find Gussie in a fury, rapidly cooling bath waiting. 'Dinner with the duchess,' Gussie scolded while rushing around the room. 'You're putting aside half mourning for the first time, wearing that blue gown. I wanted three hours . . . four!'

Cleo leaned her head back against the rim of the tub and smiled at the ceiling.

'Just look at you!' Gussie screeched. 'Moonstruck, that's what you are. That great dunce across the corridor is the same. Both of you, playing like truant schoolchildren when you're *bid to dinner with a duchess*!'

Two hours later, when Jake walked into Cleo's drawing room, she turned slowly, deliberately allowing him to have a good glance at her.

The blue dress was a masterpiece. The pearls adorning the bodice gleamed against the sky-blue silk, cleverly sewn in such a way that they drew attention to her breasts. Below the bodice, the silk fell straight to the floor. Every time she moved, her leg was almost visible.

Jake had removed his hat to bow, but his deep voice broke off in the midst of his greeting.

Cleo smiled. Since she had decided to put mourning to the side, she had given up all ambition to be a wallflower, not that it had survived the first ball she attended. She wore a deep red lip salve, a color that flattered her hair. Her ringlets were caught up and pinned with pearls, real ones this time.

Jake took one step toward her and then visibly regained control of himself. The first word out of his mouth was a curse, which made Cleo burst into laughter.

'I want to kiss you. No, damn it, I want to *ravish* you,' Jake said hoarsely. 'But I suppose I can't until after dinner?'

Cleo smiled – and stopped. He so readily assumed that they would come home together, as they would, of course. A question tumbled out of her mouth. 'What are we doing, Jake?'

He stepped close, arms around her, and kissed her just to the right of her shining lips. His arousal throbbed between them, unapologetic and longing. 'I am waiting until you change your mind about marriage.'

Cleo drew in a breath. *She* was waiting for the opal ring.

'Because,' Jake added, 'your disinclination to marry seems to me connected to your disinclination to trust a man with your heart.' He placed a kiss on the other side of her lips.

Jake picked up her pelisse, and Cleo turned about so he could help her put it on, thinking hard. He had a point. Her mother's infidelities had molded her into the woman she was.

'This is merely a suggestion,' Jake whispered. 'You don't need to carry your mother's shame.' He kissed her neck before he tucked the muff into her hands.

'Shame! My mother was never . . . !' Her voice trailed off. True, Julia had never been ashamed.

But Cleo had felt it. Her father had felt it.

Cleo had a terrible suspicion that Jake was right. It had been shaming, of course. All the men whose condemning eyes had met hers after – or before – her mother fluttered away to another lover. A hollow feeling filled her, one that she knew well.

'You are not your mother,' Jake stated. 'You could have hated her, you know. Most people would have.'

'No, Julia was lovable,' Cleo said without hesitation.

'So are you,' Jake said.

The words dropped in the room with a sense of finality.

Was that the problem? 'Of course, I am,' Cleo managed. But thoughts were going dizzily through her head.

'We'll talk about it after dinner,' Jake said. 'Now we either leave for the dinner, or I carry you back into your bedchamber, because you are the most exquisite woman I've ever seen, Cleo, and I want you again. And again.'

A side of her mouth crooked up at that.

His eyes burned at her, and his voice rang with desire – and more.

'I could get on my knees and worship you properly,' Jake said, a note of hopefulness in his voice. 'Your grandfather refused the invitation, so he would never know.'

'I'm actually glad Grandfather is not coming because . . . Do you think this gown is appropriate for dinner with a duchess? It seems rather risqué. I haven't eaten in such exalted company before.'

'You look like your namesake, Queen Cleopatra, and could rule over your country as deftly as she did, a woman who ruled most of Egypt.'

Cleo glanced down at her gown. 'It's not immodest?'

He shook his head. 'Mouthwatering. Delectable. More modest than your friend Yasmin will surely be wearing, and she wore her gowns in Napoleon's imperial court, remember?'

'Yasmin is your friend too,' Cleo objected. Over the last six weeks, they'd spent many evenings together. These days Yasmin taunted Jake with the same friendly attitude with which she addressed Cleo's grandfather.

'She's not certain of me,' Jake said, rather unexpectedly. 'Your Yasmin is a woman who knows a good deal about men. It will take an extraordinary gentleman to—'

343

'Don't you dare say "tame her"!' Cleo flashed.

'I was thinking "love her,"' Jake replied, kissing her nose. He stepped back and deliberately rearranged his erection. 'One of the more irritating aspects of wearing clothing designed by Martha is that she insists on cutting her coats back so far that there is no disguising the disgraceful state of one's breeches.' His hand rubbed slowly over the thick length outlined, rather than disguised, by tight-fitting silk.

Cleo's breath hitched. Then she remembered: Duchess. Dinner. They were already late.

'We must leave,' she said, turning away.

The desire between them felt like a knot, something tangible that could not be easily undone. Her mother's desire had been just puffs of air, in comparison.

CHAPTER TWENTY-NINE

7, Cavendish Square, London
Residence of the Duke of Trent

The Duke and Duchess of Trent lived in a mansion that was, to Cleo's eyes, designed for guests rather than comfort. The imposing front door led to a large entryway, where footmen lined the walls, ready to spring forward and accept a pelisse or greatcoat.

That entry led in turn to an imposing circular reception space where the duchess awaited her guests. The floor was made of inlaid marble that spiraled out in petals from a spherical center, lit by an extraordinary chandelier dripping with crystals.

'No sign of Trent,' Jake observed, when they walked through the door. 'I suspect he didn't make it back from Wales. She must be cross as fire.'

Despite herself, Cleo felt a twinge of self-consciousness. She *knew* Merry. She'd been asked to address her by her first name. She considered them close acquaintances, on the cusp of being close friends.

But tonight a *duchess* stood in the center of the

inlaid marble piece. Her Grace wore a pale green silk gown with a wide lace border, elbow-length sleeves, and a delightful ruffle around the bodice. Over the gown was a translucent apron with a circular hem lined with the same lace. The apron seemed to have been woven with silver thread, as it gleamed under the candelabra.

Merry was taller than most Englishwomen, especially with her chestnut curls piled high on her head. Cleo had pearls in her hair, but the duchess wore diamonds. She didn't need the adornment, though; she glowed. That was the only word for it.

The first time Cleo came to dinner with Merry, it had been an informal, intimate meal.

This was a ducal dinner party.

'Trent promised to arrive in time for dinner. To be precise, his note promised that he would arrive by teatime,' Merry said, after they had exchanged curtsies. 'I shall be very cross at him if he misses dinner entirely. I want him home, and so do the children.' She twinkled at Cleo. 'It's not fashionable for a duke to be such a good father, but I am lucky enough to have married the right man.'

Cleo smiled at her. 'My father was present in my life, and I count it as a blessing.'

'Just look at you!' Merry cried. 'Out of half mourning, I see. Does that gown come from Quimby's? Do you like my gown? Jake talked me into commissioning a gown from Mrs Quimby, and now it is my favorite garment!'

Cleo couldn't help noticing that the duchess's

breasts were entirely covered, whereas her own were practically open to the air. She made up her mind to have a stern talk with Martha. She couldn't go among the *ton* feeling as if she was dressed like a concubine. She wanted to be more proper rather than less.

She and Jake strolled into the drawing room to find twenty or so guests enjoying sherry. They moved directly toward their friends, Yasmin, Madame Dubois, Lilford and his sister.

Of course, Yasmin was seated on one side of a settee and the Earl of Lilford on the far end.

Everyone stood up as they approached; after greetings, Cleo sat down beside Yasmin.

'*Chérie*,' Yasmin said. 'I shall have to visit this costumier of yours, don't I? I assume that she made this ravishing gown. To think that I believed you a gentle dove when we first met!'

Cleo raised an eyebrow. 'A dove?'

'Sweet and lonely, wrapped in soft gray,' Yasmin said. She leaned over and whispered behind her fan. 'Note, I say nothing of the dove's swelling breast, as the poets describe it.'

'My breasts are not *swelling*,' Cleo informed her.

'Merely magnificent,' Yasmin said with a naughty giggle. 'You certainly aren't lonely anymore. You have started a fashion, by the way; I hear that English ladies are looking for American lovers to cure their ennui.'

Cleo felt a cold wave of fear. Did everyone know she had a *lover*? That was—

347

Yasmin touched her on the arm. 'I didn't mean to disconcert you. We French are flippant about such friendships.'

Cleo managed a smile.

'You really can't blame the ladies for their envy,' Yasmin said. 'Tall, rugged, manly. And his accent!'

'You like an American accent?' Cleo asked, accepting a glass of sherry from a footman and immediately taking a large gulp.

'So uncouth,' Yasmin cooed. 'Not . . . fruity, like most English gentlemen. You know what I mean, don't you? Sweet and fruity, like a jam tart.' Her eyes paused on Lilford.

Cleo watched the Earl of Lilford glance at them and turn in the other direction. 'His Lordship's accent does not please?'

Yasmin twitched. 'Just look at the man: satin breeches, a silk waistcoat, a velvet coat, silver buckles. He is a caricature of himself.'

'What do you mean?'

'Overly refined. Perfect in every way. He was a good son to his mother, no doubt.'

'Surely that is a positive thing?'

Cleo was trying to keep the conversation going, but inside she was reminding herself that she could not, under any circumstances, tug her bodice up, as that would draw attention to the fact that her gown was by far the most daring in the room. Even Yasmin was wearing a relatively demure

348

garment. She should have guessed since the dinner was in a ducal mansion.

Over her shoulder, she could see two ladies whispering to each other behind their fans, and she did not think that they would be asking for the name of her modiste. She recognized their expressions from a hundred, a thousand, such glances at her mother.

The realization tied her stomach in knots.

'One must watch for men like Lilford,' Yasmin said, shaking her head. 'The sister rules the roost, I tell you. Lady Lydia will decide who he marries, since their mother is no longer alive. What do you know of Addison's mother?'

'Very little,' Cleo said. She'd gained an impression of a remarkable woman from offhand remarks dropped by both Jake and Merry. Mrs Astor – for, of course, she retained her name when Jake changed his – was apparently cast in the American mold.

'Stay away from her,' Yasmin counseled.

'I am unlikely to meet her, as she lives in Boston.'

'The man adores you. He'll try to drag you across the ocean, if he hasn't already.'

That made Cleo feel a little better. Her confidence seemed to have gone missing. She felt exposed and raw, as if everyone was whispering about commodes and *affaires* behind her back.

Why was she so shaken by the sidelong glances of gossips? Her mother had shrugged those off for years. Besides, Jake obviously meant to propose. He had mentioned marriage several times.

Many times.

She was starting to hate the opal ring, but still . . . It existed. It was up to her to inform Jake that she had no lingering doubts about marriage. She would do that tonight.

Once Cleo was seated in the dining room – Jake on one side and Lilford on the other – Cleo met the gazes of assembled diners with her head high. She would be engaged to Jake the next time they saw her. That would stop the titters.

The thought was interrupted as the butler swept open the large double doors to the room. Down the table, guests began craning their necks to see. Luckily, Cleo was situated in the middle of the table, facing the door, and had a perfect view of the reception area.

All those seated with their backs to the door twisted about as an extremely handsome gentleman strode into view of the door, hair the color of guineas and a jaw as arrogant as that of the American to her right.

'His Grace, the Duke of Trent,' the butler announced.

Merry flew from the head of the table, out the dining room doors, and into her husband's arms. 'Darling, you are just in time!'

The tall duke folded his wife in his arms and kissed her, regardless of the table full of elegantly dressed guests. Their kiss had a core of tenderness that made Cleo swallow hard.

That's what Julia had never achieved: love and desire entwined. It came only with years of marriage, *faithful* marriage.

'Thank goodness we are in a position to watch the performance,' Yasmin hissed from Jake's other side, leaning forward to twinkle at Cleo.

Cleo was about to answer when Jake suddenly pushed back his chair, started to his feet, and strode around the table.

A large woman had strolled into view of the dining room. She had an angular face and silver hair with a delicious hat perched on one side of her head. She swiveled to look through the double doors – and as Jake rounded the table, she held out her arms.

There was no mistaking her profile, albeit rendered in a gentler version. Mrs Astor had arrived in London.

Cleo straightened her back, her heart beating fast.

Jake bowed, kissed both her cheeks, and allowed his mother to catch him in her arms. Mrs Astor's American accent cut like glass through the air.

'Dearest,' she cried. 'The moment I had dear Merry's letter, I took a packet. Can you believe that we made it here in a mere three weeks? When one thinks about how long it used to take to cross the Atlantic, it seems magical.'

Yasmin slid across Jake's empty seat and flipped open her fan. 'Speak of the devil,' she whispered.

Cleo was speechless, watching as if a play was unfolding before her, but Yasmin felt no such self-consciousness. Of course, nothing ever silenced Yasmin.

'The *maman* has heard of you,' she pointed out. 'Her Grace wrote a letter, which seems remarkably indiscreet. Though the duchess *is* American. Perhaps she felt Addison needed a kick to bring himself to the altar. A maternal shove. We have all been expecting to see a ring on your finger for weeks.'

'Please don't speak of that,' Cleo whispered, watching as the duke and duchess turned to greet Mrs Astor. Mrs Astor curtsied to Merry, then caught Her Grace into a tight hug. A ripple of chatter went down the table.

'Hugging a duchess,' Yasmin said irrepressibly. 'We French do not approve. I think we should remain seated, don't you? They are in the entry; we are at the dinner table.'

The butler was hovering, apparently uncertain as to whether he should close the dining room doors once again, but Mrs Astor nodded at him, and he rushed to help her remove her cloak.

'Fascinating,' Yasmin said, raising a sleek, naughty eyebrow. 'Clearly, Her Grace took it on herself to write to Mr Addison's mother and tell the lady that her son was on the brink of making an attachment, so the lady rushed across the ocean to determine whether you are a proper match for her son or not. I would have done the same.'

Cleo's heart was beating so quickly that she heard it in her ears. All down the table, heads were turning, looking at her because they couldn't see through the double doors though whispers had shared Mrs Astor's arrival.

She looked straight ahead, pretending she truly was in the theater and the view through the double doors was merely the opening act of a play. The butler had taken Mrs Astor's cloak and hat, revealing that she was wearing a stylish traveling dress in a flattering peach color, the jacket adorned with a lace cravat, like a feminine version of the neck cloth that all the men were wearing.

Cleo swallowed hard. If only she weren't wearing this particular gown. She gave a despairing thought to the gray dress with a military jacket that Jake despised so much. That dress was a suit of armor. This one?

She had to remember to breathe shallowly so her breasts didn't break free of her gown.

'Wait, where did the duke and duchess go?' Yasmin hissed.

All that could be seen were Jake and his mother speaking.

'Mr Addison doesn't look very happy,' Yasmin observed. 'Her Grace overstepped herself writing such a letter. Men wish to take their time before they commit to matrimony, from what I have observed.'

Mrs Astor's voice rose. In penetrating, high tones, two words were clearly audible: 'opal ring.'

At that, the chatter around the table rose to a crescendo. Cleo could feel a hot flush rising into her cheeks.

Without glancing into the dining room, Jake drew his mother out of eyesight – and, unfortunately, out of earshot.

'Well, well,' Yasmin said, flipping open her fan again. 'I don't care for opals myself. So much better to steer the man toward diamonds. Glancing at your hand, I gather that *Maman* has anticipated the romantic moment when her son will fall on his knees and offer said ring?'

'Hush!' Cleo said, wishing that she hadn't taken her gloves off to eat.

'Or perhaps,' Yasmin said, '*Maman* was asked to bring a family ring, an opal ring, all the way from America. That is somewhat romantic and might excuse the inexpensive stone. You can always buy a diamond later, perhaps for the birth of your first son.'

Cleo took a deep breath, realizing that her hand had curled so tightly around the edge of the table that her knuckles were white. The table was all looking at her again, with speculation this time.

'This evening is unfolding like a farce,' Yasmin said behind her fan. '*The Strumpet and the Opal Ring.*'

'Yasmin!'

'I know, I know.' She sighed. 'Always, I have the

temerity to speak too much, and of the wrong things. But you know, and I know, that these tiresome people have come to that conclusion. Betrothal will change everything.'

'Temerity?' Cleo asked, desperately trying to change the subject. 'What does that mean?'

'The word is the same in French,' Yasmin said. '*Témérité*. Audacity or recklessness. Madame Dubois will tell me that I regularly overstate the case, and I am simply boring.' Her smile indicated that she didn't give a fig what her chaperone thought of her chatter. 'Clearly the opal is a family heirloom, which Addison's mother brought to this country so that her son could fall to his knees and slip that priceless gem on your finger.'

The butler appeared again and bowed. 'Please continue to dine. The duke and duchess will join you in a moment.' He raised his hand, and three footmen streamed around him into the room, bearing platters of food.

Two more footmen removed the silver epergne from the middle of the table and then eased two guests seated near the head of the table down so that they could insert two more chairs.

'I didn't know you were so romantic,' Cleo managed, picking up her fork just so she'd have something to do. She poked at a slice of pheasant and shook her head when a footman offered her asparagus.

'Never will you see someone with less romance in her soul than I,' Yasmin announced. 'Except perhaps the objectionable earl. He has the soul of a rat, that one.'

'That seems unnecessarily harsh,' Cleo said, hoping that Lilford couldn't hear Yasmin. But when she glanced to her left, she met cold gray eyes suggesting that his hearing was as excellent as that of any rodent.

Yasmin elbowed her. 'They're back. Look at Addison's face.'

Cleo couldn't stop herself; she looked at the door again. She instantly felt sick. Jake was incensed: angrier than she'd ever seen him, including during their first meeting. Even from where she sat, she could see rage in his eyes as he looked at her, along with – could it be guilt? An apology?

'Furious,' Yasmin supplied, continuing her narration of events. 'He didn't want *Maman* to bring the ring. He wanted to choose the perfect stone for you himself.' She giggled.

The duke and duchess walked back into view from the door, accompanied by an extraordinarily pretty woman with dark ringlets, a small, upturned nose, and rosy cheeks.

Cleo felt as if she'd been turned to stone.

Yasmin fell silent, but she wound an arm around Cleo's waist.

The young lady was wearing an adorable, pink-striped traveling dress, high in the neck with – somewhat incongruously – an enameled cow's head pinned to her shoulder. Jake, his mother, the duke and duchess clustered about her. She held out her hand to Jake. He bent to kiss it.

Yasmin broke into a quiet, vicious stream of French curses. Not that Cleo knew the meaning of those words, but even in her numb state, she recognized the intent. Down the table, heads were turning so rapidly that she was reminded of a puppet show. You couldn't even label the conversation 'chatter.' It was more like a storm of language, all of it punctuated by hard looks at Cleo.

'We French are very cynical by nature,' Yasmin hissed. 'However, I don't mind telling you, Cleo, that I have a bad feeling.'

'She looks like a nice person,' Cleo said through numb lips. Jake had straightened and was speaking to the lady.

Yasmin's arm tightened comfortingly. 'It is awkward, yes?' she said, bending close to speak into Cleo's ear. 'When the mistress meets the wife or future wife, in this case. Believe me, I saw it happen so many times in Paris. You mustn't show what you feel. Not one *iota*, Cleo. I believe that's the same word in English as in French.'

Cleo felt as if she couldn't get a breath. Her heart was hammering, and she felt ill. 'I would like to leave,' she whispered.

'No!' Yasmin snapped. 'You will not be defeated by this girl with the cow's head on her bosom. You will hold your head high. A show of weakness is fatal.'

'It's not a contest,' Cleo said, feeling sickened. 'That opal ring Mrs Astor mentioned, Yasmin? He's had it for weeks. My maid told me.'

'*Bâtard!*' Yasmin hissed.

'It appears that he planned to give it to someone else.' Time had slowed down. It seemed to be taking an hour for the duke and duchess, Jake and Mrs Astor, and his . . . whatever she was . . . to stop chatting.

Cold settled over Cleo's bare shoulders and she glanced down at her bodice before she caught herself. She was wearing the gown of a mistress.

Her mother's gown.

'She is boring,' Yasmin hissed. '*The Heifer and the Opal Ring* will be a failure, I promise you. The audience will throw rotten vegetable marrows at the stage.'

The group turned to walk into the dining room. To Cleo's left, Lilford rose to his feet, and as if that was a signal, the entire dinner party jumped to their feet and rushed toward the door to greet the new guests.

'Come,' Yasmin ordered, standing up. 'Chin high!'

Instead of taking his sister's arm, Lilford stepped toward Cleo. 'May I?' he asked, offering his forearm.

'Yes, you may,' Yasmin replied, shoving Cleo toward the earl. 'I'm not speaking to you, but this is a good moment to break the rule. Stand before me.' She ducked behind Lilford's broad body. 'Just a moment.'

Cleo felt somewhat bewildered. She was a strong,

358

confident woman. So why did she feel so vulnerable simply because a young woman walked into the house? A woman whom apparently Jake and his mother knew?

Logically, she had no reason to believe that this woman had been given an opal ring. Or promised an opal ring.

Behind Lilford's back, Yasmin pulled down her sleeves. With a sharp wiggle, she rearranged her gown so that her breasts were on the verge of falling out of her bodice. Even more precariously arranged than Cleo's.

'Oh, Yasmin,' Cleo said, managing a lopsided smile. 'You needn't be a fallen woman along with me.'

'I have never liked prudish women,' Yasmin said, stepping from behind Lilford. She glanced up at him. 'Or men.'

The earl ignored her, offering his arm to Cleo again. Cleo caught Madame Dubois's eyes and saw distinct sympathy there. A pulse of humiliation went through her, followed by a streak of disbelief. This couldn't be happening. This afternoon, in the carriage, the things Jake had said to her . . . He loved her.

But a sickening thought followed: if he had made a prior commitment to this young lady, it wouldn't matter if he was in love. Perhaps he had promised her that opal ring, which explained why she, Cleo, had received a bear's tooth – but not a betrothal ring.

Thank goodness her grandfather had declined his invitation to dinner.

Cleo felt as if cotton wool were blocking her throat, making it hard to breathe, as if she were suffocating. The world narrowed as the dinner party stepped forward in pairs to be ceremoniously introduced to the duke's new guests.

Some of the attention diverted from Cleo after the revelation that Jake had a name different from his mother's; Cleo could hear guests speculating about Mrs Astor's remarriage as they returned to their seats. 'But no,' someone hissed, 'he was introduced as Mr Astor Addison!'

They fell completely silent, watching with curiosity as Cleo, Yasmin, and the earl moved forward to be introduced, following Madame Dubois and Lady Lydia. Cleo found herself clinging to Lilford's arm.

Mrs Astor and Jake were speaking to Madame Dubois, so Merry introduced them to 'Mrs Astor's traveling companion, Miss Frederica Cabot, my cousin, and a close family friend.'

Miss Cabot smiled prettily, and her eyes rested for just a second on Cleo's bosom. She blinked when Yasmin stepped forward.

'Are you a family friend of long standing?' Yasmin asked, once curtsies had been exchanged.

'Yes, I am,' Miss Cabot said serenely. She didn't look the slightest bit disconcerted to be coming straight from a boat to a ducal dinner party. In fact, Cleo had the idea that very little would upset

360

the young lady. 'We've known each other for many years.' She smiled. 'Since I attended one of Mr Astor's birthday parties in a cow's costume.'

'How charming,' Yasmin drawled. 'But I understood his name is Mr Addison.'

Miss Cabot giggled. 'I always forget that! I've known him by his father's name for my entire life.'

'My cousin showed an extraordinary gift for mooing at the age of ten,' Merry put in.

Cleo shot a glance at Jake, standing beside his mother. His face was tight, closed, eyelids low over eyes that gleamed with what looked like cold anger.

'A cow costume is certainly original,' Lilford said. The earl's voice and face were so controlled that Cleo never knew quite what he was thinking, but she had the general idea that he disapproved of this entire situation.

Miss Cabot gave him a tranquil smile. 'The English are far more formal than we Americans. Your evening garments are all so beautiful.' She glanced down at her pink stripes. 'I'm travel-worn after weeks at sea. American modistes are better at cow costumes than evening gowns.'

Her little nose wrinkled as she laughed. She wasn't only pretty. She was *nice*.

Cleo was swept by a feeling of utter weariness.

Suddenly, she remembered sitting by the fire with Jake, when he first walked into her dining room wearing livery. He had told her that he meant to marry someone serene and domestic, in the near future.

Here she was.

Ready to slip on the opal ring.

Mrs Astor turned away from Madame Dubois.

Cleo straightened her back, reminding herself that she was a veteran of mortifying situations. She offered Mrs Astor a reserved smile and a deep curtsy. The lady was broad-shouldered and tall, with a distinctly American air of competence about her.

'Amazing ships they have these days!' Mrs Astor cried, once introductions had concluded. 'Can you believe that we embarked from New York harbor less than a month ago?'

Lilford instantly picked up this conversational gambit, though he didn't move from his close stance beside Cleo. He was one of the most prudish men in all London, according to Yasmin's scornful reckoning, and yet he showed no reluctance to stand next to a woman whom most of the party had surely labeled a strumpet, if not worse.

Cleo could feel Jake's eyes on her. Was she being a coward by not meeting his eyes? Perhaps she was. In the core of her heart, she didn't believe that he had consciously betrayed her.

Everything in her fought that idea.

He wouldn't. He was honorable. He had planned to marry her . . .

Except it seemed he had also planned to marry Miss Cabot, and the lady clearly knew his intentions, because here she was, having crossed the entire ocean the better to accept the opal ring that everyone, including his mother, knew about. No wonder he hadn't given it to Cleo; he'd bought it for another woman.

There was nothing he could say or do that could make this better. With that thought, she raised her head and met his eyes. *She* had nothing to be embarrassed about.

She could read any number of emotions in his eyes: rage, irritation . . . a touch of panic? No shame. Cleo let her smile – her friendly, polite smile – tell him what she couldn't put in words.

Their relationship was over.

Humiliation was a familiar emotion. She'd heard it described as unbearable, and she'd thought it so when she was eight and her mother paraded a lover before the one friend she'd had of her own age – whom she never saw again.

Suddenly she realized that what she felt then and now was truly bewilderment: the incomprehension a child feels watching her father leave the room as her mother strolls in the front door, a handsome actor at her heels.

A child unable to understand why her mother finds her father insufficient.

Looking back, her father was broken, perhaps by humiliation. Perhaps because he loved a woman incapable of love.

But she, Cleo, was still bewildered. Was *she* not enough? Logic told her that Jake had no idea that his mother and Miss Cabot had embarked a boat to travel to England. But this situation explained why he hadn't offered marriage.

Remotely, she was aware of a tearing pain in her heart, as if she'd fallen off a cliff and landed on sharp rocks. He was just a man, like any other man. A wonderful man, and one whom she had loved.

But she would survive. Just as she would survive the rest of this horrific dinner party.

The strength of that conviction carried her through back to the table, where they all sat down for the dessert course, the duchess having persuaded Miss Cabot and Mrs Astor to join them.

There was some pleasure in showing no reaction at all to Miss Cabot's arrival. She made certain to laugh and chat with dinner companions on both sides – Jake and Lilford – as if Jake were no more than an acquaintance and Lilford a suitor.

Jake didn't try to say anything quietly to her, or take her hand, not that she would have welcomed it.

No, that was untrue: some vulnerable corner of her heart would have welcomed it. Instead, he sat beside her, face blank, and contributed to a lively discussion of the merits of Indian versus Chinese tea leaves, without once mentioning coffee.

That thrilling discussion was followed by the ladies retiring to the drawing room while the gentlemen remained at the table to drink port. The men all rose with the ladies, of course.

Lilford bowed, his eyes sliding from Jake's face

as if he'd caught sight of a cockroach. 'Miss Lewis, I hope you will do the honor of allowing me to escort you home in the absence of Viscount Falconer.'

'Thank you,' Cleo managed.

Entering the drawing room, she didn't hesitate. She was a veteran of women's gossip. The only way to thwart its cruelest variations was by direct action. Julia had blithely ignored the ill humor with which women from matrons to governesses viewed her love life.

So Cleo sat down beside Miss Cabot on the settee and complimented her dress, and then, for good measure, her enameled cow pin, which depicted, it turned out, a Hereford.

'I am wearing it in honor of the United Kingdom,' Miss Cabot told Cleo and Yasmin earnestly. 'This breed of cattle originated in Herefordshire, in the mid 1700s and has not yet been introduced into America.'

'You must be – you are not joking,' Yasmin exclaimed.

'I find cattle interesting, but I am well aware that few share my interest.' In short, Miss Cabot truly was just as nice as she seemed.

Cleo reserved judgment about Jake's mother. Just now, Mrs Astor was informing a skeptical group of English ladies that the Astors were one of the foremost families in America. 'I'm happy to say that inheritance taxes were repealed, and thus have not devastated family wealth, as has sadly happened to so many excellent families on this side of the Atlantic.'

'I see,' one lady said, her tone a nice mix of horror and disdain.

'Miss Cabot's family is even more prominent,' Mrs Astor added.

At that moment, Merry clapped her hands and two footmen spread out through her guests, giving each a small, elegant porcelain bowl and a silver spoon. 'We generally drink tea once we leave the men to their port,' she said brightly, looking around at the circle of female guests. 'But tonight, I wished to have a special sweet, just for us: pine-apple!'

Julia hadn't spoken in weeks, but she piped up at that. *I gave you your first bite of pineapple at the age of seven,* she said with a giggle. *I don't believe a lady should deny herself pleasure.*

Cleo found herself smiling down at the pine-apple. She remembered that day quite clearly; her mother had a gift for creating joyous celebrations. With time, she would remember those moments and not others.

'As you may know,' Merry was saying, 'we have several pineapple stoves at our country estate. What you may *not* know is that I created a tremen-dous scandal when I first arrived in this country by requesting a piece of pineapple that had been rented for a dinner party.'

Miss Cabot giggled and said, 'Rented? Who would rent a piece of fruit? That's absurd!'

Mrs Astor cleared her throat. 'Frederica, dear, we must remember that different customs can be found in different countries.'

'There are pineapple rental stores in London,' Yasmin told her. 'Wait until you see a gentleman strolling down the street with a pineapple under his arm in an absurd bid to prove his status.'

The girl blinked at her, her mouth a perfect circle. 'You must be joking.'

Merry answered that. 'Frederica, a pineapple here in Britain costs as much as a two-year-old steer.'

'No!'

'Indeed. I created a horrendous scandal by eating one,' Merry said. 'My gauche manners were discussed far and wide.' She waved her spoon. 'Please, everyone, eat your pineapple. Thanks to our pineapple stoves, the estate produces enough so that I could open my own store.'

Cleo spooned up a segment. Frederica was still staring in shock. As Cleo watched, she whispered, 'A two-year-old steer!'

'The experience gave me a profound dislike of scandal,' Merry said, smiling around the circle of ladies.

For the first time, Cleo saw a steely glint in Merry's eye. Suddenly they were being addressed by a *duchess*, a lady at the very pinnacle of society.

'Given my unfortunate experience, I would be very sorry if I discovered that any unpleasant gossip *ever* arose from a dinner party of mine,' Her

Grace said softly. 'Naturally, those who blathered would never be invited to my house for any occasion, ever again.'

Her eyes swept the circle and landed on Cleo. 'My dear Miss Lewis,' she called gaily, transforming with the flick of an eyelash into a charming, friendly lady, 'what do *you* think of pineapple?'

Cleo smiled at her. 'I am so grateful to eat it . . . My mother loved pineapple, and it is a joy to remember her pleasure in the fruit.'

'My aunt, who was as dear to me as a mother, loved hot chocolate drinks!' cried one of the very matrons who had sneered at Cleo five minutes earlier.

After that the conversation turned to mothers and their preferences.

'You must be very tired,' Miss Cabot said sometime later, rising and moving solicitously toward Mrs Astor.

'Darling Frederica is such a mother hen,' Mrs Astor exclaimed. 'The captain of the ship and I had fascinating discussions that could have gone on all night, except that she was forever forcing me to rest.'

'We must all get our beauty sleep,' Yasmin said brightly, bounding to her feet and reaching out her hand to Cleo. 'Come along, dear.'

As the ladies spilled into the reception area from the drawing room, the gentlemen rose from the dining table and came to meet them.

A footman stepped forward with Cleo's cape,

but before she could take it, Jake's large hands took it away and wrapped it around her shoulders. She fastened its pearl buttons slowly, aware of all the eyes on them.

With an effort, she curled her mouth into a smile. 'The Earl of Lilford has offered to escort me home, Mr Addison. I know you'll want to spend time with your mother.'

'Miss Lewis,' the earl said from behind her shoulder. Lilford's eyes were piercing cold when he looked at Jake.

'I will—' Jake said.

Cleo lifted a gloved hand. 'No.'

He caught her arm. 'I'm not marrying her, you goose!' His voice was low enough to escape the earshot of most of the guests except for her and Lilford.

Cleo raised an eyebrow. 'I believe the lady may be surprised to hear that.'

'You're jealous,' he said slowly. A smile spread across his face.

Cleo looked daggers at the man. If she'd had an actual dagger, she might have . . . might have damaged his waistcoat, just to make a point. Instead, she turned up her nose and swept down the corridor, deliberately wrapping her hand around Lilford's arm and snuggling close to him.

CHAPTER THIRTY

Watching Cleo, *his* Cleo, get into a carriage with another man was a terrible feeling. Jake felt an enraged howl rise in his chest.

He'd been such an utter fool.

Damn the engagement ring he commissioned – and damn Rundell & Bridges as well. How long did it take to fashion a ring? He should have bought a diamond the size of a turnip weeks ago, fallen to his knees, and begged Cleo to marry him – nay, *insisted* that she elope with him.

The days had passed like pearls on a string, each one invaluable, bookended with breakfast and evening with the woman he loved. In the night they turned toward each other and made love half asleep, murmuring, groaning . . . loving. Time passed without notice.

His fingers curled as if he could draw her back to him.

Cleo's hood slipped as she climbed into the carriage, and she was so vivid against the night sky: her hair like captured firelight, eyes sparking with anger, cheeks flushed.

370

He felt reduced to an inarticulate, ungentlemanly animal. A rough man, with no polished veneer. A man who might lose the only thing that he wanted in life.

His jaw hardened.

No, he wouldn't lose her.

Lilford's condemning look had made him feel like an ass. Except he had never said a word about marriage to Frederica. Not a word.

But his mother . . .

God only knew what his mother had told Frederica's father, because here the girl was, in a different country, chaperoned by a woman who must have presented herself as a future mother-in-law.

He wouldn't marry Frederica Cabot if she were the only woman on the face of the earth. It wasn't the first time that anger at his mother coursed through his veins: her self-assurance was such that she trampled over people's wishes.

An uneasy feeling clenched his stomach as he walked back into the mansion.

'What lovely friends you have,' Frederica said pleasantly, when he entered the drawing room.

Jake's brows drew together. Had she completely missed the drama? The uneasiness on his mother's face? Her hostess's frown? The startled inquiry that the duke gave his wife? The sharp whispers behind fans?

The Duke of Trent had returned home to a dinner party that had fallen prey to a tornado.

371

'Yes, I do,' he stated.

He hadn't had the chance to say more to his mother than a fierce declaration that the opal ring would never go to Frederica. She was regarding him now with the same expression she'd worn after he dropped the name Astor: disbelief and anger.

'You betray your dead father and me,' she had told him, back then.

Funny. He would have thought he honored his father by refusing to profit from a trade that had led to his death. Though his mother preferred to think that his father died in his sleep. It was too painful for her to acknowledge that he was addicted to a medicine that took his life. 'He simply fell asleep, so peacefully,' she had told everyone at the funeral.

Frederica was trying to coax his mother to go to bed. He watched, cynical and tired as Frederica played a role that she'd chosen for herself. Merry took one look at the three of them and whisked Frederica upstairs, her husband in tow, leaving his mother staring at Jake.

'I was rash in taking the boat,' she said, surprising him. 'I read Merry's letter and rushed to speak to Frederica's father; I should have written you for confirmation.'

'You spoke to Mr Cabot? You had *no right*, whether I confirmed my plans or no. That was for me to do.'

His mother frowned. 'Was there no opal ring, bought for Miss Frederica Cabot?'

'No one would consider the purported ring an appropriate reason for you to drag that woman across the ocean with the promise of marriage,' he said grimly. 'I have never raised the question of marriage with Frederica, or even kissed the woman. I have the right to choose my own spouse. In point of fact, the opal ring is no longer in my possession. I gave it to Merry.'

'A few months ago, you were obviously considering Frederica,' she retorted. 'We all knew that. She was a good choice, from an excellent family. If you don't want to be an Astor, you could be a Cabot!'

He stilled. 'I would never be a Cabot, no matter whom I marry.'

'One of America's first families.'

'I am an *Addison*.'

'You don't understand how difficult it has been to explain to everyone why you dropped the name that your father gave you at birth,' his mother said shrilly. 'The name that is respected everywhere.'

'Not by me.' He folded his arms across his chest. 'Do you really wish to have this conversation again, Mother?'

She narrowed her eyes. 'We never really had a conversation, Jacob. You announced your decision to change your name and while I was still thinking – God forgive me – that I was glad that your father was gone and didn't know your decision, you walked out.'

'Is there something else you wish to say?'

373

'I married your father because he was an Astor!' she shouted. 'Him! A man who wanted nothing more out of life than to prance back and forth across the stage. I married into the Astor family so that my son could inherit the name!'

Jake took a deep breath. He'd grown up in an unhappy home, so this information was unsurprising. 'Yet you want me to marry a woman for the same reason? For a name? A name, by the way, that my children wouldn't share.'

Something in her face alerted him, and he had to stop himself from shooting across the room and catching her shoulders. 'What did you do?'

'Who would marry an Addison?' she demanded, her bottom lip pushing out. 'Calling yourself Astor Addison is just a bandage over the wound.'

'I do not see it as a wound. I chose to become an Addison.'

'I understand that you don't want to be an Astor. Your uncle was hurt, but he acknowledged your right to choose a different name.'

'I am aware,' Jake said. He'd had a difficult conversation with his uncle before he left for Britain. Astor understood his objections to the opium trade, but he didn't share them. It didn't mean they stopped loving each other.

'Mr Cabot, Frederica's father, thought—'

'Mr Cabot thought, or you thought?' Jake barked.

His mother's eyes fired. 'Are you implying that I, as a woman, don't have the ability to think?'

'No. I am implying that Mr Cabot, whom I've

374

known since I was a child, would never have come up with a plan that I might change my name to Cabot. Take my wife's name, in essence.'

'People do it all the time,' his mother said. 'When a man inherits a title from an uncle, for example, it's common to adopt the name of that family from whom he inherits.'

'I am not inheriting a title.'

'Ah, but Mr Cabot—'

'I am well aware that Frederica is an heiress, Mother. I do not believe that Mr Cabot came up with the idea that I might change my name yet again. I think that *you* did, in your quest to make certain that, given I refuse to be an Astor, I would remain a member of one of the first families.'

'Not you,' she said. 'Your children. Your *children*, Jacob.'

'My children will be English,' he said, feeling the rightness of the decision settle on him like a cloak. 'I will always love my native country, but I am in love with an Englishwoman. I will settle here, and my children will be English Addisons.'

'Which one of those women you were sitting with at dinner?' his mother barked.

He raised an eyebrow. 'Does it matter?'

'Yes, it does.'

'My marriage is not your decision, Mother.' He said it gently, but it had to be said.

'I learned at dinner that Miss Lewis is the owner of Lewis *Commodes*.' The distaste in her face spoke

375

for itself. 'One of the ladies told me that the other one, Lady Yammer, was a mistress to Napoleon!'

'Lady Yasmin,' he said. 'Her mother, not herself, is an intimate of the emperor.'

Her eyes bulged with horror. 'Which one?' she repeated.

'I will not marry Frederica Cabot, Mother. I don't know what you or her father told her about this improvident trip to London, but I shall inform her of that fact myself.'

His mother seemed to crumple into herself. 'I haven't said anything to her.'

'Nothing?'

'I would have, but she never asked! She's a remarkably uncurious creature. Her father said in my presence that I had agreed to take her to London for a visit, and she smiled and said she would direct her maid to pack her trunk.'

A cynical thought drifted through Jake's mind. Frederica Cabot was exactly what he had believed he wanted in a wife: the opposite of his devious, impetuous mother.

His mother rose and shook out her skirts. She wasn't the sort of woman who would dab her eyes and show outward signs of distress, but he knew she was heartbroken.

He walked over to her. 'I'm sorry to have disappointed you, Mother.'

'I just want your children to have a name they can be proud of.'

'They will be proud to be Addisons,' he said.

'And who knows? Maybe one of them will change her name to Lewis and be equally proud of that – and of the company her mother runs.'

She managed a lopsided smile. 'I had planned to put Lewis Commodes into the house in Newport, to see whether they are worth the exorbitant price.'

He knew a peace offering when he heard it, so he folded her in his arms. 'I will live in England, Mother.'

'It's less than a month on the packet, in this direction at least,' she said, holding him tightly. 'Besides, I shall remain in London for some months. I must find Frederica a husband. I cannot possibly bring her home without a worthy suitor at her side.'

'It shouldn't be difficult,' Jake said. 'She's pretty enough, and she does have a fortune.'

His mother muttered something.

He stepped back. 'What did you say?'

'Britain is the home of the Hereford cow,' she said, and then started laughing. 'Frederica will be perfectly agreeable.'

CHAPTER THIRTY-ONE

Cleo rode back to Germain's with her fists curled, refusing to allow tears to fall. By the time she began climbing the stairs to her suite, she no longer felt like crying.

Miss Cabot's arrival was a fact. Jake had been entangled with her in some way, before he traveled to London, though Cleo doubted there was a spoken agreement. A ring had been purchased, certainly.

Yet *no one* made Jake do anything he didn't choose.

Before Jake, she'd never heard of a man changing his name on ethical grounds, but Jake had. Lewis had never been a name that meant more to the world than a label attached to the word 'Commode.'

Astor, though?

Mrs Astor clearly considered herself a princess, a titled person, due to her name: Mrs *Astor*.

Which her son had discarded.

All of which suggested that Jake would not marry Miss Cabot.

She saw no reason to call his promises to her into question. Miss Cabot would maintain her bovine serenity until the morning, when Jake would inform her that he had no plans to marry her or give her an opal ring.

After which, he would come to Cleo.

Jake's kippers and coffee were as good as, or better than, any opal ring. He loved her – not the way her mother loved men, but with steadfast loyalty.

Still, Miss Cabot's arrival had ruined her evening. Ruined her memory of their picnic in Green Park. Made her feel angry, and petty, and jealous.

She woke at dawn. Every morning, Jake walked across the corridor and found her waiting for him at the breakfast table. He had taken her to bed, night after night, and she certainly hadn't protested.

But seeing another woman's calm assurance that Jake was hers? The thought made Cleo's gut burn.

She rang for Gussie.

'You wish to go for a drive at this hour?' Gussie asked, gaping at her.

'I shall take the caravan, actually. Could you please ask O'Kelly to bring it around the front?'

'Out where?' Gussie cried. 'Where are we going?'

'*I* am going,' Cleo said. 'I shall go for a drive. A picnic. Please request a hamper and have it loaded into the caravan.'

'What happened last night?' Gussie asked. 'You weren't yourself when you came home. And . . .' She waved her hand. 'Mr Addison kept to his chambers.'

379

'No reason he shouldn't,' Cleo said, feeling very glad that Gussie hadn't accompanied her to the dinner party last night. If her dresser had even laid eyes on Frederica Cabot, there would have been an explosion.

'You're not waiting for kippers,' Gussie said slowly.

'I am tired of fish. And coffee.'

Gussie narrowed her eyes. 'That there opal ring didn't make an appearance?'

'No.'

'Then you're right,' Gussie cried, dropping the corset she was holding and rushing over to tug on the bell. 'You won't be here when he comes by. You don't wait on any man's call, not the way you would iffen you were his lady wife.'

'I should like to spend the day alone,' Cleo said.

'That's right,' Gussie said. 'No opal ring, no frolicking. There's that earl, Leluck or whatever. I've seen the way he looks at you.'

'I don't want him,' Cleo said.

She didn't want anyone other than Jake, no matter how he made her heart ache. No matter how afraid she was, underneath, that he would choose the placid American lady.

It only took an hour for Gussie to put Cleo into a walking dress, round up a picnic basket, and have the caravan brought around in front of the hotel. She bundled her into a pelisse, pressing a sachet of tea into her hand. 'The tea in the caravan will be old.'

380

'Thank you,' Cleo said, turning to give her a hug. 'I don't know what I'd do without you.'

'Wait!' Gussie cried. 'Where are you going?'

Cleo just smiled at her. 'I'm not sure myself.'

'But how am I going to direct Mr Addison to find you?' Gussie wailed as Cleo walked through the door.

You won't, Cleo said to herself, smiling.

Her mother's caravan was a trim little wagon that shone in the early morning sunshine. It was picked out in yellow stripes with blue trim and with rose-red window frames. The wheels were painted gold, and perched above them the caravan seemed rather bulbous, as if it swelled on the sides like a bubble.

'Ready to go, miss,' her coachman, O'Kelly, said, touching his hat. 'A nice drive around the neighborhood?'

'I should like to go to Green Park,' she told him. 'I visited there yesterday, and I glimpsed a meadow covered in bluebells. I do believe that we could drive into the middle of it without disturbing the peace.'

'I know where the park is, but I've heard it's dangerous. There aren't any constables assigned to that park,' he said, frowning.

'No one will attempt to rob us if we park in the middle of a meadow,' Cleo said. 'You and Chumley are enough to protect me, I'm sure.'

'I do have me blunderbuss,' he allowed. 'But, miss, I just don't know—'

'I'd like to drink a cup of tea in the open air, as I used to when my mother was alive.'

His face cleared. 'By way of a memory for the missus? Now that's a lovely thought. She did like a cup of tea in the afternoon, didn't she?'

'I thought I'd spend the day in the meadow, if it wouldn't bore you too much, O'Kelly. I miss the country.'

'It will be a pleasure.'

When they reached the bluebell meadow, O'Kelly turned the caravan off the dirt road and drove straight into the middle. Black poplars shared space with oaks, hawthorns, and silver birches surrounding the irregularly shaped meadow. The trees were all crowned with new green; beneath their shade, bluebells created misty blue fingers stretching into the herby grass.

O'Kelly helped Cleo down from the caravan and set up her lounging chair, table, and umbrella in the shade of the wagon, as it was a warm, sunny morning. 'I'll take the horses over into the shade. I'll brew a cuppa there too and bring you some in a jot or two.'

Cleo waited until he and Chumley were tucked away under the trees, enjoying a pipe and strong tea, before she pushed her chair aside and lay down on her back in the grass on the far side of the wagon. She was wearing the plainest of Martha's walking dresses, made from a pale blue linen that echoed the high expanse of sky.

Far above her, two starlings chased after each

other, dizzily wheeling through the sky. Unlike meadows in 'better' areas such as Hyde Park, no one had scythed this lawn, and the weedy grass prickled her back in a companionable way. Since she had happened to lie down next to a patch of purple goat's beard, she plucked some young shoots and chewed on them.

After a while, she propped herself on one elbow and drank her cup of cooling tea, brewed to a dark brown that resembled dirt.

Stitchwort was blooming around the wagon wheels, so she pulled a flower and tried a game her mother taught her, *He loves me, he loves me not* . . . Apparently, he loved her not, so Cleo carefully chose a flower with five rather than six petals and brought the whole thing to a better conclusion before she nibbled on the stem.

He loved her.

Jake loved her.

If he realized where she was and came to find her, he loved her. If he didn't come . . .

That was silly.

She propped up her head on a patchwork pillow made of bright scraps of Parisian silk that she'd stitched together when she was fourteen, and began to reread *Sense and Sensibility*, one of her favorite novels. An hour later, she sat up, pulled the pins out of her hair, shook all her curls out, and made a simple braid down her back. An hour after that, she toed off her slippers, untied her garters, and rolled down her stockings. Her bare toes curled into prickly grass and cool earth.

As the sun made its way overhead, Chumley took down the large wicker basket strapped to the back of the caravan and laid out an excellent picnic. He declined to join her, though, saying that he and O'Kelly were eating onion and pickle sandwiches, which was just what he wanted, but even his own wife didn't want to be around him after he ate one.

Cleo rolled on her side and ate delicacies spiced by an occasional nibble of purple goat's beard. She was happy. She would have a happy life even if Jake didn't manage to extricate himself from Miss Cabot.

Still, she felt a kipper-shaped tinge of anxiety that made her reach for the bottle of wine Chumley had uncorked and splash some into her teacup.

He *would* come.

It would be disappointing if he didn't.

She should have just told Gussie where she was going. It wasn't fair to –

Then she saw him walking across the grassy weeds: tall, broad-shouldered, striding in an indefinably American fashion, as if he had a mountain to cross before supper. He had a bunch of flowers in his hand that surely came from Lulu.

She didn't move, just lay on her side, head propped on her hand.

The relief she felt spread through her entire body like a flame. She had known he was coming – or she had told herself that she was certain – but actually seeing him made a difference. The world seemed to fall into place, the sun brighter, the stitchwort flowers a dazzling white, the birdsong joyous.

Jake walked right up to her, looking tired but firm. 'You left this morning before your posies arrived, so I brought them with me.' He sank down on his heels and offered the flowers. Frilly pink tulips nestled among lilacs in two different shades of purple, tied with a satin ribbon.

'Lulu has outdone herself.'

'She grows hopeful that my dogged persistence and her floral offerings will overcome my unfortunate looks. Are you still angry?'

Cleo sat up. 'Not unless you have a fiancée.'

His mouth eased. 'I have you.'

'I am not your fiancée,' she said pointedly.

'I bought an opal ring for Frederica, but I gave it to Merry a few weeks ago, although she had already written to my mother by that point. And my mother is impetuous, as you likely realized.'

'*You* didn't tell Mrs Astor about the ring?' For some reason that felt important.

He shook his head. 'I bought it the day before I met you. After that?' He shrugged. 'I realized I had made a mistake, and gave it away.'

'I don't like the fact you bought a ring for Frederica,' Cleo said, looking down at the bundle of flowers. 'My reaction made me feel very small.'

'I don't like the fact you were betrothed to another man for two months.'

'The ring made me feel jealousy, a lowly emotion,' Cleo admitted. 'Especially since Miss Cabot is very peaceful. Pretty too.'

'Even hearing of your fiancé made me feel homicidal,' he countered, letting out a mock growl in the back of his throat. 'Damn it, Cleo, I missed you last night.' He stood up and drew her to her feet. 'I missed you this morning. I woke up in the night, and you were nowhere in reach.'

Words caught in her throat.

'If Frederica is peaceful, you are darling. *My* darling.' He leaned forward and brushed a kiss on her mouth. Then he reached into his pocket and brought out a velvet box. 'Will you marry me, Cleo? Will you be mine, to have and to hold, 'til death do us part? In England, I might add, not America.'

Cleo swallowed the lump from her throat, ignoring the box for the moment. 'Jake,' she said huskily.

He took an unsteady breath. 'Cleo. My Cleo.'

'I . . . I agree,' she said, unable to find the right words, the ones in her heart.

He stepped forward, his arms encircling her. 'Did you just agree to marry me? I want to be certain.'

'Yes,' she whispered. She took a deep breath. 'I love you, Jake. I want to be with you every day, for the rest of my life. I – I love you so much more than anything else.'

Jake's mouth eased into a smile. 'I will love you for the rest of my life, Cleopatra Lewis.'

She touched him on the cheek, then put her arms around his neck. 'You truly don't mind staying in England? Can we leave the city now and then, perhaps live in Paris, even though your enterprises will be in London?'

His eyes were steady on hers, loving and loyal. 'Certainly. I expect there are remote parts of the world that know nothing of Lewis Commodes.'

She searched his face. 'You don't mind that I don't want to give up the company?'

His kiss was deep and loving, and it said a great deal without words. 'I don't want to give up my work; why should you give up yours?'

That was so simply put, and yet it meant so much. She nodded, unable to speak again. He wound her in his arms and kissed her so deeply that they only pulled apart to catch their breath.

He dropped a kiss on her nose before he flipped open the lid on the small box he still held.

It was a sapphire surrounded by diamonds shaped to look like leaves. 'It's exquisite,' Cleo breathed, touching it lightly.

'I wanted it to look like an elderberry, since you compared them to sapphires, but the sparkling brilliance of you is in the diamonds. I had to have it made, or I would have given it to you a month ago.'

Cleo held out her hand, her mouth trembling into a smile. He slipped it on her finger and then turned her hand over and kissed her palm.

'I shall never forget this day,' she said huskily.

'This ring, and this secret meadow in the middle of a city.'

'Someday I'll give you a secret garden of your own.'

'*You* are all I want.'

'We're the boring, loyal kind of people who stick together for life,' Jake said, kissing her again.

'We are, aren't we?' Cleo asked wonderingly, some time later.

'Boring,' he said, punctuating the word with a kiss. 'Loyal.' Another. 'Happy.'

Cleo smiled. 'Lucky.'

'God, I'm so lucky that I walked into Martha's emporium,' Jake said.

Somewhere, in the very back of her mind, Cleo heard a contented sigh from her mother and a fragment of song: *Who ever loved, that loved not at first sight?*

EPILOGUE

Three years later

'Where are we going?' Cleo asked, as Jake helped her into their carriage.

'For a drive.' Before she could ask another question, he asked, 'Can you give me your opinion of the second clause on the fourth page?' He handed over a sheaf of papers.

'Is this the contract for the orphanage grounds?'

'Yes, we finally finished negotiations.' Jake moved to sit on the seat next to her. 'I will read with you,' he said, his arm wrapping around her waist.

Or at least where her waist used to be. She was barely five months pregnant, but given the size of her belly, she was carrying an American-sized babe. A tiny lion.

A half hour later the carriage slowed and came to a halt, and Jake took possession of the papers again. 'I like your idea,' he said, dropping a kiss on Cleo's ear. 'You are a brilliant negotiator.'

'Mmm,' Cleo said, turning to capture his lips with her kiss. A few minutes later, he drew away.

His grooms had learned to unlatch the door and leave it ajar; Jake reached out and pushed it open.

'You forgot to tell me where we are going,' Cleo said.

He steadied her as she stepped down to the mounting block. In the last few months, his protective instincts had been uncontrollable. She could climb down from the carriage by herself. But she found it easier to give in.

'Wait and see,' he said, tucking her hand under his arm and nodding to O'Kelly.

They were standing in a narrow lane, the sides lined by towering brick walls. Jake led her to a wooden door adorned with peeling red paint. He had to throw his shoulder against the door, but it finally shifted with a groaning noise.

At some point in the past, this had been a garden.

Gnarled apple trees flanked the door, their branches covered with blossoms still curled tight. Grass poked out among dandelions and frothing cow parsley, with wild campion making pink patches here and there, and a swath of bluebells just open in one corner.

'A garden!' Cleo cried.

'A secret garden,' Jake said, grinning widely. He picked up her hand and kissed it. '*Your* secret garden in the middle of the city. I found it within a year of our marriage, but it took another two years to locate the owner and buy it.'

Cleo kissed him, blinking away tears. 'You make

me so happy. I smell lilacs,' she said a minute later, walking through dandelions and high grass.

Jake sniffed. 'I smell something more appealing.'

Cleo looked around. 'Campion flowers?'

'Tea,' he said. 'Tea brewed in the open air, just as you like.'

He took her hand and led her down a path that wandered into a corner of the garden. A large pergola had been built into a corner of the high wall, its arching roof hung with white netting that draped to meet emerald-green grass.

Inside the pergola, a glowing rose-colored carpet was anchored by a cluster of comfortable chairs, in which sat all her dearest friends. Viscount Falconer and Madame Dubois were seated on either side of a chessboard. Yasmin's plump baby, Benjamin, was nestled in the crook of Cleo's grandfather's arm, meditatively sucking on the head of a discarded bishop. Merry's daughter, Fanny, was seated cross-legged on the ground, reading a gossip column aloud to Byng.

'There you are!' Merry called, jumping to her feet. 'We've been waiting.'

'I couldn't get her out of the door,' Jake said, laughing as he picked up the netting and ushered Cleo inside.

'I haven't seen all of you in so long!' Cleo burst out, as they thronged forward to kiss her, even little Benjamin trotting over to hug one of her legs.

'You've been so miserably sick to your stomach,'

Yasmin said. 'We saved you the throne, *chérie*.' She gestured toward a chaise longue. 'Lie down like a Roman matron, and we will serve you grapes.'

Cleo lay down on her side, laughing, and Jake threw himself on the ground, leaning back against the sofa, one hand curling around her ankle. No matter how often doctors had assured him that acute nausea was a normal reaction to pregnancy, he hadn't left her side, bringing her endless cups of hot tea, with dry toast on the side.

Speaking of which . . . Chumley advanced down the path outside the pergola, holding a silver tray topped with a homely earthenware teapot.

'That's my teapot from the caravan,' Cleo cried.

'The caravan is parked against the wall on the other side,' Chumley said, handing out steaming mugs of tea.

'We could spend the night here now and then,' Jake said.

'Enjoy it while you can,' Yasmin said. 'I haven't had a night's sleep in two years. And since I refuse to suffer alone, neither has my husband.'

The gentleman in question just laughed.

A HISTORICAL NOTE ABOUT OPIUM, CLIPPERS, AND COMMODES

For ease of reference, I created Lewis Commodes, though it probably would have been Lewis Water Closets. What we call a toilet wasn't around in 1815, though important discoveries – the S-trap, the flush – were in process. For example, Thomas Crapper would introduce an improved flushing system in 1861 ('a certain flush with every pull'). Inventors were particularly fond of 'self-acting' water closets; you can see some elaborate, hopeful designs in one of my favorite books, Julie Halls's *Inventions That* Didn't *Change the World*.

As an American, I am sorry to tarnish the reputation of John Jacob Astor, but the truth is that Astor made a first fortune in furs, then in New York real estate, and finally by smuggling opium into China. Once adjusted for inflation, his fortune at his death was one of the largest in modern history. He became a great patron of the arts, though I made up the branch of the family that included a theatrically-minded brother and his son, Jacob Astor Addison.

I also took a few liberties with Mrs Astor's ocean crossing: packet ships only sailed monthly between New York and Liverpool beginning in 1817. Not long thereafter, they began crossing the ocean at extraordinary speeds in clippers, sailing vessels that were designed for speed (and went at a fast clip). Clippers developed in response to a wish for faster delivery of tea from China. I like to think that Mrs Astor would have been the first to jump onto a packet ship.